tunnel vision

tunnel

A novel

ision

keith lowe

POCKET
BOOKS
NEW YORK
LONDON
TORONTO
SYDNEY

An *Original* Publication of MTV Books/Pocket Books

POCKET BOOKS, a division of Simon & Schuster, Inc.
1230 Avenue of the Americas, New York, NY 10020

Library of Congress Cataloging-in-Publication Data

Lowe, Keith, 1970–
Tunnel vision : a novel / Keith Lowe.
p. cm.
ISBN 978-0-7434-2352-6
1. Subways—Fiction. 2. Young men—Fiction. 3. London (England)—Fiction. I. Title.

PR6112.O84 T8 2001
823'.92—dc21

2001041432

First MTV Books/Pocket Books trade paperback printing October 2001

10 9 8 7 6 5 4 3 2

Cover design by DeKlah Polansky
Photography by Warren Darius Aftahi

Printed in the U.S.A.

for Liza

keith lowe [redacted]

Acknowledgments

Before I wrote this book I never understood quite how many people would be involved in helping me bring it to fruition. Now that it is finished, I realize how deeply indebted I am to others—and because it is my name that ends up on the front cover, it is only fair that I should mention at least some of those people here. To start with, the book would never have got off the ground had it not been for the input and ideas of Suzy Behr, Misha Boskovic, and Eric Felton, who helped me come up with an itinerary for Andy's epic journey. I might never have found solutions to the myriad problems along the way were it not for brainstorming sessions with Laura Imber (who came up with the title) and Matt and Dan Grigson. Research would have been very difficult without the assistance of all those at the London Transport Museum and the London Underground Railway Society. I am also deeply grateful to Simon Trewin and Sarah Ballard of PFD for their ideas, enthusiasm, and brilliant agenting skills; and, similarly, to Lynne Drew, Greer Hendricks, and Suzanne O'Neill for their continued support and faith throughout the publishing process. But the greatest thanks of all must go to Liza, to whom *Tunnel Vision* is dedicated and without whose tireless help, unashamed criticism, and endless patience this book would certainly have been impossible.

Contents

keith lowe

1

Prologue

I'm standing outside Morden tube station at five o'clock in the morning with a hangover and a plastic bag full of Kodak Fun cameras. This is not a good start to the day. It's cold, it's dark, but worst of all the station doors should have opened four minutes ago. I'm late already and I haven't even started yet.

I look around me despairingly. I've never been to Morden before, but it's a pretty dreary place—the sort of place you can only imagine being dark, or rainy, or otherwise ugly and uncomfortable. The view through the doors into the station doesn't do much to make me feel better either. It's classic London Transport architecture in there—the sort of space which could be attractive, but through the use of crap-brown flooring and twenty-four of the most hideous fluorescent lights the Underground could get their hands on, somehow just isn't.

I look at my watch again—*five* minutes late. This is ridiculous.

I can't help feeling that I shouldn't be here at all. Just a look at the people who are here shows I don't belong. On my right an old tramp has passed out in the station entrance with his hand wrapped firmly around a can of Tennent's Super. On my left are two workmen, stamping their feet to keep warm. One of them smiled at me broadly a few moments ago almost as if he recognized me, and I was forced to nod a greeting to him—but I think I got out of having to strike up a conversation by turning away to look at the road. I've been trying to avoid eye contact with him ever since.

These are the people who belong here. I don't belong here. I should be on my way to Paris right now. I'm supposed to be getting married in twenty-four hours, for God's sake—I should be packing my suit and my honeymoon clothes, writing my speech. At the very least I should be tucked up in bed getting connubial with Rachel. But instead I'm out here, in the cold. In Morden.

I pull out one of the fun cameras and take a picture of the station sign. The tramp with the can of lager stirs a little at the flash, but then returns to his slumber. The two stamping men ignore me altogether, as if taking pictures of obscure stations at the crack of dawn is a perfectly normal activity, but the one who smiled at me is no longer smiling—he's started tutting loudly and glaring through the doors, looking for an official to be angry at. I can tell he regrets having smiled at me now. He probably thinks I'm a tourist. He probably thinks it's all my fault that we're standing out here instead of standing in there in the fluorescent-lit warmth of the station.

I look sadly down at my fun camera *(fun* camera?) and wonder how I ever managed to get here. I don't mean here in Morden—I caught the cab in from Belsize Park at four-thirty this morning—I mean here at this point in my life. How do you get to be the sort of person who actually enjoys the thought of catching the tube at rush hour? How do you get to be the kind of man who will happily travel the entire length of the Northern Line only to turn round and come back again once he gets to the other end? The kind of man Rachel hates (we had an argument when I got home last night about this very subject)—the kind of man people openly make jokes about.

Or, more important, how did I get to be the kind of man who makes rash bets with trainspotters?—bets I can't possibly have a hope of winning.

When I told Rachel what I've got myself into, she said I had it coming. Not very sympathetic, but she's probably right—in a way, I've probably had it coming since I was a kid. Or maybe even before then: do you think an unhealthy interest in the London Underground system could possibly be genetic? I know my grandfather was once a train driver and used to spend his days off at Crewe jotting down the numbers of British Rail trains in his notebook. Not even I'm *that* sad.

When I was a kid I was into normal things, like *The Beano* and Hubba Bubba bubble gum and thinking of new ways to get my hands on a Blue Peter badge—the tube was just a place my parents took me occasionally when their car was being serviced. I don't really remember how I first became interested in the tube. It just sort of happened—one moment I was playing with Star Wars toys, and the next I was contemplating the tube map, fascinated by faraway place names I couldn't even pronounce.

If I had to put my finger on something, I'd say it was probably the map that first grabbed my attention. It was so complicated, so detailed, and yet so *ordered.* When I was nine or ten years old, I used to study that map until I could recite it, line by line. I discovered beautiful places, with lovely sounding rural names, and in the absence of any idea about what such places looked like, I allowed my imagination to fill in the gaps. As far as I was concerned Covent Garden probably had pretty amazing flower beds, and Shepherd's Bush was . . . well, a bush owned by a shepherd. There was a farm at Chalk Farm, acres of unspoiled forest at St. John's Wood, and a friendly family from Zurich who lived down in Swiss Cottage. There was also a place called White City, which I decided must be somewhere out of the Bible, a sort of heavenly Jerusalem. That was where the Angel would go on weekends when he got fed up with Islington. Or maybe it was a place where only white people were allowed, like buses in South Africa—I found myself feeling deeply angry and upset that despite being obviously holy men, the Blackfriars wouldn't be allowed in. It wasn't until later that I learned that the names of places very rarely had any relation to what the place looked like. I remember feeling bitter as my dad explained to me that there weren't any lions in Piccadilly Circus and that Tooting Bec wasn't where our cousin Rebecca lived, who was just out of nappies and used to fart a lot. It was all terribly disappointing, but it didn't put me off my interest in the system. No way. I was hooked.

As I grew awkwardly into my early teens, I started reading up on the history of the Underground and visiting out-of-the-way stations on weekends. I used to hang around in the ticket hall at Hampstead tube hoping someone would ask me the way to Gunnersbury so that I could display my newfound knowledge. Northern Line to Embankment, I would have said, and then change onto the west-bound District Line. Unless, of course, you want to chance it and go via the Victoria Line at Euston, which can shave minutes off your journey if you time it right. But nobody ever asked me the way to Gunnersbury. Nobody ever asked me how to get to Chorleywood or Theydon Bois. In fact, nobody even asked me what the time was—they just looked at me strangely as if they were wondering what a spotty adolescent kid was doing hanging around the tube station for hours on end. The only people who ever wanted directions were tourists, and then it was only to the usual places in the center of town. As far as I was concerned, they were insulting my intelligence and I was perfectly justified in sending them to Chorleywood or Theydon Bois, anyway.

I have to admit, my school friends all thought it was a bit weird that I could quote every stop on the Central Line in order (they didn't know that if you take the first letter of each stop, you make the word *Ewnewshnqlmbothcsblbmsllsswbldte*—quite a handy mnemonic to remember). And I can't say that my ability to recite the Northern Line timetable ever did much to impress the opposite sex—when I started bringing girls home, they usually left again as soon as they discovered that my room was full of books on station architecture. I considered myself lucky if we managed to get down to our underwear without the girl leaping up in horror, screaming "Aaaargh! Tube-map underpants!!!"

And so I learned very early on to keep quiet about my hobby—it didn't take long to realize that the tube isn't considered cool in most teenage circles. And you can only be called a trainspotter a certain number of times before it begins to get annoying. Or "sad, anal-retentive bastard," which is what Rachel tends to call me from time to time. Not even she understands, and she's willing to marry me.

You see, once you get started learning about the tube, it's not as if you can just *stop.* It's compulsive. And don't go getting the idea that I'm different from anyone else who travels on the tube, because I'm not. First you learn the stations which are on your line to work, or to school or whatever—I've seen you doing it, sitting on the train glancing up at the map every now and then to see if you've remembered the order of tube stops properly. Anything to kill the time, right? But then you start looking at other lines and remembering them too. Then you start to work out whereabouts on the platform you have to stand to make sure that (a) the train doors open *directly* in front of you, and (b) when you get off the train, you will be right by the exit. Do you remember the first time you walked down the passage marked "No Exit" because you found out it was quicker? I bet you don't. I bet you do it all the time now. That's not so different from me, now, is it?

If you delved into it a tiny bit further, you would discover stuff a great deal more interesting than the bits and pieces *you* remember. Did you know that lazy pigeons regularly use tube trains to take them around London rather than flying, or that there is a new species of super-rat in the network which is resistant to all known rat poisons? Did you know that there are dozens of "ghost" stations which are no longer in use?—some of them still have wartime posters on the walls—like time capsules buried under London. Or that a proportion of the dust we breathe in while waiting for our trains is made up of asbestos and poisonous silica? Did you? Well, I can tell you that the answer is, no, you didn't. Unless, of course, you are a tube buff like me, in which case I'm preaching to the converted.

You see, the tube isn't like other railways. It's happening, it's now, it's *sexy.* You can't compare the tube with something like Connex or Virgin, or any of the other franchises which used to make up British Rail—that's like comparing Madame Sin to Noel Edmonds. The tube is the whore of railway systems—millions use her, millions despise her, and while we wish she wasn't necessary, most of us appreciate that she's actually providing a pretty useful service.

Or, to put it another way, if the Orient Express is at one end of the train spectrum, then the tube is at the other end. By saying that, I don't mean it's not as romantic. The tube is *full* of glamor, and excitement, and tragedy. How many people throw themselves in front of the Orient Express? answer me that! How many times can you stumble drunkenly into the Orient Express, strike up a conversation with a complete stranger, and end up in bed with her the next day? Not very often, that's for sure—at least, not on my salary.

The tube is the life of London: its lines are the veins and arteries, and we, as passengers, are merely corpuscles flowing (or, rather, seeping) through the system. No, perhaps that isn't the right metaphor—the Underground isn't just a physical place, but a spiritual one. It is a temple. A giant 243-mile-long temple, with whole platforms as altars, and fluorescent lights as candles. When people throw themselves in front of trains, they are merely sacrificing themselves to the god which is the tube. When congregations form on the platforms and start swearing at the electric notice boards, they are offering up prayers—and if they don't understand the two-hour waits, it is only because the tube acts on a higher plane, beyond our comprehension.

Okay, maybe I'm taking it a bit far, but you get the message. The tube is a cool place, and I like it. I love it. And if you say a word against it, you'll have me to deal with.

Now let me explain how I got myself into the mess I'm in at the moment.

It all started with a friend of mine called Rolf. Well, I say he's a friend, but I didn't invite him along to my stag night on Tuesday, and it was largely because I felt guilty about this that I went out with him yesterday. You see, Rolf is a tube friend. He's not the sort of person that mixes well with normal people. We only ever really get together to chat about the latest tube news. We usually meet in a pub and have a few drinks while we talk about rolling stock or track gauges—you know, the way you do. Sometimes we have more than a few drinks. And sometimes, like last night for instance, we drink a little *too* much. But I have to say that in general we don't usually tend to do anything rash, no matter how drunk we get. I've certainly never made a bet with him before.

There are a couple of things you should know about Rolf. The first thing is that he knows everything. I don't mean he *thinks* he knows everything—he actually does. Everything about tubes, anyway. Ask him any question on the history of the Underground and he'll tell you not only your answer, but a thousand other things about train engineering which you never wanted to know in the first place. Rolf can quote statistics for passenger flow from 1890 onwards. He can do a perfect imitation of the hissing noise made by a Piccadilly Line train stop valve. And it is widely known in tube circles that Rolf possesses the largest and most complete collection of pre-1990s tube tickets in the world. The man is obsessed.

The other thing you should know about Rolf is that he's insanely jealous of me. Not because I know more than him about Underground ticketing policy or anything like that—no, Rolf's jealous for the simple reason that I have a girlfriend and he doesn't. While he has never even kissed a woman, I am getting married to one in the morning. Not only that, but the woman in question is Rachel, and Rolf has had a thing about her ever since he first met her two years ago.

I have to say that Rolf's crush on Rachel has never bothered me that much. I mean, it's not as if he has a chance with her or anything: *she* can't stand the sight of him, and makes this obvious every time they meet. But it does mean that Rolf, in some strange way, considers me a rival. I don't think it has ever happened to him before—largely because the only people he has ever mixed with are other tube fanatics, and none of them can hope to match his encyclopedic knowledge of the system. But now, for the first time in his life, someone has something that he can't have—and that something is Rachel. Given this, I suppose it was foolish of me to even consider making a bet with him. Add to that the fact that I was drunk last night, and you can see that I was heading for disaster.

It happened after the fourth pint. We were in the middle of a debate, with a soggy, beer-stained tube map spread out on the table before us, when suddenly Rolf issued a challenge.

"The idea is impossible," he said.

"No, it's not. Anyone could do it."

"I bet *you* couldn't."

"Why not? Other people have done it. The world record is eighteen hours and nineteen minutes—given a whole day, any old fool could do it."

Rolf smiled at me patronizingly. "You have to remember, the world record holders are professionals. They spend months preparing. And even then all they need is one train cancellation to mess the whole thing up."

"Well, I reckon it's possible," I said petulantly. I resented his attitude. The problem with Rolf is that he always knows better than me.

"Oh, don't get me wrong," said Rolf. "Of course it's possible given a *few* attempts. But I don't think you can simply pick any day—tomorrow, say—and state beyond doubt that you will be able to do the whole system in one go."

I took another gulp of my beer. I was halfway through my fifth pint by now and was beginning to find it a little difficult to focus on the map, but there was something about Rolf's condescending manner that really got to me. "You always think you're right, don't you? Well, this time you're not. This time *I'm* right, and I say it's possible. Tomorrow, or any other day you choose."

"What, every single station?"

"Yes."

"In a single day?"

"No problem."

"And you're willing to put your money where your mouth is?"

I took another gulp. "Yes."

And that was it, the bet was made. Rolf could hardly keep his beaming smile under control.

Here are the terms we agreed on. I have to travel through every tube stop on the map between the time when the first station opens this morning and the time when the last station closes tonight. I don't have to include the Docklands Light Railway or the new section of Jubilee Line from Waterloo, because neither of these existed when the world record was set—but I do have to include the Waterloo and City Line, which only became part of the network recently. To prove that I've done it I have to take a photo of each stop as I pass through. That's 265 stations I've got to visit in total.

Of course, to spice up the bet a little we had to put something at stake—something worth trying for. And that's when things started to get out of hand.

"How about a hundred pounds?" I suggested. "That ought to cover the cost of all the cameras and still give me a bit of pocket money for my honeymoon."

Rolf snorted and waved my suggestion away with a drunken flourish.

"Okay," I said, "how about two hundred pounds?"

"Pathetic!" said Rolf. "Make it *three* hundred pounds and your Travelcard and I might start to consider it."

It was like a scene out of one of those films about poker players. Rolf was Mr. Big, and I was the Cincinnati Kid.

"Right! If that's the way you want to play it: how about *five* hundred pounds plus my Travelcard, against your collection of 1950s tube maps?"

Before I go on, I have to say in my defense that I haven't been quite myself recently. This wedding business seems to have got to me. I've been getting drunk quite regularly—not just last night and on my stag night but on every other night this week as well. And it hasn't been normal drunkenness either, but something more akin to madness. I seem to have regressed to doing things I haven't done for years—getting lary in pubs, flirting with barmaids, climbing up scaffolding on the way home like some pissed student or some has-been trying to convince himself he's still young. It's pitiful, I know, but I seem to have been powerless to stop myself—and the closer it gets to Saturday the worse I've become. Last night was just an extension of this, but even so I still can't quite believe how far I went.

"My 1950s maps plus my entire tube photo archive against your tickets to Antigua."

"My tickets to . . . ! I can't bet *that!*—that's my honeymoon!"

"Fine. We'll call the bet off then. If you don't think you can win . . ."

After all the drunken, macho posturing over who was right and who was wrong, it's easy to see how things escalated. I'm not a gambling man usually, but last night I seemed to be gripped by some sort of fever. Gradually the stakes were getting higher and higher, and I was quite happy to drive them up still further. I was desperate to prove that I knew I was right, that it didn't matter what I wagered because I was going to win anyway. Or maybe there was something more to it than that—I don't know. Regardless, in the end I think both of us went far higher than we ever intended, because what we ended up agreeing on was something far more important, and far more personal to both of us, than mere tube trinkets.

In Rolf's case it was the key to a safe-deposit box, which he placed solemnly on the table in front of him. In this safe-deposit box was Rolf's ticket collection—his absolute pride and joy. Rolf's collection is the main reason why he enjoys so much kudos in the tube community: it is a complete collection of every single type of tube ticket that has ever been issued in the entire history of the system. In the world of tube enthusiasts that's the equivalent of the Holy Grail—it really is unparalleled. So when Rolf placed this key on the table in front of him, I knew he meant business.

In return, I made a whole pile of things on the table in front of me: my Travelcard, my passport, my honeymoon reservations, my keys, my credit card, and my tickets for the Eurostar train—a special, one-time-only night train—that Rachel and I booked to take us to the wedding in Paris tonight. In short, all the things I have been carrying around with me for the past week for fear of losing them.

With a handshake, he handed over his key to me, and I handed my pile over to him. There were one or two more minor details, which I'll tell you about later, but basically that was that. The bet was sealed.

Afterwards we had another couple of drinks, and then I went home feeling quite jubilant at the prospect of my challenge. It was a repeat of all the other things I've been getting myself into recently—it made me feel young and free, worth something. It wasn't until I got home that I realized I might have got myself into something I shouldn't have. But by then it was too late.

Anyway, that's how I ended up here, standing outside Morden Station at five o'clock in the morning facing a task that would make Michael Palin blanch. In the cold light of day I'm forced to admit that I've been rash, foolish—childish. Every now and then I have to pinch myself to make sure it's not all some horrible nightmare: I've practically put my life at stake here, and for what?—a collection of train tickets. It makes you wonder what Rolf was putting in my drinks.

I shove the fun camera back in my bag and begin pacing up and down in front of the station doors. I am now *eight* minutes late. I'm not happy.

The two workmen aren't happy either—there is a new malevolence in the tutting of their tongues. I can tell it was probably a good thing that I didn't strike up a conversation with them earlier, because they would only have used it as an excuse to vent their frustration. Two workmen complaining about the Northern Line: that's the last thing I could handle this morning.

In fact, out of all of us out here, the only one who *is* happy is the tramp. He has woken up now and, after an extravagant stretch, has started rummaging in a large sports bag. A few moments later he pulls out a comb, which he drags through his hair for a while before replacing it. Next he pulls out a toothbrush and a tube of toothpaste, and begins brushing his teeth. Once he has finished, he spits the toothpaste out in the gutter; without any water to rinse his mouth out he takes a swig of beer from his can and uses that instead.

I become so engrossed watching this bizarre ritual that I don't notice when at last a tube official comes to open the station doors. The workmen have noticed and are right by the entrance, ready to ram their way in. And another person has appeared, as if from nowhere, waving his Travelcard in front of him.

As the tube official begins to unlock the station doors, I hesitate. This is it—my journey is about to begin. For a moment a part of me wants to pull out now, forget about the bet and go home. I still have time. I could always tell Rolf it was just a joke, that I was never really serious about traveling the whole network. But even as I think this, I know I won't do it. When the London Transport man finally pulls open the doors, I know I'm going in—I can almost hear the tube calling to me.

And besides, it would be dishonorable to stop now. A bet's a bet, even amongst trainspotters.

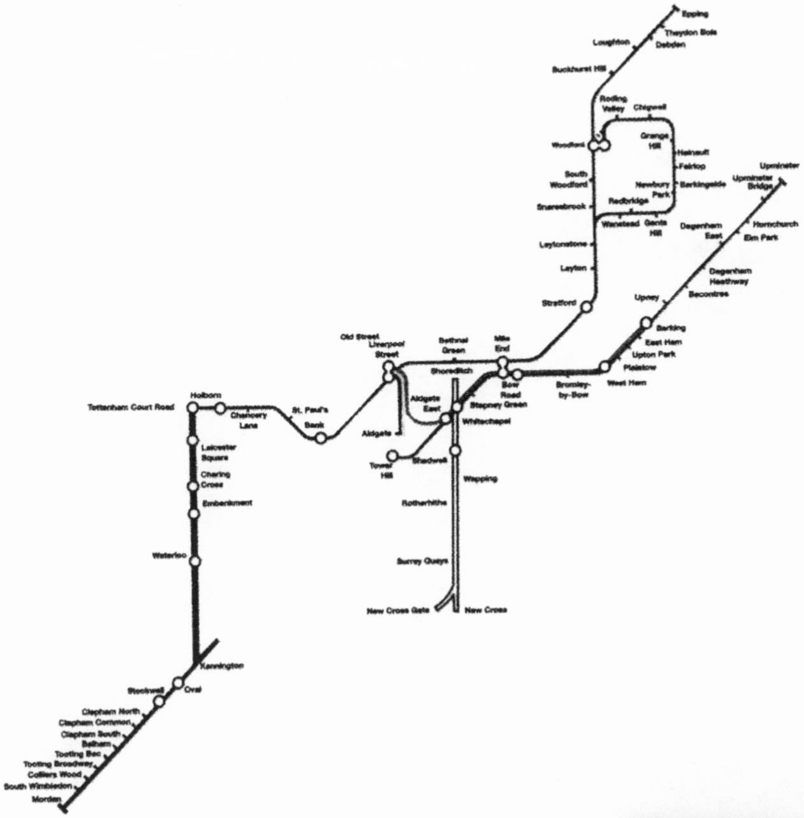

part 1

east london

Chapter 1

5:08 AM—Morden–Colliers Wood—Northern Line

The first thing that happens when the doors of the station open is a race for tickets. The man with the Travelcard looks smug and saunters down to the platforms flapping his blue Travelcard wallet in front of him as he goes, but the rest of us have to scramble our way over to the ticket machines and form a queue. I am forced to join them—Rolf insisted yesterday that I include my own Travelcard in the bet, presumably in order to make my journey just that little bit harder.

Of course, because I wasn't really alert when the station attendant opened the doors, the two workmen easily beat me to the ticket machine. I'm forced to stand behind them while they try to work out which of the three million buttons on the machine is the right one. It's extremely irritating. I know where *my* button is. I could point to it with my eyes shut—why the hell didn't they let me go first?

The only person behind me in the queue is the tramp I saw outside. He was too busy rummaging around in a bag full of small change to beat me to the machine—which is some relief, I suppose. As I stand there wondering impatiently if I'm going to miss my train, I can sense him standing close to me—in fact I can *smell* him, breathing his beery breath all over my back. It's quite unnerving. I turn slightly so that I can see him out of the corner of my eye, but it doesn't reassure me, because now I can see that the tramp is staring at me. I don't mean idly—I mean he is *really* staring. It's as if he thinks I'm one of those magic-eye posters you buy in Camden market which turn into 3-D pictures if you gaze at them long enough.

It's quite a relief when the two workmen finally manage to get their tickets out of the machine, but as they turn round a curious thing happens—*they* stare at me too. They look me straight in the face for a good couple of seconds, and smile. Then one of them shakes his head, and they walk on. It's a bizarre experience—it was like they thought they knew me or something—and for a moment it throws me.

It takes me a couple of seconds to remember that I'm actually in a hurry. Pushing the workmen and the tramp from my mind, I buy my ticket and rush down the stairs to board my train.

There's a funny thing about the Northern Line—it has its own aroma. I could smell it as soon as I entered Morden Station; it got stronger as I bought my ticket (a ticket to Epping, as one-day travel passes aren't valid until after 9:30); and now that I'm actually sitting on the train, I can feel it seeping into my clothes. It's not like the smell of any of the other lines—in fact, it's not like the smell of anything else at all. It's a sort of mixture between the odors of century-old dust, burnt rubber, and stale alcohol. The best place to encounter it is at Camden Town, but even out here at Morden it's pretty strong. The Northern Line is the oldest deep-level train line in the world—it has been accumulating this particular fragrance since

1890—and even if London Transport ever got round to modernizing the place, I doubt they'd manage to flush the smell out. It permeates everything.

As my train finally pulls away from the platform, it enters the tunnel, and the darkness of the morning outside is replaced with a thicker, more impenetrable darkness. Now that I am underground I know that the darkness, like the smell, will only intensify. This is the longest continuous tunnel in the tube system—almost twenty-eight kilometers of blackness across the center of London. Rolf has a theory that all this absence of light has the same effect as it does in Finland during the winter—twenty-five percent of all suicide attempts on the tube happen on the Northern Line. But I reckon that's just because the place is so overcrowded. Every year it carries more passengers than the Jubilee, Metropolitan, and Circle Lines put together, and yet it is the most consistently underfunded line of them all. Its trains don't work properly. Its tunnels are falling apart. It's not for nothing that its nickname is the Misery Line. If the London Underground is the whore of railway systems, this is the most down-and-out, drugged-up, and abused of the lot.

But no matter how easy it is to criticize the Northern Line, it's also hard not to feel a certain affection for it, shabby as it is. After all, it is the veteran of metro systems. Subways the world over have been modeled on it—hard to believe, I know, but it's true. As the train slides through the filthy darkness of the tunnel, I can't help feeling sentimental about it. The Northern Line always does this to me, especially when I'm traveling on a train as empty as this one. It's a feeling akin to love, I suppose. Not *passionate* love—like the sort of love you'd have for the Jubilee Line Extension or the Docklands Light Railway—but the kind of nostalgic love which grows out of lifelong familiarity. If there's any line I feel at home on, this is it.

Rachel, of course, hates the Northern Line. She hates the fact that she can never get a seat on it in the mornings. She hates the way the trains are always late. She detests the smell and the dirt and the blackness of it. She doesn't care that it's one of a kind—in fact, she wishes that it would stop being so unique and start working properly. But most of all she hates the fact that I love it so much. Which is one of the reasons why we ended up arguing last night.

As the train approaches South Wimbledon Station, I fumble around in my bag to find the fun camera I have already started. I frown slightly to myself—in my hurry to get ready this morning I'm not nearly as well prepared as I should be. Apart from my fun cameras, all I have with me is a pad of paper, an A4 blowup of the tube map, and a couple of pens—one red, one black. No book or magazine to pass the time between stations. No sandwiches for when I get hungry later on. No bottle of water, no flask of coffee, no separate bag to put the used cameras in—I even forgot to bring my copy of the train timetable. In my pockets, apart from a handful of loose change, all I have is Rolf's safe-deposit key—an object simultaneously useless and all-important. I am totally unprepared.

Glancing up from my bag once more, I notice that the drunken tramp is still looking at me. I try to ignore it, but it's difficult—he is staring at me and smiling sheepishly, as if he's trying to gather the courage to come and talk to me. It crosses my mind that he must think he knows me from somewhere—though God knows where I could ever have met a South London tramp before. And besides, the other two or three people in the carriage are staring at me too. Perhaps they think I'm famous. Perhaps I bear an uncanny resemblance to some local celebrity I've never heard of, some pub wit or *bon viveur* from Morden. Or perhaps they just like staring at people. I decide that anyone who lives right down here at the southernmost extreme of the tube map must be slightly strange and resign myself to ignoring them all for the rest of my journey.

And anyway, I've got more important things to think about, like the fact that we are pulling into South Wimbledon Station. I haul my body wearily out of the chair and stand up to take a picture of the South Wimbledon Station sign.

That's two stations down, I think to myself—only 265 to go.

It is a formidable task that I'm attempting, perhaps even an impossible one—but if anyone can do it, that person is me. I know the tube system like the back of my hand. I know its layout, I know its history, and even without a copy of the timetable, I can probably tell you most of the train times. I have a route already mapped out in my head, and if anything goes wrong along the way, I have planned a whole variety of alternative routes. What I am attempting may be madness, but it is also a challenge worthy of me.

Perhaps that's why everyone has been staring at me this morning. Perhaps they all recognize my talent, my innate transport superiority. Perhaps I naturally give off the aura of Somebody Who Knows What He Is Doing. I wish Rachel could see me now, surrounded by the respectful glances of my fellow tube travelers—then she wouldn't argue with me. Then she wouldn't call me a fool, a trainspotter, an obsessive—she would be gazing at me like these people are, with admiration.

As I sit down and wait for the train to move, I can't help but remember the argument we had last night. It's like a wound that still smarts—I want it to heal, but I can't help prodding it every now and then, just to see if it still hurts. I find myself running over the words we shouted at each other in the darkness of our kitchen, and for the tenth time this morning I start thinking up clever answers to her gibes, answers that would have put her in her place if only I had thought of them last night. But, needless to say, it doesn't help. I still can't think about last night without bitterness.

Perhaps I should tell you a bit about Rachel. Although she's a couple of years younger than me, she's far more grown up than I am. She's intelligent, usually quite mild-mannered (except in the heat of a row, of course), and hopelessly sentimental. Her father is French, and she grew up in Paris near Versailles—which perhaps explains why she's such an old romantic. It's always she who buys me flowers rather than the other way round. Sometimes she rings me up at work just to tell me she loves me, and Valentine's Day is a bigger event in the calendar than Christmas. Generally she forgives me for not being as romantic as she is. She tends to understand when I don't tell her I love her. And usually she lets me off when I forget an important date, like the anniversary of when we first met. Usually.

Rachel is a very pretty woman—much prettier than I deserve. She's got the sort of prettiness that grows on you—the sort that makes you stand back every few months and marvel at the fact that you've never really registered what big, brown eyes she has or how nice her freckles are. Last night, as I stumbled through our front door, I had one of those moments. I found myself staring at her lips, in much the same way that everyone seems to be staring at me this morning, filled with wonder. I've always thought Rachel has nice lips, but last night they seemed almost unbearably plump and kissable. What I conveniently failed to notice in my alcohol-influenced state was that those lips were also pursed with irritation.

"Hiya!" I said as I came in, probably a little too enthusiastically. "Sorry I'm late. It's the tube—you know how it is. Train got stuck in the tunnel south of Camden Town."

Rachel says I have an annoying habit of pretending everything is fine even when it blatantly isn't, and in my drunken wisdom this was the tack I had decided, quite on the spur of the moment, to take. I suppose I thought that if I was chirpy enough and friendly enough, it would make her chirpy and friendly too, and everything would be all right.

Rachel, on the other hand, doesn't mess about. "Where've you been?"

"I told you—the tube. I think it must have been a points failure or something . . ."

"No, before that."

"I went for a drink."

Rachel's face dropped. "Thanks for asking me along. I've been sitting here for hours wondering where you are. You could at least have called." She made a flapping gesture towards the kitchen table, where there was an unopened bottle of wine and two candles burnt down almost to the end. "I made a nice romantic dinner for you, but you never came."

"Oh, dear . . ." My heart sank. "I'm sorry. . . ."

"So, who were you out drinking with, then?"

I swallowed hard. "Rolf . . ." I said slowly.

"Rolf!" In a moment all her hurt turned to anger. "You were out with that . . . that geek! When you could have been here with me! Celebrating!"

"Celebrating?"

"I spend hours tidying the place up and trying to make myself look nice, and all you can do is go out drinking with Rolf?"

I frowned, trying to think. "Celebrating?"

"I told you about this last week."

"You did?"

Rachel let out a frustrated sigh. "In case you hadn't noticed, Andy, it's our wedding on Saturday. I just thought it would be nice to spend one last night together while we were still—you know—living in sin." She dropped into a chair. "I mean, I know tomorrow is our last night really, but we'll be on a train tomorrow night. I wanted to wine and dine you and then whisk off to bed. It seemed like our last chance. Tomorrow's going to be so busy, what with shopping, and packing—and I have to go and pick up my wedding dress and take it over to Sophie's . . ."

Involuntarily I felt my frown deepen. "Er, Rachel . . . there's something I ought to tell you about tomorrow . . ."

I should explain here that I haven't exactly been attentive to Rachel over the past few days. While she's been busy making last-minute preparations for Paris, I've been out every night, seeing all those friends of mine I haven't seen for years: college friends, school friends, even old girlfriends. And people I know from the London Underground Railway Society. I've had an insatiable need to see people—people who aren't Rachel. It has felt more like I'm about to die than get married. It's as if I have only a few days left to live and have been making my peace with the world before I give up the ghost and finally enter the afterlife of marriage. Like I said, I've been going slightly mad recently.

To make things worse, I've had the past few days off work and spent them looking round the new stations on the Jubilee Line Extension or checking out the latest exhibition in the London Transport Museum. Yesterday I went to visit Acton Works—which is a sort of cross between a train hospital and a train graveyard for out-of-date models. I tried to explain to Rachel that I'm not avoiding her, that on the contrary I've decided to spend the rest of my life with her, but she's still managed to get the impression that trains and stations and other "tube stuff" as she calls it are more important to me than she is.

Now that you know the history, you can see how hard it was for me to tell her about the bet I'd made with Rolf. She was never going to understand that, not in a million years. Of course, I didn't tell her the *whole* story. I didn't tell her that I'd wagered my passport, my honeymoon tickets, and all the other stuff—in fact I didn't tell her I bet anything. But even so, she didn't take it well.

"Call it off," she said.

"What do you mean, 'Call it off'?"

"I mean pick up the phone, ring him up, and call it off."

"You can't call off a bet just like that!"

"Why not?"

"Because you can't. How would I look if I rang him up to say I was chickening out? That would be the same as admitting I was wrong."

"So?"

"But I'm not wrong."

We argued for what seemed like ages after that. And she called me lots of names. She called me an idiot for spending the evening with a trainspotter when I could have spent it with her, eating ice cream off her naked body. She called me an imbecile for agreeing to spend the next day traipsing round the tube when I could be tucked up in bed with her, drinking wine and making love. And although she didn't exactly say it, she implied I was a total moron for being so interested in the tube in the first place. I'm ashamed to say that in the heat of the moment I wasn't able to come up with a single clever put-down in return.

"You know what I think?" she said, after half an hour of wrangling, crying, and shouting on both our parts, "I think you're more interested in this trip round the tube than you are in our wedding."

"Yeah—and?" I said defiantly. "What's wrong with that?"

"Andy, you're only doing this because you want to prove to your sad, trainspotter friends that you are El Tube Supremo, that you are even more tube obsessed than they are. Can't you see *anything* wrong with that?"

"No."

"And what happens if you don't make it? We're supposed to be catching this special Eurostar tomorrow night at one—what happens if you don't make it in time?"

"But I *will* make it in time."

"How do you know?"

"Because I do, that's all." I cringed as I said this, because it sounded lame even to me.

"So you mean that you're willing to risk everything—even me—just so that you can have a crack at conquering the Underground?"

"Yes."

She sighed. "Well, in that case you'd better hope you can do it, because if you're not at the station tomorrow night by the time the train leaves, I'm going to Paris without you."

For a brief, dangerous moment I considered telling her the truth—that I had to go through with the bet now, that without my passport, my tickets, and all the other things, I wouldn't be *able* to go to Paris. But for some reason I couldn't. I don't know why—my throat just seemed blocked, like there was some sort of filter there not letting the words through, and before I knew it she was walking out of the room. At that moment all desire to reason with her left me, and all I could feel was a rising anger. Taking her Eurostar tickets out of my pocket (my own were with Rolf, along with all my other things), I threw them onto our bedside table for her to pick up tomorrow. If she wanted to leave for France without me, then fine. Let her. At that moment I wouldn't have backed out of the bet for anything. Even if Rolf had called me up and begged me to reconsider, I'd still have had to go through with it. There are some things a man just can't take.

And besides, she was right, of course—even *you've* probably picked that up. I do want to conquer the tube. It's my own personal Everest. To get through today I will need all my resources and every ounce of my knowledge about the system—one slip of concentration could ruin the whole thing. Who could need more of a challenge than that? I just didn't realize there would be so much riding on it, that's all.

By the time we went to bed nothing was sorted out. We just lay there, an invisible wall down the center of the mattress, and went to sleep. Or at least I went to sleep. I get the feeling Rachel must have just lain there in silence stewing over our argument, because when I woke up at 4:15, just in time to catch my cab to Morden, her side of the bed was empty. I didn't bother looking round the flat for her, to say good-bye. I told myself I didn't have time. I just grabbed some money from the dressing table—enough to pay for the cab and twelve fun cameras from the B2 shop—and left the flat.

So here I am this morning, sitting on a train which has just entered the network of tunnels that crisscrosses London, and I find myself in a more bizarre position than I could ever have imagined. As far as I can work it out, the situation is this: If I win this bet, it will prove to Rachel that I am a bigger tube buff than even she imagined, and therefore even more worthy of her contempt. Why would she want to marry a man like me? But if I lose, then she'll discover that not only have I lied to her, I've also effectively put our wedding up for sale. Not just to anyone, but to Rolf—the single man Rachel despises more than any other on the planet. Marvelous, isn't it?—I can't win. I'm damned if I do, and I'm damned if I don't.

As my train arrives in another station, I get up to take my next photo: Colliers Wood. When I turn to sit down again, I can't help noticing the drunken tramp on the other side of the tube carriage. He doesn't say anything, but he catches my eye because he's staring at me again. Not only that but he's grinning and pointing to his forehead, tapping it in just the place where an Indian would have a *bindi.* What's wrong with the man? I have half a mind to ask him what his problem is, and why he has been gawking at me all morning. But something tells me that he is not trying to harass me, but is offering something to me instead. Perhaps it's the earnest way he keeps tapping his forehead—or perhaps it's the way he simultaneously raises his eyes to look at *my* forehead—but I get the feeling he's trying to tell me something.

As the train pulls into the tunnel again at Colliers Wood, I turn round to look at my reflection in the glass, and at last I understand the real reason why everyone has been staring at me this morning. It seems that Rachel has had the last word after all. Literally. There it is, plastered on my forehead in letters an inch high—a single word written in Rachel's off-red lipstick: TWAT.

Chapter 2

5:13 AM—Colliers Wood–Tottenham Court Road—Northern Line

I don't want to tell you about the next few minutes. I don't want to talk about the confusion of emotions that floods my brain (why would *anyone* want to write TWAT on your forehead while you were asleep?) or the embarrassment of having everyone in my carriage snigger while I desperately try to rub the word off my face with my sleeve.

And I don't want to tell you about the confusion of thoughts that race through my head, about the thousand forms of revenge I find myself planning, about how I decide to jilt Rachel at the altar just to teach her a lesson. I don't want to tell you any of this, even though I kind of just have, because it's horrible, and it makes me feel dirty and angry, and more than a little sick.

So instead I'm going to ask you a question. A difficult question that will keep you occupied for a bit. Answer me this one: If you were going to try and stop at every single station on the system in a day, what route would you take? Take a look at the tube map and try to work it out. Go on. I'll just sit here and try to rub the rest of this lipstick off while you do it. Come back to me in a few moments, after I've calmed down.

Bloody difficult, isn't it? There must be hundreds of different ways of getting round the system, but there are probably only a few which would actually work. Trying to figure them out would be hard at the best of times, but trying to do it when you're angry, and hurt, and full of revenge, is practically impossible.

There are, however, some simple rules you can follow. For a start, you want to avoid changing lines too often, because changing lines takes time. Next, you want to begin your journey out at one of the extremities, but not on a line which has lots of little branches at the ends—the last thing you want to do is start fiddling around at the ends of lines first thing in the morning when there aren't very many trains: leave that until rush hour. Don't travel at weekends, because some stations are closed on Saturday and Sunday. Oh, and one other thing: You have to watch out, because there are one or two stations which are only operational at peak hours. Don't try to go to Shoreditch Station at midday for example, because you can't, and that's that.

I decided to start *my* journey at Morden because it's one of the first stations to open. Also, I'd like to get this section of the Northern Line done and out of the way as soon as possible. It's not very nice, the south half of the Northern Line. Most of the robberies and violent crimes which happen on the Underground happen here. It's grotty, and the stations are rickety and old. Tooting Bec has one of the highest suicide rates of any station in the system (not surprising if you take a look it), with Oval and Waterloo not far behind. And besides, being a North Londoner born and bred, the idea of even *venturing* south of the river naturally fills me with distaste.

The current world record for traveling the whole system is eighteen hours and nineteen minutes, but without preparation I reckon the best I can do is about nineteen hours. That would take me up to midnight. The tube closes between 12:30 and 1:00 AM, depending on where you are in the system—so that gives me, say, forty-five minutes' grace for delays. Although, if I'm going to make it onto the Eurostar by one o'clock I'm going to have to finish sooner rather than later. As long as there aren't too many foul-ups along the way, I should just about make it.

As my train comes to another stop, I feel a little self-conscious about taking a picture of the station sign. Four or five maintenance men in fluorescent jackets joined us at Colliers Wood, and I can't help feeling a bit stupid taking pictures of station signs in front of such an audience. I know they're going to notice—it's not like midafternoon when I'd be camouflaged by hundreds of tourists doing exactly the same thing—and I know they're going to think I'm weird. As I put the camera to my eye, I can feel the maintenance men staring at me, and their staring feels like it's burning the word TWAT back onto my face again. As I sit down again, I'm trying not to look at them in case one of them says something—I know that if I try to explain, it'll only come out sounding silly.

You know what happens when you're trying to avoid looking at something—you end up staring at something else. It's as if the effort of *not* looking fixes your eyes in one place, and it becomes impossible to move them. On the tube this is pretty dangerous, because there's not a lot to stare at down here except other people, and that contravenes the most basic law of the tube—which is, don't look at *anybody.* I must have been staring at the drunken tramp—a thoroughly stupid thing to do, because he obviously takes it as an opportunity to strike up a conversation. Before I can do anything about it, he gets up from where he's sitting and comes to sit down next to me. Just like that. He doesn't even wait until the train is at a stop to give his action some semblance of an excuse.

"Going far?" he says.

"Yes," I reply, and immediately regret it, because I have just broken one of the other laws of the tube: If you don't want to talk to someone, always answer no, regardless of what the question may be.

"Where are you going?" he continued.

"Everywhere."

The drunken tramp seems to take this as some sort of philosophical statement, because he nods sagely and murmurs, "How right you are." He takes a thoughtful gulp from his beer can and continues: "That's the thing about life, isn't it? You spend your whole time certain you're going somewhere, but you're not. You're going nowhere. Or like you said, everywhere."

"Yes," I say. "Quite." He is flexing his hand round the beer can, and I notice for the first time that he's actually quite muscular. Not big, just muscular.

"I mean, how many of us ever stop to think about why we're in such a hurry?" he continues. "I sit on the tube every day and watch people rushing backwards and forwards, and I think to myself, what's the point? Why does it matter if you're five minutes late for work? If you rush about like that, there's only *one* place you're traveling to, if you catch my meaning."

"Yes," I say. He has a tattoo of a skull and crossbones on his forearm. "True words of wisdom."

But he hasn't finished yet. "Do you ever think about death?" he says. "I don't mean topping yourself, or anything morbid like that—I mean, what happens next . . . ?"

He launches into his own personal theory of life, the universe, and everything. I have to admit, he's very coherent for the sort of person who drinks Tennent's Super at this time in the morning. The tramps I usually encounter on the tube tend to be aggressive, abusive people who speak some indecipherable tramp's dialect that would confound linguists anywhere. Only last week I came across one of these at Angel Station—he shouted incomprehensibly at me, and then sat down on the seat next to me and voided his bowels. When I got up and moved to avoid the stench, he started shouting after me again. From start to finish I didn't recognize a single word he said—it made me wonder whether he was in fact speaking English at all, and not Hungarian, or Basque or something. The man sitting next to me now doesn't seem like that at all. He speaks with a clear East London accent, taking care to enunciate his words. He must be in his early sixties, he has well-kept but dirty gray hair, and though his clothes are filthy, they're also quite new looking. I decide he's not so much a drunken tramp as a homeless old muscular bloke with scary tattoos who just happens to like a tipple. At five in the morning.

The drunken man is smiling now. I think he likes me. "So tell me," he says, "what's the first stop for you on this tour of life?"

"Tottenham Court Road."

"Really? That's where I'm going too."

"Yes, well, I'm only changing there for the Central Line."

His face lights up with surprise. "That's a coincidence—so am I! Where to on the Central Line?"

"Epping, but . . ."

"Well, there's a thing! That's the very selfsame station I'm going to! Would you ever have thought it."

I begin to panic. I can see where this might lead. I don't want to end up dragging this man round with me—not today, of all days.

"No, you don't understand," I say. "When I said I'm going everywhere, I meant it. I am actually going *everywhere.*" I tell him briefly about the bet and show him the bag full of fun cameras.

"Christ," says the drunken man, "now I've seen everything."

He pauses for a while, and for a few moments I am satisfied that I have shut him up for good. As we pull into Clapham South Station,

I get up to take a photo of the sign. When I've done it, I try to gather the courage to sit down at a different seat so I won't have to listen to the drunken man anymore, but at the last moment I chicken out and end up plonking myself back down next to him again.

He, on the other hand, doesn't seem to have any of the same reservations about me. He has a look of true concern on his face, which, if he were a friend of mine, and I wasn't more than a little nervous about him, I'd probably find quite touching. "I suppose you actually *are* in a hurry, then," he says. "I mean, you've actually got a good reason to be rushing around, if you stand to lose . . . What did you say you were going to lose?"

"My girlfriend."

"You bet your *girlfriend!*"

"I didn't bet *her*—I bet . . . well, a whole bunch of things. My credit card is waiting for me in Upminster. When I find that, there'll be a note telling me whereabouts on the tube my passport is hidden; when I find my passport, there'll be a note telling me where my honeymoon tickets are; and so on. I won't have collected everything I've bet until I finish the entire system, and I need it *all* if I'm ever going to make it to my wedding." I give a short, nervous laugh—these are the extra little bits of the bet I didn't get round to telling you about earlier. Saying it out loud like this has suddenly made me realize exactly what I've gone and done.

The tramp looks stunned. "Does your girlfriend know about all this?" he asks.

"God no! I couldn't tell her that! She thinks I'm stupid enough as it is."

"Is she the one who . . . you know?" He nods at the lipstick smudge on my forehead.

Instinctively I reach up to my face, embarrassed. "If you don't mind, I'd rather not talk about it."

The tramp turns round again and leans back in his chair to stare thoughtfully at the map of the Northern Line above the row of seats opposite. I look at him, briefly, before turning away myself. I am already regretting telling him about the bet. Talking to a stranger at all goes against everything I've learned as a Londoner and as a tube traveler, but talking to a stranger like this one—a stranger who drinks strong lager in the early hours—that's almost madness. Still, I suppose it fits in with everything else I've been doing this week. I look at him again, out of the corner of my eye. Every now and then he raises his can of Tennent's Super once again. It seems to be bottomless. I am sure it should have been empty long before now.

"Tell me," he says eventually, "what route are you planning to take?"

"Pardon?"

"What's your route? After you've got to Epping, that is."

I hesitate. I'm not sure if I want to tell him exactly where I'm going. "Well," I say, a little unsurely, "first I have to get out to Upminster on the District Line to pick up my credit card . . ."

"Good," he says. "Upminster's a good start."

"And then it kind of depends on where Rolf has hidden the next item, but I thought I'd go all the way round the Circle Line in one go . . ."

"Bad move."

"What do you mean 'Bad move'?" I'm astounded. Who does this guy think he is?

"It's a waste." He is picking his nose with a long, grimy index finger as he speaks. "You should think of the Circle Line like the hub of a wheel, with all the other lines as the spokes—you want to go round it bit by bit, and shoot off up each spoke as you get to it."

"Oh, no." I find myself saying. "Oh, no, no, no, no, no, no . . ."

Before I know it he's got me going, and we're having a full-blown discussion about how I'm going to do the trip. I try to explain to him that I've got my itinerary all planned out, but he keeps finding fault after fault with it. Every now and then I get up to take a picture of a tube stop, but when I sit down again he's come up with another reason why my route's crap. I have to admit, I'm surprised by how much he knows about the tube system. I also have to admit he has a point about my itinerary. That kind of makes sense really—I planned it after several pints and an argument—it's bound to be a bit sloppy. Or very sloppy. Or downright useless. Jesus, what am I going to do?

The drunken man seems to have noticed my anxiety, because he chooses this moment to reach over paternally and put a grubby hand on my shoulder. "Don't worry," he says, "we'll stick to your plan as far as Epping—by then we should have worked something else out."

I look at him, long and hard, and I have a sense of rising panic within me. *We,* he said. He thinks he's coming with me all the way to Epping. I'm not even at Oval yet, and already I've managed to pick up some nutter.

"Since we're going to be traveling with each other," he continues, "why don't you tell me your name?"

"Andy," I say.

"Pleased to meet you, Andy. My name is Brian, but most of my friends call me Sir."

"They call you . . . ?"

He laughs—a slow, heartless laugh. "Not really. It's a joke!"

How the hell am I going to get away from him? I could try moving to another car, but I know he'll only go and follow me there. I could try and hint that I want to be left alone, but going by the conversation so far, I can tell that any hint I give will have to be pretty blunt. I suppose I will just have to wait until I reach Tottenham Court Road and try to lose him there. It shouldn't be too difficult: apart from the fact that he's half cut, he's almost an old man—he can't possibly run as fast as me. No way. No bloody way.

Chapter 3

5:39 AM—Tottenham Court Road—Northern/Central Line

I have met some pretty intrusive characters on the tube in my time. I once had a woman sit next to me for four stops on the Jubilee Line, telling me that it was unsafe to go near the armrests because touching plastic underground spreads diseases. Nutty as a bloody fruitcake. Then there was the time I had to share a carriage on the Circle Line with a whole posse of skinheads. I was only a teenager, but unfortunately I happened to be going through a rockabilly phase, complete with blue suede shoes and an unfeasibly large, sculpted quiff. The skinheads thought it would be funny to spend the rest of the journey ruffling my hair, so that by the time I got to Paddington I had a middle parting and Brylcreem smears all over my shirt.

I have to say that, when it comes to sustained intrusion, my encounter with Brian is not the worst by a long chalk—but for some reason it feels like it. Perhaps it's because I'm so tired. He carries on talking at me for the next six tube stops—by which time I know all about his back complaints and his athlete's foot (which apparently is crawling up his ankles as he speaks). He tells me all about how he's started to get scurvy and how sleeping on cold concrete has given him piles. He says all this proudly, as if delighting in the catalog of ills which are slowly eating away at him. By the time we are in Central London I'm beginning to feel quite sick. I *really* want to get away from him. As soon as I see the sign for Tottenham Court Road, I jump off the train, take my photo, and peg it through the pedestrian tunnels as fast as I can. Just the thought of his piles seems to give me an extra turn of speed.

In the end it's a good job I do run, because despite my excellent progress up the Northern Line, I'm still six or seven minutes late. Normally I'd have plenty of time to make my way over to the Central Line, but as I stagger exhausted towards the top of the stairs, I discover that the first eastbound tube is already at the platform. Not only that, but it's about to leave.

I tear down the stairs, hearing to my dismay the high-pitched beeping of the door release. Mustering a last burst of energy, I leap down the remaining steps and into the first carriage, just before the doors close.

But I'm still not alone. Oh, no. It turns out Brian has quite a pair of legs on him, after all. He's standing next to me now—and while I'm bending over double desperately trying to get my breath back, he is still as fresh as a daisy, as if I've just taken him for a stroll in the park. "That was a close one," he says. He doesn't seem to mind the fact that I ran off as soon as the Northern Line train stopped—in fact, he seems to take it for granted that I would be in a hurry to get to the first connecting train. And now, as I'm gasping for air, he still has the energy to be patronizing. "I was worried you weren't going to make it there for a second. I thought I was going to have to run ahead and hold the doors open for you."

"I knew I'd get there," I gasp, determined not to be outdone by this drunk. "No problem. No problem at all."

I wait until Brian has sat down, and then choose a seat much further down the carriage so that I won't have to sit next to him all the way to Epping.

Chapter 4

5:40 AM—Tottenham Court Road–Holborn—Central Line

The Central Line is surprisingly busy for this time of day. There are ten or fifteen people in my carriage alone. Most of them are slouched in their seats, chins resting on chests, but one or two have newspapers spread out before them and polystyrene cups of steaming coffee. There's a woman at the other end of the car with a large blue suitcase beside her, as if this tube ride is only the beginning of some much longer journey. All are sitting quietly, thoughtfully, sleepily. There is a peaceful atmosphere in here—it could almost be a Sunday afternoon.

There is nothing peaceful about the way *I* am feeling. My eyes are stinging, my joints are aching, and I feel more than a little sick—but, more than that, there is a bitterness within me that I haven't felt for years.

I curse the day I ever set eyes on Rolf. I curse the fact that I made friends with him, I curse our stupid bet, and most of all I curse Rolf himself, because he is in bed and I'm not. But all the time I know I am really only cursing myself, because I let Rolf lead me into this mess, just like I have always let Rolf lead me into things.

It's easy to think the worst of Rolf—if you knew him, you'd know what I mean. For a start he *looks* sinister. He insists on wearing a pair of John Lennon glasses, which make him look uncannily like the bloke who owned the fancy dress shop in the old children's program *Mr Benn*—stick a fez on his head and there'd be people queuing up to ask him if they could step into his changing rooms. And he's very dark. I don't mean his skin's dark, because it's not—in fact, all the time he's spent underground has left his skin pretty pale—it's more of an atmosphere I'm talking about. He's the sort of person who appears out of dark corners when you're least expecting it. He's like a walking shadow.

Rachel has hated Rolf since the very first moment they met. Not only is she jealous of the time I spend with him, she actually doesn't like the man himself. "Geek" is what she calls him generally, or, on a bad day, "Geek-from-hell." Whenever I mention his name at home, she makes motions of putting her fingers down her throat, as if she needs to purge the thought of him from her system. It's not one of her most attractive traits.

To be fair to Rolf, he wasn't overly fond of Rachel at first, either. Before he met her I think he had a mental image of her as some matron with a rolling pin who wouldn't let me come out to play until I'd finished my chores. He used to make a habit of calling her "Hitler" whenever he thought he could get away with it. (Calling someone "Hitler" is of course the highest form of insult—after all, it was Hitler's bombing of London in 1940 which put dozens of tube stations out of action for years and completely destroyed the rail link between Latimer Road and Kensington [Olympia]. In Rolf's book you can't get much worse than that.)

I introduced them to each other in a restaurant called My Old Dutch in Holborn. Neither of them wanted to meet the other, so I had to lure them both there under false pretenses. I told Rachel that the restaurant does the best savory pancakes this side of the City, which it does, and I told Rolf that it's set on the old site of British Museum Station, which it is—but I didn't tell either of them that the other one was coming.

So, you see, they were each under the impression that they would be having an intimate dinner for two, and that they would be whispering words of love, or lift design, respectively. If I had thought about it properly, I would have realized it was going to be a catastrophe. But, as you've probably gathered, I have a habit of managing to convince myself that even the most disastrous plans are a good idea.

The introductions were painful.

"At last," said Rachel, "I meet the man who keeps Andy down tube tunnels all night."

"And I meet the woman who keeps Andy at home."

"Me? Keep Andy at home? I couldn't keep Andy at home if I tried!"

Rolf looked her up and down, his eyes lingering on her body just that little bit too long. "No," he said. "I don't suppose you could."

A few sentences, that's all it had taken. They were smiling, but I knew them both too well to be taken in by it. I got the distinct feeling that those two sets of grinning teeth had somehow been sharpened and were just waiting for the opportunity to start gnashing at each other.

We ordered our pancakes, and I got on with the business of trying to get some *proper* conversation going—which was pretty difficult, because all Rolf wanted to talk about was tube stations, while all Rachel wanted to talk about was something other than tube stations. Whenever I tried to mediate, they vented their frustration by taking it in turns to call me names. They seemed to enjoy that.

I was relieved when the waiter finally came over with our appetizers. Not only because I was hungry, but because, as he laid out our food in front of us, Rolf began to question him about the history of the restaurant (or more specifically, the history of the station which used to stand here). It was a relief—after all, that's what Rolf had really come for. Once he'd got the information, there'd be no reason for him to stay, and this whole disastrous experiment could be brought to a close.

Unfortunately for us all, the waiter didn't seem to have ever heard of British Museum Station. Which meant Rolf felt duty bound to educate him.

"It was a *beautiful* station," he said. "It was designed by Harry Measures, who was particularly fond of building stations with metal supporting columns. Perhaps you have some examples of those here?"

The waiter, who seemed to be an Italian student over here to learn English, didn't really understand what Rolf was talking about. "I don't know," he said.

"How about decorative ironwork?" said Rolf.

"I don't know."

"Or original tiling? Don't try and tell me you haven't got any original tiling!"

Every time Rolf spoke he raised his voice just a little bit louder. The poor waiter became more and more flustered, and simply kept repeating, "I don't know, I don't know."

"Why don't you keep your voice down?" said Rachel frostily. "Can't you see the man doesn't know?"

"How can he not know? What on earth does he think people come here for?"

"Pancakes?" suggested Rachel.

That was it. It was open warfare now. For some reason the word "pancakes" seemed to trigger all the suppressed aggression that twenty minutes of catty comments had failed to bring to a head. At last they began to raise their voices. How dare Rachel suggest that pancakes were more important than London's heritage? And how dare Rolf make such a fuss over a station which had been defunct for over sixty years. The whole of the rest of the restaurant was looking at our table now—not that that made either Rolf or Rachel shout more softly. I found myself sliding lower into my chair, partly through embarrassment, but also in awe at the force of the storm I had let loose.

Eventually, the manager came over, attracted by all the noise. "Is something the matter?" he asked. He was smiling the sort of smile which is just waiting for an excuse to turn nasty.

"No," said Rachel shyly, suddenly realizing what a spectacle they had been making of themselves. "Really, it's not important . . ."

"Nonsense," said Rolf, "of course it's important. We want to know what happened to British Museum Station, and your waiter won't tell us."

"I'm terribly sorry," said the manager, "but the waiter has only been with us a short while and does not know very much about local history. But you are right, British Museum Station used to occupy this site . . ."

"Of course I'm right. *Nobody* knows more about British Museum Station than I do. What I want to know is whether any of the original structure of the station still exists."

"In that case, the answer is no."

"No?"

"No."

Rolf looked perturbed. "How about tile work? Perhaps in the basement you have some original Central London Railway tile work."

"No," said the manager, "we don't."

"What, none?"

"None," said the manager. He grinned, as if he knew how much such a revelation would hurt Rolf. "There is nothing left of the old tube station. It was razed to the ground, the lift shafts were filled in and covered over, and all traces of the basement were smashed to pieces to make way for the foundations of the present building. British Museum Station is entirely extinct." His grin widened. "Will that be all, sir?"

Rolf nodded.

"Good," said the manager, and with that he left us to enjoy our main courses, which had just arrived.

Rachel waited until the manager was out of earshot before finally turning to Rolf. "I've never been so embarrassed in all my life," she said, pointing a forkful of cheese and spinach crepe at him. "Couldn't you control yourself?"

"Control myself?" said Rolf. "Whatever for?"

"Well, for the sake of that poor waiter for a start."

"The waiter!" said Rolf, flabbergasted. "You want me to feel sorry for the waiter? This is British Museum Station we're talking about here!"

I chose that point to laugh loudly, as if Rolf were making a joke, but it wasn't really a very smart thing to do, because all of us knew that Rolf was deadly serious. Also my mouth was full, and laughing just meant that pieces of pancake fell out of it and rolled down my shirt. Rachel looked at me in disgust and attacked her own plate of food, muttering something about "fucking transport buffs" not quite under her breath. The rest of the meal was conducted in silence, but every now and then I couldn't help noticing Rolf shoot a sly glance in Rachel's direction. Even in the atmosphere of discomfort that surrounded us, it was obvious. He was besotted with her.

Chapter 5

5:42 AM—Holborn–Liverpool Street—Central Line

I have to tell you that the manager of that restaurant was not entirely right—there *is* something of British Museum Station left. We are passing through it now. Between Tottenham Court Road and Holborn the tunnel opens up for a while, and I can see another train through the gaps in the tunnel wall, where the other platform would originally have been. Underground, well out of the sight of anyone dining in the restaurant above, bits and pieces of the station still exist.

I remember telling Rachel a story about British Museum Station once, in the days when she didn't jump down my throat at the mere mention of the tube. We were standing together at the end of the platform at Holborn late at night, and I was trying to scare her with a ghost story. She wasn't scared at all, of course, but she still clung on to me for effect. Which was, after all, the whole point of the exercise.

Perhaps you'd like to try it with your lover next time you are in Holborn. The story goes something like this:

At the beginning of the 1930s, when British Museum Station was still open, there was a local myth that it was haunted. Many people reported seeing a figure emerging from the tunnel late at night—a figure dressed in a loincloth and a headdress, with strange markings about its face. Before long people began to say that the station was haunted by the ghost of an ancient Egyptian, who wandered down onto the platforms at night from the museum above. Londoners took this rumor so seriously at the time that a local paper even offered a financial award to anyone brave enough to stay on the station premises overnight. As far as the records show, there were no takers.

Soon after the station closed, film crews moved in to make use of the place's reputation for the 1935 comedy-thriller *Bulldog Jack*. The film is set in a disused tube station named "Bloomsbury," which has a secret passage leading to an ancient Egyptian sarcophagus in the British Museum itself. The filmmakers thought they were just exploiting a local fairy tale—but on the very same night the film was released two young women disappeared from the platform of Holborn, the next station along from the British Museum. And then marks began to be found on the dusty station walls—marks which looked like hieroglyphics. Sightings of the ghost began to increase, and strange noises were reported coming from the walls of the tunnel. People began to wonder—perhaps there *was* a secret passage leading up to the museum, after all. Perhaps mummies *were* wandering down to the tube below. Of course, the transport authority denied that any such passage existed. In an effort to avoid controversy they just waited for the rumors to die down—kept the story under wraps until it went away.

Unfortunately, nowadays there is not much left to see of British Museum Station—the platforms have been removed, and most of the 1930s adverts have been ripped down or painted over. However, if you press your face against the right-hand window as you travel westwards from Holborn to Tottenham Court Road, you can still make out the grubby white tiles of the platform walls. And if you listen carefully when you're standing on the platform at Holborn, sometimes—just sometimes—you can hear the wailing of Egyptian voices floating down the tunnel towards you . . .

If you are telling this story to your lover, this is the point where you start making ghost noises at them. Then they are supposed to giggle attractively and clutch hold of your arm in mock fear. They are *not* supposed to turn away with a tired expression on their face and tell you to grow up, which is what I'm afraid Rachel would probably do if I told her the story now.

As we pull out of Holborn Station, my reverie is broken by the loud voice of the tramp, Brian. He's sitting at the other end of this section of carriage, slouched down in his seat with his legs stretched out before him. My heart wilts at the sound of his voice—I can see I am going to have to talk to him whether I like it or not. For a moment it crosses my mind that Brian might be a friend of Rolf's, sent to hinder me at the beginning of my trip. Rolf would have known I'd start out somewhere like Morden—he knows the way I think—and I wouldn't put it past him to try to hijack my attempt. But as the tramp speaks I put the thought out of my mind. There are hundreds of places I could have started this morning—Rolf couldn't possibly put a friend of his at every one of them. And besides, not even Rolf's *that* poisonous.

"It's great having so much space to yourself like this, ain't it, Andy old son?" says Brian. "You can really spread out. If I could, I'd always travel at this time in the morning. It's so much less stressful."

"Yes," I say. "Quite."

"And if you're going to spread out, the Central Line's the place to do it, eh?" He laughs. "These trains are luxurious compared to what they used to be. I should know. I grew up on the Central Line."

"Really."

"Oh, yes. Bethnal Green is where I was born and raised."

Here we go, I think to myself; I'm about to get the whole bloody life story. I try to ignore him by looking up at the adverts—there's one for a dating agency directly above Brian's head, a picture of a man and a woman smiling at each other on a sunny garden bench—but Brian doesn't fall for it. I can't get away from the man.

"Of course, it's still the same as it ever was," he continues. "That's the thing. Up there," and he points at the roof of the train, "up there everything changes. None of the streets are the same as when I was a boy. You wouldn't recognize the London I grew up in. But down here in the tube it's still the same."

I have to fight the urge to contradict him. The Central Line has changed radically since when he must have been a kid: it has been completely refurbished; it has been given brand-new trains and brand-new technology. I am itching to tell him he's talking utter nonsense, but I can't help suspecting that he's doing it deliberately, just to draw me into a conversation. I try to shrug nonchalantly, as if I don't care what he thinks, but it doesn't work. It's as if he can read my mind.

"Don't look at me like I'm mad," he says. "They might stick new trains in the tunnels and give the place a lick of paint, but it still *smells* the same. Nothing can change the smell."

Involuntarily I find myself inhaling deeply.

"That's right—breathe it in! What does it smell of to you?"

"I don't know," I say sullenly. "Just the tube, I suppose."

"It smells of life; that's what it smells of. Life and new beginnings. It's amazing they let people like us travel on it."

"What do you mean, *people like us?"*

He ignores my question. "When I was a kid, Bethnal Green was the end of the line. I watched the whole system grow—it's much bigger now than it ever was then. Did you know that the Central Line has more stations on it than any of the others?"

"Yes," I say indignantly. "Of course I knew that."

"The thing is, me and the Central Line grew up together. I even worked on some of the stations when I was a young man—I'm a carpenter, you know. Perhaps that's why I like the smell of the place—it reminds me of my youth." He pauses for a moment, as if haunted by some memory from his childhood. "Anyway," he continues at last, "it smells much better than any of the other lines. Especially the Northern Line—that just smells of failure."

Despite myself I can't help rallying to my own line's defense. "The Northern Line's not *that* bad," I say. "I mean, it's a bit dirty, and maybe a bit old, but nothing that can't be fixed."

"It smells of failure," he repeats. "I should know, because it's where I spend most of my time. The Northern Line's where most drunks spend their time. When you're a drunk like me, you'll end up on the Northern Line too."

"There you go again! What makes you think I am *ever* going to end up a drunk?"

He doesn't answer, just looks down at my clothes. I have to admit, the differences between my own apparel and Brian's are minimal. As I was stumbling around in the dark this morning, I thought it would be easier to put on last night's clothes again rather than try to find new ones—as a consequence I'm looking more than a little crumpled. There is a beer stain on my shirt where Rolf knocked over the dregs of a pint, and someone else's cigarette ash on my trousers. As you can imagine, I don't smell particularly good, either.

"Don't go thinking I always look like this," I blurt defensively. "Normally I'm quite smart. This is sort of a special occasion . . ."

"It is?"

"Yeah. There's no point wearing smart clothes if I'm going to spend all day on the tube, is there?"

"It's all right, son," he says. "I wasn't really talking about your clothes, anyway."

"Right," I say, unsure of what else to say. "Good."

"My point is, the Central Line smells good, unlike the Northern

Line which . . ." And he goes on for a while about the differences between the various odors of the two lines. I don't really listen, because there is something else which is bothering me, a thought which for some reason my brain just won't let go of.

"Hang on a minute," I say, breaking into his monologue, "if you weren't talking about my clothes, why else would you think I'm going to end up a drunk?"

He looks at me sheepishly and hesitates. "A few reasons really, but there's no point in going into . . ."

"A few reasons such as?"

He turns away again, as if he can't look me in the eye. "It's nothing. Really."

"Come on," I say. "Spit it out."

"Well, if you must know, it's the way you hold yourself—all tense, like, and anxious. You remind me of a friend of mine who lives in a tube station—nice bloke, just a bit obsessed. You know, with things which don't really matter."

"Hang on a minute." I am getting more than a little wound up here. "You're comparing me to some tramp friend of yours who lives in a tube station?"

"Yes."

"But that's ridiculous! I have a flat in Belsize Park!"

"Fair enough," he says, as if he doesn't really believe me.

"And I have a girlfriend . . ."

"For the moment," he interrupts.

"A girlfriend," I repeat, "and a good job. I have a nice life. There's no way I'm ever going to end up like . . ." I stop myself.

"Go on, say it. Like *me.*"

"All right then—like you. There's no way I'm going to end up down-and-out. I just wouldn't let it happen."

He is not resentful as I say this—in fact he is smiling, as if there could be nothing better than living life as he does, sleeping on streets, drinking endless cans of Tennent's Super. "Let me tell you something, son," he says. "I used to have a job and a wife and all the things you have, but that didn't stop me ending up like this. There's no point in thinking it can't happen to you, because that's just blindness. You're on the edge of it and you can't even see it. I'm not trying to tell you that it'll happen tomorrow, or the next day; I'm just saying that if you're not ready for it, one day it might jump out at you unawares. So if you want to make sure you don't lose that nice job of yours, and that nice girlfriend, you'd better start thinking about what's important to you, before it's too late."

He is still smiling, and I suppose he thinks he has just said something incredibly profound. When, in fact, he has just said something incredibly irritating. Who does he think he is—the Ghost of Christmas-yet-to-come? And what good does he think he is going to do anyone by preaching? There are thousands of things I want to say to him to put the record straight, but I know there's no point—he'll simply come out with more words of bloody wisdom. I decide to button my lip. If I'm going to spend the next twenty or so stops with him, the best policy is the one I was following before I got sucked into this ridiculous conversation—stare at the adverts and ignore him.

I look upwards at the line of rectangular plastic advertisements above Brian's head and try to forget the whole discussion. My eye catches the dating agency's poster once again, and this time I notice that the woman in the picture is holding a bunch of flowers. She is in her fifties, and though she is smiling a bucktoothed smile, her expression is more one of relief than of joy. The man who is passing her the flowers is at least ten years her junior, but he too looks as if he has just been delivered from a future of unspeakable desperation. I notice with distaste that he is wearing a bright blue anorak of the sort I used to own when I was thirteen. In the top pocket of this anorak there is a small booklet. I am afraid to say that from where I'm sitting it looks uncannily like the Jubilee Line timetable.

Chapter 6

5:50 AM—Liverpool Street–Epping—Central Line

Right from the word go there have been adverts on the tube. I've got a photo at home of the Central Line platforms at Tottenham Court Road taken in 1903—the walls are plastered from end to end with ads for Oxo and Nestlé's Swiss Milk and Sunday evening concerts at the local music halls. On the Metropolitan Line in the 1880s they used to post improving tracts inside the train for the passengers to read—a bit like our *Poems on the Underground* now, only marginally less interesting. No matter how far back you go, tube passengers have never been able to escape from ads, whether they be posters advertising the benefits of Ogden's pipe tobacco or long boring monologues on how to get a better deal on your car insurance.

There's something about adverts on the tube: they aren't like other adverts. People who put ads in newspapers know they have to grab your attention immediately in order to stop you from turning the page without noticing. It's the same with billboard advertising, which has to get its message across to you in seconds as you drive past in your car. On TV the commercials have to be somehow thrilling, or sexy, or even downright outrageous, to ensure that you watch them instead of leaving the room to make a cup of tea. But on the tube, things are different. Advertisers here don't have to bother with being eye-catching, or fascinating, or even vaguely entertaining, because they know that, sooner or later, you'll get round to reading their ads, anyway. Down here there's nothing else to look at. There's nowhere you can go.

Here's a little experiment. Try looking at the word below without reading it:

RACHEL

See?—you can't, can you? No matter how much you try to see just a bundle of letters, or smudges of black ink on white paper, you can't get away from the fact that what you are really seeing is the word "Rachel"—and if you knew Rachel as well as I do, you wouldn't be able to avoid thinking of those plump, annoyingly kissable lips of hers.

It's the same with tube ads—if you stare at them enough, you end up reading them without ever intending to. And worse than that, you start to endow them with meaning, as if they were actually relevant to your life. I know more about premenstrual tablets and cosmetics than can possibly be healthy for a thirty-year-old man. I can't help it—the words tumble off the advertising boards and down rays of fluorescent yellow light, crashing through my eyes and into my brain. Like it or not, I now know all about the cost of holiday insurance (Europe *and* worldwide)—not to mention the complete history of the Jack Daniel's distillery in Tennessee—and I can quote whole lists of telephone numbers, from the one for the Samaritans to that of the Holsten Bier Fest. It's infuriating.

This morning I'm lucky enough to be seated opposite a nice

landscape photograph of Wales—but even so, I can't get away from the words

Wales—Cymru
Two hours and a million miles away

Next door to it is an advert for Cathay Pacific, claiming that it is the "gateway to the East." I snort out loud. The only gateway to the East *I* have ever known is Liverpool Street Station.

Brian has fallen asleep (fortunately), so I have nothing else to occupy me but taking photos and reading the ads—it's only after I have read them ten times over that I finally manage to turn away. For a long while I stare at my own reflection, thinking about nothing but the tube stops I have yet to arrive at.

All the stations we come to are completely empty. At Liverpool Street everyone gets out, leaving Brian and me alone in our carriage. Bethnal Green, Brian's birthplace, is deserted. At Mile End, I can see across the platforms, all empty, all quiet. Just before Stratford my train comes out of the tunnel and into the eerie blue light of a multistory car park, and I realize that I am doing something far more adventurous than flying off to Wales or even Hong Kong. I am setting out from London before dawn for the wilds of Essex.

At 6:04 my train pulls in at Leytonstone (even out here they have adverts: Pepsi, Virgin, Woodpecker cider). We have three minutes to walk over the bridge to the other platform in order to catch our next train. This is the last stopping-off point for those who want to stay inside London. From here on there is no other way for me to go but to Epping, right out at the end of the line.

I shake Brian awake and make him stumble with me to our connection. There is no one else coming with us—I get the feeling we had not only our car but the whole train to ourselves. As we cross the bridge, we get strange looks from the station attendant, a fat man with a shock of bright orange hair. It is as if he has never seen westerners out here at such a time before and can't understand what business we have this far to the northeast of London. He looks particularly suspicious of the camera I am holding in my hand. We nod to him as we walk past, but get no response. I decide that he must not understand the gesture, so I hurry on, ushering Brian sleepily before me.

"Not very friendly out here, are they?" mutters Brian, perhaps a little too loudly.

"They just have different customs out East, that's all," I say, quietly in case the man hears us.

We descend the stairs to the platform and make it onto the Epping train with one minute to spare.

Time is starting to become an issue now. I didn't think it would take this long to get out here. I left Morden over an hour ago, and I still haven't reached the end of the Central Line yet, not by a long way. I'm beginning to feel a little nervous: when I looked at my watch this morning, I just saw the time, but now I'm beginning to see the time I have *left*—just under eighteen and a half hours.

The train pulls off into the darkness once again. We are well and truly out of the tunnel now, but there are high walls on both sides of the train tracks, as if the people of this strange eastern county want to hide themselves from casual tourists like us. All I can see through the train window is streetlights peeping over the top of the walls; streetlights illuminating a foreign world hidden from unauthorized eyes.

But gradually the side walls become lower, until eventually I can see that we are traveling across open fields. Once in a while the train comes to a stop at another station—Snaresbrook, Buckhurst Hill, Debden—and I rise from my seat to take a solitary photograph.

But stations are few and far between now, and most of the time I am stretched out on the carriage seats watching Brian sleep, and trying not to doze off myself. The worst thing is that I think my tiredness is making me see things. As I'm taking my photo of Theydon Bois, the penultimate station on the line, I notice a dim figure at the end of the platform. I recognize him instantly—the same shadowy demeanor, the same John Lennon glasses glinting in the light from the streetlamp—but as the train passes by, there is no one there. The platform is empty. I shake my head a little in an attempt to clear it, but the experience makes me feel decidedly anxious. I decide to walk up and down the car for a while to try to keep myself alert.

At last, at 6:37, the train slows to pull in at Epping. This is the last stop. Fifteen years ago, when I was still a teenager, there used to be another train which went beyond here, out through the deserted station at Blake Hall and on to Ongar—but so few people were intrepid enough to venture this far that they closed that section of line off in the early 1990s. So this is it. Epping. The end of the line.

As I get out to take the last photo on my first camera, I have to say I'm not impressed. At the end of such an odyssey I expected some sort of monument, some Pillars of Hercules to mark the end of the known world. All there seems to be here is acres and acres of empty concrete crisscrossed with painted white lines and surrounded by wire fencing. It takes a few moments for it to click in my mind: it's a car park. That's all Epping seems to be—one huge car park. Great, I think to myself. Well, that was certainly worth the journey.

Now that I'm out here, I just have to go all the way back again: change at Woodford, round the loop via Hainault, and back down to Mile End, where I can change onto the District Line. But before the train sets off back the way it came, there's something I must do.

"Brian," I say, shaking him gently awake. I am smiling to myself as I do it—at last I will be able to get rid of the guy. "Brian, we're here. You can go now."

His bloodshot eyes open, and he sits up in his seat clumsily. "Thanks for waking us up, son," he says. "That's very kind of you."

"You'd better go now. We're at Epping. You'd better go."

He looks at me. "Epping. Right. Thanks." He shuts his eyes again.

"Brian, wake up!" I shake him a bit more violently this time. "This train's going back to London in two minutes."

"Yes. I know. That suits me fine."

For a moment I don't know what to say. "What do you mean, that suits you fine! You said you wanted to come to Epping—well, now we're here, and you've got to get off the train!"

"Oh, do I now?"

"Yes!"

"Well, I don't much like the look of Epping, so I think I'll go back into town."

"But . . ."

"But nothing." For the first time this morning the tramp is being decidedly grumpy. "It's still dark out there. At least it's warm on the train. I'm staying here."

My heart sinks. If it wasn't for all the commuters getting on now, I think I'd probably throw Brian off the train myself. "So if you're not getting off here," I ask sullenly, "where *are* you going?"

"I don't know. Anywhere. It's all the same to me. The only reason I fancied coming up here was because I thought it might make a change from going up and down the Northern Line all day. And I thought I could help you, of course."

"Help *me* . . . ?" I can't believe it. I practically carted this man onto this train at Leytonstone. I could have left him behind there.

"Yes. Help you." He's smiling at me now, as if he's forgiven me for waking him up. "It's okay—save your thanks. I always say that if you can't help out a mate in trouble, then life's not worth living."

I decide now that I have *got* to get away from this man. He'll drive me insane. I can't have him traveling round with me all day. I just *can't.* Where would it stop?—Would he want to come home with me? Sleep in my bed? Be surrogate grandfather to my children? In an effort to shake him off once and for all, I decide to tell him, straight out, that I'm going to be taking a different route than him.

"Well, I'm going to Upminster next, on the District Line . . ." I begin.

Brian's face lights up. "That's very kind of you."

"Eh? Kind of me . . . ?"

"To offer. And the answer's yes, I'd love to come with you. Just as far as Upminster. It should be a bit warmer by the time we get there."

"Hold on a minute . . ."

"I'll even take the pictures for you if you like, so you can have a lie-down. Teamwork—that's what I like."

"I don't believe this," I mutter to myself, but deep down I do believe it. It's typical. I go to say one thing and end up giving the exact opposite impression. It's the story of my life.

But even as the train sets off for Central London once more, even as I'm planning ways of ditching him once we get to Upminster, there is a part of me that can't help acknowledging the fact that traveling round the tube by myself for a whole day could get pretty boring. And if I were to look within that part of me, deep down, I know there would be a serious danger of discovering that somehow, for some reason, I'm secretly glad of Brian's company.

Chapter 7

6:45 AM—Epping–Woodford—Central Line

7:15 AM—Woodford–Mile End via Hainault—Central Line

At 6:45 our train leaves Epping, and I travel with Brian to Woodford, where we change trains again to go round the Central Line loop. At 7:15 we catch a Northolt train via Hainault, and before long we are making our way back on our circuitous route towards London.

It's frustrating doing it like this—going all the way into London, coming all the way back out to Upminster on another line, and then going all the way back into London again—but it's the only way it can be done. There are strict rules governing "roving." For example, it would be great if there were some shortcut between the Central Line and the District Line, but I would only be allowed to take it if it involved public transport—catching a cab to Upminster is not allowed. And even if there were a fast tube to Upminster—one of those ones which miss out some of the stations like there is on the Metropolitan Line—none of the stations I missed would count. So if our train seems a little slow as it chugs past golf courses and rugby pitches and pieces of open countryside, I must simply grin and bear it. There is no alternative.

At 7:36, after Newbury Park, the train enters the tunnel again, and I know we will soon be back in London proper once more. The closer we get to the center of town, the busier the tube car gets, and I am glad Brian is here to save my seat for me while I get up to take photos of the station names. I am also glad of the conversation. For the past three or four stops he has been quizzing me on my knowledge of the tube, particularly on the bit of the Central Line where he grew up. I have to admit that I feel quite chuffed at having such an attentive audience (and I mean *audience,* because despite all their looking elsewhere, I know everyone else in the carriage is listening too).

At 7:43, as we pull out of Wanstead, I sink back into my seat with a feeling of satisfaction. I have already taken photos of the next few stations on the way out to Epping, so I can afford to relax a little.

We have finished the loop by 7:45. So far, everything has gone exactly according to schedule.

I love this time of day on the Underground. Despite the obvious discomfort and the heat and the grumpiness of the hordes of people who cram their way onto the tubes between seven-thirty and nine-thirty, there is something life-affirming about the rush hour. This mass migration from *A* to *B*—it shows we are alive, it shows we can function well as a society. When else, and where else, would you get company directors and barrow boys squashed right up against one another? When would you find old women and teenage boys jammed together, physically intimate? The tube is the great equalizer. In here, black people, Asians, and whites mingle peacefully with tourists, tycoons, and tramps—there is no seniority, no privilege, and no discrimination.

While Brian is thinking of more questions to ask me, I look

around at the other people in the carriage. It is still quite early, but there are already plenty of people standing. They are beginning to jostle for position, scavenging seats like their lives depend on it, and I know that if I had to leave my seat now, I'd have a job getting it back again. When at last somebody actually does leave a seat free, a scramble develops between a white woman and a young Asian man to get to it first. I can see madness in their eyes, as if they know they are damned to repeat this ritual every day for the rest of their lives. Unfortunately for the Asian man, the woman is better at calculating the angle at which the seat-leaver will depart. She wins by inches.

Standing in the aisle a few feet away there is a man in his late fifties, with a bushy handlebar mustache. Beside him is a young girl who has twenty-five rings through various bits of her face (I have already counted them). The man, like most of the people in the carriage, can't help staring at her. I can see the ends of his mustache quivering to the beautiful jingling sound that comes whenever she turns her head, and at every twitch of her pierced lips, he winces visibly. I have to suppress the urge to lean forward and tell him that she probably has piercings in far more painful places than her lips.

Beyond these two, a seated middle-aged woman is putting on makeup using her hand mirror. I watch for a moment as she applies mascara to her eyelashes, terrified that the train will make a sudden jolt and she will plunge the stick into her eye, but she finishes the job successfully and the danger is averted. She is less lucky with her lipstick, though. As she places it to her lips, the train *does* give a sudden jolt, and she is left with a scarlet streak up one of her cheeks.

Other than these people I can see only a few other faces between all the legs and bags and bodies: an expensively dressed black man in his thirties, with a head as bald as a Cadbury's cream egg, a smug Australian man in bright clothes (far too bright for the tube at this time of the morning), a bossy-looking woman with fat ruddy cheeks who reminds me of the French teacher I had when I was fourteen. All these people are packed together like chickens in a battery farm, and yet none of them complains or tries to take it out on their fellow passengers. Nobody screams, or cries, or makes any indication that they are anything but comfortable—the place is a picture of tolerance.

But just as I am congratulating myself on living in such an accepting society, just as I am thinking of writing a letter to the Queen recommending that she award a medal to the tube travelers of London, someone gets on the train who shatters all my illusions.

"Kiss me!" he says, as he steps between the closing doors. "Kiss me!"

The newcomer is short, and brown, and looks as if he might come from somewhere in Southeast Asia—Indonesia perhaps, or the Philippines. He is somehow shiny-looking, as if he has not yet been tainted with the dust of the Underground.

"Kiss me, kiss me!" he says as he squeezes through the crowd. The man with the handlebar mustache looks at him in horror, as if this is the last straw, but most people seem to understand that he is not offering his lips round the carriage but mispronouncing the words "Excuse me." Not that they *do* excuse him, of course. Not at all. Everyone is making it as difficult for him as they possibly can, for the simple reason that it is obvious that he has never done this before. You can tell it a mile off—he is a novice. A tube virgin.

For all their tolerance, the one thing people on the Underground cannot countenance is novices. You can always tell a novice on the tube: he's the one standing on the wrong side of the escalator with a queue of people behind him waiting for a chance to lynch the guy. He's the one who asks you stupid questions—like where the exit is—and who then bothers to introduce himself, as if he expects to bump into you again sometime. If you met him on the street, your natural instinct would be to help him out, but after you've been stuck behind him in a corridor while he bumbles along trying to read his map, you get an incredible urge to send him off in the wrong direction, just for the hell of it. And if he doesn't understand much English, you suddenly find yourself talking in fluent Cockney rhyming slang. That's the thing about the tube—you can't be nice to beginners, it's just not allowed. Down here beginners are fair game.

I heard a story once about a Chinese guy on the Northern Line who had never been on a tube train before. There were no seats, so he had to stand up in the aisle—and as it was one of the old Northern Line trains, he found himself standing between two rows of dangling straphangers. Of course, never having been on the Northern Line before, the Chinese bloke had no idea what these dangly things were for. For several stops he stands in the aisle with nothing to hold on to, staring at these dangly things as if he's afraid to touch them, and stumbling into the other passengers every time the train turns a corner. So there he is, stumbling about, when suddenly the train comes to a halt in the tunnel, and the voice of the driver announces that the train is being delayed. When he hears the driver's voice, the Chinese man's face lights up. At last, he's worked it out—the dangly things must be microphones—after all, they do *look* like microphones. So he grabs hold of the nearest one and starts talking into it, having what he thinks is a conversation with the driver. Of course, no one else in the carriage thinks to correct him. Oh, no. They've had this bloke stumbling into them for the past few stops and they're fed up with it, so they just watch and laugh, until the train starts up again and deposits the man at the next stop.

So there you go—that's the way we treat novices on the Underground. They don't get help, they get laughed at, and that's if they're lucky. Of course, the story about the Chinese man probably isn't true. It's probably just one of those tube myths which circulate for a year or two and then disappear back to where they came from. But it demonstrates my point.

The guy who's getting on now has all the hallmarks of the beginner: the tourist map, the knapsack, the T-shirt which used to be trendy about eight years ago. As he gets on, the whole carriage seems to groan audibly, and everybody glares at him as if to ask what the hell a Filipino is doing in Leytonstone. To my shame, I have to confess I'm thinking exactly that myself. It is as though the Central Line at rush hour has brought all my latent xenophobia to the surface.

"Kiss me!"

He repeats it until he finds a space to stand—as it happens, directly in front of me. The black man with the bald head exchanges a look with me and raises his eyes to the ceiling, as if he's never seen anything so ridiculous. The Australian man in the too-bright clothing is smirking callously, but also a little nervously—after all, it can't be that long since he was a tube novice himself. For a moment the woman with the pierced face looks decidedly put out. She is no longer the center of attention.

Brian seems oblivious to the studies in anthropology which are going on around us. In fact, he is looking quite uneasy. He doesn't seem to see the individuals in the crowd like I do, just the crowd itself, crushed together all the way down the carriage.

"Jesus!" he is muttering now. "How many people can you fit in one carriage?"

I turn to look at him. He is beginning to sweat. "About two hundred," I tell him. "Two hundred ten tops."

"Jesus!" he repeats. "I hate the rush hour. It makes me feel funny."

I spy a chance to get rid of him, once and for all. "You can get out if you like," I say hopefully. "I'm sure I can manage on my own."

"I can't. I'm coming with you to Upminster. I promised."

I glance nonchalantly round the carriage. The middle-aged woman with the lipstick streak is staring straight at me with a sour expression on her face, as if she can read my thoughts. "Yep," I continue, "two hundred and ten people in each carriage. That's coming on for seventeen hundred people in each train. Over two million passengers traveling on the tube each day, most of them in the rush hour. Makes you wonder how it's possible, doesn't it?"

"God, how do they all breathe?"

His own breathing is becoming a bit labored now, and he is getting wheezy. I wonder if he can add asthma to his list of ailments. "Do you really want to know?" I ask him.

"Yes!" There is panic in his voice. "I mean, is there enough oxygen for everyone?"

Part of me relishes his claustrophobia, but I can't keep it up. No matter how I try, I just can't help feeling sorry for him. And besides, there are people listening—and Brian has asked me a direct question about the tube. "If you must know," I sigh eventually, "there's more than enough oxygen. There are one hundred and twenty-seven fans dotted around the system. Not only that, but most stations these days inject filtered, ozonized air into the corridors. And even if they didn't, you'd still be safe. At the beginning of the last century people managed, and there wasn't any ventilation at all—the place smelt a bit, but it wasn't dangerous."

"So you mean I can breathe easy?" says Brian, oblivious to his own pun.

"Yes."

"Well, thank Christ for that!"

He rummages in his bag, presumably in search of another can of Tennent's Super. I feel as if I've let him off too easily.

"No," I continue, "you don't need to worry about there being enough air. If I were you, I'd be more worried about crashing."

"Crashing?" He stops rummaging.

"Yeah. Especially on the Central Line. Did you know that since the war there have been more collisions between trains on the Central Line than on any other? That's not the sort of statistic London Transport advertises. And what's more, most of them have happened around Stratford, which is . . ."—I look up at the tube map above my head—which is the next stop, as it happens. I feel like a naughty schoolchild. "So if the train gives a sudden lurch as we are coming into the station, start worrying!"

I can see that it isn't only Brian who has been listening to my words. I am receiving concerned glances from the woman who looks like my old French teacher, and the man with the handlebar mustache is looking with renewed anxiety at the girl with the pierced face, as if he can think of nothing more degrading than being found in a crushed tube carriage next to her. The Australian man in the bright clothes is grinning, as if to say "Train crash?—Cool!"

The only person who hasn't understood what I have been talking about is the Filipino man in front of me. He has, however, understood at least one of my words. "Kiss me," he says, leaning down towards me, ". . . Stra'ford?"

As he says it, the train enters Stratford Station. "Yes," I say, "this is it."

"Stra'ford?" he repeats, annoyingly.

"Yes." I point out of the window at the platforms we are passing. "Stratford."

The Filipino hesitates for a moment as if still not sure, but then starts making his way down the carriage towards the doors.

Brian has started rummaging in his bag again and has located another can of beer, which he opens now, spraying a few drops on the coat of the man with the handlebar mustache.

"That stuff you were saying about crashing," he says after taking a swig, "it doesn't happen very often, does it?"

"No. Not very often."

"Good." He looks better now, almost relaxed. He is holding his can of beer like a drowning man clutching a rubber ring.

"In fact, last time there was a crash on this line was about fifteen years ago."

"I suppose it's much safer now than it used to be, now they have all their computers."

"Yeah, it's pretty safe. If you look at the fatality rate per number of journeys taken, the tube is over three times safer than going by car and almost four times safer than walking."

Brian looks at me with an expression of wonder on his face. "How do you know all this useless stuff?"

"I study it."

"Why?"

I notice myself stiffen slightly, and I am about to protest that there's nothing useless about knowing about your surroundings, when I am distracted by a minor commotion by the train doors.

The Filipino man is there, banging on the glass in frustration because he can't get it to open. It is obvious he can't read English, because in his effort to escape he is repeatedly pressing the red button, marked "Close." He turns desperately to the woman standing next to him.

"Kiss me!" he implores, but the woman turns away from him, embarrassed.

Eventually the train begins to pull away from the station. In desperation, the man pulls the emergency lever, and the train screeches to a sudden halt.

"For God's sake," says the Australian man to the girl by the doors, "why didn't you just kiss the guy?"

There are a few titters from further down the carriage, but most of the passengers where I am are stony-faced. They want to get to work.

The Filipino is going frantic. Despite his best efforts the doors *still* have not opened. He resumes his attack on the Close button, hitting it now with his palms. The rest of us just sit there in silence, waiting. For a while I think the Filipino is going to cry.

At last the doors open, and a London Underground official appears, followed by two Transport Police. He seems to fill the doorway, not only with his body (which is extremely large) but with his presence. He exudes authority, and I can sense a collective sigh of relief gathering amongst my fellow passengers. "All right," the London Underground man gruffly announces to the whole carriage, "who pulled the emergency brake?"

There is a moment of silence before *everyone* in the carriage points at the Filipino simultaneously. "He did!"

The official looks down at the Filipino and snorts with annoyance, as if he too recognizes the man as a tube virgin. The Filipino looks back at his savior lovingly. "Kiss me . . ." he croons.

"Right, that's enough of that!" says the official, and nods to the two policemen. They step forward, one on either side of the Filipino, and march him out of the carriage. At last, the doors shut, and the train finally pulls away again. The other passengers all turn back to whatever it was they were doing before the commotion as if nothing has happened, satisfied to be on their way again.

I can see by the look on Brian's face that he is horrified. "Nobody helped him!" he is saying. He glares round the carriage at all the others, who are doing a very good job of ignoring him. "I can't believe nobody helped him!"

"Well, *you* didn't help him, either," I point out.

Nobody else in the carriage says anything. The woman who looks like my old French teacher goes back to her book, the black man with the bald head goes back to reading the adverts above my head, and the middle-aged woman at last notices the streak of lipstick on her cheek and starts to attack it hurriedly with a tissue.

The man with the handlebar mustache resumes his contemplation of the girl with the pierced face. The Australian man smiles at me, as if he has found the whole episode very amusing. I scowl back at him. There is nothing funny about what has just happened. Nothing at all. I look at my watch. This train is now seven minutes late.

Chapter 8

8:01 AM—Mile End–Aldgate East–Whitechapel—District Line

8:13 AM—Whitechapel–Shoreditch–New Cross—East London Line

8:35 AM—New Cross–New Cross Gate—On foot

8:39 AM—New Cross Gate–Whitechapel—East London Line

8:54 AM—Whitechapel–Upton Park—District Line

I spend the next hour trying to weave my way through the spaghetti of lines east of the City. Boxed in by commuters everywhere I go, I can't really muster the energy to be brisk about it—I move like a zombie from one line to the next, taking photos through a haze of sleepiness. At one point I am in such a daze that I forget to change lines and have to double back on myself—another five minutes lost. But I can't be too angry with myself because I am now, at long last, on the way to my first collection point: Upminster, where my credit card is waiting for me in a green envelope taped to the back of a chocolate vending machine.

Brian has been strangely quiet for the last few stops. After the incident with the Filipino he continued quizzing me on my tube knowledge for a while, but he hasn't said much since New Cross—he's just been following me around like some faithful hound. He seems cheerful enough, though, and he has been singing quietly to himself (some song from a 1950s musical, I think). I'm just beginning to enjoy the silence between us, when he breaks it, abruptly, to ask about the line we are now on.

"What's the most interesting thing you know about the District Line?" he says.

I sigh (loudly, so that he will hear it). "Haven't I told you enough about the tube for one day?"

"Go on!" he urges me. "I challenge you to know something interesting about it. I bet you don't. It's the most boring line on the Underground."

"No," I say. "The *Bakerloo* Line is the most boring line on the Underground."

"Well, it shouldn't be a problem, then. I'll give you thirty seconds to come up with something interesting about the District Line, or you'll have to buy me a drink once we get to Upminster."

It doesn't occur to me to tell him that the pubs won't be open when we get to Upminster—I'm sure Brian knows some drinking hole that will be willing to serve him booze before eleven in the morning. And besides, the last thing I want is to lose any sort of challenge today.

"Right," I say. "Statistics from 1996 show that the District Line is the second-busiest line on the Underground."

"I said interesting!" He smiles.

"Okay, okay! How about the stations? Lots of them are listed."

"No. Still not good enough. You have ten seconds left."

"The trains are mostly D78 stock?"

"No."

"With a capacity of 1,372 passengers?"

"No. Boring."

I am racking my brains for something, but I'm afraid he's probably right. There is nothing interesting about this line—not for a train nonenthusiast. In a last desperate effort to come up with something to satisfy my drunken companion, I tell him the only thing of note I can think of.

"I met Rachel on the District Line. On the platform at Kensington (Olympia). Does that count?"

"Ah," says Brian. "Now, *that's* interesting."

And before I know it, I'm telling him all about the genesis of the world which is me and Rachel. Funny how these things happen, isn't it? I was looking forward to a long, quiet journey out to Upminster—but here I am gabbling away again. The funniest thing is that I'm glad to be doing it. It feels important to remember how Rachel and I met, and I want to make sure that I get it exactly right. For myself.

Here's how the story goes . . .

Chapter 9
How I Met Rachel

August 1998—Kensington (Olympia)—District Line

I was sitting on a bench on the platform at Olympia, extremely drunk, extremely fed up. I was drunk because I had just spent the evening having a reunion with a bunch of people I used to know years ago at university—it's obligatory to get drunk on such occasions. And I was fed up because I'd wasted most of the night plying one of them with wine (a woman called Sonya whom I'd always fancied in tutorials), only to find out she'd got married five years ago to a racing driver. After her husband came to pick her up from the wine bar (in some unbelievably flashy Italian car), I wasn't really in the mood to socialize. Instead, I spent the rest of the night plying *myself* with wine, which, as you can imagine, is enough to make you both drunk and fed up in one go.

I don't really know how I got from the wine bar to Olympia—it's all a bit of a blur. The only thing I remember is that I shared part of my journey with another man who was even more drunk than I was.

His name was Ziggy (at least, I think his name was Ziggy—he had zigzaggy teeth, anyway), and he told me a sexist joke which went like this:

How long does it take to get a woman into bed? . . .

Unfortunately, I can't remember the punch line. Given the extent of Ziggy's drunkenness, it's entirely possible that he didn't even tell me the punch line—but anyway, at the time it didn't seem important. It was the question itself which mattered. I remember it circling round and round my brain as I stumbled towards the station, and thinking to myself that on current form I'd *never* get a woman into bed. As far as jokes go, that's not very funny.

So there I was, sitting on a bench on the platform, alone, with the contents of my head sloshing around miserably. To pass the time, I was drunkenly imagining that I was sitting at the bottom of the Adelaide pool at Swiss Cottage Sports Centre. I don't know if you've ever noticed this, but tube stations always sound like swimming pools when you're drunk. It's better when you're at a proper underground station, but even some of the open stations like Kensington (Olympia) do it: there's a certain quality about the echo. Tonight, the muffled sound of voices was reverberating off the walls of the exhibition hall, and there were squeals of laughter coming from some women at the other end of the platform—the sort of noise little girls make when they're splashing around in the shallow end. Just by me there were a couple of fifteen-year-old boys pushing each other up and down the platform: I couldn't help imagining that some show-off lifeguard would start blowing a whistle at them and tell them to keep away from the edge. All it needed to complete the picture was a woman to walk past wearing a swimsuit. Which is strange, because that's exactly what happened.

She must have been in her early twenties, and she was walking down the platform in a blue, all-in-one bathing costume. She had a jacket on as well, which was obviously far too big for her, but even so it was only long enough to cover the tops of her thighs. And anyway, it kept swinging open as she walked. When she saw that there were people on the platform, she self-consciously pulled her jacket around her, but it didn't hide the fact that she was practically naked. She even had bare feet.

She came over to my bench and sat down beside me, and as she did so I couldn't help noticing her jacket ride up her legs. She tried to pull it down to cover herself, but that only meant it slipped off one of her milk-colored shoulders in a sort of six-of-one–half-a-dozen-of-the-other type situation. I was mesmerized. She turned and looked at me briefly, as if she knew exactly what I was thinking.

"What are you looking at?" she said indignantly.

"Nothing," I said.

"Good. Because I've had enough of people looking at me for one night."

"Really?" I turned away and put my head back in my hands. "Lucky you. No one's given *me* a second glance."

I figured it was probably best not to say anything more. The poor girl probably wanted to pretend she wasn't even there. Whatever the reason for her state of undress, this was the stuff of bad dreams—being stuck in a tube station with virtually no clothes on, having to get home somehow without anyone seeing you. Just the thought of it was making me feel sober.

We sat on the bench together, not saying anything, for what seemed like an eternity. It was taking twice as long as it should for the train to come, as if the minutes had to wade waist-deep through water to arrive. It was frustrating for me—it must have been hell for her.

Eventually, even in my drunken state, I couldn't help my curiosity getting the better of me. "Do you mind if I ask . . ." I began.

"Yes."

"Fine," I said. It was obviously not a good time. "Sorry," I added.

"If you must know," she said at last, "I've been modeling cars at the motor show in Olympia. It was all my stupid flatmate's idea. I've never been so embarrassed in all my life."

"Didn't you take any clothes with you?"

She pounced on the question as if she had been expecting me to ask it. "Yes. Yes, I bloody well did. Only that's not much help when they're locked away in a changing room and you're storming out in protest. The only thing I could get my hands on was my supervisor's jacket."

"Storming out in protest?"

"Abso-fucking-lutely. Tonight I've been whistled at, I've had my arse pinched—even the supervisor tried to touch me up. It's like they think I'm a piece of meat or something. So I stormed out in protest—all right?"

"Oh," I said. What else could I say to something like that?—especially as it was taking up most of my energy not to stare at those legs myself.

When the train eventually pulled up, I was almost as relieved as she was. I can't say it had been exactly comfortable sitting on that bench with her—it was a sort of mixture between shared embarrassment, sexual tension, and a desire to laugh at her for being so stupid. Getting on the train at least gave us something to do. Something normal and everyday.

We shared our carriage with the two teenage boys, which wasn't ideal, because they kept on looking over at my companion and giggling. In a sudden flash of chivalry I removed my coat and offered it to the woman to cover her legs, which she did with a grateful smile.

"So where are you going to?" I asked.

"West Ham."

"West Ham! And you're going home like that?"

"It's not as if I have a choice, is it?"

If she had been going back to Hampstead or Richmond or somewhere out in a nice middle-class suburb, I wouldn't have minded. Or if it had been Camden Town, it would have been fine—it's practically compulsory to walk down the street in nothing but a swimsuit there. But West Ham? It's not the sort of place I'd want to walk around seminaked in the middle of the night, even if I wasn't a woman. Which I'm not.

I was suddenly overcome by a desire to help her out, and of course, the machinery of my brain being well oiled with wine, I came up with another of my brilliant plans. "Well, it just so happens that I'm going to West Ham myself," I lied, "so if you like, I'll take you home." Almost imperceptibly she drew back, and I knew at once that I'd overstepped some hidden mark. In a hurry to correct my mistake I added, "Don't worry, I'm not some weirdo. When we get to the station, we can catch a cab and I'll drop you off."

"Right," she said warily. "Okay. Thanks."

That's the problem with being chivalrous: once you've started you just can't stop. It begins with giving a girl your coat, and before you know it you're accompanying her halfway down the District Line in the wrong direction. It's not like you even have any choice in the matter, so what can you do, except throw yourself in at the deep end and try and get to know her a bit better?

At Earl's Court I found out the woman's name was Rachel.

At Victoria three *very* drunk men got on and started laughing uncontrollably because Rachel was wearing two coats. It's great stuff, alcohol.

By Westminster we were chatting quite nicely, and I felt like kissing her. That was the first time I noticed what delightful lips she had. For a moment Ziggy's punch-line-less joke came back into my head, and I was forced to turn away because I started blushing. But I couldn't help it—Rachel was beautiful. It was like a dream come true—alone in a tube carriage with a beautiful woman. A beautiful seminaked woman. A beautiful seminaked woman with the most kissable lips in London. I was in heaven—but of course it didn't last, because just as we were leaving Westminster Station, she finally asked me what I did for a living.

It's strange but, when it comes to chat-up lines, saying I work in a bookshop has never really worked for me. And for some reason most women don't seem to find the tube a turn-on—in fact, the mere mention of public transport seems to turn even nymphomaniacs into stone. That's why I found myself now telling Rachel I was a racing driver. A bit of a stupid thing to do, considering I don't even know how to drive.

"Goodness!" said Rachel. "A racing driver! How come you're not driving home tonight?"

"Well, I . . . er . . . I had a bit to drink tonight, so I thought it'd be best to leave the car there."

"What sort of car is it? I bet you drive something dead flashy."

"Yep. It's a . . . a Fiat."

"A Fiat," she said, unimpressed.

I felt like kicking myself. For some reason Fiat had been the only make of car I could think of at the time. "Oh, but it's not just an ordinary Fiat," I burbled, in an attempt to salvage the situation. "No, it's the top of the range. It's a Fiat . . ." I desperately tried to think of the name of the car Sonya's husband drove her away in tonight, or indeed any name that might sound even a little exotic. "A Fiat Tagliatelli," I said at last, triumphantly.

"I don't remember seeing any of those at the motor show tonight."

"Oh, no, you wouldn't have done—they're very exclusive. Only twenty of them ever made. Of course, I don't drive it very often—it reminds me too much of work. And besides, cars count for over eighty percent of the pollution in London. Unlike the tube, which runs off electricity generated by natural gas and low distillate oil, and which is therefore a far more efficient means of transport."

She looked at me strangely. "Right," she said. "Still, it's a shame you didn't tell me when we were back in Kensington. I could have driven it for you, seeing as you live so close to me. I've always wanted to drive a . . . What sort of car did you say it was again?"

"Er . . . a Linguini. Perhaps I could give you a ride in it some time."

I almost kicked myself as I said this—how the hell would I pull that one off?—but Rachel seemed impressed, because she looked at me and smiled broadly. "That is something," she said, "that I wouldn't miss for all the world!"

We carried on chatting as we passed through Embankment, Temple, and Blackfriars. Rachel turned out to be twenty-four years old—just under three years younger than I was at the time. She had just left college, and was now working for a PR agency. I asked her all sorts of questions about herself, lavishing attention upon her, partly because I wanted to turn the conversation away from cars, and partly because I loved watching her lips move. We went through station after station, and for once I was oblivious to the tube around me. For the first time since the evening began everything was going along swimmingly. I wished the journey could last forever.

At Tower Hill an Italian-looking man got on and started staring at Rachel lasciviously. I suppressed the urge to put my arm round her protectively (a wise decision, as it turned out, because whenever I've done that since, she has snapped at me for it—she says it feels like I'm claiming her or something). At Aldgate East everyone got off, leaving me and Rachel alone in our carriage. By the time we got to Mile End, Rachel had begun to shiver.

"Here," I said, "why don't you take my jumper."

This *wasn't* being chivalrous. As far as I was concerned, this was being coldly calculating. Not only was I trying to continue the theme of me being all nice and caring, I also figured that the more things of mine she borrowed the more likely she was to give me her phone number—after all, I'd have to get them back at some point. Plus I'd get to watch her take her coat off so that she could pull the jumper over her swimsuit—a prospect which I have to admit didn't exactly upset me.

"But what about you?" she said.

"Oh, don't worry about me. We racing drivers don't need jumpers, you know. In fact, you can borrow it if you like. Give us your phone number, and I'll come round and pick it up tomorrow."

Unfortunately for me, Rachel was not stupid. "Hang on a minute," she said. "How come you're being so nice to me?"

"No reason. I'm always nice to people."

"You're not trying to chat me up, are you?"

"No . . ."

"Because if you are, you can forget it. I've had enough people trying to chat me up tonight."

"Don't worry, I'm not trying to chat you up."

"All night I've had people staring at my breasts and running their eyes along the length of my legs. It's obvious they're imagining what I look like naked and thinking what they'd like to do to me if only they could take me home. I'd hate it if that's what you were thinking."

"I told you," I gulped, "I'm not trying to chat you up!"

"No?"

"Of course not."

"Oh." She paused and thought about this for a while. "So I suppose what you're trying to tell me is that you don't find me attractive."

"No, that's not what I'm saying at all."

"So you do find me attractive."

"Well . . . Well, of course you're attractive, but that doesn't mean . . ."

"So you think I'm attractive, but only attractive like your sister, or your aunt or something. Not like a woman you fancy."

I panicked. "No. I do fancy you. I mean, I would fancy you, if it wasn't rude. I mean, I would fancy you if you wanted me to, but as you don't . . ." I was floundering, and I knew it. There was nothing for it but to come clean. "All right," I said at last, "if you want to know the truth, I *was* trying to chat you up."

"I knew it!" she said, punching me violently in the arm. "Typical!"

"Yeah, I know. Sorry."

We sat in silence until the train neared Rachel's stop. I felt despicable for trying to seduce someone in such a vulnerable position. Not only that, I felt stupid, because we had been getting on so well, and I had gone and ruined it. If the truth be known, the main reason I'd tried it on was because Ziggy's question had been going round and round my head all night—How long does it take to get a woman into bed?—and I kept imagining that the joke was on me. How sad is that? I was trying to impress a man who had passed out almost an hour ago in a doorway in Kensington.

Rachel kept looking round at me, as if she expected me to say something, but I was too embarrassed even to apologize further. I desperately wanted to get this farcical journey over and done with so that I could hurry back to my own, empty bed in Belsize Park. Eventually, to my relief, we pulled into West Ham Station.

"Look," I said, as we got off the train, "I fancy walking home—why don't I just wait with you for a taxi, and then we can go our separate ways?"

She looked at me, disappointed. "So, you don't want to come back to my place, then?"

Her question threw me. "Well . . . I don't know."

"If you've had a few drinks, you'll probably be needing a cup of coffee," she said, smiling nervously. "It's the least I can do after all your help."

"Yeah," I said, gathering confidence once more, "I suppose it *is* the least you can do."

"And if you're going to take me for a drive in your fabulous Fiat Macaroni, you're going to need to know where I live."

"How right you are," I said. "How right you are."

This is the story I tell Brian: I first met Rachel on a journey between Kensington (Olympia) and West Ham—until today, probably the most eventful journey of my life. Before I knew it I was on my way back to her place, and I hardly need to say that she didn't keep my coat on for the rest of the night . . . But we'll leave it there—I'm not going to say any more, because that would be ungentlemanly.

Suffice it to say that the answer to Ziggy's question is twenty-two stops.

Chapter 10

9:07 AM—Upton Park–Barking—District Line

Brian wipes a grubby tear away from his face. "That's so romantic," he says. "That's probably the most romantic-est thing I've ever heard."

Our own journey has taken us out beyond West Ham by now. It is just gone ten past nine, and we're pulling out of Upton Park. I watch Brian wipe his eyes and wonder what in my story could have triggered his tears. It's supposed to be an amusing story, for God's sake—he shouldn't be feeling sad for us. It makes me wonder if he knows something I don't, some terrible end our relationship is doomed for. But then again, maybe I just told it wrong.

"How did you get out of the business about the flashy car?" Brian continues. "I mean, you were supposed to be taking her for a ride in it the next day."

"It turns out she never believed me in the first place when I said I was a racing driver. No, she thought I was joking all along—said she found it quite endearing."

Brian shakes his head in disbelief. "You lucky so-and-so," he says.

"I suppose it's not surprising she didn't believe me really, seeing as she was wearing my coat. Famous racing drivers don't tend to buy duffle coats from Oxfam. Still, it makes you wonder, doesn't it? She thought I was being endearing, when in fact I was being a bit of a prat."

We both sit and ponder this for a while as the train gathers speed, and I can't help being reminded of the lipstick word Rachel wrote on my forehead this morning. It has taken her three years to work out that I'm not that endearing after all. It crosses my mind that perhaps she meant more by that one lipstick word than I thought. Perhaps she doesn't want to marry me after all.

"Still, you got together with her," says Brian, after a while, "and that's the main thing. Not only that, but you're still with her. What's it matter how it happened?"

"Yeah, I suppose you're right."

"'Course I'm right. Just you make sure you keep hold of her, that's all." He takes a melancholy sip of his beer and stares out of the window. "You lucky so-and-so," he repeats. "I get drunk on the platform at Olympia all the time, and I've never once copped off."

I am tempted to point out that there's a difference between being drunk in a station and going there specifically to *get* drunk, but I don't have the heart. For the first time today Brian seems a little deflated, as if his tramp's armor of street wisdom and Tennent's Super has finally been pierced. I look at him, and I am suddenly reminded that he is not just a tramp but an old man—much older than my father. My distaste at the idea of a tramp "copping off" is replaced with distaste at the idea of an old man "copping off." He should be at home with a pipe and slippers, and a wife bringing him cups of hot milk. He should be looking forward to his retirement, and spoiling his grandchildren with sweets behind their parents' backs. Not sleeping rough in tube stations.

"Weren't you ever married, Brian?" I ask.

"Still am."

"But . . . but where's your wife, then?"

He hesitates, as if thinking whether to answer me or not. "We're separated. She left me almost ten years ago."

"Where did she go?"

Brian sighs, as if he doesn't really like me asking such questions. "She ran off with another man, if you must know. A bloke who lived at the end of our road. A kitchen salesman."

"Jesus, that's terrible!"

"Yes," he mutters. He is staring out of the window. "Yes, it *is* terrible. Still, it can't be helped now, and there's no point in moping about it. Life goes on, as they say. She has her life, and I have mine."

As if to drive the point home he takes another swig on his beer can. It is meant to be a full stop on the conversation, and I understand it as such—there are some things which are too painful to discuss with strangers on a tube train. I decide it might be better not to pry any further, so I follow Brian's eyes through the window to the acres of train tracks and flat waste ground that exist between Upton Park and Barking. For the first time today it has started to rain.

Chapter 11

9:13 AM—Barking–Upminster—District Line

I have to say the world we're passing is a strange one. Everything looks sort of *square.* The oblong council blocks we passed at Bow Road were quickly replaced with big rectangular warehouses, and at Bromley-by-Bow there was a rubbish recycler's where paper and cardboard have been mashed into massive cubes. Now, at Upney, we are passing row upon row of boxlike pebble-dashed houses, with row upon row of boxlike garden sheds at the ends of rectangular strips of garden. Even the train I'm on isn't so much a tube as a carton—it's like traveling in a giant version of one of those boxes Jaffa cakes come in, only without all the bright colors.

Or actually, maybe *with* the bright colors—if not on our train, then at least everywhere else. As we trundle through this boxy world, we seem to be surrounded by color—enormous curves and swirls, painted as if in protest at all the right angles which surround them. Just after Barking we passed a train in a siding which was *covered* in bright blue, red, and orange graffiti, and at Dagenham East there is a whole length of wall—there must be at least half a mile of it—

coated in a stream of multicolored lettering. Some of it is quite beautiful. All the graffiti artists have names like Dodo, Jaf, Hag, JC, Zero. I suppose you've got to have a short name if you're going to sign it in spray paint next to a 630-volt electric rail with 40-mile-an-hour trains on it.

I watch all this in silence as we chug through Elm Park and Hornchurch and Upminster Bridge. We are approaching Upminster now—the most easterly station on the system, eighteen miles outside Central London—and once we get there, we will simply turn round and come back again, like as not on the same train.

"So," says Brian, "are we meeting your mate when we get to Upminster?"

"No," I say.

He is confused. "But I thought you were picking up your credit card there."

"I am, but not from him."

"He's left it with someone else, then?"

"Kind of." I look around me uncomfortably, just to make sure no one's listening. "Actually, if you must know, it's strapped to the back of a chocolate machine."

Brian stares at me in disbelief. "A chocolate machine," he repeats.

"Yes. You know how they have those machines back-to-back on open-air platforms? Well, Rolf said he'd hide my card in between them. It seemed the only safe place."

Brian turns away again. "This gets better and better," he mutters.

Ignoring him, I pick up my bag and go and stand by the doors, ready to get out. It's a little premature, because the train probably won't pull into the station for at least another minute or so, but I can sense another of Brian's lectures coming on, so I figure it's probably sensible. It turns out to be a mistake. Even as I stand up the train begins to slow, and as I wait by the doors it grinds gradually to a halt. The station is about two hundred yards away. We have stopped a mere stone's throw from our destination.

I don't need to tell you what it feels like, because I'm sure it's happened to you too: you think you've arrived somewhere, when something goes wrong at the last minute. Perhaps the train in front of you has had to stop for some reason, and so you can't get into the station. Or maybe the points have chosen that moment to fail, and you have to wait for twenty minutes while someone comes and sorts it out. I've even been on a train which entered a station too fast and activated the automatic emergency brakes—when we screeched to a halt, there was nothing but a thin sheet of metal and glass between me and my platform, but because a couple of carriages were still in the tunnel, they couldn't open the doors. At times like these it's not the fact that you've stopped that pisses you off; it's the fact that you're nearly there. There's nothing more frustrating in life than the thought that you almost made it.

The thing is, whenever this happens, there's always someone who stood up too soon, and today it's me. Today it's my turn to have everyone looking at me, like they're thinking I'm a fool for getting out of my seat before the train got where it's going. For a while I hover in the aisle, unsure whether to sit back down again or hang around like a git by the doors. In the end I compromise by leaning back against the pole and trying to look casual.

The train stands, motionless, and in total silence. I have to admit, I am starting to get a little anxious—we should have started up again by now. Brian is looking at me with a worried expression on his face. "What's happened?" he asks.

"How the hell should I know?"

The impatience in my own voice tells me exactly how anxious I really am. Every minute counts today, and I can't really afford to stand around like this, waiting indefinitely for my train to move. And what's more, my credit card is strapped to a chocolate machine—

while I'm stuck in this tube carriage, *anyone* could find it. As the time passes I become more and more restless, until I find myself pacing backwards and forwards in front of the doors, as though my own movement will make up for the lack of movement of the train. Five minutes pass. Ten minutes. And still there is nothing.

"What the hell's going on!" I blurt impatiently, to no one in particular. "I can see the bloody station from here—we could have *walked* there by now!"

Even as I'm saying this, I am watching through the glass of the doors to where a train is passing us, going in the opposite direction.

"Jesus, that's our train!" I am consumed with irritation—if this bloody rust-bucket had moved ten minutes ago, I could have been on my way back to town by now. I watch helplessly as the carriages slide past us, out of reach. It seems full of happy, smiling people. Happy, smiling people who don't have to be anywhere on time, but will probably be on time anyway. And as they cheerfully roll on, my own carriage stays motionless.

"Andy." Brian's voice is calling me calmly. "Andy, there's no point in shouting. It ain't going to help."

"What else am I supposed to do while I'm standing here?"

Another man, about the same age as Brian, is sitting nearby. He chooses now to add his own penny's worth. "He's right, you know—shouting never did do no one no good. Perhaps if you sat down . . ."

He doesn't need to finish the sentence. I should never have stood up in the bloody first place. I plonk myself down in a seat by the door, and, as if it has been waiting for me to do just that, the loudspeaker crackles on and the voice of the driver rains down on us. "We are sorry for the delay. This is due to a signal failure at Upminster Station. We will try to get the train into the station just as soon as it is safe to do so. I repeat . . ."

There's something profoundly irritating about such announcements. Before they are made, you curse the fact that nobody is telling you what's happened—but knowing what's happened never helps. What you really want to hear is someone telling you that the wait is over. Anything else just makes it worse. This announcement, like all such announcements, produces a general groan throughout the carriage.

"It's always *we,* isn't it?" I hear one of the other passengers grumble. "Never *I'm* sorry, always *we* are."

I say nothing, because apparently I am not allowed to say anything anymore.

We wait another few minutes. I do some quick calculations in my head. If I'm going to make it round the system in nineteen hours, then I only have about forty-five minutes to spare. But I have already lost five minutes by missing our stop at Whitechapel earlier, and a further seven minutes because of that Filipino pulling the emergency handle. Add that to the—I look at my watch—eight minutes we have been standing still, and we have a total of twenty minutes wasted. I sigh heavily, but I am at least partly relieved. As long as we start moving *now,* I should still just about make it. It's a tight margin, but I still have just under half an hour to spare.

Fortunately, I don't have to live through this torture for much longer. I am about to leap out of my seat and give the carriage doors an almighty kick when suddenly the train gives a lurch and crawls, painfully slowly, towards the station. At last we reach the platform, and the train opens its doors to disgorge its irate passengers. It is 9:41. Since I started the day, I have lost a total of twenty-one minutes.

There is an end-of-the-line atmosphere at Upminster, intensified by the fact we have all been so still for the past ten minutes. While all the other passengers grab coats and bags and hurry out towards the exit, Brian and I walk along the platform in search of the chocolate machine. We find it about halfway down, and sure enough, taped to its back with electrician's tape there is a green envelope. Tearing the envelope open, I find my credit card inside, along with a handwritten note which says simply:

12:00, central buffers, Cockfosters

"What does that mean?" asks Brian.

"I suppose it must be where he's hidden the next item. My passport, perhaps. Or my Eurostar tickets."

Behind us the train we have just disembarked from makes a humming noise, as if its engines are warming up. Grabbing Brian by the sleeve, I leap back onto it, for fear that it will start back on its way to town without us. But the train does not move anywhere. After a few moments all the lights in the carriages suddenly turn off, and a voice comes sailing down the platform towards me: "All change please! This train is being taken out of service. All change please!"

As I step back onto the platform, Brian also sidles out of the carriage. "What are we going to do now?" he says. He looks nervous.

"I don't know about you," I say curtly, "but I'm getting on the first train back to London."

Brian looks at the darkened train behind us. It is the only train at any of the platforms. "It doesn't look good," he says.

I ignore him because there is an LT man walking down the platform towards us, still calling out his chant: "All change please!" As he nears us, I collar him.

"Excuse me—when's the next District Line train going back in?"

He looks at me blankly. "It isn't," he says.

A wave of trepidation sweeps over me. "What do you mean, it isn't?"

"I mean we're not running any tube trains at the moment. Signal failure. You'll have to take a bus. District Line trains are now running from Dagenham East only."

"Dagenham East!" I gasp. "That's *miles* away!"

"About five miles away, to be precise," he says, and starts to walk away.

"Wait!" I cry desperately. "It's only a signal failure *here*—surely it won't hurt to run trains? This is the end of the line—there aren't any other trains to crash into!"

"That's where you're wrong, sir. We run overground services from this station as well, so if we're going to keep those going, we have to stop the tube trains. Like I say, you'll have to catch a bus."

"B-but . . ." I stammer, "but I haven't got time!"

"Sorry, mate. There's nothing I can do." And with that he carries on walking down the platform.

I slump down onto a station bench. Dagenham East! There's no way I can get there in the twenty or so minutes I have to spare. I can't believe it—I have been beaten by a single signal failure. Some tube adventurer I turned out to be.

"So that's it," I say. I think perhaps I might be in shock. "Not even five hours into my day, and I've already lost the bet."

Brian is staring at me with a concerned look on his face. "Aren't you even going to try?" he says.

"No."

"Why not?"

I feel like hitting him. "Because there's no point. If I took a bus to Dagenham East now, it would waste at least half an hour—and that's if I can find out which bus to take. Even if everything worked perfectly, I'd still have to break the world record for the rest of the trip just to make it round in time. It's just not possible."

"What if you took a cab to Dagenham?"

"I can't. By the terms of the bet I am only allowed to use public transport. Catching a cab would be cheating. And besides, there's no guaranteeing I'll even be able to find one."

Brian sits down on the bench beside me. "Maybe we could *steal* a train." He means it as a sort of wry joke.

"Just leave it, Brian. It's over."

"But there must be something . . ."

"I said it's over! I've lost the challenge, okay. I've lost my bet. I've lost . . ."

At last the enormity of what I've done hits me, and I can't quite believe I have been so stupid. Despite all her harshness with me yesterday, despite her ultimatum and the emotional blackmail, in the end Rachel was actually right. I *am* a twat. I must have been insane to think I could do the system in a day without any time to prepare. I must have been totally off my trolley. And now I'm going to pay for it, because even if Rachel does still want to marry me, when she finds out what I've just gambled away, there's not a chance in hell that she's going to forgive me.

Chapter 12

9:55 AM—Upminster—District Line

We sit and stare at the train carriage before us. It seems somehow symbolic—the lights are off, and the doors are closed. There isn't a single spark of electricity in the whole damn thing. I remember the conversation I had with Brian earlier, about becoming a tramp, and suddenly the idea doesn't seem so far-fetched. After all, if Rachel kicks me out over this, I'll be homeless. And without a home or a girlfriend to go back to, the prospect of joining Brian in some doorway for a can of Tennent's Super doesn't seem so unwelcome anymore.

As if he has heard my thoughts, Brian lifts his can to his mouth for one final swig—but before it reaches his lips, he stops. He is looking straight ahead, beyond our tube train, to where another train is pulling into the station. "Hang on a second," he says. "Did that man say there were overground services running through this station?"

"Yes."

"Where do they go to?"

"I don't know."

I'm not really interested in Brian and his overground services. If he wants to go and get on some obscure overground train, then I wish he would just do it and let me sit here in peace (although I have to say it annoys me a little that he is only willing to leave me alone *now,* when my own journey has failed).

Brian is being far from peaceful. He is standing up now, looking for the LT man we spoke to earlier. Spying him walking down the platform towards us, he shouts over to him excitedly. "Oi! Excuse me! What time does the next overground leave for London?"

The LT man points to the train which is coming to a stop across the tracks on the other platform. "That's one there," he says.

At last I realize what Brian is getting at. I sit up, and for a moment I allow myself a glimmer of hope. "Where's it going?" I ask.

"Fenchurch Street."

I look at Brian, disappointed. "That's not on the tube map," I say.

"So?" His eyes are alive with excitement. "Fenchurch Street is only two minutes walk from Tower Hill, and then we're right back on the District Line in the middle of town!"

I gape at him, unable for a moment to take the information in. "Jesus," I gasp, "what the hell are we hanging around here for? We *have* to catch that train!"

I leap off my bench and, grabbing Brian's bags and mine, I push past the LT man and run as fast as I can towards the bridge to the other platform. By the time I reach the stairs Brian has overtaken me, showing incredible pace for a man of his age. My lungs are already bursting, but I'm determined to keep up with him—if he's going to get to that train, I'm going to make damn sure I do too. We run over the bridge and down the stairs to the train, but it is already pulling away.

"Quick!" screams Brian. It is an old-fashioned train, with doors that open manually—as Brian runs along the platform beside the moving carriage, he manages to grab hold of one of the handles and throw the door open. He scrambles in, and then hauls me and my bags after him. I am afraid to say that I am in too much of a state even to get on the train properly—as it leaves the platform my legs are still hanging out of the open door, and Brian has to drag me into the carriage before we can close the door behind me.

I am so out of breath I can hardly stand up. I stumble, exhausted, into a crowded carriage full of people, all looking vaguely disapproving of our method of entry—but I don't care. All I care about is the fact that we have made it.

I look over to where my companion has collapsed to get his breath back.

"Brian," I pant, "I could kiss you!"

He looks momentarily perturbed. "No, you couldn't," he says warningly.

His squeamishness warms me to him, and for a moment I really *do* want to kiss him. "You silly old fucker!" I smile.

The train speeds on towards London through Hornchurch and Elm Park and all the other stations we have just been to. It stops momentarily at Barking, and then tears away again, overtaking all the slower District Line trains as it goes. Through Plaistow and West Ham and Bow we race, and then beyond the tube lines, through Limehouse and on to the City. I am bowed by a newfound respect for overground trains—if they all go this fast, I might give up using tube trains altogether.

By the time we arrive in Fenchurch Street, we have made ourselves an extra twenty minutes. Before the train has even stopped Brian has the door open, much to the frowning and tutting of the other passengers, ready to leap out onto the platform. I feel as though I have only just got my breath back from the last lot of running, and here I am about to start running again, down the platform, down the stairs, and out along the street to Tower Hill. But as I take off after Brian, I don't mind—in fact I'm grinning all the bloody way. I can't help myself. The bet's not over yet. We are right back on schedule.

part 2

north london

Chapter 13

10:14 AM—Belsize Park

Rachel was back in bed when the phone rang. It was gone ten, and she was wondering whether she was going to get up. She had already packed most of her things this morning, just after Andy had left at four-thirty, but she still had loads to do today. She was supposed to be collecting her wedding dress this morning. She was supposed to be going shopping, to buy last-minute things like camera film, sunscreen, after-sun lotion—things for the honeymoon. And she was meeting Sophie for lunch. There was plenty she should be doing right now, starting with answering the telephone, but somehow she didn't seem able to begin. She was having trouble convincing herself that it was worth it. And staying in bed was so easy.

She let the phone ring six times, and then listened as the answerphone kicked in. If it was important, she'd get up, but it was probably just another friend of hers calling to ask directions to the church in Paris. Whoever it was, the chances were pretty low that the call was important enough to get her out of bed. And if it was

Andy, calling to apologize for leaving her here all alone wondering what the hell he was playing at, then sod him.

She lifted her head off the pillow, half hoping that she would hear Andy's voice coming out of the answerphone imploring her to pick up, but instead all she heard was a long low-pitched tone. Whoever it was had rung off.

She flopped her head back onto the pillow again. Why was she marrying such a twat? Other women didn't have twats for husbands. Other women didn't marry men who made stupid bets they couldn't possibly win, and who abandoned them in the early hours of the morning only twenty-four hours before their wedding. Other women didn't have to put up with their fiancés being obsessed with the London Underground. So what was wrong with her?

Or perhaps other women did have to put up with that sort of stuff as well, and they were just too embarrassed to tell anyone. Perhaps that was what marriage was all about—letting your husband get away with being a twat. Turning a blind eye to the fact that he seems to love tube stations more than he loves you. And putting up with him not calling you when you're lying in bed waiting for the opportunity not to answer the phone.

She would have understood if it had been his stag night last night. If his friends had stripped him naked and dropped him off on one of the Shetland Islands for a joke, if they'd locked him in a disused tube station, or tied him to the front of a Circle Line train—well, that would be understandable. She didn't care if Andy's friends acted like idiots, because she wasn't marrying Andy's friends. But this business—this ridiculous bet Andy had made the last minute before their wedding—this was all Andy's own doing. He had *chosen* to do this.

She rolled over to stare at the wall for a bit. There was a stain above the mirror left over from when the upstairs flat's bath had overflowed—Andy said it looked a bit like a map of the Central Line. But then Andy said everything looked like something to do with the tube. If he ever went to a psychiatrist and was shown those inkblots, he'd probably say they all looked like trains or something. Where other people saw pictures of couples having sex, Andy would see an image of the signal box just outside Willesden Junction.

She let her eyes drift sadly across the other items on their bedroom wall—the mirror, the wall lamp, the picture her aunt had painted for her a few years ago for her twenty-fifth birthday. The vintage Underground map. She had just got to the bookshelf (with its copies of *Pride and Prejudice* and *Bridget Jones's Diary* sitting side by side with *Rails Through the Clay* and *London Under London)* when the phone rang again.

She listened to it ring—once, twice, thrice . . . and six times, until once again the answerphone picked up the call. Let it be him, she thought—*please,* let it be him. She felt like a schoolgirl again, praying for her boyfriend to call her. Only she wouldn't run to the phone like she would have then; she'd deliberately *not* run to the phone, give him the same medicine, let him wonder where *she* was.

She listened as her own voice beseeched the caller to leave a message, and then the beep, and then . . . Nothing. This wasn't right—Andy wasn't playing her game. How could she be expected to feel all victorious if he didn't even leave a message? She hit Andy's pillow halfheartedly. Not only was he a twat, he was an inconsiderate twat—and she'd make a point of telling him so just as soon as he deigned to talk to her again.

She sat up in bed, and as she did so a thought struck her. Perhaps he'd left a message on her mobile. He knew she was supposed to be up early this morning—she had so many things to do—perhaps he had simply assumed that she'd already left the flat. Reaching down to the floor beside the bed, she picked up her bag—after a few seconds rummaging, she located her mobile and switched it on.

There were three messages on her answering service. One of them was from her friend Sophie, asking if they were still meeting for lunch today. The second was a call from the department store where they had their wedding list—apparently most of the items on their list had been bought now, leaving only some glasses, a set of saucers, and an engraving of Turnpike Lane tube station by night. That, at least, was *one* sigh of relief. The last message was from the dress shop, saying her wedding dress was ready.

She was about to curse Andy out loud when the phone in the sitting room rang again. This time she would answer it. Pushing the covers aside, she swung her feet over the edge of the bed and onto the cool softness of the bedroom carpet. She hurried out into the hall—that was the fourth ring now—and through to the sitting room. It had better bloody well be Andy, she thought. She wouldn't have wanted to get out of bed for anyone else. It had better be Andy, calling to apologize. But she knew it wasn't. There was something, a certain irritating quality about the ring, that told her she was doing all this hurrying merely to answer a wrong number.

"Hello," she said, picking up the receiver. She flopped down onto the sofa.

"Rachel?"

"Yes, who's that?"

There was a pause, before the line went dead.

That's odd, she thought as she replaced the handset—must have been cut off. She shivered. Looking down, she realized she was only wearing a T-shirt. It was one of Andy's—one of those T-shirts from the London Transport Museum with a big, red-and-blue tube sign on the front of it, saying "Belsize Park." It came down to the tops of her knees, but even so, it was not quite warm enough to be wandering around the house without more on.

She was just about to get up and find her bathrobe when the phone rang again. Uncertainly, she picked it up once more.

"Hello?"

"Rachel." It was the same voice again—a familiar voice, a man's, but Rachel couldn't quite place it.

"Who is this?"

"I'm calling about your boyfriend," the voice said. "He's in trouble."

"What do you mean? What sort of trouble?"

"The sort of trouble you should know about if you're going to marry him. He doesn't deserve you, Rachel. If you only knew where he was right now. If you only knew what he was doing!"

Instinctively, Rachel stretched her T-shirt down over her knees. "What are you talking about? Who is this?"

"He's willing to risk you and all you have together. You should leave him. He's not worthy of you. You shouldn't marry him."

"Tell me who this is. If you don't tell me who you are, I'll . . ."

The line went dead.

Rachel put the receiver back on its cradle for a second time. For a few moments she sat where she was, staring at the phone, half expecting it to ring again. She felt quite unpleasant, like some stranger had just groped her on a train. Only this wasn't a stranger, because she recognized his voice. She thought hard for a moment . . . but no—she couldn't quite place it. It was probably just one of Andy's friends playing some pathetic joke on her. The thought angered her. Some of Andy's friends didn't know when to draw the line. She could just imagine Mickey, or Andy's work colleague Phil, thinking something like this was funny. But this morning, after spending several sleepless hours in bed alone, Rachel didn't have much of a sense of humor.

After a few moments she stood up. Now that she was out of bed, she might as well have a shower and get dressed. It didn't look as though Andy was going to call her, so sod him. She'd go out without talking to him and carry on with her day as planned. If he could do it, why shouldn't she?

Grabbing hold of the bottom of her T-shirt, she pulled it briskly over her head and threw it down on the sofa by the phone. What had the voice said?—"If you only knew where he was right now . . ." What an irritating thing to say! Christ, if she knew where he was right now, she'd go and find him and tell him to stop being such a selfish, untrustworthy, *uncommunicative* twat!

She stepped out into the hallway in the direction of the bathroom, and as she did so she caught sight of her own shadow flitting across the hallway wall. She used to be scared of her shadow once, when she was a kid: it used to chase her up the stairs in the night when she ran from the loo back to her bedroom. She didn't get scared by such things anymore, but this morning something certainly clicked within her anyway. It was sudden, like a cog had just turned slightly in her brain and everything now fitted into place—she now realized whom the voice on the other end of the telephone belonged to. A quiet man, shady-sounding, unwillling to give his name—it suddenly seemed so obvious. But rather than put her at ease, the discovery made her feel much worse. Because the man who had rung her was not the sort of person who would make practical jokes. He was probably the one friend of Andy's who lacked any sort of sense of humor at all. He was also the one friend of Andy's that Rachel couldn't stand. He gave her the creeps. The man who had rung her was Rolf.

Chapter 14

10:16 AM—Fenchurch Street–Tower Hill—On foot

We run along the platform, through the barriers, and out of the station. We throw ourselves down a flight of steps and into the maze of ancient streets that make up the City of London. It's like entering a ghost town, a disused labyrinth of pedestrianized walkways and buildings made of metal and glass—empty places devoid of any life and movement other than our own.

Brian leads the way because he knows the roads round here, while I follow, panting, determined not to fall too far behind him or make him slow his pace. My lungs feel as if they are about to burst through my rib cage, but as I leap uncertainly down another short flight of steps, I remind myself that this is a race, that there's no time for rest, no time for caution, and somehow the thought makes me feel strong.

Do women get this feeling—this primitive joy at hurling your body against its physical limitations? Do they feel the pleasure I feel, pursuing this challenge like it's a stag bolting out of sight in some primeval forest? Can they understand? Can they understand me?

Brian and I keep running—we run all the way. It's not far from Fenchurch Street to Tower Hill tube, but it feels important not to slacken our pace, not even slightly. We run down streets with ancient names—Crutched Friars, Seething Lane, Pepys Street—neglected places, long-forgotten, and our running fills those streets like unexpected storm water rushing through ancient channels. We take the shortest possible route, slicing corners as we pass them, tearing diagonally along trafficless roads without regard for the cars that might at any moment appear from some side street to plow us down. There is no thought in my mind beyond reaching my immediate destination—all time has telescoped down to this moment, this single moment of motion. Our hurried footsteps echo off the walls of the buildings. Before us, the Tower looms.

Anyone who has ever run a race—I mean *really* run one—will know this feeling, this complete absorption in the movement of your limbs, the pumping of your heart. It's like being under the irresistable influence of a spell. Your body has a life of its own, every set of muscles working in harmony, without the need for prompts from a mind which has become blank. You don't make decisions or think about where you're going, you just run. This is the way I am. I am like liquid, flowing over curbs, round corners, between parked cars—all obstructions are negotiated smoothly, instinctively. There is no resistance to this movement—it is all part of the spell.

The only sound I hear is the sound of my feet and the sound of my too-fast breathing, but there is a rushing in my ears—not a sound exactly, more of a sensation. Somewhere deep within me I recognize this feeling, and it unnerves me because I have felt it before, but then the thought is lost in the wealth of other bodily sensations that are beginning to overwhelm me. My chest is in pain. It feels as though it wants to burst with the sheer amount of blood my overworked heart is trying to force into my lungs—thin blood, lacking in nutrients, because I haven't eaten or drunk anything since yesterday night. I know I am not used to such bursts of exercise, but I don't have time to stop, not now, and so still my body moves, my legs and arms pumping like pistons to keep me flying through the streets.

As we turn a corner I see our destination ahead of us—the tube station, its mouth gaping like a gateway to the underworld—and beyond it the traffic streaming down Tower Hill. Suddenly the emptiness of the world we've been running through disappears, and we are surrounded by activity. Lines of cars seem to hurtle along the street before us, pedestrians in business suits scurry across the road between them, and beyond, past the Tower itself, the river flows unstoppably towards Wapping and Rotherhithe.

A party of schoolgirls, ushered by two flustered teachers, is walking two-by-two towards the station entrance, and Brian and I are forced to increase our pace to ensure we reach it before they do. As the party of girls arrive at the top of the steps, we sprint past them, not looking at our feet as we run over the edge, trusting blindly that somehow they will find the right footholds on the way down.

By some miracle I manage to arrive in the station ticket hall upright, but I am still traveling at pace. I try desperately to slow down, but it's too late. A woman is striding towards me, towards the exit—she looks determined. She has only a split second to see me before I run into her, not nearly enough time to change her course or get out of my way, and I am so out of control there is nothing I can do to stop it happening, either. As our bodies collide I feel my feet leave the floor, and for one glorious moment I am weightless, suspended in the air, like a puppet the moment before his strings are cut.

I am staring straight into the woman's face while we fall—her expression is one of total bewilderment and panic. As we collapse together onto the station floor, her face comes closer, close enough to kiss, and when my body crashes into the concrete, I can feel her body landing on top of me, the bones of her hips digging painfully into my groin.

For a second we lie still. She is breathing fast, and I can smell mints on her breath—but in a moment her panic has turned to anger. "Jesus Christ!" she shouts at my face. "You total fucking idiot!"

"S-sorry," I stutter. "I'm sorry—are you all right?"

"Let go of me!"

I look down to see that I am clutching her arms.

"Twat!" she spits, as she extricates herself from my grip and climbs hurriedly to her feet. Before I can get up, she is gone, cutting a swath through the hordes of schoolgirls who are staring down at me, their excited eyes greedily lapping up my confusion.

I hear a voice behind me, "Are you okay?" Brian's hands reach under my armpits, and he hauls me back up onto my feet. "Come on. We have to buy tickets."

I feel winded by my fall, but there is no time to worry about this while I follow Brian to the ticket machines at the side of the hall. My body feels somehow lighter now, and once again I hear that rushing in my ears. As I hurry haltingly through the groups of other customers in the hall, my feet stumble slightly. For some reason all fluidity of motion has left me. My fingers don't seem to work properly as I fumble in my pockets for the right money. I am no longer a graceful animal moving smoothly through the world on pure instinct—as I try desperately to shove a crumpled ten-pound note into the ticket machine, my body begins to shake—with exhaustion, perhaps, from all my running—and I can feel the sweat breaking out all over my skin.

I am still short of breath, no matter how fast I try to suck the air in, and I'm worried I'll never be able to get my breath back. That woman seems to have knocked it all out of me—"twat," she called me—and my heart is racing. Brian is running away again now, and I'm forced to follow him, bundling through the ticket barriers and down the steps to the platform, where a Circle Line train is pulling up. Something within me remembers my cameras, and I pull one out, panting, to take a picture of the station sign, but by the time I've done this, the stairs seem to be full of schoolgirls. I can see Brian on the other side of them all, running to hold the carriage doors, but I can't get past because there are so many. I am still struggling for breath as I press up behind a big group of them, trying hard not to tread on the back of their heels, but the train carriage is still out of reach, ten yards away across a sea of bodies. I start to panic, and my breathing gets faster. Some of the schoolgirls are looking at me again now, with the same combination of excitement and alarm they had as I tumbled onto the floor of the ticket hall with that woman, and I realize I must look a state. My hair is stuck to my forehead with sweat, cold sweat, and my clothes are crumpled and stained. My hands are covered in black tube grime, and on my forehead there is still a smudge from Rachel's lipstick—I catch a glimpse of it in a makeup mirror one of the girls is holding. I suddenly realize why the girls are staring. They think I'm a tramp. They think Brian and I are two of a kind.

It's now that the world begins to spin, and the roaring in my ears becomes too loud for me to hear anything else. I'm falling forwards towards the doors of the tube car, and there I see Brian waiting, with thousands of other people who are staring at me with eyes that say "twat," and I'm thinking, God, I must look terrible, I must look like Death in an anorak, and shit, is this the way Rachel sees me?

As the world goes suddenly dark, I seem to be surrounded by schoolgirls—blue stockings, satchels, pencil cases, hair in ponytails and bunches, a mirror, sensible shoes, cries of "Miss! Is he all right?"—schoolgirls with mouths that glint with metal braces. Schoolgirls everywhere.

Chapter 15

10:26 AM—Belsize Park

After she'd finished her shower, Rachel stood in front of the mirror and looked at herself, naked. She'd always done this, ever since she was a schoolgirl. Of course, then—when she was little—it had been uncertainty that had made her look, a sort of frightened curiosity over the freakish changes her body was going through. But it was different now. These days she was more comfortable with all her lumps and curves and tufts of hair, and she looked at herself more with a sort of voyeuristic admiration than anything else. Viewed from the outside it was quite a good body, really. It was nice to look at. It was attractive.

This morning she was almost nostalgic as she looked at her image in the mirror. Because sooner or later this body was going to change. She could see it already in the shape of her hips, which were ever so slightly wider than they used to be a few years ago—and no matter how straight she tried to stand, there was a definite sag to her tits, especially the left one. It was only going to get worse. Once she was married, she'd probably stop shaving her legs, not only in winter but in summer too: she'd seen it happen with some of her friends—they got married and they could no longer be bothered. Her friend Anna no longer even shaved her armpits, and while Rachel sort of respected her for it, it also made her a bit squeamish—that was just one step *too* far away from the schoolgirl's body she used to have.

But then, who knows?—soon Rachel might have schoolgirls of her own. After she'd been married a few years, she might get pregnant, have twins or even triplets, and then it wouldn't matter if she shaved her legs or not, because she wouldn't have time to be attractive anymore anyway. She'd balloon to twice her normal size, grow enormous udders like a prize milk cow, and have calves like some Romanian peasant woman—thick and swollen and puffy. And then afterwards, after it was all over and she was surrounded by screaming children, she'd be left with stretch marks like stripes across her belly and nipples like fat brown pieces of chewed-up chewing gum. When she stood in front of the mirror in ten years' time, she probably wouldn't recognize herself. She shuddered to imagine what she might see then. A row of bellies, each one hanging over the last? Tits like deflated balloons? Cellulite like cottage cheese covering her ever-expanding thighs? She couldn't for the life of her understand why Andy was the one who was getting all het up about the wedding—it struck her that *she* was the one who had the most to lose.

The thought panicked her. Perhaps she should get out now while she still could. Perhaps she should run away—go to her mum's to hide, and wait for the world to forget about her. It would be quite simple to do: she'd already packed all her things, and it wasn't as if Andy was here, begging her to stay. If she left right now, drove to the coast and caught the first ferry to France, she could be in Cherbourg by nightfall, safely tucked up in her old bedroom. Then she wouldn't have to go through with tomorrow. It would all be so easy . . .

Abruptly, she turned away from the mirror. She had to hurry now, get dressed and get on to the shop to pick up her wedding dress. She had so much to do today; she didn't have time to stand here daydreaming. She'd arranged to be at the dress shop at eleven, and after that she was going over to Sophie's. Unlike some people, she liked to stick to her arrangements.

She reached down to pick up her clothes, but as she did so she couldn't help but give the mirror one last look—one final lingering glance at her still youthful body—and it was a look of sadness. Tomorrow she would be signing a contract for life. Tomorrow, whether she liked it or not, she would have to accept once and for all what she'd known for years. She was never going to be a schoolgirl again. She was a woman, a grown-up, with all that that entailed. Fat, stretch marks, pubes—that was just the tip of the iceberg.

Chapter 16

10:23 AM—Tower Hill–Great Portland Street—Circle Line

I have never fainted before. It's a most unnerving experience—it feels like you've been asleep for hours, when in fact it only lasts a short while. It feels like you can fit whole lifetimes into that brief period of unconsciousness. While I am out, I have a sort of dream. I dream that Rachel is crying, and that I can't help her—I don't know what is wrong. I'm looking at her from a great height, and yet I can see every tear that rolls down her cheek as if it is magnified. There are reflections in them—reflections of a man dressed in dark clothes.

When I open my eyes, I find myself sitting in a tube seat by the doors of the carriage. Brian is leaning over me looking worried, and one of the schoolteachers is fanning my face with a clipboard and asking if I am okay. My first instinct is to panic.

"Where are we!" I shout, struggling to my feet. "How long have I been asleep?"

"Calm down," says Brian. "We're still at Tower Hill."

"How can we be? I fell asleep . . ."

"You fainted," Brian corrects me. "You were unconscious for a few seconds, but that's all. The train has only just started moving."

I look about me, confused. The schoolgirls are all still staring, of course. I don't think they've ever known such excitement on a simple tube journey.

Their teacher calls on one of them to hand over a bar of chocolate, which the girl does, grudgingly, and then the teacher passes it over to me. I smile gratefully at the girl as I munch on her sweets—it is the first thing I have had to eat today. The girl scowls back, as if she thinks my fainting is all just an elaborate ploy to get my hands on her Toffee Crisp. I make a resolution: Next time I see a shop, I will buy some food.

After a while the train rolls into Aldgate Station. I'm still feeling a little wobbly when the doors open, but I manage to get to my feet and take a snap of the station sign. As I do so a man in a black suit gets on the train—the sight jogs something inside me, something disturbing I saw while I was unconscious. Once I am sitting back down, I make another resolution: As soon as the opportunity arises, I will give Rachel a call.

While the train rumbles on towards Liverpool Street, Brian interrupts my thoughts.

"What are we going to do about the next envelope?" he asks.

I reach into my jacket pocket and take out the note Rolf left us at Upminster. "Twelve o'clock," I read out loud, "central buffers, Cockfosters." I ponder it a moment before putting the note back in my pocket. "It looks like Rolf's doing pretty much the same as he did with the last envelope, I suppose."

"So what's the plan?"

"Well, there's no point in going to Cockfosters now, because the envelope won't be there until after midday. So I reckon we should probably carry on with our route—Northern Line first to Edgware and High Barnet. Then we'll come back down and do Walthamstow and Cockfosters later."

"Perhaps we should make our way up to Cockfosters right now, see if we can catch Rolf when he comes. Then maybe we could get the bastard to give you your stuff back."

"Brian . . ." I nod towards the schoolgirls, none of whom seem in the slightest bit shocked by his swearing.

"Sorry," says Brian.

"Let's just stick to the plan, okay?"

The schoolgirls and their teachers get off at King's Cross. We would have got off here as well if it wasn't for Euston Square and Great Portland Street. It's unlikely that we will be able to do these two stations on the way to anywhere else, so we may as well get them out of the way now. Once we have photographed them, we will double back and make our way up to North London from here.

Slowly, our train pulls away from King's Cross Station. As it does so I have to smile: one of the schoolgirls is waving good-bye—I think it's the one who gave me her Toffee Crisp. I suppose after the show I've put on this morning she probably thinks she knows me quite well. She, on the other hand, is just another girl in another blue uniform to me. I do wave back to her, but only briefly. Just as the train is beginning to pick up speed, I raise my hand, before the girls and their uniforms disappear and we are swallowed up once more in our journey.

Chapter 17

10:39 AM—Belsize Park–Golders Green—By car

Rachel was in a swearing mood this morning. She always swore when she drove, but this morning her expletives began before she even got behind the wheel. Because this morning, by the time she had showered, eaten a banana, and made her way downstairs, Humphrey had a ticket on him.

"Fuck it!" she muttered as she snatched the ticket from under the wiper. The bloody traffic wardens round here didn't miss a trick—that was the third this month. "Don't worry, Humphrey," she said as she opened the car door and threw the ticket onto the front passenger seat. "One day we'll find the tosser who keeps giving us tickets and run him down."

She started the engine and pulled out of her apparently illegal parking space in one smooth, easy move. She immediately felt a little better. For a fourteen-year-old VW Beetle, Humphrey couldn't half maneuver. And he was reliable too. No matter how much Rachel swore and cussed behind the wheel, Humphrey was always as steady as a rock. He was certainly one of Rachel's joys in life. He was dependable, he had character—and she always knew where he was, which was more than you could say for some people.

Rachel loved being in Humphrey. It was like a second bedroom in here: small, but cozy. The backseat was covered in clothes, there were pairs of shoes strewn across the floor, and the dashboard was mostly obscured beneath a litter of tapes, various items of makeup, and the bottles of essential oil she kept in here to stop Humphrey getting that horrible smell that other cars had. She always felt at home in Humphrey. It was the one place she could be as messy as she liked without having Andy nag her—a room of her own.

"Bollocks," she mumbled as she arrived at the end of Belsize Avenue—the lights had just turned red.

In a way, Humphrey *was* a second bedroom. She'd stopped short of sleeping in him, but she had got changed in here, several times. The last time was on her way to Sophie's party, parked in a side street in Finchley. She'd only intended to put on a little makeup in the rearview mirror, but then she realized she had a backseat full of clothing—so she tried on a couple of tops until she'd found the one that suited her best, and then wriggled out of her jeans to put on the red skirt she'd bought in French Connection last year. It was only when she was down to her knickers that she realized that she was effectively sitting in a see-through box on the side of the street, and that there was a crowd of eleven-year-old boys watching her through the window. She'd never put on a skirt so quickly in all her life. Why didn't they put curtains on car windows, like they did with hearses?

As she steered Humphrey out onto Haverstock Hill, she rummaged through the debris on the dashboard to find an appropriate tape. She fancied something gentle, perhaps a bit melancholy, to suit her mood. All she came up with, however, was *Soundz of the Asian Underground,* a tape Andy's friend Mickey had bought him for his last birthday (along with the inevitable jokes about it being an album of train noises from the Singapore Metro). It wasn't the sort of thing she usually liked, but she put it on anyway, and found it unexpectedly soothing. The car filled with the sound of tablas, and for the first time this morning Rachel found herself smiling.

How could Andy possibly imagine that traveling by tube was better than this? Here she was in her own cozy little self-contained bubble, surrounded by her own things, listening to music she liked. Since when did the tube offer you any of that? She had her own seat—in fact, she had seats to spare—there were no noisy schoolkids banging her with their bags, no armpits shoved in her face, no greasy men touching her up—and even if she wasn't exactly invisible as she sat in traffic swearing to herself, she felt like she was, so that was almost as good. It was the only way to travel.

Although, having said that, she had to admit that sitting in traffic swearing to herself seemed to be playing an increasing part in her daily journeys. She was just hitting traffic now, at the foot of Rosslyn Hill. Eleven o'clock, and Hampstead was already jammed. Hampstead was always jammed. She'd complained about it to Andy once, and he'd sarcastically suggested that the council should pave over Hampstead Heath to give cars the freedom to go wherever they wanted. There were times, when she'd spent half an hour crawling up the hill at a speed of just under two miles per fortnight, that she had thought that a pretty inspired idea.

In an effort to avoid the bottleneck, Rachel decided to turn right onto Downshire Hill. As she did so she noticed a car behind her follow suit. She wondered if he'd had the same idea as she, or whether he was just following her on the off chance she'd be able to lead him round all the traffic. That was the sort of thing *she* did. Especially with taxis—if she ever saw a taxi turn off the road in heavy traffic, she *always* followed it. Taxi drivers knew all the best routes.

She knew it was silly, but she was a bit annoyed that the man behind had followed her. It was *her* shortcut, and she didn't want anyone else using it—at least, not so obviously. Once people cottoned on to the fact that there was an alternative route, then everyone would start using it, and before you knew it, the shortcut would be just as busy as Hampstead High Street was. She'd seen it happen before, in other parts of London. And then, of course, the council would move in and fill the whole area up with speed bumps, and soon it would be just as quick to stay in the traffic she'd been hoping to avoid, crawling along behind some bus at a speed marginally slower than walking pace.

She didn't go all the way to the main road at the bottom of the hill, because she had a feeling the traffic up there would be just as bad. Instead she took an earlier turning, up through the backstreets of Hampstead. It was a little bit of a maze up here, but fine if you knew your way. And it was quite a scenic way to go—the houses were all so lovely that she often forgot to feel jealous of those rich enough to buy them.

The car behind her followed her lead, which surprised her, because not many people knew this way. Perhaps he was a local on his way home—although she would have expected someone who lived round here to have a nicer car than the shabby old Renault this guy was driving. There was even rust on the bumpers—not very Hampstead at all.

On a whim she took the next right turn, and then right again, so that she was going back on herself. Sure enough, the car behind did the same. She knew it—the bastard *was* following her. She'd teach him to try to muscle in on her short cuts! At the next junction she turned right again, and for the next five minutes she led him round and round in circles, just to make sure her follower was completely confused, before making her way back to the main road towards Golders Green. He'd never be able to find his way through those streets a second time, not without a guide. Serve the fucker right! Diving into the stream of traffic on the main road, she finally lost him, secure in the knowledge that her shortcut was safe.

Andy always told her off for doing things like this—the aggressive streak she displayed when she was driving seemed to shock him. But then Andy wasn't a driver, so he didn't understand—and anyway, he wasn't here, so bollocks to him. She could hoot her horn as much as she liked. She could switch the radio to Capital Gold and sing along to sixties music at the top of her voice. And she could shout obscenities about the quality of other people's driving to her heart's content. It wasn't *really* aggression—it was just driving. It was the way all people in London drove—she'd be absolutely mortified if any of the other drivers ever actually overheard the names she called them.

This morning, as she nudged her way between two BMWs in the lane next to her, she had lots of swearwords in her. It was as if some goblin had visited her in her sleep and filled her up with expletives.

"Bugger bum shit tit fuck arse," she shouted as the BMW driver behind refused to let her in. "You fucking old git!"

She felt like a kid in one of those pick 'n' mix sweet shops. She could have as many *fucks* and *arses* as she wanted, a few *shits,* a liberal sprinkling of *wankers*—or she could forgo these and have two *cunts* and a *motherfucker* instead, as these were more expensive than all the rest. This morning, for some reason, she wanted to gorge herself.

"Fucking shit-for-brains! Didn't anyone ever *teach* you how to drive?"

Her swearing followed her down the hill like a fast-flowing stream, but by the time she arrived in Golders Green, she felt better. Swearing was like squeezing spots—unpleasant, but strangely satisfying at the same time—and once she had finished she felt somehow cleansed.

She managed to drive round and round and round and round

and round in search of a parking place without so much as a whispered "bollocks," and eventually she was rewarded with an opening on Golders Green Road, about a hundred yards from the dress shop. The space was tight, but she slid Humphrey into it in one easy movement. She felt proud of herself. That was the way people in adverts parked.

Across the road, about twenty yards down a side street, someone else was attempting to do the same thing, badly. If she hadn't had other things on her mind, she might have watched, smugly, as he tried three times to get his car into the space. If she hadn't been concentrating on locking Humphrey and getting on to pick up her wedding dress, she might have noticed that the car was familiar to her, a certain shabby old Renault, with rust on the bumpers. Not very Hampstead at all.

Chapter 18

10:40 AM—Great Portland Street–King's Cross—Hammersmith & City Line

10:46 AM—King's Cross–Golders Green—Northern Line

Once we're back at King's Cross, the race begins again. Now that I've had a rest, there is no excuse not to get a move on—so when the doors of our train open, we sprint down the Hammersmith & City Line platforms to the ticket barriers. Once through them we run down the steps into the ticket hall to the next set of barriers—the ones that lead to the deep-level tubes. The ticket hall here is crowded—it is always crowded—so it takes a few seconds to fight our way through the people round the ticket gates. Once we are through we have two sets of escalators to descend before we can find the Northern Line.

The first thing I do when we arrive on the northbound platform is to check the display board. There is a Golders Green train due in one minute—I have just enough time to fulfill one of my earlier resolutions. Pulling out my newly found credit card, I make my way over to one of the public phones.

"What are you doing?" asks Brian.

"I'm just going to call Rachel quickly, let her know where I am."

Pushing my credit card into the telephone, I ring my own number. Irritatingly, it is engaged. I glance up at the display board to find that the last minute has ticked away—the train is due any second. I put down the receiver quickly and call Rachel's mobile number—but to my consternation I find that that number is also engaged. What's wrong with the woman!—how can she be on both phones at the same time? I start to dial the number a second time, just to make sure I have got the right one, but at that moment my train comes thundering into the station. I feel a tug on my sleeve from Brian—it's time to go.

Putting the receiver down, I pull my credit card out of the phone and join Brian at the edge of the platform. My phone call to Rachel will just have to wait. As the doors of the train slide open, I climb inside, and within moments I am traveling northwards, towards Belsize Park, Golders Green, and beyond.

Chapter 19

11:05 AM—Golders Green

While Rachel waited to be served in the dress shop, she rang home, just to see if there were any messages on the answerphone. There was one, from Andy's mother. Rachel listened for two, three, four minutes—Andy's mum always left long, rambling messages—before finally ringing off and putting her mobile back in her pocket. Still nothing from Andy.

She sat down dejectedly on the chair by the counter. She was waiting to be served by Esther Hillman, the owner of the shop, but unfortunately Esther was tied up with another customer at the moment, going through a catalog of dress designs. Rachel watched them and remembered doing the same thing herself months before. The same patterns, the same fabrics, even Esther's sales talk was remarkably similar—the only difference was that while Rachel had been unable to contain her excitement, this customer seemed only able to complain.

Rachel found herself cringing as the woman criticized each design in turn, sometimes quite scathingly. It wouldn't have been so bad had she not been so obviously rich. She was about the same age as Rachel, but from her manner Rachel could tell that she probably hadn't had to work a single day in her life. She reeked of money. She was wearing the sort of clothes you could buy only in those shops in Covent Garden where they didn't have price tags. And she had a watch on that was probably more expensive than Humphrey. On the other hand, she also had absolutely enormous hips—so there was *some* justice in the world after all. As Esther signaled to her that she would be over in just a second, Rachel couldn't help staring at the woman's backside. Give her a bustle, she thought—finish the job off.

While the customer turned away to look at some fabric, Esther came over to the counter.

"Hello, dear." She smiled. "Come to pick up your dress?"

"If I can, yes."

"Of course you can. Just give me a moment while I attend to *Madam,* and I'll come and sort you out."

Rachel liked Esther. She was in her early sixties and, while she was generally good-natured, had a definite cantankerous streak that made Rachel smile. For example, she insisted on introducing herself to customers as *Miss* Esther Hillman. She'd stand in her shop, surrounded by wedding paraphernalia, and make absolutely sure that everyone knew she had never been married herself. "Does a cobbler mend shoes in his spare time?" she'd say, if questioned. Or, "When you're a baker by trade, you don't eat cakes at home." Advice which old big-hips here would do well to follow.

Eventually Esther passed her difficult customer on to one of the shop assistants and came to sort Rachel out with her finished dress.

"I suppose you want to try it on, one last time?"

"I don't think so . . ." Rachel began.

"Oh, but you must!" said Esther, with a flourish. "You never know, we might still need to make a few nips and tucks. The last thing you want to be worrying about on Saturday is your dress."

"But I don't really have time for nips and tucks. Sophie is taking the dress over to Paris for me this afternoon. I'm meeting her in an hour."

"Well," said Esther, "do it for your own peace of mind, then. Or if not for yours, then for mine."

Rachel hesitated. "Okay then . . . I suppose you're probably right."

She followed Esther through to the fitting room and started taking off her clothes. Once she had the dress on, she stood in front of the mirror and watched as the dressmaker scrutinized every inch of her body for possible flaws.

"Well," Esther said eventually, "if I say so myself, that is one fantastic dress!"

"It is," said Rachel quietly. "It's a great dress."

"Not only that, but it suits you. I hope you don't mind me telling you that you have a lovely body. Your husband-to-be is a lucky man." She glanced through the doorway to the shop floor, where her previous customer was still looking at fabric with the shop assistant. "Just think what he could have ended up with."

Rachel smiled. "She does have quite big hips."

"*Quite* big! Darling, they're enormous. And she has legs like tree trunks! It'll take an extra six yards of material just to cover them up."

Rachel laughed, and then said, "Thanks, Esther. It really is a lovely dress. It's good to know that at least one thing has gone right today."

"Do I take it that some of the other arrangements are not going so well?"

Rachel started unzipping the dress. "Well," she said uncertainly, "having the wedding in Paris has posed a few problems . . ."

"But I thought your father was sorting everything out over there."

"He is—and he's found the loveliest place for the reception—but there's still all the organizing to get people over there. And . . ." She paused. "I don't know . . ."

"What, darling? What is it?"

"Well, it's Andy."

"What about Andy? What's wrong with him?"

"That's exactly it. What *is* wrong with him? And more to the point, where is he? I've hardly seen him for the past few days, and this morning he got up at four-thirty to go and wander round the tube all day. He's acting . . . I don't know—sort of strange."

Esther shrugged nonchalantly, as if she couldn't quite see what the problem was. "He's a man. He's getting married. What do you expect?"

"I suppose so. It's just, I got a phone call this morning, and it made me feel . . ." She paused for a moment before stepping out of the dress and picking up her trousers. "I don't know. You'll probably tell me to ignore it, that it's just last-minute jitters."

"Hell, no! If you've got last-minute jitters, you shouldn't be marrying the man. Darling, nobody should get married unless they are sure. I see enough brides coming through here to know that. It's one of the most important decisions of your life—you can't take it lightly. Just think, if I'd ignored *my* doubts, I'd be married to Solly Cohen right now—I'd be spending the rest of my life playing bridge with his sisters. Please God, preserve us all from such a fate!"

Rachel smiled wanly. "So you think I should hold back?"

"I didn't say that. But you do have to sort it out in your head. Why don't you talk to him, see how you feel?"

Rachel didn't say anything. It was sound advice, if only she knew where the hell to find him.

"Anyway," Esther continued, "I don't understand why girls like you are so determined to marry at all. I mean, it's good for business—believe me, I'm not complaining—but it always seems such a shame. Whatever happened to living in sin?"

Rachel got dressed and listened to Esther chatter away about the other women who came into her shop, about how many of them were now divorced, or remarried, or having affairs. It was not really what Rachel wanted to hear, not today, but there was nothing she could do about it beyond making her excuses and leaving. *She* wasn't like that, was she? She wasn't fickle, unfaithful, ready to give up?

"Of course, it's not only the women," Esther continued. "The men are just as bad—I just don't get to see them as often, that's all. We don't get many men coming in here to be measured for dresses. Although we have had one or two . . . !"

Rachel buttoned up her trousers and made her way back out into the shop. Once out of the fitting room Esther became her normal, professional self once more—the indiscreet chatter stopped, and while her assistant packed up Rachel's dress, she went to see how old big-hips was getting along with choosing her fabric. Rachel stood by the till, and watched, waiting for Esther to come and tell her how much she had to pay. She was restless. She wanted to go.

She was just wondering whether to make her check out to "Bridal Paths" or "Miss Esther Hillman," when she noticed a face staring at her through the window. Well, perhaps not exactly staring at her—it was only a brief look, really—but it still gave her a shock, because it was a face she recognized. She looked round at Esther and the shopgirl. They were both busy and hadn't noticed the man looking in, and when Rachel turned back to the window, he had already gone. But he had been there, glancing at her as he passed the shop. It was too much of a coincidence for her to let it pass.

"Excuse me a moment," she said to Esther, and, leaving her checkbook on the counter, she strode over to the door.

"Rolf!" she called once she got outside.

The man was there, about twenty yards away, hurrying up the street. Rachel ran after him. When she caught up, she put her hand on his shoulder.

"Rolf," she said, stopping him, "I thought it was you."

"Oh," said Rolf, "hello." He looked sheepish. Not only was he hanging his head, but he kept on looking at the ground, at the road behind her, at the shops—anywhere but directly at her. He was definitely up to something.

"Was it you who called me this morning?"

"Me? No . . ." He had a handful of green envelopes, which he clutched to his chest.

"Yes, it was," said Rachel curtly, not even attempting to keep her irritation under wraps, "I recognized your voice."

"Okay, so maybe it was . . ."

"Well, in that case, tell me something—what did you mean when you said Andy might be in trouble? Is there something going on that I should know about?"

Rolf hesitated. "Perhaps . . ."

"Don't give me that. Either there is or there isn't. If something's wrong, I want to know."

"I'm afraid I can't tell you about it yet. But you'll find out soon. Once it's all . . . finished."

Rolf had stopped looking away now and was staring directly at her. The effect was unnerving—his gaze flicked from her eyes, to her mouth, to her chest, and back up again. It was almost as if he were trying to pierce her, dissect her with his eyes. Suddenly he reached forward with his hand to touch her hair. Rachel was forced to lean back abruptly to avoid his touch.

"Look," she said hurriedly, "I don't suppose you know where Andy is right now, do you?"

"No," said Rolf. He looked irritated at her movement away from him. "Not exactly . . ."

"Not *exactly?* What does that mean?"

"Nothing. Anyway, sorry, but I've got to go." He started backing away. "Sorry," he said again.

"So am I," said Rachel.

"Good-bye." He hurried off quickly. Rachel shivered—there was something about the man that was just . . . creepy.

As an afterthought she called after him, "Are you following me?"—but he scurried off without answering. "Well, if you are, then stop it."

Something Esther had said earlier came back to her. "Of course, it's not only the women," she had said. "The men are just as bad." For the first time this morning Rachel allowed the question to form properly in her head—was Andy having an affair? There was definitely something wrong—why else would Rolf have bothered to call her up? She should probably have asked him about his bet with Andy, just to make sure it wasn't some ridiculous cover story, but she hadn't thought of it in time. Whatever. There was something happening, and Andy was in the center of it.

It wasn't until she was back in the shop that she realized that she had forgotten to do up the buttons on her shirt. The shopgirl pointed it out, with a blush, as if it were she and not Rachel who had just flashed her bra across half of Golders Green. Rachel herself simply started buttoning her shirt up. She was almost used to this sort of thing by now—it was just a repeat of the eleven-year-old boys hanging round her car outside Sophie's watching her change into her skirt. But she wasn't as calm as she looked.

"Fuck it!" she said as she did up the final button. It just came out before she could stop it. She felt a little ashamed, because the shopgirl, the big-hipped woman, and even Esther Hillman all looked up at her, slightly shocked. For a moment she thought of explaining, but she realized this would probably only make things worse, so she buttoned her lip as well as her blouse.

As soon as she could, she wrote out her check and, picking up her dress, left the shop for good.

Chapter 20

11:44 AM—Interlude at Finchley Central (1)—Northern Line

My journey continues. I suppose I could tell you all about how I got from Golders Green to Edgware, how I then caught a bus to Mill Hill East, and all that sort of stuff. But I'm not going to. Instead, I'm going to interrupt my commentary, because I want you to do something for me. I want you to shut your eyes and imagine what the tube map looks like. No peeking—just shut your eyes and picture it. When you've got it, come back to me. I'll give you ten seconds.

Okay, so what does your image look like? I don't suppose for a moment that you had to shut your eyes—everyone knows how the tube map looks. It has nice straight color-coded lines. It has stations which are spaced out evenly, with clear and simple interchanges. There are no bends or kinks, just neat, crisp corners. In short, it looks a bit like an electrical circuit diagram.

Well, let me tell you that that picture you are imagining is wrong. It's merely an invention by a guy called Harry Beck—an extremely clever designer who made the map readable. A *real* tube map looks nothing like that. A *real* tube map is a topographical mess of lines, straightforward at the edges but more and more complicated the closer you get to the center. A bit like life really. Except with life we don't always have someone like Harry Beck to come and untangle it all for us.

The reason I'm bringing this up now is that I'm just getting off the tube at Finchley Central, and the first thing I see is an educational poster all about how the tube map was created. Apparently Harry Beck used to live somewhere near here—a piece of tube history that I'm afraid is completely new to me, although I can't say I find it altogether surprising. Finchley Central is exactly the sort of place someone like Harry Beck *would* live.

It's 11:44, and we are changing here for the High Barnet branch of the Northern Line. It's a beautiful autumn morning, and the sun is shining down onto the platform, making the tarmac glisten. All around the station the trees are turning yellow and brown, as if gleefully preparing for the season of announcements about "the wrong sort of leaves on the line." One or two of them are even dropping a few premature leaves now, as if impatient for their moment of glorious disruption. There is a squirrel sitting on one of the fences, holding his hands to his face like he's biting his fingernails—as if he's worried I'm not going make it round the system in time. It really is a lovely day. If you ignored the sound of distant traffic, it would be easy to imagine we are in the countryside, a million miles from London, and tube trains, and stupid bets.

We have to wait a while for our connecting train, so we take the opportunity to have a pee behind one of the station buildings. Afterwards, Brian turns to me with a sheepish look on his face.

"Do you mind if I nip off for a bit?" he says.

I am surprised—this is the first time today he has expressed any wish other than to stick to me like glue. "Nip off? What for?"

"I need something."

"Oh." I turn away, disappointed. "You mean beer."

"Well, yeah, actually, I do. Not that it's any of your business. There's a shop just round the corner, so I thought I'd stock up. If you're lucky, I'll get you some food while I'm there—something to wipe that sour look off your face."

I give him a fiver and ask him to grab me some bread and cheese. "Be quick about it, though. We've only got seven minutes till the next Barnet train—if you're not back in time, I'm catching it anyway."

I sit down while I'm waiting for him to return. My body aches from all this traveling. In the past hour it feels as though we have passed through most of North London. If I see another row of semi-detached housing, or another average high street full of average cars and average people, I think I'll scream. I am in a world of Woolworth's and Boots and M&S, where the people never change and nothing ever happens. For the past hour it has felt as though the train has been wading through double-glazing and doorbells that go *ding-dong.* And now at last I have arrived at the very hub of this great suburban wheel—Finchley Bloody Central.

In Finchley Central they wash their *Mondeos* on Sunday mornings before settling down to do some DIY. In Finchley Central they twitch their net curtains and gossip about the woman from number 22 who's just had a hysterectomy. Even the tube station I'm sitting in now is middle-class—set away from the main road on a leafy suburban lane, with tidy, open-air platforms and wooden benches for bored teenagers to smoke on. And it has this poster on Harry Beck's design classic, so that even a trip to the tube station can be an educational experience.

The thing is, despite my horror of the place, there's a part of me that likes it here. There's a part of me that likes all the hedge trimmers and Habitat vases. I suspect I could quite easily move here, fill my house with tasteful pine furniture from Ikea, and end up leader of the local Neighbourhood Watch scheme. Perhaps if my own lines hadn't got crossed, led me astray at some point, this is where I'd be now, with a responsible and well-paid job, with a wife and family. Instead of hiding myself in a Belsize Park flat I can't afford, and filling my head with tube trivia.

I look across the platform at Harry Beck's map, with its straight lines and easy-to-read station interchanges. I have to admit there is a small part of me that resents Harry Beck. His map may be good for tourists and beginners, but for my purposes today it would certainly be much easier if it was better at telling the truth. For example, from the tube map you'd think that Edgware and Mill Hill East are hundreds of miles apart, when in fact I caught a bus between them a short while ago—it took me only fifteen minutes. At other places it's even worse. Heathrow and Uxbridge are at opposite ends of London on the tube map—in real life they are practically next door to one another. This is the sort of information that could save me today. But it is exactly the sort of information that is missing on Harry Beck's modern classic. His world of harmony and ease is false.

I glance up at the electronic station board—a High Barnet train will be here in one minute. Where the hell is Brian? For a moment I imagine the worst—that he has taken my fiver and run off with it—but as the train pulls into the station, I see Brian's wiry form appear at the station entrance.

I don't have time to feel guilty for my lapse of trust. "Brian!" I screech. "Hurry!"

He runs across the bridge to my platform, a plastic bag full of food and beer swinging from his hand. I wedge myself in one of the carriage doors to stop them closing before he gets here—a dangerous thing to do, because I've seen someone get thrown off a train for doing that. Fortunately, Brian gets to me before the doors shut, and we are on our way again.

But before these doors close, there is one final thing I have to tell you about tube maps.

Almost every year a new version of the map is published, and no two successive versions are exactly the same. For example, the map I am using to plan my journey today is an early 1997 version and has two special features. Firstly, *Baron's Court* is spelled without an apostrophe. And secondly, Mornington Crescent—the station after which they named the Radio 4 game—has a big red cross through it, to denote the fact that it was closed at the time for rebuilding.

The tube map changes constantly as time goes by. And no matter how minute these changes might seem in the big scheme of things, they do make a difference. If you had a whole collection of maps, like I do, you'd understand. A missing apostrophe can cause all sorts of problems. A red cross can change your life.

Chapter 21

11:44 AM—Interlude at Finchley Central (2)

"So," said Sophie, her mouth overflowing with cheese-and-spinach quiche, "where do you think he's got to?"

They were sitting in a cafe by Finchley Central Station, just round the corner from Sophie's flat. Rachel had dropped off the dress at Sophie's, but Sophie was so hungry she had insisted on going out immediately to the cafe for something to eat. So here Rachel was, watching her friend stuff her face, and answering questions about her current predicament.

"I suppose he must be doing this tube thing—that's the only explanation. But there's something wrong about it. It doesn't quite make sense. I mean, if he's so set on doing this bet, why can't he wait until we get back from our trip? Why does he have to do it now?"

Sophie finished her mouthful. "Well, maybe he's not going round the tube after all. Maybe he's doing something else. Organizing a surprise for your honeymoon or something."

"Maybe . . ." Rachel was doubtful.

"Have you tried ringing his friends?"

"I called the bookshop and asked them, but he hasn't been in. I spoke to Phil, who works with him, and he said he hasn't seen Andy since the stag night—he said the last thing he remembers was the stripper giving Andy a hard time for pinching her bum. So that was really helpful. Then I tried ringing a few of his other friends, but everyone seems to be out."

"I wouldn't worry about it too much," said Sophie, taking another forkful of quiche. "He's probably just sulking somewhere. Christ, if you wrote 'twat' on *my* forehead, I'd never talk to you again."

"But he is a twat. And not only that, he's up to something; I know he is. That was the whole point of that creepy phone call this morning. That was what Rolf said: 'If you only knew what he was doing right now.' Maybe he isn't traveling round the tube after all. Maybe he's doing something else. Something . . . wrong."

Sophie smiled, spinach and cheese oozing between her teeth. "Have you tried ringing the stripper?" she said. At least, that's what Rachel *thought* she said—it sounded more like "Have oo pry wigig a fwippa?"

"Do you have to stuff your face while you're talking? I thought we were supposed to be going out for lunch with each other this afternoon."

"Sowee," said Sophie. "I mungwee."

"Pardon?"

She finished her mouthful. "I said, sorry, I'm hungry. I've been up since six this morning packing the car up, and I haven't had a chance to have breakfast yet. I've got a boot full of wedding presents for you."

Rachel brightened. "Have you . . . !"

"Yes—presents which I'm going to have to bring all the way back to England again as soon as you've opened them."

She tucked into her quiche once more, pausing only to take the odd swig of milk from her glass. It always amazed Rachel how Sophie could eat so much and yet never seemed to put on any weight. It also amazed her how she could be so slovenly about it. There she was, shoveling pastry into her mouth, crumbs all down her front, completely un-self-conscious about how much she was eating—and completely unaware of the fact that she had a milk mustache any five-year-old would be proud of. It was disgusting.

Rachel turned away from her friend, and in doing so spotted someone even messier than Sophie, entering the cafe. It was a tramp, by the looks of him. He was carrying a big bag and a couple of four-packs of extra-strong lager, and he appeared to be out of breath. Rachel watched as he strode up to the counter, ordered two large sandwiches to take away, and hastily started shoving his cans of lager into his bag.

"I suppose he *could* have gone off with the stripper," Rachel said eventually, turning back to her friend. "It's not inconceivable."

"For God's sake, Rachel!" said Sophie, "I was only joking about the stripper."

"Yes, but he might have done, mightn't he? You know what sort of thing goes on at stag parties. They might have hired prostitutes, for all we know. Andy might have got a taste for that sort of thing."

Sophie started to laugh, just managing to swallow her mouthful before she started choking. "God, can you imagine that! Andy in a brothel. He wouldn't know where to put himself!"

Rachel smiled, despite herself. "I'm serious, Sophie. He might have wanted one last fling or something. One of the others might have put him up to it—you know what men are like when they're drunk."

"I can just see him now, strung up in some dominatrix's lair, being whipped to within an inch of his life!"

"Sophie!"

"Well, come on, you're being ridiculous. Andy wouldn't sleep with a prostitute on the eve of his wedding. Apart from the fact that even the *idea* would scare him half to death, Andy's not like that."

"But what about that phone call I got this morning? The one from Rolf."

Sophie pushed aside her empty quiche plate. "Has it crossed your mind that this Rolf bloke might be lying?"

"But why would he want to do that?"

"Maybe he's jealous. Maybe he doesn't want you taking his playmate away from him. Or maybe he has a phobia about weddings. There could be a hundred reasons."

She was interrupted by a shout from the counter. The tramp was telling the man who was serving him to get a move on—he was in a hurry, he had a train to catch. The server looked intimidated, which wasn't really surprising—the tramp was a muscular man, and he had tattoos all over his arms. Everyone in the cafe stared as he grabbed the sandwiches out of the server's hand and literally ran out of the shop.

"Wow!" said Sophie. "A tramp in a hurry. I don't think I've ever seen that before."

They both watched as he ran off down the street in the direction of the tube station, slamming the door behind him as he went.

"So," said Rachel, "you don't think Andy's having an affair, then?"

Sophie didn't say anything, just raised her eyebrows at Rachel and started peeling a banana.

"Well, I suppose we've just about covered everything," said Rachel, "except where Andy is."

Sophie held the banana up to her mouth. "Like I said," she said, "he's probably just sulking by himself somewhere."

Rachel smiled palely and watched her friend take another enormous mouthful.

Somewhere in the distance she heard the sound of a train rattling to a stop. It was time to change the subject.

Chapter 22

11:52 AM—Finchley Central–High Barnet—Northern Line

12:04 PM—High Barnet–Bank—Northern Line

12:52 PM—Bank–Tottenham Court Road—Central Line

1:02 PM—Tottenham Court Road–Euston—Northern Line

1:10 PM—Euston–Walthamstow Central—Victoria Line

1:28 PM—Walthamstow Central–Finsbury Park—Victoria Line

1:40 PM—Finsbury Park–Cockfosters—Piccadilly Line

What do you see here, above? Nothing but a list of trains, I suppose—about as interesting as reading a timetable. But to me it is important. Because I know people who actually do read timetables, and I'm beginning to see what the attraction is. The 12:04, for example—that tells of a long, easy journey from High Barnet to

Bank, during which time Brian and I chat inconsequentially and finish off the sandwiches he bought at Finchley Central. Or the 12:52, which tells of tension, a quick trip through the center of London, just to get to the other branch of the Northern Line. The 12:52 also tells of frustration, because these are all stations Brian and I have seen before, early this morning, when we caught the tube out to Epping at 5:39. So you see, there is a beauty even in a list of trains. Because every train time, and every destination, shows a journey—and every journey has a story attached to it.

Our story at Tottenham Court Road is one of curiosity, because as we are fighting our way through the lunchtime crowds, we discover a problem we haven't encountered before—someone has collapsed at the foot of the stairs and there are two medics in fluorescent vests attending to him. One of these medics keeps shouting to the crowds to keep moving, that there is nothing to see, but they ignore him, slowing to a crawl as they peer at the body of the man, sprawled out on the station floor. But Brian and I are not curious. We turn and run the other way, to the passage marked "No Exit." Within less than a minute we have bypassed the crowd and are standing on the Northern Line platform to greet our next train.

We have only three stops on this train, an anxious story, before we hit Euston and have to start running again—up the stairs into the main subway, and then back down, as we descend once more to the Victoria Line platforms below. Brian almost has a fight with a street musician in one of these tunnels. He trips over his guitar case, spilling coins all over the subway floor—the man screams after us to come and help him pick them up again, but we are forced to run on, leaving him to scrabble around after pennies on his own.

The Victoria Line is quick and efficient, and takes us speedily through Highbury, Finsbury Park, and Tottenham Hale. At Seven Sisters a group of young black women get on, with long nails painted with patterns and perfectly sculpted hair. They look like walking statues carved in ebony, stately and beautiful—Brian stares at them like he can't quite believe his eyes. When one of them turns on him and tells him to put his eyes back in their sockets, he doesn't quite know what to do.

Once we reach Walthamstow Central, we turn round and go back the way we came, down the Victoria Line to Finsbury Park. And there we change for the train to our next prize—the envelope hidden at Cockfosters. I turn my thoughts to what I will find once I open that envelope. I still have five items missing—my Eurostar tickets, my honeymoon reservations, my passport, my keys, and my Travelcard. I have a feeling that Rolf will have hidden only the most trivial of these items out here. I know him—he won't want to give me too much too soon—and yet I cannot leave the envelope unfound because I need directions to the next one.

And so, you see, this last journey tells a story of trepidation. As we travel through Turnpike Lane, Wood Green, Arnos Grove, Brian and I talk in hushed tones about what will be waiting for us at the end of the line. And as our train slides past Southgate, Oakwood, and on towards Cockfosters, we wonder what our next destination will be. Because this ending is merely one of many. Because once we reach the end of the Piccadilly Line, a new mission will be waiting for us.

Chapter 23

1:42 PM—Back again in Belsize Park

Andy had once written a poem to Rachel. It was a few years ago, but she still remembered the first line. It went:

The sun is shining, and Rachel's in my bed . . .

She had found it by her pillow one morning when she woke up. Of course, she hadn't known what it was at first: she'd picked up the piece of paper assuming it was some boring practical note asking her to pick up some shopping or take his washing out of the machine for him. But as she lay on her back reading it, bleary-eyed, and realized what it was . . . it wasn't like anything she had ever felt before. She seemed to be waking up all over again. Her whole body fizzed. It was suddenly as if she was made entirely of bubbles which seemed to be bursting all at once, popping so fast and so beautifully that she couldn't keep track of them. It was like being immersed in warm champagne. And she found herself crying, because the sun *was* shining, and she *was* lying in his bed. Andy's bed. Andy's wonderful bed.

Nobody had ever written a poem to her before. She must have read it a dozen times that morning, and after she'd finished reading it, she lay the paper over her face, as if the physical words would somehow seep off the page and into her eyes, her mouth, her nose. And once she was filled with them, once she was certain the words were suffused throughout her body, she got up and went to work.

It was funny, because she couldn't remember the rest of the poem now. She had a feeling that she couldn't remember it because the words weren't really that memorable, because Andy had never exactly been another Shakespeare—but it didn't matter, because somehow, that morning, she had changed. And when Andy told her for the first time that he loved her a few weeks later, she was able to take it calmly, and say what she needed to say in reply, because nothing else mattered.

But it all seemed wrong now. She was standing in the doorway looking at Andy's bed, which had become *their* bed, and it was empty. No champagne, no bubbles—nothing. The sun was shining, but who the fuck cared?

She had only arrived home a few minutes ago. She'd dropped Sophie off in Finsbury Park and then come straight back: she had originally planned to join her in buying a few final things before going to Paris, but she had begun to panic about the packing she'd done this morning. It had been so early, and she'd been crying—she was bound to have forgotten everything important. And besides, perhaps Andy had come home in the past couple of hours and was waiting for her there. Or perhaps he had rung, left her a message. So she ended up leaving Sophie on Stroud Green Road, and hurrying back to Belsize Park.

When she arrived home, the door was still double-locked and Andy's coat was still missing from the peg in the hall where he always hung it. Her heart sank a little when she realized that he wasn't there. Despite herself she'd checked the bedroom anyway, just in case: she'd still hoped she might find him lying in his bed—*their* bed—sheepish from their argument last night, but happy to see her. But, of course, he wasn't there. So now here she was, disappointed, standing in the doorway to their room, feeling bitter.

She went through to the sitting room to check the answerphone, but only through a sense of duty, to complete what she had come home for. He hadn't rung, of course. There was a message from his mother wishing them both luck, and another from Rachel's friend Patrice. There was even a message from her father, in English, explaining in his thick French accent that everything was now arranged and that tomorrow would be the most perfect day ever. But from Andy, nothing.

She dropped down onto the sofa, and lay for a while, staring up at the ceiling. She felt like crying. What had she done to deserve this?—she only wanted to know. Was Andy still angry with her? Was he deliberately keeping her guessing, trying to get back at her for what she'd written on his forehead in lipstick? Or perhaps he had had an accident—maybe he was in hospital somewhere, unconscious, unable to tell the doctors who he was or where he lived. Oh, please, God, don't let that be the case. She wanted to cry, to let the day's frustration out somehow, but she couldn't because something, a lump in her throat, was stopping her. And she knew that no matter how hard she tried, she would not be able to make her tears come, because she recognized exactly what that lump in her throat was. It was anger. Pure, unadulterated rage.

Because when it came down to it, why the fuck should she be crying? What had she done, apart from worry herself sick about why her wayward twat of a boyfriend had been acting so strangely? She wasn't the one who had gone out on the piss every night for the past week, surrounded herself with strippers and tarts and God knows who—she wasn't the one who was wandering round the tube in pursuit of some obscure tube buff's Holy fucking Grail. Christ, she thought, she'd almost be *glad* if he was in hospital—it was a better excuse for abandoning her here than the one he was using at the moment.

She got up off the sofa and went through to the kitchen to pour herself a glass of the wine she had bought for dinner yesterday—perhaps that would calm her down a little. Perhaps she would finish it off, get a bit pissed. It seemed like a good idea. She uncorked the bottle and felt the madness subside a little—a development which she also found worrying. Was this how alcoholics were made? She told herself that pouring a glass of wine made her feel grown-up, made her act grown-up, think more rationally. But there was always the possibility that she wasn't gaining control of herself but quite the opposite—maybe it was oblivion that was beckoning to her.

She took her first sip, and her anger seemed to dissolve into the red liquid in her glass. She lifted the glass again, this time taking a deep draft—the tang of the wine swelled on her tongue, and she could feel the lump in her throat soften slightly. She wanted to be angry. She wanted to cry, and scream, and hit things, but in the end she couldn't, because she didn't really know what to be angry about. When he came home, when he admitted that he had been thoughtless, selfish, inconsiderate, then would be the time for all that—but until then she had no idea what to do. It was all probably some big misunderstanding, some unintentional breakdown in communication. He'd probably come home completely unaware that he had done anything wrong—they'd have an argument, she'd throw her shoes at him, and then they'd say sorry and fuck each other's brains out. That was the way it usually happened. It wasn't so bad, not really.

She took a sip of wine and thought back to all the arguments they'd had over the past three years. The first had been on their first morning together, when Andy had tried to wriggle out of the bullshit he had given her about owning some flash car—he had been convinced he'd got away with it, that she really believed him, when it was blindingly obvious that he hadn't the faintest idea about sports cars. And then he'd tried to tell her that he had only been joking, that he hadn't been feeding her some crap line. It took her a whole day in bed to convince him that she really didn't care that he had been fibbing. He was only really arguing with himself. She liked him—she fancied him—and for her that was enough.

Since then they'd argued about pretty much everything. When they moved into their flat together, they argued about where the furniture would go. They squabbled about whose pictures would go on the walls, about whose turn it was to do the washing up, and about why their telephone bill was so expensive. There was a running war they had every Saturday evening over whether they would watch *Great Railway Journeys* or *Blind Date,* which usually ended up with the two of them rolling around on the sofa fighting over the TV remote until both programs were forgotten. One evening they had an hour-long dispute over who was better at Scrabble, which was only resolved when they played a game and Andy beat her by 120 points ("Well *you* try making a word out of six es and an *i,*" she'd said afterwards). Another time they had a massive row over whose fault it was that the dinner had burnt. Andy had said it was her fault because he was on the phone to his mother, and so she should have been looking after it. Typical—*he's* cooking dinner, and yet somehow Rachel was supposed to know telepathically that he's abandoned it so that he can chat to his mum. They argued about that one for two hours before they got so hungry they gave up and went out to get take-aways. They finally made it up to each other on the sitting room floor, making love in a litter of pizza boxes and half-empty Coke cans.

There was nothing like a good fight to light their fire. One minute they'd be screaming at each other, the next they'd be pulling each other's trousers off. Sometimes they'd make love in tears, apologizing between desperate kisses. Sometimes they'd laugh at themselves while they embraced, embarrassed at the pointlessness of their wrangling. Once they even made love *during* an argument. They shouted abuse as they thrust furiously against each other, using sex as an excuse to bite and scratch one another—or maybe it was vice versa, she wasn't sure. Afterwards the quarrel seemed to disappear. It was as if it had only been an expression of sexual frustration in the first place.

Sometimes it was the argument itself that was exciting. When all it took was a minor disagreement to get them going, Rachel always knew they were in for a good one. They'd taunt each other, teasing all the tender spots with cheap shots and insults. And before they knew it, they'd be locked together in conflict, whipping each other up into a crescendo of passion and anger, reaching desperately for that wonderful release of invective before they collapsed, exhausted, into tears. There was something primeval about it when they argued like that. Confrontation was their foreplay, apologies their postcoital caresses. And afterwards they'd feel closer and more tender towards each other than ever before.

She had hoped it would be the same today. Really all she wanted was to have him back, to reassure herself that everything was okay, that he wasn't pulling out of marrying her at the last minute. She wanted the sun to shine again and to lie in his bed with him. But she couldn't, because he wasn't here, and it was all happening too quickly anyway. Why did they have to be getting married *tomorrow?* If it had been next week, then they could get all the squabbling out of the way—as it was, it looked as if they'd be arguing at the altar.

She drained her glass of wine and then filled it again, almost to the top. It gave her a perverse sense of pleasure—if Andy could go out and get drunk, then so could she. She'd get completely smashed and then tell him exactly what she thought of him. But even as she told herself this, she knew she wouldn't do it. She didn't really like drinking, and besides, she'd already told him what she thought of him. She'd written it in letters an inch high across his forehead. What she really wanted was to be able not to think that anymore. What she really wanted was for Andy to be the same man who wrote her poems and was happy just to have her there with him. After all, that was why they were getting married, wasn't it?

She shuffled out of the kitchen and made her way down the hall to the bedroom. When she got there she noticed her Eurostar tickets sitting on the bedside table where Andy had left them last night. The sight shocked her, and once again she began to panic about whether she'd forgotten to pack everything or not. Hauling her suitcase onto the bed, she went through the contents piece by piece until she was satisfied that there was nothing important missing, and then she did the same with her hand luggage.

Once she had finished she emptied her glass of wine and lay down on the bed beside her suitcase. She lay in almost exactly the same position she had lain in this morning, waiting for the phone to ring—and yet Andy still had not called, and she was still alone. And as she lay there, staring aimlessly at the ceiling, she wondered if somehow this was the way it was always going to be, that she would always be waiting for Andy, that she would always be lying here, alone. It was a sad thought. It made her feel heavy, and tired. Closing her eyes, she pushed the thought to one side and let herself drift sadly towards sleep.

Chapter 24

2:06 PM—Cockfosters—Piccadilly Line

Cockfosters is at the end of London. We have broken out of all the semis and suburban shops and are now traveling through birch woods, across open fields. There are rows of sidings to our left and one or two trains-in-waiting—trains which look as though they've been forgotten, abandoned to the graffiti writers and the pigeons. Our own train is sauntering now, easing its way towards the terminus. Its job is almost done.

I pull out Rolf's last message and read it again: "12:00, central buffers, Cockfosters." I can't help feeling slightly nervous. For a start, the time says twelve o'clock—that's over two hours ago. Presumably that means Rolf expected us to get to Cockfosters sometime shortly after midday—are we really running that late? And secondly, if the envelope has been sitting here for two hours already, what's to say that someone else hasn't already found it? Anything could have happened to it in that time. Although I try not to imagine the worst, somewhere lurking in the back of my mind is the image of some teenager wandering home through the streets of

North London with my honeymoon tickets sticking out of his coat pocket.

Slowly, our train edges its way between two bright orange shelters and slides into the central bay of the station. As it comes to a smooth stop and the doors open, Brian and I are ready to leap out and run down to where the buffers are.

"Quick!" I tell Brian, "if we find it fast, we might be able to get back on this train when it turns round."

We hurry down to the end of the platform. There they are—a few feet from the front of the train—the buffers that mark the very end of the Piccadilly Line. They are protected behind iron railings designed to stop people climbing down onto the tracks—railings which Brian and I must ignore. Squeezing between these and the driver's compartment, we clamber round to the red metal frame that straddles the track.

"What are we looking for?" asks Brian.

"I don't know. The same as what we found at Upminster, I suppose—an envelope taped to the metal."

Unfortunately, in our hurry to get to the buffers and find our prize, we have forgotten something. Hearing a muffled shout from somewhere, I look up—the driver of the train we were just on is only a few feet away, staring straight at us from inside the driver's cab. We should have waited.

"Oi!" The driver climbs out of the cab. "What the hell do you think you're doing?"

"Ignore him!" I whisper to Brian. "Find the envelope."

"Are you tired of living or something? Those rails are live!"

Brian and I bend down to look under, behind, around the buffers. I am beginning to get a little distressed—we should have found it by now. A big green envelope should stand out against the red metal. It should be obvious.

"Are you *deaf!"* The driver is getting angry now. "Right, that's it—I'm calling the super."

He doesn't need to call the station supervisor, because he's on his way already—I can see him hurrying through the ticket barriers towards us. It looks like we're in trouble.

"Shit!" I say. "Maybe we got the wrong buffers."

"I don't think so," says Brian. He pulls me over to his side of the frame and points. There, on the side, is a small piece of silver tape stuck to the metal. Sticking out from underneath it is a tiny piece of ripped green paper, the same color as the envelope Rolf left us at Upminster. Somebody must have got here before us.

The station supervisor has reached us now, panting after his short run from the ticket barriers. He is not what you'd call a slim man. His arms are so pudgy he can't put them by his sides properly—they jut out at an angle from his enormous trunk. His gigantic trousers seem to dig into his flesh, making an indentation round the entire circumference of his waist, rather like the seam you get between the sections of an inflatable raft. He has the ruddiest cheeks I've seen in years.

"What is it with you people?" he pants breathlessly across the railings. "Why do you insist on climbing onto the rails?"

"I'm sorry," I say, "I can explain . . ."

"Come out from behind there. I could have you two arrested if I want."

"Really, if you'll let me explain . . ."

The driver of the train chooses this point to become offended. "Oh! so you'll talk to him, but you won't talk to me!"

"Please . . ." I clamber out from behind the railings, "this is all a mistake . . ."

"Too right it's a mistake," says the supervisor. "You'll be lucky if I don't have you banged up!"

"No, you don't understand; it's all part of a joke . . ."

"Oh, a joke, is it? Very funny. *Very* funny indeed."

It seems the supervisor is less interested in hearing my explanation than in telling me off. I am on the verge of losing my temper with him—after all, I really do have more important things to think about right now. Without the envelope that was attached to the buffers, I may as well call an end to my trip. Not only have I lost what was inside this envelope, I have lost the directions to the next one, and the next, and the next: the chain has been broken, and there is no way of telling where to pick it up again. In the face of this, what the supervisor is getting upset about seems ridiculously insignificant. So *what* if he can have me arrested? So *what* if the rails are live? If I got imprisoned or even fried on the tracks, it would at least give me an excuse to tell Rachel as to why I missed our wedding. The way things are going it looks as though I'm going to need one.

"Look," I say, "I don't do this sort of thing for fun, you know. You don't think I'd come all the way out to Cock-bloody-fosters just to use your buffers as a climbing frame?"

"Wouldn't be the first time," says the supervisor. His cheeks are even redder now than they were a few minutes ago.

"Well, it would be the first time for me. Now, if you'll excuse me, I'll be going."

I push past the driver, which seems to irritate him no end. "Oi," he says, "I *do* exist, you know!"

"Come on, Brian."

I start making my way back down the platform, but Brian lags behind. "What about the envelope?" he asks.

I don't answer, partly because I am too annoyed, and partly because I don't have an answer. And, if I must say it, partly because the question isn't relevant anymore. The question he *should* be asking is, "What about Rachel? What the hell are you going to say to her when you get home?"

I lead him away from the two London Underground men and step back into one of the train carriages. But as I sit down in the silence of the stationary car, I can't help but wonder—what *about* the envelope? Who could have taken it? It wasn't as if it was in an easily accessible place, like the one in Upminster was—it was out of the way, behind a set of barriers, taped to the underside of one of the train buffers. That's not the sort of place someone stumbles across things by accident. And how would whoever took it get there in the first place? Going by our recent experience, it was pretty impossible to climb onto the tracks right in front of the ticket hall without someone noticing you. So why would you do it? Whoever took that envelope must have had a reason to be climbing round the buffers. Whoever it was knew that the envelope was there. Either that, or . . .

The thought makes me leap from my seat. My sense of impending hopelessness has melted away now and been replaced with irritation—irritation at myself for allowing my argument with the supervisor to cloud my judgment.

"Where are you going now?" asks Brian as I stride to the doors.

"Stay there," I tell him. "I'll be back in a minute."

Hurrying out of the train, I run back down the platform towards the buffers. The station supervisor has turned away and is waddling back towards the ticket hall. As I tap him on the shoulder, my hand seems to sink into his uniform—my God, even this man's *shoulders* are fat!

"You again, eh?" says the supervisor as he turns. It's like watching the revolution of a planet. "What do you want now?"

"Oh," I say, "er, just to apologize, and to ask you a question. What did you mean when you said, 'Wouldn't be the first time'?"

He stares at me blankly, two piggy eyes buried deep within hollows in his cheek flesh.

"You know," I try again, "when I said that I didn't come out here just to climb on the buffers, and you said 'Wouldn't be the first time.'"

"I know what we both said; I'm just waiting for that apology you promised me."

"Oh, sorry," I say. And then I shrug and say it again. "Sorry."

He watches me, squinting. "You people think I've got nothing better to do than shout at passengers. Well, I'll have you know that I've got a station to run here. That requires a lot of work. And when people like you come and start messing around on the tracks, it just makes *more* work. What you were doing was dangerous. A kid *died* two weeks ago because he was walking on the tracks, trying to get to our sidings to spray graffiti on the trains. Had a weak heart, the inquest said. And another one was severely injured when he climbed on the roof of a train—he fell off when it started moving and broke both his legs. Now, those are just kids. You and all your mates should be old enough to know better."

"*All* my mates? What do you mean?" I feel a wave of excitement shoot through me.

"You know exactly what I mean. You're the second lot I've had climbing round those buffers today. You should be ashamed of yourselves."

"So, you mean, you saw someone else on the buffers, then?"

"Yes, a couple of hours ago."

"They, er . . ." I hesitate. "They didn't leave anything there, did they?"

"What, you mean this?" The fat man reaches into his pocket and pulls out a green envelope—its contents jingle slightly as he does so.

"Yes," I say. Hearing the jingling sound, I make an educated guess as to what is inside the envelope. "It's all just a silly joke, really. This friend of mine stole my keys and said he'd hidden them on the buffers. I'm really just the victim in all this. I had to come all the way out here to get them."

I reach out to take the envelope from him, but he snatches it away again quickly. "How do I know they're yours?"

"I can describe them," I say, and I do so. I am trying to be as quick as I can, because I can hear the train warming up behind me, ready to go.

The supervisor seems to sense my impatience, because he takes his time in checking every last detail of the keys I have just described before handing the bunch over to me. He folds the envelope in half and puts it back in his pocket.

"Um," I say uncertainly, "I don't suppose I could have the envelope too? Could I?"

He looks at me suspiciously. "Why?"

I think quickly for a plausible explanation. "Just I'm supposed to be meeting my friend later. I have to . . . er . . . well, I should give him a piece of my mind really for playing such a stupid trick on me. But I need to see the envelope to find out where I'm meeting him. So, if I could . . . ?"

I hold out my hand impatiently. The damn train is going to go any second, with Brian and all my cameras on it.

The supervisor dips his sausagelike fingers into his pocket and pulls out the envelope once more. But before he hands it over, he takes a peek. "I don't know about directions, mate—it looks more like a telephone number to me."

"Thank you." I snatch the envelope out of his hand and take off back down the platform to the train, calling over my shoulder as I run, "Thank you. And I promise this won't ever happen again. I promise."

I make it back to my carriage just before the doors shut.

Brian seems impressed when I turn up beside him, bearing the crumpled envelope in my hand. "Well," he says, curious, "what does it say?"

I unfold the paper, and read the numbers out: *690–12:20–891.*

We stare at each other for a couple of seconds and then back at the piece of paper, before Brian says, "What the hell does that mean?"

"I don't know."

Brian looks at me anxiously. "What are we going to do, then? Where do we go now?"

I turn away. I feel suddenly very tired. "I don't know."

I lean back into the firm upholstery of my seat and stare hopelessly through the window. Gradually the trees give way to houses once again, streets and streets of them, stretching out southwards before us across the eternity that is London. In my hands I clutch the bunch of keys Rolf has made me fight so hard to get—not my passport, not my Eurostar tickets or anything else irreplaceable—my keys. The *important* items are hidden somewhere else, and the only clue to their whereabouts is this piece of paper with its mysterious numbers scrawled in Rolf's handwriting. If only I wasn't so tired, I might be able to figure out what they mean.

Despite my anxiety about where we're going next, I can't help feeling lulled by the comforting rhythm of the train wheels on the tracks. Just the sound is reassuring. And the feel of my keys is hard, solid in my hands—I am reminded that no matter how distant the end of the day seems, I *am* slowly winning back my possessions, one by one. The exhausting process of tearing round the tube is at last beginning to yield results.

Putting the keys into my jacket pocket, I settle further back into my seat. I really am exhausted—I'm in desperate need of a break. If only I could sleep. Next to me Brian is already beginning to doze—I can see his head drooping, only to jerk back upright periodically whenever it reaches his chest—and I have to fight the urge to join him.

But the rhythm of the train is hypnotic, and the motion soothing as the rocking of a cradle, and gradually, inevitably, my eyelids drop.

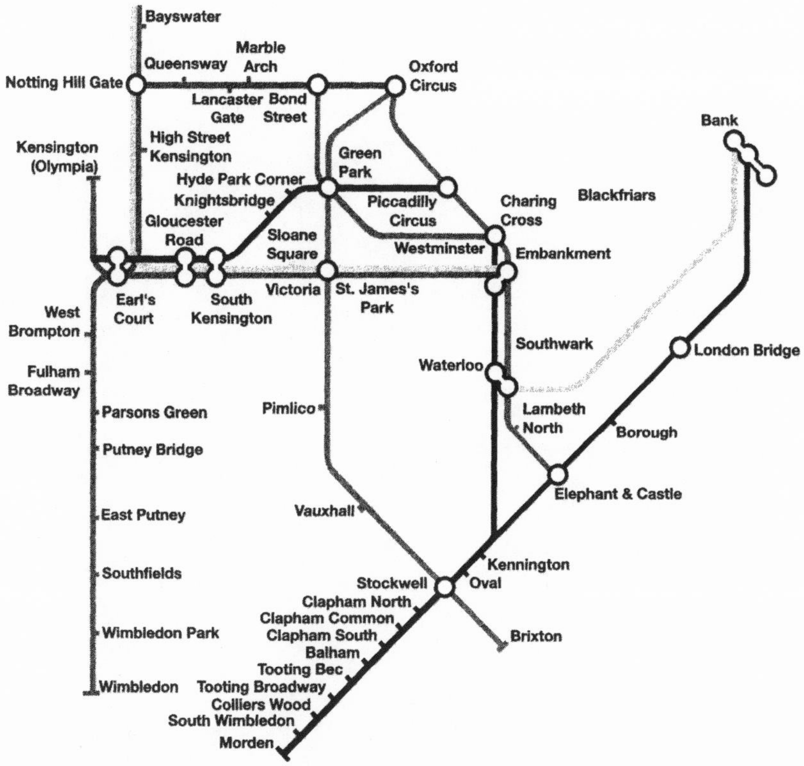
Bayswater
Marble Arch
Queensway
Oxford Circus
Notting Hill Gate
Lancaster Gate
Bond Street
Bank
High Street Kensington
Kensington (Olympia)
Green Park
Hyde Park Corner
Knightsbridge
Piccadilly Circus
Charing Cross
Blackfriars
Gloucester Road
Sloane Square
Westminster
Embankment
Victoria
St. James's Park
Earl's Court
South Kensington
West Brompton
Southwark
London Bridge
Waterloo
Fulham Broadway
Pimlico
Lambeth North
Parsons Green
Borough
Putney Bridge
Elephant & Castle
Vauxhall
East Putney
Kennington
Southfields
Stockwell
Oval
Clapham North
Clapham Common
Wimbledon Park
Clapham South
Brixton
Balham
Tooting Bec
Wimbledon
Tooting Broadway
Colliers Wood
South Wimbledon
Morden

part 3

south london and west end

Chapter 25

2:34 PM—The Vestibule of Hell—Piccadilly Line

See how the tunnel yawns before me! It is dark, as a sepulchre is dark, and from it cometh an odor such as exists not on the surface of the earth. I am fearful, for a wind stirreth from within, and bloweth at the dust which hath settled about my feet.

And though I wish to go out from this place I cannot, for I have been chosen. I am drawn into the tunnel's maw; I fall into it as a pebble falls into a well. I move, and yet I walk not; I am carried, and yet I have paid not my due. And all about me there is darkness.

And yet still I see, for above my head there shineth a sickly light, which doth illuminate the faces of the damned. Before me they sit, still as statues wrought from wax. I see kings, and children, and beggarwomen: they multiply before me till they fill my carriage. And yet still they multiply, without the windows of the carriage and beyond into the everlasting blackness. Faces pass before mine eyes as on a continuous film, and amongst them I see mine own face, and it frightens me, for it shineth with a pallor more wan than death.

And though I try to cover this vision I cannot, for my hands have been bound behind my back. And though I try to close mine eyes I cannot, for the lids of those orbs have been plucked from my face. And my fear groweth.

But within my fear I hear a voice and I am comforted. And the voice saith thus: "Fear not the vision thou dost behold. For the darkness is my body, which lieth deep beneath the earth. And the faces of the multitude are my blood, which giveth me life. Verily, though thou art drowned in the multitudes and swallowed up by darkness, even so shalt thou be delivered."

Thus speaks the voice, from whom and from whence I know not, and yet I draw great solace from it. Yea, though I hear not the voice thereafter, I fear no evil, and for a while I am at peace.

My carriage passeth out from the tunnel and into the light of the Temple. And at the Temple the doors of the carriage open, like unto curtains parting, and Rolf cometh in. And I see that Rolf is clad in garments of azure and black, scarlet and silver, green and gold, and all the other colors of the map. On his fingers are one hundred rings and round his neck he weareth a garland of tickets. In his hands he beareth a golden box beset with gemstones. And in the golden box beset with gemstones there is a casket made of clay upon which is written my name, and it is ready to bear my soul.

And Rolf seateth himself upon my right side and saith unto me: "Thou hast denied thy wife and for this thou shalt pay. Even now thou hast gone beyond thy stop. Even now thou sittest upon the wrong train. This is my word."

Thus speaks Rolf. And when his words are finished I look up, and behold that I am traveling upon a line I know not, for it is set about with brimstone and smoke. And all around the train there spring flames, and there is much sweat upon my brow. And I am sore afraid, for the train is gathering much speed and I am going down into the darkness of the pit. And though the train goeth yet faster and even still faster, Rolf is laughing, for before us there is a great rock. And my fear groweth, for the train will smite the rock. And still we go faster, and still Rolf laughs, and we get nearer and I want to scream because any second now we shall be torn asunder. The fire burns brighter than a furnace, and the smoke is so thick I cannot breathe, and though I try to run I can't get away because we're going too fast and I know there's no escape now—we're going to crash. We're going to fucking crash.

Chapter 26

2:35 PM—Somewhere on the Piccadilly Line

I awake with a start.

My first reaction is one of relief: I have been dreaming. But as I gather my wits, the cold realization dawns on me that I have nothing to be relieved about. One of my worst fears has come true: I fell asleep. And not only me—Brian has fallen asleep too. His head is resting on my shoulder, and he has dribbled slightly on the sleeve of my jacket.

I try to get my bearings. We are on a Piccadilly Line train, I know that much. We got on at Cockfosters and were traveling south to Piccadilly Circus; the last stop I remember taking a photo of was Covent Garden. But now . . . shit, we could be anywhere!

Taking care to remove Brian's head gently from my shoulder, I lean forward to the woman sitting opposite me.

"Excuse me, can you please tell me what the next stop is?"

She looks at me coldly. "Hyde Park Corner," she says.

It is all I can do to stop myself cursing out loud. We have missed Piccadilly Circus by two stops.

"Brian," I say, shaking him roughly. "Brian, wake up."

He sits up with a start. "What?" he says. "What? Where are we?"

"Piccadilly Line. It's two-forty-five, and we're still on the bloody Piccadilly Line. Do you know what that means?"

"No," he says, rubbing his eyes with both hands. He looks like an overgrown child, bewildered at how he could be so late for school. "Which stop are we at?"

As if in answer to his question, the train arrives in Hyde Park Corner Station and begins to slow. "Hyde Park . . ." says Brian. "We're not supposed to be here!"

"Tell me about it." I try to keep the hostility out of my voice. After all it isn't Brian's fault we overran our stop. "Come on," I say. "We've got to go back."

Once the train has ground to a halt, we hurry off through the sliding doors. As we make our way through to the opposite line, I half expect to stumble onto a bustling platform full of people waiting to travel into town, but when we get there, the platform is empty. It doesn't bode well. At this time of day an empty platform this close to central London generally means you've just missed a train. I cock my head and look at the electronic notice board to see how long we'll have to wait.

"Five minutes," I mutter grumpily.

For a while we stare miserably at the notice board, waiting for the number of minutes to reduce visibly before us. They don't, of course. The more you stare at one of those boards, the longer the minutes take to tick away. I'm half expecting it to flash up the word "Correction," and then a message saying the next northbound train isn't *really* due for another six months.

"I'm sorry," says Brian after a while.

"It's all right. It's not your fault."

"But you haven't had any sleep since we started. I should've taken over for a while, let you get a bit of shut-eye."

"Yeah, well, there's nothing we can do about it now anyway, so let's just forget it."

For a few moments this seems to assuage Brian's guilt. "How much time have we wasted?" he asks.

I look at my watch. "Five minutes from Piccadilly Circus, five minutes back again. Plus however long it takes for this train to come."

"Four minutes!" says Brian triumphantly, as the number on the board changes.

"Four *London Transport* minutes," I correct him. "That could mean anything."

It's almost heartbreaking, standing there on the platform by ourselves, waiting for the next train to crawl its way into the station. We're both tired, and groggy from the sleep we've snatched, and it's difficult not to be ratty with each other. It's probably not a good idea to discuss our progress—not in these circumstances—but somehow it seems to be the only thing either of us can think about.

"How are we doing for time?"

I glance at my watch. We have been on the tube for exactly nine hours and forty-seven minutes. In other words we're just over halfway through the day, and this is what I tell him.

"So how many stations d'you reckon we've done?"

"About a hundred and twenty."

"That's good," says Brian. "Isn't it?"

I nod, but only halfheartedly. We are supposed to be halfway through the day by now, but we still have 145 stations to go. And we have to do *all* of them if I'm ever going to get my things back.

"Have you worked out what your mate's note means yet?" says Brian.

"I think so. Kind of."

I pull the note out of my pocket and unfold it once more.

"690–12:20–891," I read out loud. "It's a weird way of writing it, but I think 12:20 must be the time—twenty past twelve . . ."

"Right," says Brian. "And what about the other two numbers?"

I look at them again. "They seem to be . . ." I don't want to say it, because I'm not sure. "It's a bit of a wild guess, but the only thing I can think of is that they're rolling stock numbers."

"Rolling stock numbers? What are they?"

"You know, numbers of train carriages."

"So what the hell does that mean?"

"I suppose it means Rolf has hidden his next envelope on some tube carriage somewhere. Either carriage 690 or carriage 891."

Brian stares at me blankly. "But how are we going to find them? There must be hundreds of tube carriages on the system. Thousands even."

I don't answer his question, because I don't have an answer: we could spend weeks wandering round the tube looking for a specific car.

And besides, my thoughts are interrupted by the sound of the train pulling into the station. When it stops and the doors open, Brian and I bundle our way onto it as quickly as we can. Not that it makes any difference, of course—we could crawl onto the train and the net result would be the same, but leaping onto it quickly gives us the illusion that we are at least doing something to speed up our journey.

The train has other ideas, though. Its doors don't slam shut, ready for it to rapidly leave the station. It doesn't accelerate to high speeds in a matter of seconds, making our cheeks wobble with the sheer G-forces involved. No, it just sits there. Quietly. For an agonizingly long time. It's as if it's waiting for something to happen.

After a minute or so, I stand up to poke my head through the doors and see if I can work out what's holding us up. But there's nothing to see—the platform is as empty as it has always been, ever since we arrived. It seems like there is nobody in this damn station—nobody wants to get on, nobody wants to get off. I try to tell myself we must be waiting because there is something in the tunnel ahead of us—another train perhaps—but I know this can't be so: there hasn't been a train through here for at least five minutes. I look at my watch—*seven* minutes.

When at last the doors do begin to close, I catch something through the corner of my eye. Further down the platform someone darts onto the train at the last moment—a dark, shadowy form that seems to detach itself from the platform wall. It's not the sort of thing I would normally notice, but there is something about the figure I recognize. Of course, I'm probably only imagining things. The figure was at the other end of the platform, and it was only a fleeting glimpse—how could I possibly recognize him? I tell myself not to be stupid and that it was probably only someone arriving on the platform just in time for the train. But as the train pulls away, I can't help noticing that there isn't an entrance to the platform where the shadow came from. Whoever it was, they must have been there all the time.

Chapter 27

2:44 PM—Piccadilly Circus—Bakerloo Line

Have you ever wondered what it would be like to live underground? I don't mean specifically on the tube—I mean anywhere. Think about it for a moment—what would it be like to spend the rest of your life in a cavern or a tunnel? What would it be like never coming up to the surface to see daylight, never seeing trees or grass or sky ever again, but being surrounded forever by solid rock and earth. Does that sound like a good idea to you? Or does the thought make you uncomfortable?

There are so many negative connotations linked to being underground that I sometimes think it's impossible to feel good about it. Underground is dark, and lifeless. Underground is where the air is stale and plants don't grow and light cannot penetrate. It is where you are put when you die, stuck in a box for all eternity in a space only just big enough to fit your body. It's no wonder Brian feels claustrophobic when things get tight down here. When confronted with the idea of being squashed in a small space with a couple of hundred others, surrounded on all sides by countless tons of rock, most people can't help feeling at least slightly claustrophobic—even me. Perhaps that would explain why I seem to have just had some sort of hallucination, a vision of a man appearing where no man should have been. Perhaps that's why I've just had a dream about riding on a train to hell. It's not that surprising. Hell is underground. Underground is hell.

Brian doesn't seem as philosophical as me. At least, he isn't daydreaming about the nature of subterranea like I am.

"Well?" he is saying.

"Well, what?"

"Well, where are we going next?"

"Piccadilly Circus . . ."

Brian sighs impatiently. "I know *that.* But where then? We still haven't sorted out where we're going to find your mate's tube carriages. We don't even know what *line* they're on."

"Yes, we do," I say. I point to the note in my hand: *690—12:20–891.* "If they *are* carriage numbers, I'm pretty sure they're Piccadilly Line rolling stock, because they only have three digits. And look at the time—twelve-twenty—it's only twenty minutes after the time he wrote on his last note. My guess is that Rolf must have hidden the next package somewhere on a Piccadilly Line train while he was in Cockfosters."

Brian sighs deeply. "So how are we going to find these two train carriages, then?"

I don't answer him straightaway. The thought of wandering all over the Piccadilly Line looking for a couple of train carriages is ridiculous—it could take hours. There must be an easier way of doing it, or Rolf wouldn't have worded his note like this: I know Rolf—he likes to set a challenge, but not one which can't be solved. There must be a way of working out where these carriages are going to be, at what time, so that we can meet them along our way. And that's when I have an idea.

"Paul," I say.

"Pardon?"

"My friend Paul. He works at the Northfields depot. If anyone knows where to find a piece of rolling stock, Paul will."

"So they keep tabs on all the carriages at the depot, then?"

"I suppose they must do. But Paul will know anyway—it's his hobby."

Brian stares at me in disbelief. "His *hobby?"*

"Yes. You know, like stamp collecting."

"You mean you're friends with someone who memorizes train numbers? For fun?"

"Yeah."

He shakes his head as if he can't quite believe what he's hearing.

"What's wrong with that? Paul's a good bloke."

Brian unzips his bag to find the rest of the sandwich he bought at Finchley Central. He mumbles something to himself I can't quite hear. Although, I don't try too hard to hear it—it's bound to be something derogatory. I learned long ago not to pay too much attention to the things people say under their breath.

At Piccadilly Circus we get off the train and change onto the Bakerloo Line. I like the Bakerloo platforms at this station. They are bright and cheerful, with red, green, and cream tiles in elegant curves around the roundel signs. Whatever you might feel about the Underground being claustrophobic, the other side of the coin is that it is also quite a *cozy* place. Because stations like this are deep below the surface, they are always warm, even in the bitterest of winters. And it is anything but dark—the lights follow the curve of the platform, illuminating every bit of the station in bright, warm-colored light. There are no shadows here.

I should really call Paul as soon as I can to see if he knows anything about these two train numbers, so the first thing I do when I arrive is walk down the platform looking for a public telephone. There are quite a few people waiting for the train to arrive, so I must thread my way through them—but when I finally find a phone, it's out of order. I try it a couple of times, but there's nothing I can do. Swearing under my breath, I turn to face the tracks. I'll just have to wait until I find another chance.

Despite the number of people on the platform, it doesn't feel in the slightest bit crowded here—there's a sort of family atmosphere about the place. Beside me a young mother is playing with the child in her push chair. Beside her, four young men in cheap suits are discussing loudly what they are going to do at the pub tonight, and a bit further along a couple of girls are giggling with each other. At the end of the platform are three very trendy looking people—two men and a woman: one of the men has a camcorder and is filming the other two as they chat.

Yes, it's a bright cozy platform, with a family atmosphere to it. Everyone here looks like they have reason to be, and they all look supremely normal. And yet I can't help feeling . . . I don't know. It's hard to put my finger on it.

"Brian," I say, after a while, "do you ever feel like we're being watched?"

"Of course," he says. "We *are* being watched."

"We are?"

"Yep. Everywhere we go."

He points down the platform at a security camera which is focused in our direction.

"A friend of mine got arrested the other day for pissing on the train tracks at Camden," he continues. "Drunk and disorderly, they said he was. Of course, he denied it, because nobody had been around when he did it, but they had the video evidence, so there was nothing he could do. They fined him two hundred quid."

"Two hundred pounds! Just for pissing on the tracks?"

"Well, they said it was to teach him a lesson. They must have thought it was dangerous, what with all the electricity going down the tracks and all, but they needn't have worried. Eddie's got terrible prostate trouble—there's no way he could've reached the live rail."

I get an involuntary image in my head of 630 volts zapping its way up an arc of urine, before I mentally shake myself and try to get back to the point.

"What I mean is, do you ever get the feeling someone is specifically watching *us.* Perhaps even *following* us."

"What, today?"

"Yes, today. Right now, as we speak."

"But why would anyone want to spy on us?"

"Well, they wouldn't normally. But I know Rolf, and he'd be curious to know how I'm getting on. I just thought . . . I mean, it's crazy really—but I thought perhaps he might be following us."

Brian looks around suspiciously at the other dozen or so people standing around us. No one is looking at us—their heads are all turned to face the tunnel, waiting for the train to arrive in its mouth. Brian eyes them each, one by one, before turning back to me. "Is he here?" he says in a low voice. "Which one is he?"

"Well, no, he's not actually here. I just thought maybe he might have sent someone to tail us. Rolf has lots of friends who'd be willing to help him keep track on our progress."

"So you mean you've noticed someone hanging around?"

"Well, not exactly. It's just a feeling really . . ."

"Oh," he says, visibly relaxing, "just a *feeling.* I get those all the time—they don't mean nothing."

The train is coming now, gliding down the platform until it comes to a halt, and the doors open directly in front of us. After the exiting passengers have alighted, Brian and I step inside the carriage. There is nowhere to sit, so we stand by the doors. I look at all the other passengers in the carriage. I suppose Brian is right—I'm just being paranoid. Nobody here looks familiar. They couldn't be following us—doing it without being noticed would be impossible.

While we are waiting for the doors to close, I poke my head out of the carriage, just to check that there's no one lurking about on the platform. There isn't, of course. The platform is wholly empty—there is nothing there except the security camera, still pointing at me, motionless. I smile at it, wryly. On a whim, I stretch my arm out just before the doors close and give it a little wave.

I don't know about you, but I can't help feeling a bit weird about having so many closed-circuit television cameras all over the place. I mean, what are they *watching* anyway?

There are security cameras everywhere in the capital now—over three hundred thousand throughout London at the last count, and the number is rising daily. They've even got cameras on the front of buses now for identifying people who park their cars in bus lanes. There are cameras inside buildings; there are cameras outside buildings; there are speed cameras on the roads—in Finchley there are even special camouflaged cameras, so that you don't even know you're being watched.

On the Underground they love them, and they're putting them everywhere—King's Cross Station alone has twenty cameras just to monitor the station entrances. If you ask me, it's all getting out of control. When I'm standing alone on a platform, the fact that there are cameras looking at me doesn't make me feel safer at all—quite the opposite. Half the time you can't even see them—they're enclosed in big spheres made of black glass suspended from the ceiling of the tunnel, so that you can never be sure if they're pointing at you or not. They can see you, but you can't see them. It's spooky.

And what do these cameras pick up? People pissing on tracks? People throwing themselves on the tracks? People begging? People mugging, pickpocketing, and sexually molesting each other? The problem is, crime doesn't really happen on the tube, not like it does in the world outside, anyway. So all the security cameras are really recording is thousands upon thousands of hours of people reading books, picking their noses, throwing money to musicians, and any number of boring, inconsequential things to fill the time while they wait for their trains. There are probably hundreds of hours of tape just with me in it. The police could probably compile a dossier on me, trace my movements through the tube network over the past five years.

In return for Brian's story about his friend who got fined for pissing in the station, once we're sitting down in our carriage, I decide to tell Brian a story of my own. It's about a mate of mine called Arnie.

"Arnie works for London Underground," I say. "He's a sort of glorified security guard—his job is to sit in a control room staring at a set of monitors, just to make sure that everything's going all right on the platforms in his station. It is such a mind-blowingly boring job that he's taken up drinking, just to while away the hours. That's all he does all night—stares at CCTV pictures of people pacing up and down impatiently as they wait for trains, and sips his whiskey. He smuggles the stuff into work by bringing it in in a thermos flask, so that people will think it's coffee.

"I went and joined him after I'd finished work once and chatted to him over a few drams while we watched the cameras, but it was so dull I started to fall asleep. Arnie's been doing this job for years—it's no wonder he's turned to drink."

Brian fidgets slightly in his chair when I say this. I figure he's probably uncomfortable about me talking about drink like this, but I decide to ignore him. It's not like he's gone out of his way to spare me from delicate subjects today.

"Anyway," I continue, "one night, after a few too many, Arnie was sitting there watching the screens, and he saw a space alien getting off the train. It didn't really grab his attention at first, because watching CCTV is a bit like watching normal telly, and seeing aliens on telly isn't that odd. But when a second alien got off the train, it finally clicked that this wasn't telly at all—this was actually happening on the platforms below. Aliens were getting off the train. After the first two, another one appeared, and then another, with giant buglike eyes, and antennae on their heads. And then further down the platform, from one of the other carriages emerged a bush—a giant, walking bush."

"A bush?" says Brian, skeptical.

"Yes," I say. "Of course, Arnie, who had been cooped up in this control box all evening with nothing to keep him company but a flask of Johnny Walker, was absolutely terrified. He immediately leapt up out of his chair and ran out into the station to warn everyone. I mean, as far as he was concerned the station was being invaded by spacemen. He was trying to grab hold of the loudspeaker and warn members of the public to evacuate, when the station manager caught up with him and managed to calm him down. You see, it turns out that one of the local nightclubs was doing an alien theme night and allowing free entry to anyone who came in fancy dress. Arnie was suspended for two weeks and has been forced to take random breath tests ever since."

I give Brian a sideways glance. "The funny thing is that although Arnie accepts his mistake about the aliens, to this day he is still convinced that he saw a bush walk off that train. When he was telling me the story, he swore it—he even knew what *type* of bush it was—privet, I think he said."

"A bush?" repeats Brian, in disbelief.

"Yes. Privet. When I told Rachel this, she just laughed and said, 'See? It just goes to show—if CCTV can't even distinguish between a bush and someone carrying a pot-plant, then what bloody use is it anyway?' But Arnie is positive that it wasn't someone carrying anything—it was an actual bush. You can't argue with him. My own theory is that the bush was going to the same nightclub as the aliens, dressed as a triffid."

"Triffid, eh?" says Brian when I've finished telling him all this. He doesn't look amused. "Do they look like privet bushes, then?"

"No, Brian, it was a joke."

"Oh," says Brian, but he's still not smiling.

I try again. "The thing was, he was pissed. He was just seeing things."

Brian shoots me a look. "Take it from me," he says firmly, "it doesn't matter how much you drink, you don't start seeing things like that. Not on scotch, anyway."

"So what are you telling me? That there really was a bush getting off that train?"

"You never know," says Brian indignantly. "Maybe there was."

"Yeah, *right.* I suppose it was just on its way home to see Mrs. Bush, then. And its little bush kids."

"There's no need to be sarcastic." Brian reaches into his bag for something, but then seems to change his mind. "And anyway, what makes you such an expert on what people do or don't see?"

I shrug disconsolately. I don't know what I've said to piss him off. "Okay," I say sullenly, "maybe you're right—it was a real bush. What the hell do I know?"

I sit back in my seat, my arms folded, my lips pursed. I have a real urge to tell Brian to stop being so touchy and lighten up a bit, but I'm too tired to argue. Perhaps that's why Brian's being so ratty with me too—both of us are exhausted.

I stare at my reflection in the window opposite—I see a tired man, slumped in a chair with his arms crossed. I notice I have big gray bags under my eyes. Actually, I look awful. I'm certainly not a good advert for the benefits of drinking and staying up all night. I look down at my clothes and find them grubby from all my tube traveling. I have grime underneath my fingernails. When I blow my nose, what comes out is black—the accumulation of hours of inhaled tube dust. (Almost fifty percent of tube dust, by the way, is made up of iron from the grinding of the train brakes—that's why it's so black. And it gets everywhere: in your pores, in your nose and mouth—the way my eyes feel it's as if bits of iron have crawled their way into my sockets, to grate against the backs of my eyeballs every time I blink or look from side to side.)

It's while I'm doing this—looking up at my reflection, looking down at my clothes—that I catch sight of him again. A dark figure. He's standing in the next carriage, watching me through the connecting doors. It's only a fleeting glimpse, so I can't be absolutely sure it's the same person I saw join the train at Hyde Park Corner, but in my heart I know it's him. For that one moment, that one split second when I catch his dark eyes trained intently on my own, something inside me recognizes him—but then he's gone. I blink a couple of times and shake my head, but when I look back, he is not there. The space on the other side of the connecting doors is empty.

"Did you see that?" I ask Brian.

"What?"

"That man. In the next carriage."

Brian looks over. "A man? What man?"

I return my gaze to the empty space in the window, and an element of doubt takes hold of me. "It's nothing," I say after a moment. "Ignore me. I'm imagining things."

Brian, who obviously thinks I'm making a reference to Arnie's bush vision, snorts his disapproval. "Imagining things, eh?" he says sarcastically. "*Very* funny."

I continue to look over at the blank space in the window of the connecting door. For a moment I consider telling Brian what I saw, but only for a moment. Something tells me that this is a thing I should keep to myself. Because at least now I know that these are not ghosts I'm seeing. Somehow, Rolf is following me.

Chapter 28

2:45 PM—Belsize Park

As Rachel slept her mind filled with dreams. They weren't like the dreams she normally had, which always felt like stories—feature films running effortlessly before her unconscious eyes. This afternoon they were just fragments, one running into another, a muddle of sensations . . .

It was dark, and she was floating. Andy was cradling her head, just as he had done when he'd asked her to marry him, and he was singing to her—a lullaby—but she couldn't hear the words because of the noise from the trains. Esther the dressmaker was at the end of the platform, plucking a goose for a feast—the air was filled with feathers which rained down on her like snow. Rachel became so engrossed in watching the feathers that she didn't notice when Andy had gone, and now she was alone in the dark. The wind from the trains whistled around her, and then Rolf was there with his hand down the front of her knickers, pulling her away with him down a tunnel. She didn't want to go with him because she was looking for Andy, but his hand felt so good. For a while she rubbed herself against him, but then the wind became stronger and she found herself flying away, borne on the wind like a leaf. She felt light, but she was anxious about flying so fast, because she had no control. Soon she found herself in a vast cavern, limitless in size. Andy was there, in the distance to one side—he was beckoning and calling to her, but she was too far away to hear what he was trying to say. She wanted to change direction, go and join him, but she couldn't because her wings were quickly becoming enfolded in wrapping paper. She looked down to find that there were people she had never seen before all around her. They were tying her up with ribbons and telling her how happy she'd be when Andy unwrapped her. The lights from the trains sent flashes across her eyes and made her frown . . .

Rachel turned over once again, and as she turned, a whole jumble of images turned with her, which made her eyelids flicker and her feet twitch anxiously: a phone ringing, a crow with its claws on her genitals, a race, a trap, a death . . . For a moment she hovered close to consciousness, her mind about to snap her out of her dreams, but then she felt a warmth within her—just as she did when Andy rested his hand on her belly to soothe her when her menstrual pain was bad. The feeling comforted her. Gradually, she slipped back into sleep.

Chapter 29

2:46 PM—Piccadilly Circus–Elephant & Castle—Bakerloo Line

Right, I have to shake myself now, wake myself up. I have to forget about what I've seen, for the moment at least, and prepare myself for the next stage of the journey. I tell Brian to gather his things and get ready. And while we're at it, you'd better prepare yourself too. Forget about tiredness, and how the hell I'm going to find time to ring Paul at the Piccadilly Line depot; forget about Rolf and Rachel and the man who's following me, and focus. This is not the time to slack off. Because we're about to hit South London, and things are going to get hectic.

If traveling round the tube were a quiz show, then South London would be the quick-fire round. You've got to have your wits about you down here, because you're leaping off trains and changing lines so often, it's easy to lose track of where you are. You can save valuable minutes by knowing in advance at which end of the platform the exits are, and those minutes often mean the difference between catching a train and missing it. You have to be able to think quickly and have the energy to run repeatedly up stairs and down long corridors. I suppose it's sort of like the Underground equivalent of the *Krypton Factor*—with a touch of *Mastermind* thrown in, because without a specialist's knowledge of the tube, you wouldn't have a hope.

You might like to trace out the route we are about to take on the map *before* we start, because otherwise you'll never be able to keep up. Remember, this is a quick-fire round. The route we are taking is as follows:

Bakerloo Line from Piccadilly Circus to Elephant & Castle,
Northern Line to Bank,
Waterloo & City Line to Waterloo,
Northern Line to Stockwell,
Victoria Line to Brixton,
Victoria Line back up to Victoria,
District Line to Wimbledon.

Got that? Okay. So, fingers on buzzers. And here we go.

Chapter 30

2:47 PM—Piccadilly Circus–Wimbledon—Various

QUESTION: When you catch the southbound Bakerloo Line train at Piccadilly Circus, which end do you get on? Front or back?

ANSWER: We get on the front end of the train—that way when we arrive at Elephant & Castle, we are directly by the stairs that lead us up to the Northern Line.

(If you didn't get this question right, then you are disqualified, because if we had been at the back end of the Bakerloo Line train, we wouldn't have made our connection. As it is we have to scramble up the steps just to make it onto a northbound Northern Line train before the doors close.)

Q: What do you do now you're on the Northern Line? Do you stay where you are, or do you worry about trying to change carriages in time for your next connection?

A: We chill out for a few minutes. We don't have to worry about changing carriages because where we got on will leave us right by the exit at Bank. (Instead, we can listen to the three dust-covered builders sitting beside us talk about what they would like to do to the girl who is fast asleep opposite me. It's not very nice, what they are saying, but at least it takes my mind off the journey and stops me looking over my shoulder every two seconds.)

Q: You arrive at Bank and leap straight out of the train and into the corridor that leads you to the Waterloo & City Line. How long is the corridor?

A: Bloody long. I had forgotten how bloody long. It seems to curve for miles, a subterranean wormhole decorated only with fluorescent lights. After running for a while, I have to slow down and take a few breaths—I use the opportunity to look back, but there is no one following us: the only person I can see in the whole tunnel behind us is a woman in a business suit and high heels. Now, however, is not the time to slow down. If we miss the shuttle to Waterloo, we will have to wait up to five minutes for the next one. I pull myself together and start running again.

Q: The Waterloo and City Line shuttle leaves Bank at 3:17 PM. How long does it take to get to the other end?

A: Three minutes. It's only one stop—hardly justifies being called a whole line, really.

Q: You arrive at Waterloo—what happens here?

A: We have to run up and down stairs and escalators like insane fitness freaks. I counted the number of stairs you have to negotiate to change lines here once. Do you know how many there are? One hundred and twenty-eight, that's how many. I am rapidly becoming exhausted. Brian, on the other hand, is still sickeningly full of energy. Which is probably a good thing, because by the time we reach the Northern Line platforms, he has to physically support me.

Q: Your southbound train leaves Waterloo at 3:23 PM. While you try to get your breath back, you notice something: the man sitting opposite you is wearing a fishing hat. Why?

A: This is a trick question. There is no excuse for such behavior on the tube. There are no fish here. There is no water. As far as I know, fishing hats are not the latest fashion.

Q: *As you stumble off the train at Stockwell, where do you go to change onto the Victoria Line?*

A: *Through to the tunnel next door. The changeover from Northern Line to Victoria Line at Stockwell is easy because both southbound platforms are parallel to one another. I am lucky here, because as Brian and I race through onto the platform, there is a Victoria Line train waiting for us.*

Q: *Once you get to Brixton, at the end of the Victoria Line, what do you do?*

A: *We change onto the parallel platform for the ten-minute trip back up to Victoria. Once again, the train is sitting there at the platform, just waiting for us to get on. Things are going extremely smoothly. If this* had *been a quiz show, I would now be well on my way to winning the luxury holiday for two in Barbados.*

Q: *And what happens at Victoria?*

A: *Yes, what* does *happen at Victoria? Once we've run up all the stairs and escalators into the main station, and followed the signs for the District Line, what do you think we come across? Well, I'll tell you—a dead bloody end, that's what. At the foot of the stairs that lead to the westbound District Line platform there is a sign saying that there are no trains going to Wimbledon at the moment because of a points failure at Earl's Court. After all our success throughout the rest of South London, we seem to be scuppered at the last hurdle. Our holiday to Barbados has been whisked away from right under our noses. This isn't the* Krypton Factor *after all—it's more like* Wipeout*.*

Q: *So, what now?*

A: *To start off with, I just stand at the foot of the stairs for a few moments, staring at the sign. I mean, what would you do? Confronted with a closed line you'd probably just swear a lot and give up—but I'm standing motionless for a reason: my brain is working overtime. We may be slightly scuppered for the moment, but after all this is Victoria—not only the busiest* tube *station in London but also the busiest* mainline *station. I make a decision: if we can't get to Wimbledon on the District Line, we'll get there by overground. Somehow.*

Q: How?

A: Well, there's a Connex South Central train going from here to Clapham Junction in about three minutes' time . . .

Q: So what do you do?

A: Brian and I make sure we're on it. We have to—we have no choice. Tearing across the station concourse, we make our way over to the correct platform, where the train is waiting for us. Once we've scrambled our way onto it, we sit down and rest for a bit as the train eases its way out of the station and into the open air. It's actually a bit of a relief to be out in the open again—it's nice to be able to look at the scenery rather than just passing underneath it. As we cross the river, Battersea Power Station looms towards us, before the concrete-tower blocks take over, lined up like dominoes across South London. Despite the worry over where the hell we are going, watching the world float by like this soothes me, calms my brain. I allow myself to switch off for a while.

Q: And how long does this bliss last?

A: Seven minutes, that's how long. Seven minutes is all I get before we arrive at Clapham Junction, and I have to start up all over again.

Q: So now what?

A: Jesus, I don't know! Clapham Junction is like the train equivalent of Spaghetti Junction in Birmingham. There is nothing here but train tracks—acres and acres of the things. After our train has negotiated its way through them all, cutting obliquely across this wasteland of parallel lines to pull up at one of the thousand and one platforms, there is nothing for us to do but get off the damn thing and run along the subway trying to find the platform where Wimbledon trains stop. Fortunately they all seem to stop at the same platform.

Q: What time is it?

A: It is 3:52.

Q: And what time does the next Wimbledon train leave?

A: At 3:53. Actually it's a train bound for Dorking, but what the hell, it stops at Wimbledon on the way, and that's all that matters. I'm feeling pretty smug with myself because I've just realized that we have actually saved *time by coming this way. Just like this morning, we have bagged ourselves an extra fifteen minutes by taking overground trains rather than sticking to the tube. As we pull into Wimbledon station at four o'clock exactly, I can barely stop myself from grinning, because there on the platform is a District Line train, doors open, ready to leave for Earl's Court in just a couple of minutes' time. It looks like we've made it. We are right back on schedule.*

Q: And how does this make you feel?

A: Proud. Chuffed with myself. I have made it successfully through the trickiest part of my journey, and thanks to my own resourcefulness, it has come off with barely a hitch. I feel like some sort of tube hero, leaping gracefully from one train to another, like Errol Flynn swinging on chandeliers. Eat your heart out, Rolf. And eat your heart out, Rachel—it seems I am "El Tube Supremo," after all.

This quick-fire round is ended.

Well, it's *almost* ended. I just have one more thing to do before I can get on this train to Earl's Court. According to the display board, I have two minutes before it leaves, so I run down the platform to the public telephone. Pulling out Rolf's note, I quickly dial Paul's number.

Chapter 31

3:58 PM—Wimbledon—District Line

Paul has worked as a tube train mechanic at Northfields for the past thirty years. You could say it's the perfect job for him. He loves trains, but especially *his* trains: once he has worked on a tube car, he will follow its movements on a daily basis. He is like a mother duck, keeping track of his chicks as they glide this way and that along the subterranean streams of the Piccadilly Line.

When I get through, Paul seems utterly unperturbed by my question. He doesn't seem to think it is odd at all to ring someone out of the blue and ask them about rolling stock movements.

"Let me see," he mutters down the phone at me, "690 and 891—they're coupled with 890, aren't they? I think they went in for servicing last night because one of the door releases was a bit sticky."

"So you mean they're still with you, in the depot?"

"Not my depot, the other one, at Cockfosters."

I curse out loud. Of course! Rolf must have gone straight from Cockfosters Station to the depot, just five minutes walk away. If we'd done the same thing, we'd have our third envelope already—

as it is we're going to have a nightmare getting it. If we have to go all the way back to Cockfosters, I can kiss the Eurostar good-bye.

My cursing seems to worry Paul. "What's this all about?" he says. "Is there something wrong with these cars that I should know?"

"No, I just need to see them, that's all. I was just up in Cockfosters earlier—I could have gone to see them then."

"Well, why don't you come down here to Northfields?" he suggests. "They're bound to come back through here sooner or later."

"But I thought you said they needed servicing?"

"Yes, but it's only a sticky door. They should be able to fix that in no time. If you hold on a second, I'll just give Cockfosters a call on the other line. They should be able to tell you when they're due out again . . ."

There is the sound of him putting the phone down and then the noise of voices in the distance. I look up at the display board once again. Our train is due to leave in one minute.

When Paul comes back to the phone, he sounds jolly. "I just had a quick word with Nigel, and he tells me your carriages will be rolling off into the station in half an hour's time. They're pretty much back in service, good as new."

"In half an hour, you say?" I can't help getting excited.

"Yep. It should be departing Cockfosters at four-thirty on the dot—just in time for the rush hour."

"Paul," I say, "you're an absolute star."

I say good-bye to Paul and ring off. Looking up at the display, I see we have almost run out of time—our train will be leaving the station at any moment. Brian makes a move to sit down in the carriage, but I stay where I am.

"I just have to make one more quick phone call."

"But we have to go . . ." says Brian urgently.

"Don't worry. I'll be quick."

I shove my credit card back into the telephone and dial Rachel's mobile number. It rings once, twice, three times. I want to talk to her, just to let her know where I am. She'll only get worried otherwise, and then she'll just have another excuse to be angry with me.

On the fourth ring, the train begins to hum, as if it's warming up to leave.

"Come on, Rachel, pick up the bloody phone!"

It rings again and again, but as my train continues to warm up, I figure she isn't going to answer it. Suddenly, without any further warning the carriage doors begin to close. Brian wedges himself between them to hold them open and gestures to me wildly. It is time to go.

Slamming the phone down, I grab my credit card and bundle over Brian's legs into the carriage. As I do so Brian steps away from the doors, and they slam shut behind me.

"Well," says Brian, "that was close." I think he's annoyed with me.

"It's okay," I say. "I made it, didn't I?"

"Oh, yeah, you made it. But what would you have done if I hadn't held the doors?"

I don't answer him. It's unnecessary to answer him. I just sit back and try to enjoy the fact that for once I can relax. And I *can* relax—up to a point. For the next twenty minutes all I have to do is take a few photos, cross off a few stations on the map, and plan what we're going to do when we get back up to town. Now, at last, I can concentrate on getting the next envelope.

Chapter 32

4:00 PM—Wimbledon–Earl's Court—District Line

The problem with relaxing is that you finally realize how tired you are. I hadn't really noticed while I was running around, but now that I'm sitting down I can feel the backs of my eyes burning with the desire to sleep, and all the muscles around them are taut, stiff from the effort of keeping my eyelids wedged open for so long. My arms feel as though they're two inches longer from carrying my bag of cameras around all day; my feet are in real pain . . . in fact, all my muscles ache, except those in my legs—*they* have gone numb and right now are melting like processed cheese into the upholstery of the train seat.

Brian looks tired too. As he sits beside me he lets out a deep sigh, before pulling a can of beer from his bag and opening it. The sight of him drinking irritates me for some reason. I try to ignore it by taking out my tube map and studying it. I count the number of red crosses and frown. We have done 132 stations in total—not quite half the number on the map.

After a short while, Brian turns to me. "What did your mate say about those two train carriages?" he asks.

"Just that they're in the depot. Cockfosters depot, as it turns out, which is why the time on Rolf's note was so close to the time for the envelope that had my keys in it. Bit of a shame we didn't think about it while we were up there—we could have popped in at the depot there and then."

"So what do we do now?"

"Well, our carriages aren't going to be leaving Cockfosters for another half an hour, so that gives us plenty of time to get some other stuff out of the way before we hook up with them. I reckon we should do the West End now, and then come back down to Hammersmith to wait for our train there."

Brian lets out another sigh, as if he's frustrated with the relentlessness of our journey. It's a bit irritating really. I mean, nobody *asked* him to join me today, did they? If he doesn't want to do it, nobody's forcing him—he could always bugger off at any time. I watch him take another swig and then wipe his mouth with the back of his grubby tattooed hand, and it annoys me.

"Brian," I say tiredly, "why *do* you drink so much?"

He sighs again, before saying, "Because I'm stressed."

"No, you're not. You're the most laid-back person I've ever met. Look at me—*I'm* the one who's stressed."

"Well, maybe you should drink more," says Brian. "Then you could be like me."

I turn away, disappointed with him. "That's not much of an answer."

"It's not much of a question. I could ask you why you like the tube so much, but what would you say? You like the tube because you like the tube; that's all there is to it. It's an unhealthy habit that takes your mind off the things that really matter."

I think about this for a moment. "But the tube matters," I say.

"No, it doesn't. It's a distraction."

"But it does matter," I insist stubbornly. "Just think where we'd be without it. How would anybody get to work? The economy would collapse if we didn't have a decent transport system—life would be chaos. It's important to care about such things."

"Yeah. In moderation, though, mate."

"The tube is our history," I try. "It's what defines London as a city. It's part of *all* of us."

"See? You're doing it now."

"Doing what, exactly?"

"Using the tube as a distraction. At least I know what I'm doing when I take a drink—but you . . . you haven't got a clue. You think all this tube rubbish is *normal.*"

"It *is* normal."

"See? There you go again."

"What do you mean *there I go again?"*

"You're trying to keep the conversation stuck on the tube, like that's the only thing that matters. If you actually stopped to think about it for half a moment, you'd realize that the tube is the thing that matters *least of all.* Why are you so determined to win this bet, for Christ's sake? The tube'll still be there if you don't make it. Rolf'll still be there. You'll still be there. There's only one person who might not be there—*that's* what really matters."

I feel the blood running to my face. "All right, if you're so against distractions, why don't you answer my question? Why *do* you drink so much?"

"I told you. To take my mind off things."

"What things?"

Brian sits and thinks for a moment, and takes another sip, as if he needs the taste of beer in his mouth to remind him why he's drinking. "Okay," he says decisively after a few more moments. "You and me have got different problems. Your problem is that you don't know what you want. You're about to marry this girl, but you never really *decided* to be with her; it's just something that sort of happened. And she asks you to do stuff you don't want to do, and she makes you feel stuff you don't want to feel, but you put up with it because if you actually *thought* about it for a second, you probably want to keep her happy. Because, without having to make an actual decision about it, you quite like having her around. That's *your* problem."

He says it as though there's no room for argument. I'm about to tell him to stop avoiding the bloody question—but before I can interrupt him, he continues.

"*My* problem is that I've already made my decision. I decided years ago who I wanted to spend the rest of my life with. I just can't have her, that's all, because she's decided on somebody else. And that's why I drink."

I look at him, his stubbly, sad old face, his tattooed hands made steady by the alcohol. "But drinking isn't going to make that any better," I say.

"I *know* it's not going to make it better. It's not about that. I told you, it's a distraction."

The conversation seems somehow to have come full circle. It's like a lot of conversations we've had today: it hasn't gone anywhere—not really. I mean, I know a bit more about him, but when it comes down to it, we've just come right back to where we started from. Brian drinks to distract himself. And that's that.

But it strikes me that if Brian's trying to distract himself from the loss of his wife, then he's not doing a very good job of it. Anyone who knows as clearly as this the reason why he drinks is surely only going to remind himself of it every time he opens a beer. It seems that Brian is stuck in a circle of his own. He drinks to forget his wife, but because he knows this to be the case, each time he has another drink, he only remembers her more strongly than before. And so he must drink again . . . He reminds me of one of those roundel tube signs—a red circle with a blue bar across it bearing the name of his wife. Each time he tries to escape from her name, he just finds himself revolving 180 degrees and returning to it once again. She is like a symbol, a logo, stamped across his whole life. Much like the tube is stamped across mine.

Our train is pulling into another station now: Southfields. I am about to stand up in preparation for taking my photo, when Brian surprises me by saying, very decisively, "I want to tell you a story."

"What sort of story?" I say, pulling myself to my feet. I can hear my knees creak.

"It's a story about death."

"Oh," I say, "cheery, then."

"Death ain't a bad thing to tell stories about. That's a mistake a lot of people make. Thinking about death once in a while is a good thing: it reminds you to be alive. That's why I want to tell you this story. It's a sort of cautionary tale."

The train comes to a stop, and the doors slide open, and I'm worried that if I let him go on at me, I'll miss my opportunity. "Hang on a minute," I say, "just let me take a picture of this sign. Then you can tell me all the stories you want."

Brian looks at me and snorts sarcastically, but I ignore him. Stepping over to the doors, I pull out my fun camera and hold it up to my eye.

Chapter 33

SOUTHFIELDS

Chapter 34

4:05 PM—Wimbledon–Earl's Court—District Line

"Okay," he says once I've sat down again, "the story's about a body. Not just any body, but a body they found in the aftermath of the King's Cross fire in 1987. It was a story told me by one of the coppers who had to work on the cleanup afterwards. A right nasty job."

He looks at me briefly just to make sure I'm still listening, so I nod reassuringly.

"I don't know how much you know about the King's Cross fire. You see, most of the people who died there died of smoke inhalation, but there were also a lot of people burned. Thirty-one of them was burned beyond recognition. Round the escalator where the fire started the heat was so intense it melted the metal side plates. It was a terrible mess there: ash, soot, twisted metal, and melted rubber everywhere. And of course the bodies.

"It was the job of the police to try and put names to each of the people they found. They set about doing this straightaway, and pretty soon they had found out the identity of practically everyone. I say 'practically' because there was one body that they couldn't identify. Without a name, they called the body by its number. Body 115.

"It was strange, because although his body was the most damaged by the fire, the police had so much forensic evidence about Body 115, they all thought he would be a doddle to identify. You see, at some point in his life the man had had an operation where they'd put a metal clip into his brain. Not only that, but the clip was a bit unusual—it was made by a Japanese manufacturer, and only four hundred of them had ever been imported into this country. According to this, copper things like that are a forensic medic's dream come true—but unfortunately, when they went to the health authorities for a list of candidates, there was no record of which clips had gone to which patients. And so they had to start again.

"The next thing they tried was his fingers. One of the guy's fingers was relatively unburnt, so they managed to get a fingerprint off him—but unfortunately this didn't match up with any of the five and a half million prints in the police national collection. Instead they tried his dental records. Body 115 was wearing a strange pair of dentures when he died, and the lower set had a couple of letters etched into them: 'FH.' So the police advertised in all the dental journals. But no one came forward to give any information.

"Then two months after the fire, a medical artist at the University of Manchester managed to come up with a reconstruction of the man's face. So they posted the picture up all round King's Cross—but again, no one came forward.

"So they turned to the people who were lying near Body 115 at the time of his death. Perhaps he was traveling with a friend, they thought—perhaps if they matched him up with one of the other victims, they might get somewhere. The body found next to him belonged to a known vagrant, so maybe Body 115 was a tramp."

Brian looks at me to make sure I'm still following. "That's when I first met the copper who told me this story," he explains.

"Right," I say, "I've got you."

"Okay, so they think maybe he's a tramp, just like me. So they go all round the center of town asking people like me if there have been any disappearances, if any homeless man suddenly vanished around the time of the fire. But nobody reported anyone missing, which is hardly surprising, because I can tell you that the police cleared the booking hall of homeless people just before the fire started. I know, because I was there at the time.

"Anyway, at this point they're beginning to run out of leads. Scotland Yard checks the man's details against their missing person's list and comes up with three hundred or so possibilities, but none of these turn out to be the right man. In desperation they even consulted a psychic at the College of Psychic Studies. The psychic suggested a few leads, but in the end they all led nowhere.

"They were just about to give up, when suddenly something interesting happened. Two years after the fire, and after more than six thousand hours of police investigation, they finally came across an unclaimed suitcase that had been left at the King's Cross left-luggage office just before the disaster. Inside they found more than five hundred pounds in wage packets, some denture powder—remember this man had dentures—some clothes that would fit a man of the same height as Body 115, and a merchant seaman's ID card belonging to a man called Hubert Rose. There was even a photograph of Rose on the card which looked just like that of the artist's reconstruction. 'Bingo!' they thought. This was it—the police were sure they'd found their man. The only problem was that, while they were double-checking, somebody noticed that none of this bloke's fingerprints, which were *all over* his ID card, matched up with those of the dead man. No matter how much they wanted Hubert Rose to be the man they were looking for, he wasn't—he was just a red herring. So now they were right back at square one.

"To make things worse, now the police didn't have one mystery to solve, but two: one person without a name, and one name without a person. Well, they'd already tried just about everything they could with Body 115—but there were still a few things they could do to find Hubert Rose. So they contacted his family, but none of them had seen him for over twenty years. They tried his friends, and that was the same. The missing person's bureau couldn't help, either. In desperation they got his family to appear on *The London Program,* but no one ever came forward to say they knew him or where he was. Hubert Rose had disappeared without a trace.

"As for Body 115, there came a point when the police just had to give up. They had searched every possible avenue and come up with a blank. After two years they finally closed his file and buried him in a vacant plot of the St. Pancras and Islington Cemetery. To this day nobody knows who he was."

As he finishes his story, Brian sinks back into his chair, clutching his beer and staring at the seats in front of him. He seems quite calm, serene almost—like he has said what he had to say and can now sit back and relax.

"That's a terrible story," I say quietly.

"Yes, it *is* a terrible story. It just goes to show how easy it is to disappear in this city. The guy with the ID card is no more traceable than the charred remains of the body. *He* could be either of us."

"But he's not. Thank God."

Brian takes another swig of lager. "No," he says, matter-of-factly, "he's not. But he could be. That's just my point. He could be."

I turn to look at him, and for a second I think I get what he's going on about. It seems his story is not about death but about being *alone.* The thought jolts something in my head: is this the real reason why Brian drinks?—not to forget his wife, but to forget his loneliness?

I watch him sip his beer, and for a moment I find myself imagining that he is the missing merchant seaman in the story. The idea isn't *that* far-fetched. After all, I don't actually know very much about Brian. I don't know his surname. I don't know anyone who knows him, or who has even met him—certainly no one who could back him up and verify that he is who he says he is. I don't know where he lives, if he does live anywhere. I know nothing about his past except that he was once married, was once a carpenter who lived in Kenton, and he could quite easily have been making that up. When all is said and done, I can't even be sure that anything he has told me today is true—as far as I know he could be Hubert Rose himself, or anybody else, for that matter. He could even be a spy for Rolf.

As the train decelerates I turn away again to see, almost with surprise, that we are arriving at Earl's Court. It's time to change once again. Time to travel up the little spur to Kensington (Olympia), the station where I first met Rachel all those months and years ago. It almost feels like an impertinence to interrupt the mood by getting off the train and beginning our chase again, but it is necessary. Life goes on. And I'm sure Brian agrees with me when I say that stories like that are not for dwelling on—they are simply tales to remember once in a while, to remind you to thank your stars. Because one day, when you're shopping, or mowing the lawn, or reading in bed, or even spending a day traveling round the tube for a bet, it will happen to you too—and it's a good thing, a healthy thing, just to keep this in mind. I suppose this is just Brian's way of telling me not to mess up my life. We will all of us die one day—in the meantime let's just hope that when that day arrives, there will at least be someone to miss us when we're gone.

Chapter 35

4:19 PM—Belsize Park

Rachel woke up to the sound of the phone ringing. It was very confusing because she had been dreaming about a telephone anyway, and now here one was in real life, ringing incessantly and calling her out of her slumber. She lay for a moment, her face tensed up, her head full of the noise from the other room. Mercifully, after a couple more rings the noise of the bell stopped and was followed by that of the answerphone kicking in. She turned onto her side and buried her head under the pillow. In a few moments whoever it was would have left their message, and then she could go back to sleep.

It was only at this point that she suddenly remembered that she was waiting for Andy to call, and that this might very well be him now. The thought woke her with a start and jolted her head out from beneath the pillow. Stumbling to her feet, she ran clumsily through to the sitting room and picked up the receiver just as the answerphone was getting to the end of its message.

"Hello?" she croaked, "Andy? Is that you?"

"No," said a voice quietly. Rachel sat down. She recognized the voice immediately—it was the same person that had called this morning.

"Rolf?"

"Andy's not coming home," said the voice. "He's busy. He's chasing his tail."

"What do you mean?"

"I mean what I say. His tail. He's chasing his tail. Why are you marrying him? Why are you marrying someone so obviously beneath you?"

She grasped hold of the words in her mind, turned them over, tried to understand their meaning. She was confused. She had just woken up, and there was something about this conversation—random, beyond her control, a little frightening—that was unmistakably like the dream she had just been having. The images of her dream flashed through her head once more: she had been in a public call box—the phone had been ringing, but when she'd picked it up, there was no sound on the other end; it just continued to ring and ring, while outside there were thousands of wedding guests waiting in a queue. And now she was talking into the phone. "I'm marrying him because I love him."

"No, you don't, Rachel," said the voice. "No, you don't. You don't love him. You only think you do. You can't marry someone like that—he isn't worthy, he isn't . . . pure."

"What are you talking about? What do you mean, he isn't *pure?"*

"Just exactly what I say—aren't you listening? He isn't pure. He doesn't love you like he should do—*purely."*

She wasn't dreaming, was she? This wasn't an extension of her thoughts, her fears? She shook herself mentally, trying to find her balance. She wanted to put down the telephone, shut off from this unwelcome voice, but something inside her told her not to—after all, when you were confronted with monsters in your dreams, weren't you supposed to turn and face them, talk to them, find out what they wanted? Besides, she had a feeling that as soon as she put the phone down, Rolf would only call straight back.

"What do you want, Rolf? Why do you keep calling me?"

"I just want to stop you making a bad mistake, that's all."

"You want to . . . Let me get this straight—you want to stop me getting married? Is that what this is all about?"

Rolf hesitated. "Well . . . yes."

"Listen, Rolf, I don't know what's going on in your head, but I'm in love with Andy. And I'm going to marry him. Sure he's not perfect, but neither am I."

There was silence on the other end of the line.

"And neither are you," she added, as an afterthought.

"Okay, okay," said Rolf's voice, hastily. "I might not be perfect, but I'm better than him. I can *beat* him . . ."

His voice trailed off, as if he had said something he shouldn't have. For some reason Rachel found it particularly irritating. Perhaps she *should* put the phone down, after all. Perhaps she should just tell him to leave her alone and then hang up—it was a tempting thought. But something kept her there against her better judgment. She couldn't help getting the feeling that there was something more to this conversation than she realized, something she really ought to know.

"Is this about your little bet with each other?" she asked, "because if it is, I'm not interested in who is better than the other. As far as I'm concerned, you're both acting like children.'

"Oh, so he told you about the bet, did he?"

"Yes, he told me all about it."

"And did he tell you about *what* we bet?"

"Not exactly . . . no . . ." She was thrown. "Why? What was it?"

Rolf laughed nervously. "You'll see," he said. "You'll see."

"What? What will I see?"

But he was gone. As the phone went dead, she felt all her anger bubble up to the surface once more. Not only had she not had the satisfaction of hanging up on Rolf, the bastard had hung up on *her.* And he'd left her with so many questions! What on earth had he been going on about? And, more to the point, what had her idiot boyfriend gone and got himself into? It was ridiculous—she felt like some duped parent finding out for the first time that her child had been led astray—the only difference was that she was supposed to be marrying this child, this big useless kid, in less than twenty-four hours.

She put the receiver down heavily on its cradle and was distracted once again by the sound of the phone. Or, not exactly the phone this time, but the answering machine—it clicked loudly, and then whirred as the tape rewound.

When she realized their conversation had been recorded, her first reaction was to reach for the erase button—and not just because she wanted to keep her answerphone clear. The whole exchange had been creepy from start to finish, and she had an urge to get rid of it, wipe it from existence. But at the last second, just as she was about to delete the recording, she held back. Perhaps she should keep it, after all, at least until she'd played it back to Andy. It might do him good to show him what his trainspotter friend was really like.

And besides, no amount of deleting would be able to remove the conversation from her memory, which was all she really wanted to do. Because now, whether she liked it or not, she had something else to worry about. It was plain from this conversation that there was more to Rolf's telephoning her than could be explained by mere geekiness: somehow this weirdo—this obsessive—had got it into his head that their occasional, uncomfortable exchanges had meant something. The thought made her feel faintly sick, but it was unavoidable: somehow, for some reason, Rolf had decided that he was in love with her.

Chapter 36

4:28 PM—Kensington (Olympia)–High Street Kensington—No. 9 Bus

4:33 PM—High Street Kensington–Bayswater—District Line

By the time we get to Olympia, I'm beginning to feel suspicious again. I think I must be developing some sort of paranoia, because despite the fact that there is obviously no one following us, I can't seem to shake off this feeling that somehow we are being watched. As we run along the platform and out of the exit, I find myself looking behind me—repeatedly—but there is definitely no one running after us. In fact, there aren't that many people here at all, just a couple of old men, a woman in a duffle coat, a teenager. If Rolf *is* having us followed, he's certainly keeping a low profile.

There's no train to change onto here. Somehow we have to make our way through the streets to High Street Kensington Station, half a mile away. Brian leads me on a run up to Hammersmith Road, where through a piece of good fortune we manage to catch a no. 9 bus. I'm extremely grateful for this. It seems that each time we start running, I lose my breath more quickly than before—while this morning I was sprinting from platform to platform, the most I can manage now is a sort of slow jog, and the time I need to recover my energy afterwards is becoming longer and longer. I think an extra half a mile on foot along the main road would probably have finished me off.

At High Street Kensington we catch a District Line train northwards, and my mind turns once more to the next envelope I have to find. It's about now that the two carriages mentioned in Rolf's last note will be leaving the depot, and the thought worries me. I can't imagine whereabouts on a train carriage Rolf could have hidden my envelope—there simply aren't any nooks and crannies on a tube train, for obvious reasons. He would have had to stick it to the ceiling, or behind one of the adverts, or who knows where else. Now that the carriages have been released onto the Piccadilly Line, my envelope is free for anyone to find.

Of course, there is a chance that it might still go unnoticed, even if it is in an exposed place. Train commuters are notoriously unobservant. Not only that, they're uninterested: a green piece of paper strapped to a window or a train door would be simply another piece of litter to them—they'd ignore it like they ignore everything else. But unfortunately such commuters aren't the only people who travel on tube trains. And not everyone is as unobservant and closed off to the world around them as your average nine-to-fiver.

For example, the carriage Brian and I are on at the moment is full of Italian teenagers. Kids like these don't act like normal passengers. They don't stand quietly, with bored expressions on their faces, waiting for their stop to come. They aren't even *trying* to look bored. Instead they're flirting with each other, swinging on the handrails, using the windows as mirrors to brush their hair in, and gratuitously drinking cans of Fanta. I watch them anxiously for the next couple of stops. If one of *them* were to spot a green envelope shoved down the back of a seat, they wouldn't be able to resist it.

The Italians aren't the only tourists on our carriage. At Notting Hill Gate a couple of Scandinavians get on—two enormous men, each about six-foot-eight tall. They don't carry neat little designer knapsacks like the Italians, they carry rucksacks—enormous great things, big enough to carry gravestones in. They are a couple of suntanned giants, with bright blue eyes and blond beards that look as though they've been cultivated by several months in the wilderness. They both have shoulders that'd make a brick shithouse look like it was made of Legos, and great slabs of muscle, like a series of buttocks, down their arms.

At Bayswater, I have to squeeze between them to take a picture of the station sign. I think of scowling at them angrily, for taking up all the space. But at the last minute I decide against it. After all, they *are* six foot eight.

The train hovers at the station for about thirty seconds before the pneumatic hiss of the door release signals that we are about to move off again. However, just as the doors of the train are closing, an old lady pulling a trolley bag struggles onto the platform. One of the Scandinavians by the door sees her and so grabs hold of the sliding doors and hauls them back open again. He doesn't just prevent them from closing, he practically rips them off their hinges.

Everyone at my end of the carriage glares at him. You are not supposed to hold the doors back, not even for a little old lady. It's one of the laws of the tube. There is a general muttering around me, as my fellow passengers whisper their disapproval to one another—but, like me, nobody says a word out loud.

All the other doors in the carriage close, and then open, and then close again, but the tourist steadfastly holds his open while the old woman hobbles forward. It's agonizing watching her struggle along with her bag. Christ, she's slow! I've seen *snails* run for a train faster than her. I've seen *paraplegic* snails move faster. It is unbelievably frustrating.

In an effort to speed things along a bit, I step off the train and carry her bag for her. As I do so, all the doors open and shut again, and for a moment it crosses my mind that this is all a joke—the blond giant is just waiting for me to get off the train before he lets the door close behind me. But he doesn't. He holds the door firm. In fact, he holds the door too firm. As I help the old woman to step into the carriage, I hear a loud twang! When the Scandinavian tourist finally lets go of the door, it stays motionless. All the other doors open and shut, repeatedly, but this one stays exactly where it is. Somehow the man seems to have broken it.

We wait for a few minutes, wondering what's going to happen next, and I can feel my face flushing—not only with irritation, but also with guilt for my part in breaking the train doors. Of course, I tell myself, it's not really my fault—it's *his* fault—I would have let the old dear miss her bloody train. But that doesn't stop me from feeling that I had a part in it. And now I'm going to have to pay for it, in time.

After a short while, one of the station officials appears and examines the broken door. Then he stares straight at the Scandinavian tourist. London Underground staff have a sixth sense about this sort of thing. "All right," he says, "who did this?"

"I did," says the old woman defiantly.

"Very funny," says the official sarcastically. "Who really did it?" He looks at the tourist again.

"Don't be cheeky, sonny," says the old woman. "I broke the door. You should do something about your rickety old trains. They're falling apart."

While the station official is giving the door another look over, she smiles at me and the Scandinavian tourist, and puts her finger to her lips to signal us not to tell the truth.

"Well," says the station official, "you've done a bloody good job. This train's not going anywhere like this. I'm afraid everyone's going to have to get off."

"What!" I blurt out. "Surely you're not going to make everyone get out, just because of one faulty door?"

"That's exactly what I'm going to do, sir. This train is now dangerous."

"But I'm only going another couple of stops!"

"I don't care how many stops you're going—you're doing it on another train."

I glare angrily at the tourist who started all this, but he doesn't see me. He is getting off the train merrily with his friend. This doesn't affect him—it's just another story to tell his family back home over dinner, while they gobble herrings together, or whatever it is that makes Scandinavians all so bloody enormous. I have half a mind to turn him in to the station official.

"Come on, Brian," I hiss through my teeth.

We get off the train and stand on the platform with all the other passengers. While we stand there, I hear an announcement over the train loudspeakers: *"Due to passenger action, this train is now out of service. All change please. All change."*

The station official is walking the length of the platform, telling everyone in the rest of the train to vacate their carriages. It seems to take an eternity for everyone to get the message—probably because half the passengers on this train don't speak English.

It's while I'm fantasizing about taking a language course, just so that I can learn to say, "Everybody off the bloody train!" in several European languages, that I hear a second announcement. This one isn't on the train loudspeakers. It is coming from the main station public address system.

"Attention please. All District and Circle Line services between High Street Kensington and Edgware Road have been suspended

until further notice. Passengers are advised to find alternative means of travel. I repeat . . ."

Brian and I look at each other. Neither of us can quite believe it. *"All* services," says Brian. "Why?"

"Let's find out," I say urgently.

We grab hold of a second station official and ask him what's going on, but he doesn't seem to be any wiser than us. "If you hang about for a few minutes, sir," he says, "I'll let you know as soon as I find out."

"I don't have a few minutes . . ." I say, but the station official has moved on. He disappears into a crowd of teenaged Italians, bombarding him with questions about what is happening.

"What are we going to do?" asks Brian. "If *all* services are suspended, then there aren't any trains going in either direction."

"I know," I say impatiently. "I know. We've got to think of something else." I rack my brains for a solution. "Okay," I say, "we're at Bayswater Station. That means Queensway's just a hundred yards up the road. If we run up there, we can get on a Central Line train to . . . somewhere."

"Yes, but where? I thought you said we were going to Hammersmith to meet up with this train that's got your envelope on it. We can't get to Hammersmith on the Central Line."

"Okay," I say, thinking quickly, "okay, maybe we can forget about Hammersmith. Maybe we can go out to Ealing Broadway and catch the District Line down to Acton Town instead. Our train should be passing through there in . . ." I look at my watch. " . . . in about thirty to thirty-five minutes. We should be able to catch it, no problem. Then after we've picked up our envelope, we can do west London and come back here once London Transport have sorted out this chaos."

"Will that work?"

"I think so. We'll just have to swap around our itinerary a little. Come on, we'll work it out when we get to Queensway."

• • •

We race along the platform and up the stairs which lead to the exit. I'm so exhausted now that running is the last thing I need to do—especially through crowds like this. It's the crowds that make it so tiring—the fighting your way through hordes and hordes of people.

At the top of the stairs things get even more crowded, as countless others try to squeeze out of the station to find their way to alternative transport. One or two are holding things up even further by arguing with the ticket inspectors about whether they can get their money back. Brian and I fight our way desperately through the mob, wading our way through Italian, Spanish, Japanese, and French tourists with something akin to a breaststroke action, before we finally break out into the daylight and are free to start running down the street.

Chapter 37

4:41 PM—Queensway—Central Line

One hundred yards up the road we come to Queensway tube station. When we arrive there is a queue of people waiting for the lift, so we run down a side passage and enter the lift from the wrong side—unconscionable queue-jumping, I know, but that is allowed on the Underground as long as it's done without any pushing or shoving.

"I don't like this," I say to Brian, as we make our way down to the westbound platform. "I don't like this at all. First there's signal problems at Upminster this morning, then a points failure at Earl's Court, and now the Circle and District Lines have been suspended completely—no explanation, nothing."

"Sign of the times," says Brian. "The whole system's falling apart."

"But why didn't they give an explanation? They always give an explanation."

We hover near the edge of the platform. The next tube is not due for another five minutes, a fact which makes me slightly nervous—

after all, if we don't make it to the Piccadilly Line in the next half hour, the train with our envelope on it will shoot by without us. We don't have time to lose.

"And it's strange that it happened at Bayswater," I continue, thinking out loud. "Every time we've been delayed today, it's been in a place where we've had some sort of obvious escape route. It's weird. It's like someone's *playing* with us."

I look down the platform at the security camera and can't help feeling that it is trained on me, watching my brain tick as I stand here, waiting for the approaching train. I stare into it and try to ascertain its purpose. Are you playing with me, Rolf? Or are you trying to guide me into some perfectly thought-out trap? In my pocket I can feel Rolf's safe-deposit key, and it is like I am carrying a piece of him, attached to me like a leech.

I think back to the other delays that have happened today—a signal failure this morning at Upminster, a points failure at Earl's Court, and now this—and suddenly it strikes me that there is something that all three delays have in common. They have all happened on the *District* Line. The odds of three such major faults happening independently, on the same line, within a few hours of each other must be minuscule. No line is *that* inefficient. Surely this can't be a coincidence?

I desperately want to sit down now—I feel sick with tiredness—but I have to keep standing for fear of losing my place at the platform edge. Unconsciously I spread myself out, trying to take up as much space as I can to maximize my chances of being by the doors when the train arrives. And I wait. I wait for the tiny change in pressure that comes as the engine of the train compresses the air in front of it like a piston. And I wait for the sound, the squealing of the rails, like the sound a piece of ice makes when you hurl it across a frozen pond.

But it doesn't come. There is no change in pressure; there is no rumble of approaching trains. Gradually the platform is beginning to fill up, and still the train does not come; and at last I begin to sense that something is wrong.

People are becoming impatient—I can hear muttered swear-words and the odd person clicking his tongue behind me. The squeeze is becoming dangerous now as the crowd begins to strain towards the edge of the platform. I sidle closer to Brian. Down the platform I can see rows of heads stretching out above the tracks to look down the tunnel, as if by doing so they will tempt the train to hurry forward. And once again I get the feeling: there is something wrong.

It does not come as a surprise when I see him. It's only a fleeting glimpse, but it verifies the foreboding within me: he is here. I see his dark form detach itself from the wall about halfway down the platform and disappear, a shadow dissolving into the crowd. I don't see his face, of course—just his profile, from a distance, and then the ripple through the crowd as it swallows him up—but I know it's him. It can *only* be him. No one else in the whole station is moving.

I feel a tug on my sleeve and look round to see Brian staring at me. "Are you all right?" he asks. "You look a little pale."

"I don't feel great," I admit.

"Perhaps you should sit down for a bit." He looks back, but the crowd behind us is like a thick hedge. "Maybe when we get on the train . . ."

I look across at him. "I don't think a train is coming."

He starts to reassure me, but then stops, as if something in my face has told him that I know what I'm talking about. There will be no train.

We stand for another few moments before the announcement is finally made—there is a person under a train at Marble Arch, and as a consequence all westbound traffic has been canceled until further notice. A groan goes up along the platform, and somebody behind me says loudly, "Bloody hell," but in general nobody moves. They have no choice. They simply have to wait until services resume.

"Brian," I say uncomfortably, "we can't stay here."

"But what can we do?"

"I don't know," I say, glancing down to the end of the platform where I saw the shadow disappear. "Just, please, let's get away from here."

I am feeling suddenly very unsteady on my feet. As Brian leads me through to the back of the crowd, it feels as though my knees are going to buckle beneath me any second, and the feeling makes me anxious. It's a true relief when I hear a train coming into the opposite platform—eastbound, towards town. It sounds ordinary, familiar, a haven of normality arriving on the other track. At once all my anxiety is channeled into one thing—I must get on that train. I don't even care where it's going, I just have to get away from here. Without thinking, I take hold of Brian's sleeve and drag him away from the crowd. Even as we leave the westbound platform, I can still hear the sound of radios, and people muttering, echoing down the corridor behind me.

Chapter 38

4:48 PM—Queensway–Oxford Circus—Central Line

The carriage on our new train is much busier than I expected. No one usually goes *into* London, not at this time, but today, perhaps because of all the delays, there isn't even space for us to sit down.

Brian and I stand in the aisle, holding on to the poles as the train starts up. "What are we going to do?" he says.

"I don't know." For some reason my mind has gone blank. I'm too tired to make decisions.

"Next stop's Lancaster Gate, and then Marble Arch. Maybe we could take a bus somewhere?"

"Maybe, but a bus could take forever. It's rush hour."

"Or we could get out at Bond Street. We could take the Jubilee Line from there, back down to the Piccadilly Line. If we're quick, maybe we can catch Rolf's train as it comes through Green Park."

"Yes," I say, but I am unsure. That's precisely what Rolf expects us to do. But then, what options do we have now? We *have* to get to that train. We *have* to get our next envelope. Green Park is the only place we can go.

I stare at the window for a while, before I suddenly feel Brian's hand on my arm. "Andy," he says gently, "are you feeling okay?"

"I'm a bit . . . nauseous."

In the changeover at Lancaster Gate we have been thrust further into the car—Brian squeezes me through to one of the seats reserved for elderly or disabled people, and asks the man there if I can take his place. Once I am sitting down, he holds his hand out.

"Give me the camera," he says. "I'll take the pictures from now on, while you have a rest."

I look at his hand and hesitate. I don't want to give the camera to him. There are a thousand things that could go wrong. He might forget to wind it on at one of the stops. The flash might not work, or someone might get in the way of the station sign, leaving me with a useless photograph of some stranger's head. Brian might not aim straight. But none of these is the real reason why I hesitate. The plain fact of it is that there is still a part of me that doesn't completely trust him. I mean, how long have I known the man?

"Andy," he says firmly, "you're in no fit state. Now, give it to me."

Reluctantly I hand the camera over. But perhaps I'm not completely reluctant. I'm really too tired to make any kind of a fuss, and in a way it's a relief to let the damn thing go. At last I am free to give up this whole affair. It is literally out of my hands.

After a few more people get on, the doors close and the train begins to move. The last to get on are a couple of girls—young women in their early twenties. One of them takes a seat beside me to my left, while her friend is left standing in the aisle to my right. They look tired from work, but relieved to have finished for the day. The one who is standing reaches up to grasp the rail above my head. I am so close to her that I can see a slight discoloration under the arm of her blouse, the yellow hint of a sweat stain.

As the train starts to move off once more, I hear the crackle of the digitized voice announcer coming from a speaker above my head. Her name's Sonia, this voice. I'm not making it up, Sonia is its official name. I read somewhere once that all the digitized announcers on the tubes have names.

Tonight Sonia is going nuts. No sooner has the train started off than her voice kicks in: "Please let the passengers off the train first," she says, although we are accelerating towards full speed and no one would even think of trying to get off the train. "Mind the gap between the train and the platform. This train terminates here."

Everyone in the car looks at each other and smiles. Near me there is a man in a pair of Elvis Costello glasses reading a copy of *Military Illustrated.* He looks up from his magazine and raises his eyebrows at the girl in front of me. "Typical!" he says, with venom. The woman looks back at him, and then at me, and grins, before turning away—and as she turns away I can see the discolored part of her blouse strain slightly from her armpit towards her breasts. I shut my eyes and listen to Sonia speak.

I rarely listen to the voice announcers, but I have to admit that there is something attractive about this one. There is a certain authority in her voice, as if she is absolutely certain about every word of her gobbledygook. She sounds young, but also mature, with a hint of coquettishness. In fact, she sounds quite sexy. I wonder wearily if the tube authorities thought of that when they chose their speaker. Was it an unconscious choice by some male London Underground manager? Or was it deliberate—an attempt to make the tube line more user friendly, more attractive—more alluring?

Rolf once admitted to me that he sometimes becomes excited by some of the digitized voice announcers. It was the only time Rolf has ever confessed to having any sexual feelings at all. I wonder what he would do if he were in my position now, alerted to the sound of the speaker's voice by the nonsense she is talking. Would he become distracted by the sultry tone of her voice? Would he become so involved that he'd miss his stop or forget to photograph one of the stations' signs?

"The next station is Epping," says the voice. "Change here for the Metropolitan Line."

I think the only reason Rolf is excited by this voice is that he is on the Underground when he listens to her. I can't imagine Rolf becoming aroused by the voice of an announcer in a lift or an airport. I can't even imagine him fancying a real woman, not without the added stimulation of the tube in some form—a skulking man in a mac committing *frottage* on crowded Northern Line trains. But with these digitized announcements you can almost imagine that it is not the voice of a woman you are listening to, but the voice of the train itself. Rather than fantasizing about the body of the woman who speaks those words, you can lose yourself in the reality of it all: the train is actually speaking. She is speaking to *you.* As her body slides naked through dark tunnels, she is seducing you with the only words she can say, the only words she is programmed to say. When she announces the name of the next station, really all she wants to do is tell you how much she wants you, how much she is enjoying the feel of you inside her, standing with your hands upon her straps and poles, your body snugly pressed against the upholstery of her seats. She tries desperately to inject sexual overtones into her voice when she invites you to stand clear of her doors, or mind the gap, wooing you with the names of stations in the hope that you will ride her all the way to the end of the line. Yes, that's exactly the sort of fantasy that would turn Rolf on.

As the train starts to slow in the tunnel, the girl with the stain on her shirt leans across me to say something to her friend. I can smell her perfume as she does so, the faintest residue of the scent she put on this morning while she was dressing for work, mixed with the more earthy smell of her own skin.

"Sorry, love," she says, once she realizes how close she is to me.

"Don't mind me," I say hurriedly. "I won't even notice you're there."

I shut my eyes and allow the girl to continue leaning across me. She is talking to her friend about one of their colleagues at work, a young trainee she is having problems with. Although I have my eyes closed, I can still sense her closeness. I know I shouldn't be enjoying it, not on the eve of my wedding, but I'm too tired to fight the feeling. Instead I sink deeper into my seat, bathed in the girl's presence, and allow my mind to wander towards her.

As the train gives a slight lurch, she falls sideways and knocks into me, the softness of her breast enfolding my cheek. I open my eyes briefly to glimpse the white curve of her blouse pulling away from me. "Sorry," she says again. I look up at her and smile briefly, so as not discourage her from standing so close, and then shut my eyes again. I can still feel the afterglow of her breast on my cheek, as if the touch receptors on my skin are reluctant to let go of the sensation. What would Rachel think of me now? How would she like it if she knew I was thinking of another woman's breasts? I get the impression she no longer cares what I think. She regards me as a twat—she said so this morning while I slept.

I fidget slightly in my seat and settle myself just a little further forward—enough to make contact with the office girl likely should the train lurch again. My face feels hot with her proximity, as though her body is radiating heat towards my cheeks and forehead, and I am beginning to feel intoxicated, drunk with her closeness. She is so sumptuous, so desirable. She is so *there.*

Surely this woman must know the effect she is having on me. Surely she can't be so unaware of her breasts that she will leave them hanging beside a stranger's face for several minutes at a time. Or perhaps she is not so innocent, after all—perhaps she knows exactly what she is doing. Maybe she enjoys the thrill of contact as much as I do, and is hiding behind a conversation with her friend in order to experience it again and again. I read a newspaper article once which claimed that in a questionnaire seventy percent of the women admitted they had become sexually excited by being pressed up against other people on the tube, compared to forty percent of the men. Is this what she's doing? Am I her plaything? Does she find me attractive—not a twat at all, but a *man?*

"This train is Latimer Road," croons the voice announcer as the girl's breasts brush across my cheek once more. "Stand clear of the gap. Mind the next station, please."

As the train comes to a stop at the station, in my mind I create the fantasy that the girl in front of me is one of Rolf's spies. She's here to entrap me. She thinks she's distracting me from taking my pictures of station signs, but what she doesn't know is that I have Brian with me, that he is taking the photos now. I smile to myself while she leans across me: she can try to seduce me with the softness of her body as much as she wants, because I am safe until we reach Bond Street. I can afford to call her bluff, sit back and enjoy her seduction, and feel the warmth of her body radiating across the inches which separate us. If I wanted to, I could lean forward at any time and bury my face in her softness, feel her flesh wrap itself around my nose and mouth, engulfing my face completely. Or I could reach out with my hand and touch her breasts, bulging there beneath her shirt, draw them close to me, flick open the buttons so that I can reach in and caress her nipples. She wouldn't protest, not if she were sent by Rolf to seduce me. She would utter some encouragement as I leaned forward to kiss her, something meaningless but seductive. "Stand-clear-of-the-doors-please, stand-clear-of-the-doors-please, stand-clear-of-the-doors-please. This is a Central Line train calling at all stations to Hainault via Newbury Park."

I snap my eyes open, suddenly aware that I have been falling asleep. The space in front of my face is empty. The seat beside me is empty too. For a moment I think I have been imagining the whole thing, the girls, the voice announcer, even the bet—but as I look about me, I see Brian standing by the doors with my camera in his hand. I am not so fortunate as to have been stuck in a dream for the past thirteen hours. I take another look up and down the carriage. The girl and her friend are nowhere to be seen, and I can only imagine that they must have got off at the last stop.

I shake myself and look over to the doors where Brian is standing. "Where are we?" I ask, unsurely.

"Next station is Bond Street."

The information throws me for a second. "Bond Street? Already?"

"Yes. We're changing here for the Jubilee Line, remember? We're going down to Green Park to the Piccadilly Line."

"Right," I say.

But I don't feel right. There is something wrong with doing it that way; I can feel it—it is the obvious thing for us to do, and for that reason alone it is dangerous. Perhaps Rolf has friends on the Jubilee Line too. Perhaps he is just waiting for us to go there so that he can finish us off for good. I take a few deep breaths and try to clear my head, and as I do so a plan starts to form . . .

I pull out my blowup of the tube map, to see if there is another route we can take to the Piccadilly Line. My eyes are greeted with a succession of neat red crosses, obliterating the names of all the stations throughout two thirds of the map, but I can still see where the lines go.

"Okay," I say decisively, "this is what we're going to do. We don't get off at Bond Street—we get off at Oxford Circus and take a train down to the Piccadilly Line from there."

"But that'll take longer . . ." starts Brian.

"Trust me. If the train we want left Cockfosters when Paul said it would, we'll have time. Just."

"Whatever you say," says Brian. He looks tired too now. I honestly believe that he would do anything I told him to at the moment. Which is good, because if he thought to question me, he'd probably realize that staying on this train until Oxford Circus is madness—we'd waste far too much time, and we'd seriously run the risk of missing our train.

But then again, if Rolf *is* following us, if we're going to shake him off our tail, perhaps a bit of madness is what we need.

Chapter 39

4:56 PM—Oxford Circus–Piccadilly Circus—Bakerloo Line

4:59 PM—Piccadilly Circus–Green Park—Piccadilly Line

At Oxford Circus we change lines. Everywhere we go now there are crowds, hordes of faces and bodies and backs of heads, blocking our way, clogging up the corridors which lead between platforms. On the trains they stare blankly at us, through us—in the stations they ignore us altogether, focusing only on the train and squeezing into the carriages amongst all the other blank, staring faces. I stumble along from one platform to the next, more on automatic pilot than with any sense of purpose. I have almost forgotten that I am in a race. It's all I can do to remember which train we're on, and where we're going.

At Piccadilly Circus we change again, barge through the crowds to the Piccadilly Line, where a train is just pulling into the station.

"Is this one ours?" calls Brian as we shuffle impatiently behind a mob of people trying to squeeze onto the platform.

"I don't know—check the numbers on the carriages."

We make our way towards the train, and I pull out Rolf's note once again to remind us of the carriage numbers we are looking for. The first two carriages we come to don't match, so we hurry down to the next carriage to check that number too—still no match. And now the doors are about to close, so Brian and I are obliged to leap on to the train and wait until the next stop before we can continue our search.

"Dear-oh-dear," says Brian as the tube takes off towards Green Park. "Are you sure this is the right train?"

"Not at all. I'm just hoping."

"What happens if it's not?"

"Then we wait for the next one, and then the one after that. That's all we *can* do."

We stand by the doors, gripping hold of the handrails as the train sweeps into the darkness of the tunnel. I have to say I'm not feeling too good. The presence of so many people has pushed the temperature in here right up, and I can feel my shirt beginning to stick to my skin underneath my jacket. I gaze blearily down the length of the carriage at everyone else, the office workers and schoolkids who sway and nod every time the train rounds another bend.

"Look at this train," I say after a while. "I don't see how we're ever going to find the envelope, even if we do locate the right carriage. How the hell are we going to search the place with all these people in the way?"

Brian follows my eyes and smiles grimly. I remember his claustrophobia this morning and immediately regret bringing the subject up.

"Even if the carriages were empty, there's no guaranteeing we'd find it, not without a toothcomb search. These are big carriages. Rolf should have been a bit more specific."

"Maybe there's another clue on the note," says Brian. "Have you looked on the back of it?"

I turn the note over in my hand and look at it, but it still says exactly the same as it has always said. I stare at it, and for the first time something about it grabs me—something obvious. "Two carriages," I murmur. "How can one envelope be on two carriages at the same time?"

I stare at the note for a moment, not really looking but thinking to myself. I'm trying to remember something. What was that thought I had when we first picked this note up: *Weird way of writing it.* Compared to the other notes Rolf has written, it *is* weird. No specific location. Two carriages instead of just one. And the time given not at the beginning or end of the note, but between the two numbers.

It's this last thought that does it. "Between the two numbers!" I say out loud. "*Between* them!"

Brian looks at me curiously, but I don't have time to explain my outburst, because our train is just pulling in at Green Park Station. When the train comes to a halt and the doors open, we leap straight out and sprint forwards to the next carriage. Brian is ahead of me, so he gets there first, to the number printed on the end of the car: 690.

"Got it!" he shrieks back at me when he sees it. "This is one of the right ones!"

I try to keep my head. "Okay," I say, "let's check out the next one."

The platform is swarming with passengers now, both people waiting to get on the train and those who are shuffling their way down the platform towards the exit. Worse still, the exit is behind us, so we are effectively fighting against the tide. Pushing our way forward, we ignore the fact that we are bumping people as we go, and make our way as fast as we can to the next carriage on, the second from the front of the train. We can see its number before we even get there: 891. Sure enough, it is our second car.

"Right," I gasp as we shunt ourselves forward, "when we get there, look on the outside of the train, between the two carriages.

He must have taped our next envelope to the coupling or something, somewhere round where the two carriages join. Quickly! We have to get it before the train leaves!"

At last we find ourselves at the junction of the two carriages. I look behind the plastic cover which shields the gap between the two carriages, and there it is at the bottom: taped to the front of car 690 is a green envelope, covered in thick black dust.

"Grab it!" I shout.

Brian reaches down and, with a bit of tugging against the thick tape Rolf has used to attach the envelope, he finally plucks it from the metal of the step. I want to open it here and now, but beside us the doors are beginning to slide shut. Taking Brian's arm I throw myself into the nearest car. As the doors close we tumble into the mass of bodies already occupying the carriage. Some of the people here look at us disapprovingly, because it was crowded enough in this carriage without two more people forcing their way in, but I have to say I really don't care. Because in Brian's hand, wedged between Brian and myself, is the thing we have been chasing all afternoon: the third of our envelopes.

"Well?" says Brian. "Are you going to open it or not?"

Nervously I take the envelope from his hand. Sliding my finger beneath the flap, I carefully tear the seal and take a look inside.

Chapter 40

5:02 PM—Green Park–South Kensington—Piccadilly Line

I'm an optimist at heart; you might have gathered that. I tend to think things will be easy, even when they blatantly won't be. I tend to think things will always end happily ever after. I am forever underestimating the length of time complicated tasks will take, and I always assume that everything in life, buses and trains included, will run according to its timetables. As you can imagine, I'm frequently disappointed.

It's the same with this envelope. After all the tearing around after this train, after all the delays and changed plans, I have subconsciously convinced myself that this newly found envelope will contain one of my more important items—my honeymoon reservations or my Eurostar tickets. But when I open it up, all I find inside is my London Underground Travelcard, and I can't help feeling let down. My Travelcard's of no use to me whatsoever. Apart from the fact that I won't be needing it once I'm on my honeymoon anyway, it won't even be valid once I'm back. It expires in a week.

"What does the note say?" asks Brian.

Placing the Travelcard in my jacket pocket, I reach back into the envelope and pull out a piece of lined paper. Unfolding it, I read out loud: "*Eight-thirty PM—Harrow & Wealdstone—Display board.*"

"Is that all it says?"

I turn it over and look at the back. "Yes, that's all." I smile wanly and slide the note into the same pocket as my Travelcard.

Brian and I stand in silence for a few moments, thinking about it and rocking gently from side to side with the motion of the train. Harrow & Wealdstone is a long way away, right out at the end of the Bakerloo Line. I can't help feeling a little angry—Rolf is certainly not making it easy for me, sending me right out to the far reaches of the system. Not only that, but I'm going to have to wait for another three and a half hours before I can collect my next item. The bastard is torturing me.

"Well," I say after a while, "at least the next envelope sounds relatively simple to find."

"Yeah," says Brian, "no problem at all."

"And once we've got that envelope and the next one, we'll be well on our way to finishing."

"Yeah," says Brian, "and everything will be all right."

It seems Brian is every bit as much an optimist as I am. I'm unused to hearing him say such overwhelmingly positive things, so I look up at him, and the sight that greets me gives me a shock. Brian is not looking too well at all: his fear of crowded spaces seems at last to be getting the better of him. His eyes have gone all starey, and his forehead has broken out with beads of sweat. His face looks sort of *taut.* It's like his claustrophobia is expanding beneath the surface of it, stretching his skin like the skin of an overblown balloon.

I look at the carriage around us. It must be hell for him in here—we are crammed in this train like we've been vacuum-packed, without enough room even to turn around. I try to make a little space for him, but really it's impossible. All I manage to do is back myself into the breasts of a twenty-something office girl—they mold themselves around my elbow like a pair of beanbags.

"Are you okay, Brian?" I ask. "You look a little . . . I don't know—pale."

"It's okay. I'll be fine when we get out of this tunnel."

"Is there anything I can do for you? I sort of owe you one for before . . . you know, when I had to sit down. I don't know what I would have done if you hadn't been there to take over for a bit."

"It's all right, mate. We've all been there—when we're tired, or sick. Or drunk."

He smiles, so I decide to keep talking, to try and take his mind off things.

"I don't know what came over me, really. Maybe it was the suicide announcement that did it—it's those words, 'a person under a train.' I don't suppose there's any other way of announcing it, really, but even so, it's pretty graphic. I've never seen it happen, but I can't help imagining it . . ."

I tail off, realizing suddenly that this might not be helping—talking about suicide probably isn't the best way to ease someone's claustrophobia. So I fall silent, but after a few moments Brian surprises me by saying, "I've seen it happen."

It is the last thing I expected him to say. "You *have?"*

"Yes. To a friend of mine. A girl called Janey."

"Jesus, that's terrible."

"Yeah, well, it happens a lot. Being homeless can get pretty depressing sometimes. For some people it must seem like the easy thing to do."

He starts reeling off a list of the friends he's had over the years who have taken pills, fallen off bridges, slit their wrists. He goes into detail, probably a little more detail than I feel comfortable with—but it seems to make him feel better. It's as though talking about something like this eclipses his claustrophobia—a minor unpleasantness drowned out by the image of something far worse, and far more gruesome.

The other people in the carriage pretend not to listen to him, but they do. You can tell by their faces—they lose that blank inward stare for a moment and focus on the pair of us, just for a split second, before switching their eyes away again. They don't want us to notice them listening, because they don't want Brian to stop talking: a few tales about people topping themselves is entertainment for the journey, something to think about on the way home from work. It breaks the daily commuting routine. But personally, I'd rather not listen. In fact, I try *not* to listen—I've had enough of Brian's gruesome stories for one day.

"I've got a friend who dosses down in Charing Cross called Suicide Sam," Brian says, "because every now and then he throws himself under a train. He's been knocked out a couple of times, and last time he lost two of his fingers under the wheels, but he hasn't succeeded yet. I suppose someday he'll get it right—that's if he doesn't end up permanently hospitalizing himself first."

Beside me the office girl moves slightly, and her breasts wrap themselves a little more completely round my elbow. I am trying not to be distracted by them, but they're difficult not to notice. Even some of the other people in the carriage notice. A schoolboy next to me seems unable to avert his embarrassed gaze from them—large, soft bosoms, enfolding my arm. And a woman in her thirties is watching both the bosoms and the boy, a faint smile on her face, as if she enjoys the schoolboy's uncontrollable interest. But somehow it doesn't seem right, not while Brian is talking. It makes me feel uncomfortable to have sexuality and death squeezed so close together in the same small space.

"Then there was Mick the flower seller. We should have seen it coming with him, after he lost his stall. He did it with paracetamol and half a bottle of gin—went to sleep and never woke up again. . . ."

What was I saying before about Brian being an optimist?

"Then there was Kate Brady . . ."

It's more like he's reciting some sort of inventory or timetable than telling me the names of former friends of his, and it leaves me feeling distinctly uncomfortable. It's a relief when we finally pull up at Knightsbridge Station. When the doors open, Brian is forced to one side as a variety of people push their way past him and out of the carriage. They are replaced with several more people from the platform, making the area by the doors even more crowded than it was before. I manage to extricate my elbow from the office girl's bosoms and take a photo of the station sign: it's only by sheer determination that I manage to do it—I have to reach into my bag for the camera and then rise above the crush to take the picture before the doors close. It is far from easy.

"What's next?" asks Brian tensely, once the doors have shut and the train is moving off again. He seems to have forgotten his gruesome list.

"We go to Hammersmith," I say. "Then we take the Hammersmith & City Line up to Baker Street. From there we can begin to make our way up to our next envelope."

Brian looks briefly about the carriage, as if braving the sight of all the squashed bodies. But he seems slightly better than he was a few minutes ago—his gaze even lingers on the breasts of the office girl for a few moments, before returning to me. "How much time have we lost?" he says.

"I'm not sure. It must be at least half an hour by now."

"Do you think we're going to make it?"

"I don't know," I say. "I just don't know."

Even as I say this, I am still assuming somewhere inside me that we *can* make it. In fact, not only that we *can,* but that we *will.* Like I said, I'm an optimist—and as long as nothing more goes wrong, I'm still within the time limit of forty-five minutes over schedule. To tell you the truth, right now it's difficult to see what else *could* go wrong—I mean, if one of Brian's friends can repeatedly throw himself under trains and come out with only a couple of fingers missing, then making it round the tube system by half past midnight can't be that difficult. Of course, it's just when this last thought pops into my head—this last, poisonous, jinxing thought—that it all goes wrong.

You see, that's the problem with being optimistic: it doesn't prepare you for failure. When things go wrong, you have absolutely nothing to fall back on, because things going wrong is not an option you ever thought about before. I have foolishly thought that since we have been delayed so much today, by the law of averages things will now go smoothly. But just because I've encountered one signal failure today, it doesn't mean for a moment that it won't happen again. Just because we've seen trains delayed by suicide, points failures, passengers pulling the emergency handle, that doesn't mean there aren't an infinite variety of other delays the tube can throw at us.

But even a pessimist wouldn't have foreseen this one. It sends a jolt through the car, and there is a violent screeching noise as all of the wheel brakes the length of the train are applied. In an instant our whole carriage is thrown into disarray as over a hundred passengers lurch forward and collapse on top of one another, and the noise all around me is deafening—the screaming of people, the squeal of brakes, the grinding noise as the side of the carriage scrapes its way along the wall of the tunnel—and while I'm falling to the floor, I swear I see sparks flashing across the windows. It's all over in a moment. In the space of only a few seconds our train has ground itself to a sudden and violent halt.

Chapter 41

5:07 PM—Car 891—Piccadilly Line

The inside of our carriage is chaos. Brian falls on an old Indian gentleman, the office girl falls on Brian, I fall on the office girl, the schoolboy falls on me, the thirty-something woman falls on the schoolboy, and so on down the carriage. We are like dominoes toppling, human dominoes that scream and kick and panic as they fall. All of a sudden the world has become a tangle of limbs and hair, squashed faces, trapped fingers—one of the people on the floor beside me seems to have broken his nose in the pileup and is holding it, desperately trying to stem the flow of blood.

My own face has found a soft landing in the cleavage of the office girl. I lie there for a few moments, relieved to have found safety in the mayhem, but then I realize that the office girl is struggling to get out from underneath me, kicking at the floor with her legs. With difficulty I pull myself upright and help her to her feet. Next to me the thirty-something woman is doing the same for the schoolboy.

The natural reserve of rush-hour commuters is lost in the chaos.

All around me people are talking. "What the hell is happening?" one passenger is asking another, and someone else says, "Have we crashed?" An old man causes ripples of laughter by claiming loudly that this is the only bang he's had in years. On a more serious note another man is claiming to be a doctor and asking if anyone is hurt.

I look up and down the carriage. As far as train crashes go, this must be a pretty minor one. The carriage doesn't seem to be damaged in any way. No one seems to be hurt badly. There are just a few people shocked—the schoolboy, for example, who looks as if he wants to burst into tears. The thirty-something woman is holding his head tightly to her chest, and whispering soothing words to him.

"Are you all right, mate?" I ask Brian, as I help him up from the floor.

"Yes, yes," he says, impatiently, dusting himself off. "Just a few bruises. What do you suppose has happened?"

"Well, we can't have crashed, not going at the speed we were going—otherwise there'd be a lot more damage than there is. We must have just stopped suddenly for some reason."

"What do we do now?"

"Just wait, I suppose. Maybe the train will start up again."

Even as I say this I know it's just wishful thinking. Tube trains don't stop so suddenly for no reason. Something's very wrong—if I had to take a guess, I'd say that this train has been derailed. And as far as our journey goes, that means it's pretty much the end of the line.

I watch Brian's face for a moment, see the disappointment on it, and I know exactly what he's thinking. He's thinking how utterly unlucky we have been today. He's inwardly cursing the inefficiency of London Underground, the selfishness of the suicide, the bad design of the train or the tunnel or whatever it was that can have caused a derailment at such an inopportune moment. He's thinking that if only we'd been traveling yesterday, or tomorrow—then we would have avoided all these disasters and been well on our way to winning our bet.

But *I'm* not disappointed like he is. *I'm* angry. You see, I know something that Brian doesn't. I can't curse our luck, or the driver, or the train. I can't pray that we might be delivered somehow, that by some miracle our luck might change. Because it's obvious to me that this derailment has got nothing to do with luck at all. As far as I'm concerned, it's quite clear that all of this is a setup.

I think back to the last disastrous couple of hours traveling, and it is evident that we have been led into this situation. First there was the signal failure, then the train at Bayswater being damaged, Circle Line services being canceled—the suicide. And now this, the final coup de grâce in a nightmarish handful of delays. It's just too much to be a coincidence.

I have thought all afternoon that Rolf was having me followed—he must have been watching, waiting for the right time to strike. And before you start thinking I've gone mad, let me tell you that it would be quite simple. I mean, I haven't actually seen the suicide, have I? How do I know it actually happened? He doesn't have to arrange the *accidents* to send me off course, just the announcements—and Rolf has friends throughout London Transport. It is just conceivable that he has played me like a pro.

No one else in the carriage suspects that this could be a setup. To them it's all just blind chance—I think they're grateful it hasn't been more serious. The old Indian gentleman has found himself a seat to sit on and is mumbling to himself—prayers of thanks, perhaps. The office girl is straightening her skirt and pulling her top straight where the lace of her bra has become visible. There are three or four men, Brian amongst them, hovering round her and asking her if she's all right—she smiles innocently, like she thinks their concern for her is quite touching. All around me there is chattering and joking and even laughter—it seems totally alien, especially on the tube, especially given the situation: strangers are communicating with one another. Right in front of me the thirty-something woman is kissing the forehead of the schoolboy tenderly—has she *no* shame? And although there is nobody seriously hurt in the whole carriage, the man who said he was a doctor is squeezing his way down the length of it making sure there are no injuries, and making sure everyone knows that he's now in charge. I have a sudden and quite irrational urge to punch him.

When the loudspeaker finally crackles into life, there is a general shushing, and at last the noise of all the chattering dies down. The silence is uncanny—it's like we're all standing round the wireless, waiting for some modern-day Neville Chamberlain to tell us we've declared war.

The voice that speaks to us is clear, and slow:

"This is your driver speaking. I'm sorry for the emergency stop. The situation is that the front two cars of the train have been derailed. There's no need to panic—everything is perfectly safe—but this train is not going to move anywhere now until the engineers arrive to put the train back on the rails. As a consequence, you're all going to have to walk down the tunnel to the next station, which is South Kensington. It's only a few hundred yards. I've radioed the station, and they're sending a help party down the tunnel to lead you all. In the meantime, can I ask you please to make your way slowly towards the front of the train. I repeat, there's no need to panic. So can you make your way slowly to the front of the train, and there'll be someone to guide you down the tunnel to South Kensington Station."

"Great," I say to Brian. "Fucking great."

"Well, at least we're both okay."

I glare at him, because it's probably the most annoying thing he could've said.

"Okay? You call *this* okay?"

"Yes, I *do* call this okay." He is angry with me, impatient. "We're both in one piece, aren't we? Not only that, but we're near the front end of the train. So stop your whining. We should be out of here in no time."

But as we begin to shuffle our way like sheep towards the front end of the carriage I can tell we are *not* going to be out of here in no time. Our carriage was packed when we derailed, and so, doubtless, were the carriages in front—it'll take forever for all these people to make their way through the connecting doors and out through the driver's cab into the tunnel. I decide that it's best not to say anything, but I know we're finished. This is the last catastrophe in a disastrous journey.

I look at my watch. The time is 5:36. I shuffle along after Brian as fast as the crowd will let me, but no faster. All the urgency has left my pace. When a gap opens up before me, I don't dart forward to fill it, and I don't press close on the backs of the people in front in an effort to hurry them on. And why should I? I'm not going to spend the rest of the day making myself a target for Rolf's sabotage. As far as I'm concerned I'm finished. The bet is off.

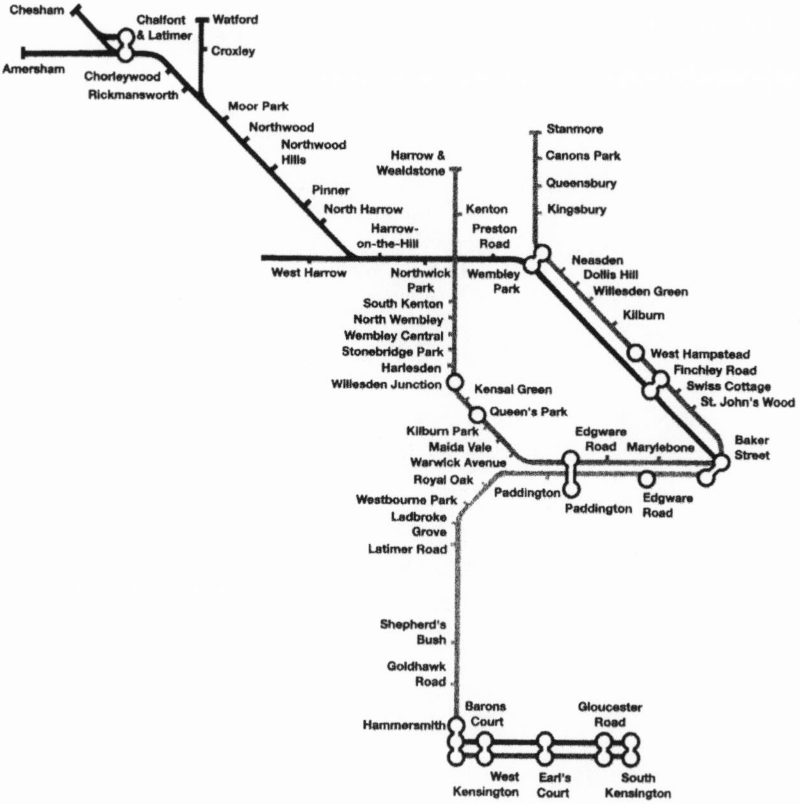

part 4

northwest london

Chapter 42

5:21 PM—*Tunnel between Knightsbridge and South Kensington—Piccadilly Line*

"What's the point?" I ask Brian as we trudge down the tunnel.

It took a good ten minutes to get to the front of the train, and now we and all the other passengers are making our way down the tracks towards South Kensington Station. Our way is lit by London Underground staff with flashlights, who manage to illuminate the darkness just enough for us to be able to see where we are putting our feet. It looks strange down here like this. Somehow it doesn't seem like I'm in the tube—it could be any train tunnel, anywhere.

"What's the bloody point?" I repeat. "We must have lost so much time by now there's no *way* we're going to make it to Monument by half past midnight."

"Well, if that's your attitude," says Brian, irritated, "you're probably right."

We tramp on in silence. Behind us I can hear a man and a woman laughing excitedly—this is an adventure for them: they have never walked down a tube tunnel before. I wish I could share their enthusiasm, but this is not a novelty for me. Perhaps another day I would have waited for them to catch up, joined in with their laughter, perhaps even told them one or two tube tales—but today I just don't seem to be in the mood.

After a few more yards I begin to slow down. "We may as well forget it, Brian. We were running late as it was. It's hopeless to carry on."

"Don't be ridiculous," says Brian curtly. "Things are never hopeless."

"But there's no way I'm going to make it to the wedding now. We may as well just face it." I stop in the tunnel. "Christ, what am I going to tell Rachel?"

In the darkness I can make out Brian's figure looming towards me, and I feel a sudden yank around my throat causing me to lurch forward. Brian has grabbed hold of my shirt. "I'm going to get you round all your damn tube stations if it's the last thing I do," he says, as he starts to drag me physically down the tunnel. "You and all your whinging! You thought we were finished in Upminster, but we weren't, and we're not finished now. Not unless you give up before you've even tried."

"But it's impossible," I complain as I stumble after him, trying to free my shirt front from his grip. "Everything would have to go like clockwork from now on if I'm to get the rest of my stuff. There isn't room for even a single further delay."

"And how do you know there are going to be any more delays?"

"There are always delays."

"Of course there are, for God's sake! But how do you know they're going to happen this evening?"

"I . . . well . . . I don't."

"Exactly," he sighs, exasperated. He stops and turns to me. "Just suppose a miracle happens and every train from now on runs on time. What would happen then? Eh?"

"Well, I suppose, conceivably we could make it . . ."

"So when we get to this station up ahead, where would we have to go?"

I think for a second. "We'd have to get the District Line to Hammersmith. We could change there and make our way up to northwest London . . ."

"So if we were going to have a chance of making it, we couldn't afford to miss a single train, right? Say, for example, if it's too overcrowded?"

"That's right."

He grabs me again by my shirt and gestures wildly at the tunnel full of people. "Well, where the bloody hell do you think all this lot are going? There's a whole trainload of passengers here who are going to need to find alternative transport. At least half of them are going to want to use the District Line. If we don't get a move on, we're going to be at the back of the queue!"

At last what he is saying sinks in. I suppose I have to hand it to the bloke—Brian is doing his best to win this bet, even though it's not strictly speaking any of his bloody business.

As he storms off down the tunnel overtaking all the other passengers in the darkness, reluctantly I start to follow him. It's not easy going. I have to watch where I'm putting my feet because the gravel on the tunnel floor has holes and divots in it, and Brian has this habit of breaking into a run every time there's a space between passengers. But before long we can see the station platforms shining ahead of us, and despite the fact that I can't really see why we're bothering, I have to admit that the sight is heartening.

"Light at the end of the tunnel!" Brian calls out.

"Right," I say, and hobble on unenthusiastically in his wake.

Soon we are clambering out onto the platform at South Kensington. Now that we're in the light of the station, we can see all the other passengers, daubed with dust from the tunnel, making their way to the exit in groups of two or three. None of them seem to be in a hurry—perhaps the accident has knocked all the rush out of them—one or two have even stopped to admire the paintings of animals on the platform walls. Brian and I run past them all. We sprint through the narrow exit and charge up the steps that lead to the District Line.

It's only once we get to the top of the stairs that we see what we're up against. I have to say that no matter how negative I was while we were in the tunnel, there was always a spark of hope alive in me. It's hard to despair when you've got someone like Brian virtually dragging you onwards, and somewhere deep inside me I still believed that it was possible to beat Rolf, beat the system, and win this bet. But once we reach the top of the stairs, we are confronted with a sight that knocks the last bit of hope out of me. It literally stops me in my tracks. I feel like saying to Brian, "See?—I told you there was no point." But I don't. I just stand there, deflated. In front of us is a solid mass, an impenetrable human wall hundreds of people thick.

Chapter 43

5:25 PM—South Kensington—Piccadilly Line

I don't know what to do. I just don't know what to do. It has been one disaster after another today, and I'm too tired to think anymore. I've run out of ideas.

The situation is hopeless. The way forward is a crush of bodies too dense to pass through. Even the way back is becoming impossible now as all the people behind us begin to arrive, and the stairway is becoming as crowded as the platform. I have only been in a station this crowded a few times in my life: the last time was at Fulham, and I had to wait for nine trains before one had enough room in it for me to get on. *Nine.* We are already so far behind schedule I can only realistically look at this as the final straw.

There is a train entering the station now. A voice announcement comes over the loudspeakers: it instructs people not to move forward, because the platform is so full the people at the front are in danger of being pushed onto the tracks.

While I'm dithering by the edge of the stairs feeling sorry for myself, I can see Brian steeling himself and remember once again that I'm traveling with a claustrophobic. The crush is obviously becoming too much for him. I look up at him and wonder if I should try and muster the energy to comfort him, but before I have time to think about it properly, he grabs hold of my hand. "Come on," he says, and starts pulling me forward.

I want to reach out to him and calm him down, tell him that the crowd will abate soon if he can just relax with it for a while, but I don't—partly because I'm too tired, and partly because of the throng around us, staring at us while we blatantly flout the request of the announcer. And besides, Brian's actions don't appear to be done in panic. There is something methodical in the way he is pushing his way through the crowd. He shoves people out of the way one at a time—a schoolkid here, an old woman there. He shoulder-barges each of them, without discrimination, without any regard for the dirty looks the crowd is giving him.

I suppose he can get away with it because he's a tramp covered in tattoos—but unfortunately I'm not, so as I follow in his wake I have to apologize to absolutely everyone. Nobody says anything back, but it's quite plain by the way they look at me that they're not impressed. By the time we're nearing the front, one or two people are beginning to shove me back, but still nobody says anything. I know that they are only really jealous of Brian's audacity and mine: I can even feel one of them slide in behind us, taking advantage of the space we are making to advance himself a few extra feet.

As we reach the front of the platform, the train comes to a stop, with a pair of doors just a few steps away. I half expect Brian to thrust his way past the last set of people in front of us, but he doesn't. We have to wait until a small mob has got onto the train before it's our turn. And of course, when it *is* our turn, there isn't any room left. The train is absolutely jam-packed.

I want to give up now—I'm *aching* to give up—but Brian is determined to push forward. With one foot still on the platform, he leans into the open doorway as if he's at the back of a rugby scrum and starts shoving violently against all the bodies packed into the carriage.

"Hey!" complains one of the passengers, a young Scotswoman, "watch what you're doing!" But Brian ignores her and just carries on pushing until he has cleared a space for himself, about eighteen inches square, to stand in.

"Come on!" he says to me once he is on the train.

"You must be joking!" I mutter. "There's no way I'm going to fit in there!"

"Don't be silly—of course you will." He turns his head to shout at the other people in the car. "Come on everyone! Move up a bit—there's room for one more!"

There is a general mumbling throughout the carriage as everyone shuffles along a token inch, but combined, miraculously, they make just about enough space free.

Suddenly a signal goes up further along the platform from one of the station attendants—the doors are going to close. Brian reaches out his hand to me and hauls me into the car. At the same time I am shoved violently from behind by someone else who is trying to squeeze himself on. The newcomer jams himself behind my right shoulder to ensure himself a space on the train, twisting me round in the process, so that as the doors shut they catch my other shoulder and the back of my head. For a moment I am scared that my bag will become trapped between them, and I have to bend forward and drag my bag between my legs to prevent this from happening. But eventually I am safe. The doors do shut. And, with a shudder, the train begins to move.

"See?" says Brian. "I told you there was room."

I only manage to grunt in agreement because I am so twisted and my chest is so crushed I can't get the wind up to utter any actual words. I'm still not sure it wouldn't have been better to stay on the platform—I can barely breathe in here. I am crushed right up against the glaring face of the Scottish girl Brian had been pushing. And somewhere behind my right shoulder, out of sight, is a stranger who has followed me onto this car. But at least we're here. Somehow, we have made it onto the train.

Chapter 44

5:38 PM—South Kensington–Hammersmith—Piccadilly Line

ThistrainissocrowdedIcanbarelybreathe.Youcan'ttellwhereonebody endsandthenextbegins,andtheheatisunbearable.Everyoneispushing everyoneelse—notbecausetheywanttobutbecausetheyMUST.They pushwhentheymustinhale,theyarepushedwhentheybreatheout.The wholecarriageswellslikeabellows,expandingandcontractingwiththe collectivebreathingofthecrush.

Myrightarmhasgonenumb:IthinkI'mmeltingintotheScottishgirl.I'm exhausted.I'msodrainedIcanbarelystandup—infact,theonlyreason I*am*stillstandingisthatthejaminhereiskeepingmeupright.Thereisno swayingbackwardsandforwardswhenthetrainturnsacorner.Weare packedsolid,notasingleairspacebetweenourbodies.Perhapsthat's whyIcan'tbreathe.There'snoairinhere,onlytherumblingofthetrain. There'snowheretoESCAPEto,nowheretofindanyspaceexceptthe insideofmyownhead.

Fromthisangle,allIcanseeisbodies—acrushofarmsanbreastsand torsosfillingmyfieldofvision.Igetasuddenimageinmyheadofbeingina pit,amassgravefilledwiththecadaversofmyfellowpassengers.They hadtodigthroughsuchplaceswhentheywerebuildingthetube—plague pitswherehundreds,eventhousandswereburied,squashedintogether andburiedundertonsofearth.I'veseenpicturesofthemachinerychurning uponehumanskullafteranother.SomeofthemenworkingontheVictoria Linehadtotaketimeoutbecauseitwassoharrowing,diggingthroughthe dirtthathadoncebeenhumanflesh.

Thethoughtismakingmequeasy,soIturnmyheadupwardstolook awayfromeveryone'sbodies,lookuptowardstheceiling,quellmyNEED toscream,run,escape.AllIcanseenowisfaces.Hundredsofthem.Irealize withashockthatthefacesofallthepeopleinthecarriagewithmelookeven morelifelessthanthebodiesthatsupportthem—hundredsofslackmouths, hundredsofsaggingcheeks,acresofpaleskin,madeyellowbythestriplights thatilluminateit.Nobodylooksatanyoneelse.Nobodylooksatanything— theireyesaredead,turnedinuponthemselvestoavoidtherealityofthe horrendouscrush.Itwistmyheadtoscanthecrowdedcarriage,tryandfind afacethatlookssomehownormal,buteverywhereIlookitisthesame.

ItisthenthatIrealizethattheonlyfaceIcan'tseeistheonebehindme. Themanwhopushedhiswayontothecarriagebehindme,themanwho ensuredthathefollowedmeonhere*he*isinvisible.Icanfeelhisbodyjammed upagainstmine,andIamamazedbyhisboldness.Justthethoughtofhim behindme,so*close,*ismakingmyheartrace.Isthisthemanwhohasbeen followingmeallday?IsthisRolf'sspy?Istruggletoturnroundandlookat himintheeye,butnomatterhowItrythereisnotenoughSPACE.Forthreelong minutesIamforcedtostandwithmybacktohim,mystalker,unabletosee hisface.WheneventuallyourtrainpullsintoEarl'sCourtStation,thereissuch acrushofpeopletryingtogetbothonandoffthetrainthatinthemeleeIlose trackofhim,andbythetimeIgettoturnround,therearesometwentynew facesinthecar.Hecouldbeanyoneofthem.

Asthetrainstartsupagain,Istudythefacesofthenewcomers,butthey areasblankasthepeoplewhowerealreadyinourcarriage—oneortwoof themlookbackatme,reenteringtheworldforafewmomentstowonderwhy itisthatI'mstaringatthem,butit'sonlyforafewmoments,andthenthey turnbackinsidethemselves,behindtheirmasks,manikinswithNO soul.WhoeverRolf'sspyis,he'sgood.Noneofmyfellowpassengersstands outfromtheothers.Noneismorenervous,ormoreanimated,ormore attentive,orsuspicious-looking.Theyareallthesame.I'minacarriage fullofwaxworks.

Asthetrainrattlesthroughtheground,Idomybesttomakeroomfor myself,strainingmyneckabovethesweatingbodies,intheHOPEthatI mightsqueezemywayoutofthiscrowdandintotheshallowairspace atthetopofthecar.Butthecrushistoostrong,andallIcandotopreventthem forcingtheverylifeoutofmeiscurlmyshouldersandputmyarmsbefore mychest,fetuslike,toprotectmybreathing.Idon'tknowhowmuchlonger Icanstaylikethis.IfeelasthoughI'mslowlybeingsqueezedintoapaste. But then at WestKensington afewpeoplegetout, andthecrush eases slightly,and atBaronsCourt afewmore, until at last I am free to breathe once again. Gradually the carriage returns to normal—busy, but bearable—and all those people who remain here gratefully begin to take in deep breaths, as if to do so were some kind of wonderful luxury. I myself don't bother, because I'm about to get off, anyway. As soon as we hit Hammersmith, Brian and I must change trains and start all over again—a new line, a new station, a new crowd. And I know that I cannot truly breathe until this journey is over. Until then there can be no rest for me. No escape, no space, no . . .

No nothing. The bet is all.

Chapter 45

5:44 PM—Belsize Park

Rachel was watching a couple of pigeons fight over a crust of bread on the flat roof of the extension downstairs. She didn't really have time to be watching pigeons—she had just finished packing the thank-you cards and was on her way to call her father when they'd caught her eye. There was something mesmerizing about them. Somehow, given the alternative of wedding-induced anxiety, the idea of watching a couple of birds fight it out over a lump of bread seemed relatively attractive.

The pigeons were always on the bloody roof. She and Andy had once spent an entire summer trying to shoo them away, but in the end they had given up—the birds were far more persistent than either of them could handle. Ever since then Rachel had developed a grudging sort of admiration for them. Often, when she was upset or angry or confused, she soothed herself by sitting and watching them as they pecked and squabbled and strutted around the roof, and she had come to realize that she and Andy had never had a chance against them. The persistence they had shown against her feeble shooings was there in everything they did: feeding, fighting—even mating. They were quite easily the most stubborn creatures she'd ever come across.

Today, as she watched these two birds snatch the bread back and forth repeatedly, she had an irrational urge to exterminate the lot of them. The whole point of staring at the pigeons like this was to calm herself down—she wanted to be soothed by visions of some pigeon paradise, where everything was simple and all you had to worry about was eating, sleeping, and fucking. But the more she watched, the more they seemed like human beings—endlessly tussling over some manky old crust that was barely worth having, apparently just for the sake of it. Actually, the comparison with human beings didn't seem so far-fetched. They certainly never seemed to run out of things to fight about. And was she imagining things, or didn't they mate for life? In which case it must be just as tricky for a pigeon trying to select a partner as it was for a human being. The idea made her shudder, and she thought of Rolf. She could just imagine him as one of those grotty pigeons—the creepy ones with bedraggled oil-black feathers and clubfeet—pursuing her tirelessly round and round and round the roof downstairs in an effort to mate with her.

She began to feel anxious again and unconsciously shook her head slightly. She had enough to do this evening as it was, and now she had yet another thing to worry about. If Rolf *had* been a pigeon, she would quite happily have blasted him out of the sky. She had spoken to him three times today already, and he still hadn't got the bloody message—something had to be done about him before he turned into some sort of stalker.

She turned away from the window with a sigh and carried on through to the sitting room. Picking up the phone, she dialed her father's number in Paris, but after a few rings his machine answered. She thought of leaving a message, something about

Rolf, but then put the phone down again without doing so. She didn't want to worry him. And besides, he was probably out for the evening now—she seemed to remember him saying something about going to play canasta tonight with his friend Jean-Luc.

She loitered halfheartedly beside the phone—who else could she ring? If she told her mother about Rolf, it would only make her hysterical. Patrice worked late, and she didn't have his work number—and as for Sophie, she was probably halfway to Paris right now, along with Rachel's wedding dress and a car full of presents. Rachel didn't feel like talking to anyone else. The last thing she wanted on her wedding day was for the church to be humming with rumors and gossip.

Eventually, reluctantly, she came to the conclusion that there was only one thing she could do. Since there was nobody else to advise her, she would have to call Rolf herself—tell him where to get off. And she'd have to be blunt about it. It was plain he had some bee in his bonnet about her—a bee which needed swatting rather than the feeble shooing she'd directed at her pigeons. If she wasn't firm to the point of harshness, he'd only reinterpret her call as some sort of pathetic come-on. The man wasn't just thick-skinned, he was armor-plated.

She looked at the phone, and hesitated. She wasn't sure if she could face talking to Rolf a fourth time today—especially since the previous three times had been so unsuccessful: the man didn't seem to be able to take fuck off for an answer. For a few minutes she entertained various other options—writing him a threatening note, sending a bunch of thugs round to break his kneecaps—but nothing feasible came to mind. She felt at once powerless and quite angry: where the hell was Andy when you needed him?

She was still gathering the courage to pick up the phone, when she noticed the light on her answering machine flashing at her. Quite unexpectedly, it gave her an idea. She remembered accidentally recording her conversation with Rolf earlier—perhaps she could use it against him somehow. Surely there was more she could do with the recording than merely playing it to Andy to prove to him what his friend was up to. Perhaps she could threaten Rolf with it—blackmail him somehow. It seemed too good an opportunity to waste. All she had to do was work out some way to use it.

Slowly, a plan started to form in her head. Of course, in order for it to work it had to be obvious that Rolf was in the wrong. For a moment it crossed her mind that she might not have remembered their conversation rightly, that there wouldn't be anything overtly incriminating in what Rolf had said to her. There would be no point in threatening him unless she had recorded him saying something that was obviously wrong. Tentatively, she leaned over to the answering machine and pressed *play.*

She listened, as the tape played back their earlier conversation.

"Why are you marrying someone so obviously beneath you?" Rolf's voice was saying.

And then came her own voice: "I'm marrying him because I love him."

It was strange hearing her voice being played back over a tape recorder like this. At the time she'd said those words she'd been half-asleep, and the whole episode had seemed surreal, like a part of one of her dreams. But now, on hearing it again, her voice sounded solid, wide awake, certain of what she was saying.

She hit the forward button and then listened to some more: "Let me get this straight," her voice was saying, "you want to stop me getting married?" And then there was Rolf's voice replying, "Well . . . yes."

Perfect! she thought. She stopped the tape and rewound it to the beginning. Then she played it again and paused the tape just before the part where Rolf asked his first incriminating question.

Now all she had to do was call Rolf. Picking up Andy's address book, she leafed through it until she came to the right page—then, with a deep breath, she dialed Rolf's number.

The phone rang several times. When at last she got an answer, her heart leapt into her mouth—but it was only Rolf's own answering machine kicking in. Or rather, one of those British Telecom answering services—the ones where you can stop the message and rerecord it if you want to.

Gathering her wits about her, she waited for the voice on the other end to finish, so that she could leave her message. She just wanted to get it over and done with.

"Rolf," she said at last, steeling herself. "It's Rachel. This is not a social call—I just thought I'd return the harassment. I also thought you ought to know that I recorded our conversation earlier today. If you don't believe me, listen to this . . ."

She held the receiver over the tape machine and played back the incriminating part of the conversation. She felt a little evil, doing what she was doing, like some blackmailing *femme fatale* from an old black-and-white movie. But then, maybe a bit of nastiness was what was required here. Rolf had obviously put her on some sort of pedestal—perhaps this would snap him out of his little fantasy world, show him that she was just as capable of unpleasantness as the next person. And she *was* capable of unpleasantness. Sometimes she could be so malicious she surprised even herself—not at all the fluffy princess Rolf obviously thought she was. Perhaps this would teach him a lesson.

"Now," she continued, the receiver back at her mouth again, "if you ever ring me again, or follow me, or hassle me in any way, I will play this tape not only to Andy, but to all your friends in the London Transport Museum, the Underground Railway Society, and all the other geeky institutions you belong to. I will make sure you'll never be able to show your face in any of these places again."

She paused for a second, before adding, "I am not interested in you, and I never will be—got that? The only person I've ever been truly interested in is Andy, which is why I'm marrying him. I don't care if you have some stupid bet together, and I don't care who wins—it's Andy I'm in love with."

She paused for a second more, but as she couldn't think of anything else to say, she put the phone down.

For the next few minutes she sat, wondering if she had said all the right things. She was sure she should have tried to sound more threatening. She should have said something about playing the tape to the police perhaps—or even to her lawyer. But instead she'd gone on at the end about being in love with Andy, about him being the only person she'd ever been serious about. She supposed it didn't hurt to ram home the message that she was in love with someone else, but surely there was something else she could have said?

But then, it was true—she'd never really been in love until she'd met Andy. Not properly, in a grown-up way. Even when he was being a twat, Andy was far more right for her than any other man she'd met, and she couldn't imagine anyone being able to take his place—least of all Rolf. That *was* why she was marrying him.

Irritated, she hauled herself off the sofa and went back to the bedroom to finish her chores. She didn't feel quite ready to have nice thoughts about Andy. The bastard still hadn't called her. And by the sound of things, he'd got himself into more trouble with Rolf than he'd let on. Besides, if it hadn't been for Andy, she wouldn't have been in this mess in the first place—after all, Rolf was Andy's friend. By all rights it should be Andy who was sorting this out, not her.

Still, she was glad she'd made that phone call. It might not do what she hoped—Rolf would probably find some way to convince himself that she hadn't really meant what she'd said—but at least it was a start. At least she felt like she was *doing* something.

Feeling happier, she decided it was time to try to forget about it. She could spend the rest of her life worrying about Rolf, or she could get on and do something constructive—like looking for her address book, for example. There were going to be a million postcards and thank-you notes to be sent while she was on her honeymoon, and since it was beginning to look like she would be sitting in Antigua by herself, she might as well make sure she was able at least to write to her friends.

She went back to the bedroom to search through the pile of things she'd left on the bed. On her way there she automatically glanced out of the hall window—absentmindedly, she noticed that the pigeons had stopped their endless to-ing and fro-ing with their piece of crust. Somehow the birds seemed to have resolved the issue: now there was only one pigeon on the roof, enjoying the bread all on its own.

Chapter 46

5:49 PM—Hammersmith–Baker Street—Hammersmith & City Line

At Hammersmith Station we have to leave the Underground to change lines. We have to go up the stairs, through the arcade of shops, out into the street, across the road, and then into another station which is also called Hammersmith. It's bloody disorienting having two separate stations called Hammersmith, but that's the tube for you. There are two stations called Edgware Road, as well. Why make things simple when you can confuse the hell out of everyone?

Brian and I keep pace with the crowd as it surges towards the exit stairs. I have to suppress the urge to turn round and look to see if there is anyone following us. It would be impossible to tell with all these people here—they could all be following us. And at the same time I can't help feeling that somewhere in this throng he is there, keeping track of us with his dark beady eyes. Or if not him in person, at least one of his stooges, carrying out his instructions so that they can report our every action back to him. I desperately want to confront the crowd behind us, see if I can spot the one face in all that mass that has his eyes trained on me, but I know that it would be useless. Even if I found our stalker, it wouldn't avert what lies in store for us. And I know that there *is* something in store for us. Rolf hasn't finished with us yet. I can feel it—he is planning something.

It is 5:58 when we cross the road into the other station at Hammersmith. Fortunately there is a train waiting for us at the platform, and we only have to wait a minute or two before it departs. Brian and I get the last couple of seats available in our carriage, which is a relief, because waves of tiredness are beginning to hit me again.

In my exhausted, half-paranoid state I'm feeling more worried now than ever. While my body is slumped in a seat by the doors, my mind is working overtime: Does Rolf know where we are? Has he worked out what our next move will be? If he *is* watching, he'll soon be getting desperate—after all, we're still going, despite everything—so who's to say what he might resort to next? The Hammersmith & City Line is far too crowded at this time of night for anyone to consider using physical force, but who's to say they wouldn't strike later, when we're out in the suburbs, in an empty carriage somewhere far from Central London? And who's to say they're not watching us now, waiting to pick their moment?

I look around me at the other passengers. As our train starts up I keep my eye on them, just to see if any of them are watching me. Any one of them could be one of Rolf's cronies—there's no telling what sort of person he'd choose to follow us. A burly man with a thick neck gets on at Goldhawk Road, but he only stays for one stop—and to be honest, he doesn't look like he could be one of Rolf's cronies. Members of the London Underground Railway Society and Subterranea Brittanica just don't look like that. At Shepherd's Bush a tall black man wearing an anorak and a pair of cheap specs gets on—much more like it—but at Ladbroke Grove he gets off again: I watch him making his way towards the exit.

Brian's voice snaps me out of my thoughts.

"You know," he says, stretching out on his seat, "I bet your mate Rolf wouldn't have done as well as we have today. Not with all the delays we've had."

"Yeah," I say curtly. "Well, Rolf probably *wouldn't* have had the delays we've had."

Brian takes a sip on the can he's been nursing for the last couple of stops, before saying thoughtfully, "I'd really like to meet this Rolf bloke one day. I'd like to see if he's as much of an expert as you say he is."

"Oh, he is. Believe me."

"But I can't believe he's more obsessed than you are."

I snort loudly. "You think *I'm* obsessed! Christ, Rolf's *five* times as bad as I am. *Ten* times, even. He's the most obsessive, compulsive, antagonistic, weird *bastard* I've ever met."

"But I thought he was a friend of yours."

"He is. Sort of."

He looks at me blankly. "I don't understand. Either he's a mate or he's not."

"Look," I say, irritated, "can we just leave Rolf out of it, please? He's the one person I really do *not* want to talk about right now."

Brian goes quiet, and I immediately feel guilty for snapping at him. I sigh deeply. I can see this is going to be one of those conversations.

"Look," I say, "if you must know, it's just that he's . . . He's not always . . ." I have to stop to find the right words. "I suppose what it comes down to is that I don't trust him."

Brian shrugs. "So he's *not* a mate, then. You *trust* your mates."

"But it's not as simple as that. I mean, we spend a lot of time doing stuff together. And we do things I'd never do with anyone else. Important things. So he's not just anybody. He just has a knack of getting me into trouble, that's all."

He is staring at me, and I can see that I'm going to have to explain further.

"The thing is, Rolf has a way of getting people to do things they'd never do normally. He's blagged his way into the Northern Line central control room before. He's managed to get more than one station manager to lend him their keys. I've even watched him convince a ticket inspector to let him off a ten-pound fine—*that's* how good he is. And he's got loads of friends in high places. I mean, I wouldn't be surprised if he's managed to engineer a few signal failures to slow us down today. He's sort of . . . well, he's devious. That's how he gets *me* to do things too." I pause for a moment, before adding, "Rachel hates him."

"Good for Rachel."

"Yeah. Except she takes it out on me. Look . . ." I push back my fringe to show Brian the tiny scar I have on my cheekbone just by my hairline.

He raises his eyebrows, pretending to be impressed.

"Rachel gave me that. She was so upset with me for going to visit a disused station with Rolf that she threw a hairbrush at my head. It was our anniversary, you see. Two years from the day we met."

Brian shakes his head in disbelief. "'Scuse me for asking this, but if this Rolf bloke keeps getting you into such trouble with Rachel, why are you still friends with him?"

"I don't know. I just am."

"Listen," says Brian, "I used to have a friend like that. Always clever. Always right. Always got his own way. And never once did he give me anything but trouble. I tell you, people like him are no good. It sounds like all your mate Rolf cares about is messing up your wedding. The next thing he'll do is try to get his hands on your Rachel."

I snort loudly. "Surely you're joking! Rolf—and Rachel . . . !"

"Why not? You yourself said he fancies her."

"But that's just a schoolboy crush!"

"Is it? He seems to have done a good job of getting you out of the way on the day before your wedding. For the *whole* day. Sounds like the actions of a desperate man to me. You should ditch him as soon as you can. Tell him where to go."

I turn away, still reeling from the preposterousness of what Brian is saying. "I couldn't ditch Rolf. Word would get round. It's a small place, the world of tube enthusiasts."

"So? My street was a small place, but I still ditched *my* mate once I realized what he was like."

"Yeah," I say, in a last effort to make him understand, "but your mate wasn't a tube enthusiast, though, was he?"

He stares thoughtfully at the floor. "No," he says eventually. "No, he wasn't a tube enthusiast at all. He was a kitchen salesman."

As the train decelerates I turn away again to see, almost with surprise, that we are arriving at Westbourne Park. I get up to take a photo, but only reluctantly—this is one conversation I don't want to let Brian get away with. Not only is he telling me who I can and can't be friends with, he's also comparing my life to his, and that's something I can't be doing. So what if his wife ran away with a kitchen salesman? So what if he ended up living at the bottom of a can of beer? I'm not like that. *Rachel's* not like that.

On the other hand, Rolf is like that. I take my photo, and when I sit back down beside Brian, it is this seed of doubt which prevents me from starting up our conversation again. Instead I lapse into silence. I appear to have underestimated Rolf today—severely. The idea takes me almost by surprise, and I spend the next couple of stations mulling over it. It's a difficult combination of thoughts to come to terms with: the fact that your fiancée thinks you're an idiot, coupled with the fact that one of your friends is trying to steal her away from you. If you're already feeling vulnerable and paranoid like

I am, it's even worse. It's enough to make you think other, more harmful thoughts. It's enough to make you want to do irrational things.

As we approach our stop, this is the way my mind is going, spiraling downwards into black thoughts and suspicion. But then something happens to distract me from all that—a simple thing, which has an unexpectedly profound effect on me. In a moment I forget all that Brian and I have talked about. All thoughts of fellow tube enthusiasts, of Rachel, of Brian's kitchen salesman, are banished from my head. Because here, walking down the carriage towards me, is Rolf's spy.

Chapter 47

6:05 PM—Baker Street–Kingsbury—Jubilee Line

She has a perfect face—one of those cheekbony faces that only models have, with eyes the size of chocolate Minstrels. There is a mass of dark, tussled hair like strands of licorice, tumbling onto her shoulders and the tops of her breasts. She is wearing a yellow blouse, which shows off her tan nicely—it is tight enough for her pierced navel to appear in between the bottom buttons, a single silver stud shining out from the tiniest glimpse of bare belly. In fact, she's about as far away from a trainspotter's crony as you can get. Not the sort of person I was expecting at all.

But I know she's Rolf's spy. I know it sounds crazy, but I just know. Not only does she have a copy of *Underground News* poking out of her bag (and in my experience, women that look like her don't tend to read journals about train stock movements), but I can tell from the way she fixes her eyes upon me from the moment she steps into the carriage. She picks me out, and once she has spotted me, she starts making her way over. She actually enters the train at the other end of the carriage from me, so she has quite a way to walk. The woman is determined.

Of course, as soon as I catch her eye, I immediately look away. It's an automatic reaction—I never look at beautiful women on the tube, because I'm always afraid that they'll catch me staring and know that I desire them. Instead, I watch the other passengers. None of them seem to have the same scruples as I do: men and women alike, they all watch the newcomer step through the doors and into the car. One old man in the aisle reaches up to his hat, as if he feels compelled to tip it to her. Brian is gawping at her with a big grin on his face and fumbling with his beer can in an effort to put it away in his pocket. The woman beside him is gazing at her with an expression somewhat akin to wonderment.

I trace the woman's movements through the other passenger's eyes—she reaches up to the pole, her breasts lifting slightly, and the buttons on her yellow blouse strain just enough for onlookers to catch a glimpse of white lace between them. She squeezes between a married couple, her back to the woman, oblivious to the jealous looks she is giving her. She passes right down inside the car, turning heads as she goes, until at last she comes to a stop in front of me.

At last I allow myself a quick glance—after all, it would be unnatural for me not to look at the person who has come to stand before me—and as I look up at her, she smiles at me. Not a big smile, not an invitation to talk, just a small impersonal smile to acknowledge my existence. She has full, plump lips. I smile back, and then drop my eyes to the hollows of her collarbones, then lower still . . .

I can see the outline of her bra through her blouse. This is not something I try to notice; it is something I can't help myself from seeing—her breasts are large and prominent, and they are only slightly above my eye level. I almost feel guilty for looking at them. I say almost, because at the last moment I realize that this woman is not here accidentally at all, and her little smile at me is far from innocent. This is no normal commuter. This is no casual traveler from *A* to *B*. This woman is a decoy, a lure, and she is here to ensnare me.

I know she will make her move soon, because it is almost time for me and Brian to change lines again. As we pull into Baker Street I have to stand up, brushing past this Aphrodite to get to the exit. Rather than taking my seat as any normal person would, she follows me to the doors, and that is the final giveaway. Why would anybody go to all the effort of walking down the full length of the carriage when they are going to get out at the next stop anyway? For one stop she would surely have stayed by the doors. Unless of course she wanted to be noticed. Noticed by me.

As the train slows I deliberately avoid looking at her, to make sure I don't give her the impression that I know what she's up to. Brian, on the other hand, is openly ogling her. I nudge him gently to try to get him to stop, but it doesn't work. He is ignoring me.

I have already made up my mind what I will do. When the doors open, I will grab Brian by the hand and make him run. We need to get to the Jubilee Line platforms as soon as possible if we are to make good time here. The Jubilee Line is a deep-level tube, rather than one of the shallow cut-and-cover versions like the Hammersmith & City, so we have to go a long way down into the ground via stairs and escalators to find it. If we run all the way, there is no way this woman can follow us without becoming completely conspicuous.

But my plan is ruined before the doors of the train even open. Just as we are coming to a halt, I feel a tap on my shoulder. I turn to find the woman looking at me with her enormous hazelnut eyes.

"Excuse me," she asks, "please, can you show me the way to the Jubilee Line?"

For a moment I hesitate—perhaps I have got this all wrong. Not only is her appearance the last thing I would have expected from one of Rolf's spies, but her voice is also wrong—although her English is deliberate and correct, she has a marked Italian accent. Where would Rolf have found an Italian woman to do his dirty work—let alone one who looks like this?

Once she has finished speaking, she smiles broadly, as if proud to have spoken so well, and her eyes linger on mine just long enough to be flirtatious before she flicks a glance in the direction of Brian. I am immediately torn. Should I tell her where to go, or should I be chivalrous and show her to the Jubilee Line like she asks? This could so easily be a ploy to slow me down. Or worse—perhaps Rolf is trying to tempt me. Whoever she is, I'm going to have to give her an answer, because the doors of our train carriage are about to open.

I decide that even if she is following me, the best thing to do is call her bluff, so I give her my biggest smile, and say, "The Jubilee Line?—why that's exactly where we're going! Of course, I'd be happy to show you the way!"

As the doors open she saunters out in front of us, as if she wants to detain us, make us wander slowly with her while Rolf organizes some major delay on the platforms below. Well, I'm not having any of it.

"Come on!" I say, grabbing her hand. "We must hurry!"

She gives a startled cry as I pull her down the narrow alley that leads to the Metropolitan Line platforms.

"Don't worry," I call out to her chivalrously, "I have a train to catch, that's all. If you want the Jubilee Line, you'd better follow me!"

And with that I let go of her hand and race off down the Metropolitan Line platform towards the stairs that lead down to the deep-level tunnels. Brian is running beside me now as we race down the stairs and along the corridor which leads to the escalators, and I notice that he keeps on glancing behind him to check on the progress of our new companion. I slow down for a second to have a look for myself. To my surprise I find she is keeping up very well. As she runs down the stairs after us, her breasts, which were so alluring earlier, now seem cumbersome and comical, bouncing up and down with every step.

When we arrive at the bottom of the escalator, I can hear the sound of a train rumbling out of the tunnel. I don't bother to wait for the other two—I run straight for the northbound platform, and there I find a 1996 stock train speeding into the station. As it slows to a halt Brian appears by my side, followed by the Italian woman, out of breath and more than a little confused.

"Jubilee Line!" I say, and give her a little bow as I press the door-release button.

She looks at me curiously, and then gives me a big smile that makes me want to melt. "English people are so strange!" she says as she steps onto the train, keeping her beautiful eyes trained on me all the way.

"Well, I never!" whispers Brian before he follows her on board. "That's one chat-up line I'd *never* have thought of."

There is only one seat free, so Brian lets the Italian woman have it. She smiles prettily at him and goes to sit down, leaving me and Brian in the aisle.

"I think our new friend is quite taken by you," he says once she has gone.

"Of course she is," I say.

"Is this a technique you try with all the ladies, then? Take them into a tube station and then run away?"

"Works every time," I say. "It's a lesson I learned from my best friend, Mickey Price, when I was a kid. When I was about six years old, a new girl came to our school. She was beautiful, and everyone fell instantly in love with her—all the boys crowded round her and asked if they could kiss her. But not Mickey. He pushed through the crowd and told her that unlike the others *he* would never kiss her unless she could *catch* him. So of course she chased him, and when she caught him, she kissed him, slap bang on the lips."

"So your friend Mickey was the brainy one." Brian grins.

"Not really. You see, Mickey truly didn't want that girl to go near him. When she finally caught him and kissed him, he punched her in the arm. The other girls had to pull him away in case he hit her again."

"That's terrible," says Brian.

"Yes, it is. But sometimes girls just have to realize that no means no."

I glance over at the Italian woman as I say this, and nod courteously.

"So are you going to talk to her, then, or what?" says Brian.

"No," I say, "I don't think so."

"Why not? She's looking at you."

I smile knowingly. "Let her look."

At St. John's Wood a few people get off, leaving some seats free at the other end of the carriage. Once I have taken my picture, Brian and I go and sit down. After the brief buzz of adrenaline from running to catch our connection, I am beginning to feel a bit nauseous again, and the chance to sit down is welcome.

From where we sit we can see the Italian woman, further down the carriage. Every now and then she glances over, and it's obvious she's keeping an eye on us. I catch her at it once: she smiles briefly at me, before looking away, and I can't help feeling a thrill within me. She really is astoundingly beautiful. It would be so easy to go over and talk to her, find out where she's going, perhaps get her telephone number.

As we pass through Swiss Cottage and Finchley Road, I notice that Brian is busy watching her too. At West Hampstead he stares at her for a good minute, but then he catches me looking at him and, embarrassed, turns away to read the adverts. But only for a short time. After a few moments he turns back to me.

"Can I ask you a question?" he says.

"If you like."

Brian looks me straight in the eye. "Have you ever been unfaithful to Rachel?"

"No."

He raises his eyebrows, as if he doesn't quite believe me. "You must have considered it, though?"

"No," I repeat.

"What, never?"

"Well, maybe in the odd daydream—but never in real life."

Brian laughs nervously. "Come on!—you *must* have done. Everyone *thinks* about it once in a while—it's human nature. There must have been a time when you were tempted."

I want to say something, to deny it, and get back to thinking about how to escape from the Italian woman. But for some reason I remain silent.

"There *was,* wasn't there!" says Brian triumphantly.

"Okay, maybe I was tempted. Once."

"Just the once?"

"Yeah, once!" I say indignantly. I look up at Brian, and I can see he is smirking at me, as if he doesn't believe me. "I never *did* anything."

Brian sniggers. "What was her name?"

"She was called Fiona. She used to work in the shop next door to mine."

"And was she good-looking?"

"Stunning."

"So?" he says impatiently. "What did you do?"

"I told you—nothing. We used to go for coffee together occasionally, but that's all. She probably didn't even fancy me."

"Oh." He is disappointed.

"Anyway, even if she had fancied me, I wouldn't have done anything. I've never been unfaithful to Rachel, and I don't intend to start now. Especially on the day before my wedding."

We sit in silence for a while. I can't help glancing over to the Italian woman to see if she is still looking at us, and I am slightly disappointed that she isn't, even though I know she is keeping tabs on us anyway. She really has got an exquisite face. Rolf has chosen well.

"I was unfaithful to my wife," says Brian after a while.

I stop looking at the Italian woman and turn back to him. I am a little surprised. "But I thought it was she who . . ."

"Yeah, she did. But I was unfaithful first."

I don't know what to say. I don't really want to know about this just now—there are much more important things in progress—but at the same time, a confession like this isn't something you can just ignore. I have to respond in some way, so I look at him and say, "Oh."

"I never wanted to be unfaithful. I always really loved my wife—still do. Only, we were going through a bad patch and stuff, and, well . . . it just sort of happened."

"What do you mean *it just sort of happened?"* I say. As I do so I find myself glancing across at the Italian woman again—can such things just *happen?*

"Well," Brian continues, "I was doing some joinery on a big old house in East London, and one day the owner's wife called me into the bedroom to help her with something. But it was obvious what she really wanted, and so I thought, why not? Rita, her name was. Lovely woman. Sparked up my whole life, she did."

"But didn't you feel bad?"

"Of course I felt bad. That was what was so *good* about it. Once I got to feeling guilty, I started being extra nice to my wife to make up for what I'd done. For the first time in my life I told her I loved her. From the way I was acting, you would have thought I didn't care a damn about my wife, and I knew that, so I started to make a special effort to let her know that I cared about her. Anyway, then my wife started feeling appreciated a bit more, so she started being nice to me as well, and for a while it was like we were courting all over again. I tell you, Rita was probably the best thing that ever happened to my marriage. Life had a sort of edge to it because of the way I was carrying on with her. Life was exciting. And I brought my excitement back home with me—into the bedroom, if you catch my meaning."

He grins at me, a lascivious grin, but it fades fast.

"The only problem was, it didn't last. After a while my wife expected me to be my extra-nice self all the time, and when I wasn't she accused me of not loving her again. She wanted me to tell her I loved her all the time, and I didn't want to tell her at all. Things started to turn sour all over again. It was horrible—it was even worse than it had been first time round. I tried to talk to Rita about it, but of course she didn't want to know, and so soon it all began to go wrong with her as well, and in the end it all just finished up being a big mess."

I nod my head at Brian wisely. "That's the way these things always end up," I say. "That's why it's always better to keep control of yourself."

"I don't know about *that,"* says Brian. He looks slightly offended. "I don't know what's so good about keeping control."

"Well, it's better than *losing* control."

"Is it?"

"Of course it is."

He shakes his head. "I don't think so. Perhaps if I'd lost control a bit more with my wife, I wouldn't have had to lose it with Rita."

"But if you'd kept yourself in control *all the time,* you wouldn't have had the problem with Rita in the first place."

Brian looks upset. He has pursed his lips and is refusing to look at me. For a moment I think he has finished, so I look back over to the Italian woman to see if she's watching us, but then Brian suddenly turns to me. "You know," he blurts, "I'm *glad* you had a little thing for this woman who works in the shop next door to you. I would have been *more* glad if you'd ended up kissing her."

"And I suppose you'd have been ecstatic if I'd taken her round the back of the shop and shagged her senseless. That would have made your day. Well, I'm sorry to disappoint you."

"Don't be stupid," says Brian. "All I'm saying is that it makes you more human, that's all. I bet your mate Rolf's never been unfaithful."

"Huh! I don't even think he's ever had a girlfriend."

"Well," says Brian decisively, "there you go, then."

I don't know what he's getting at exactly, but he seems to be satisfied. I'm a bit confused about why he's suddenly being so hostile towards me, but I don't really have time to think about it, because this is the moment when the train begins to pull into Kingsbury Station. This is the moment that I have to start thinking about getting up to take a photo again. But more important, this is the moment that the Italian woman gets out of her seat and, without so much as a glance at either me or Brian, walks over to the doors and leaves the train for good.

Chapter 48

6:35 PM—Kingsbury–Stanmore–Wembley Park—Jubilee Line

Why did she leave us at Kingsbury? It feels wrong, somehow, for her to have left so soon. Surely if she was one of Rolf's spies, it would have been more logical to stay on the train, follow us right to the end, and keep Rolf posted as to our whereabouts with a mobile phone. I have to admit that I was quite looking forward to being followed by her. Pathetic, isn't it?—I'm quite happy to have my journey sabotaged, and along with it my wedding, as long as it's by some beautiful stranger. I wonder what Rachel would say if she knew. I don't know, maybe the Italian woman wasn't a spy, after all—it's hard to know what I think anymore. But then, if she wasn't following us, why didn't she say good-bye?

When we arrive at Queensbury a few minutes later, more people get off the train. If the Italian woman has handed the spying over to someone else, it's not easy to see who it could be. There are two old ladies at the end of the carriage, but neither of them look like they could keep up the sort of pace they'd need to follow me and Brian. At Canons Park a couple of Asian teenagers get on, but I can't imagine them being in league with Rolf—he won't even *talk* to kids, and I'm pretty sure most kids wouldn't want to talk to him, either. Soon there aren't that many people left—the train's becoming emptier and emptier the further we go from Central London. Surely if someone is following us now, they will show themselves. Surely I'll be able to recognize them.

But nobody does show themselves. By the time we arrive in Stanmore at 6:42 PM there are only two other people in our carriage, and when the doors finally open with a waft of cold air, even they go. We are at the end of the line.

We have about five minutes to wait before the train turns round and goes back to Central London, so while Brian nips off to the end of the platform for a pee, I decide to check out the rest of the train. Leaving my bag on the seat, I walk down the platform towards the station house, dipping my head into each carriage as I come to it. I do this warily, because I know I must be at my most vulnerable now—I'm alone in Stanmore station, without even Brian to protect me should anyone decide to jump out at me. But the further I walk along the platform, the more I begin to realize that there *isn't* anyone to jump out at me. In fact, there isn't anyone at all. This whole train is entirely empty. No spies, no thugs, no stalkers. There is no one here but me and Brian.

As I rejoin him a few minutes later and wait for the train to start up again, I look about our carriage miserably.

"God, I hate empty trains," I say.

"Me too," he says. "They always remind me of my first girlfriend."

"They do?"

"Yeah." He sighs heavily. "Maureen Butcher, she was called. She lived across town from me, so I seemed to spend my whole life traveling home late at night—you know, because she wouldn't let me sleep over, if you see what I mean. I spent a whole year traveling backwards and forwards across London to see that girl, and I never got to have sex with her. In the end she just told me that she wasn't interested. Sitting in empty trains in the middle of nowhere always makes me feel the same way I used to then. It's depressing."

I nod slowly. I know exactly what he means. "I get the same thing with buses," I say. "Waiting at a bus stop at eleven o'clock at night. I wasn't allowed to stay at my first girlfriend's because her parents wouldn't let me. So I used to have to spend eternities standing at the bus stop waiting for a 143 not to come."

"What was this girl's name?"

"Katrina Morpeth. She was fourteen, and I was fifteen."

"And what happened in the end?"

"She chucked me for my best friend, Will."

"Oh," says Brian understandingly, "a bit like my wife and her kitchen salesman."

We sit there in the brightly lit carriage together—just me, Brian, and forty empty orange and brown seats—as our train starts up and begins its long journey back to Canons Park, Queensbury, and beyond.

Brian's right—it is depressing. I suppose it's something to do with the fact that we're out in the suburbs. When you find yourself on an empty train at Oxford Circus, you rejoice, because you've got all that space to yourself—but out here it just feels sort of lonely. It's the same feeling you get late at night out in country stations: because you know that the reason the train is empty is simply that it's *always* empty, because you're traveling from nowhere to nowhere. The only good reason to sit on one of these trains by yourself late at night, if a good reason exists, is to go and see a woman. Or, as Brian says, to come home after having seen one.

That's the thing about being single—you end up doing all kinds of things you wouldn't dream of doing if you had a partner. Like hanging around hopefully in dodgy nightclubs until the lights come on and the bouncers kick you out, alone, into the street. Or flirting embarrassingly with some barmaid in town who has seen it all a thousand times and just wants you to leave her alone. And at the end of it all, there is always the long tube ride home, on an empty train, by yourself.

It's at times like these that I thank my stars I've got Rachel. At least I don't have to trek across London in the hope of getting inside her knickers. At least I don't have to spend lonely hours wondering whether she likes me or not, or agonizing over whether she'll be offended if she catches me looking at her breasts. I don't have to prove myself to her, and I don't have to win her over to get her to fancy me. When I'm on a tube by myself late at night, it's not because I've spent the whole evening failing to chat someone up, but because I'm going home to Rachel, in our nice warm bed, in our cozy flat.

Sort of makes you wonder what the hell I'm doing here now, doesn't it?

Chapter 49

6:58 PM—Wembley Park–Watford/Chesham/Amersham—Metropolitan Line

7:59 PM—Amersham–WestHarrow–Northwick Park—Metropolitan Line

8:28 PM—Northwick Park–Kenton—On foot

The next couple of hours is the same routine—empty trains, strip-lit carriages, and nobody to talk to or look at except for Brian. We're traveling the outer reaches of northwest London now, ticking off stations and killing time till eight-thirty, when we can pick up our next envelope in Harrow & Wealdstone. For long stretches between stops Brian drifts off into a snooze, his snores echoing the rumble of the wheels on the track as we travel down the Met Line from Wembley Park to Watford, Chesham, and Amersham—some of the loneliest and most far-flung stations on the system.

I keep thinking we're going to catch up with Rolf—after all, I know he's out there somewhere, with my belongings. I imagine us finding him out on some platform in the middle of nowhere, and perhaps tying him to a bench so that he can't sabotage our journey any further. But we don't catch up with him. He seems to have melted into the network around us without a trace, watching us wherever we go, invisible and ubiquitous.

Inexorably we travel onwards—through Moor Park, Northwood, and Pinner—just me, Brian, and our empty seats. I keep myself awake by standing up occasionally and pacing up and down the carriage. Staying awake is the only challenge here. As long as the train keeps moving, we keep moving—there's nothing either of us can do to speed the journey up. And likewise, there aren't any mistakes we can make, not really—not as long as I stay awake and keep taking photographs.

But I'm afraid to say that all that is about to change. Because after West Harrow, and Harrow-on-the-Hill comes Northwick Park. And Northwick Park is where we get off, and leave the tube altogether.

For a while now I've been quite worried about how we're going to get the Bakerloo Line out of the way. I've never particularly liked the Bakerloo Line. It's so *boring*. There's nothing to distinguish it from any other train line in the world. It's not particularly reliable, but neither is it particularly unreliable, so it's difficult to work up much enthusiasm even when you're cursing the damn thing. It's not that old, but it's certainly not high-tech either, and while it does have accidents and delays and floodings and crimes, it doesn't have *that many* accidents or delays or floodings or crimes—just enough to make it average. That's pretty much all you can say about it. The whole thing is average. Boring, dull, and average.

My problem today is how to get it done without having to go all the way into the center of town and back out again. The nearest link between the Met Line and the Bakerloo is at Baker Street—if I were to go all the way back there to change, it would take almost an hour out of my journey.

Fortunately Brian has an idea.

"Kenton," he says.

"Pardon?"

"Kenton Station. It's on the Bakerloo Line, near where I used to live. If we get out at Northwick Park, we can walk there."

"Really!" The thought reawakens a modicum of enthusiasm in me—after all, if it's true, this will save us bucketloads of time. "Are you sure, though?"

"'Course I'm sure. I used to live round here, didn't I? It's a five-minute walk."

It's too good an offer to turn down, really. I'm too tired to ask Brian any more probing questions, like how far we'll have to run, or whether he is sure he knows the way. I just decide to follow his lead and trust him. So when our train eventually pulls up at Northwick Park, rather than simply taking a picture and slumping back in my seat, Brian and I find ourselves standing by the doors, readying ourselves for a mad sprint through the streets to the other tube line.

There are two exits from Northwick Park tube station—one of them goes out towards the hospital, while the other one rather reassuringly has a big sign over it saying: *"Kenton Station situated in Kenton Road."* This is the one we go through. I figure Brian will probably know where Kenton Road is. We hurry out of the station and turn left down a long street full of big suburban houses.

It's got quite windy since we were last outside—the height of the houses seems to funnel the wind towards us so that we have to run against it. My legs feel like they are made of cast iron. I know we should be running, but it's all I can do to keep up a steady jog. Silently I curse the wind that is hampering us. I curse my legs for feeling as if they are about to give way. I curse London Underground for not building a straightforward link between the two stations, and

I curse Brian for coming up with a plan which means more running. Haven't I run enough today? When is all this running going to stop?

I also curse the street we are running down—not for any particular reason other than that at the moment I hate the whole world. But there is definitely something about this part of the world that seems more hateable than elsewhere. It's so *suburban.* All the houses are big—not *too* big, just big enough to be larger than anything I will ever be able to afford. They all have nice long hedges screening their fronts—carefully tended by some underpaid gardener, no doubt—and their driveways are filled with big, expensive cars (not aristocratic cars, like Bentleys, Ferraris, or Jaguars—no, these are middle-class cars: top-of-the-range Fords, Nissans, and Range Rovers). I dare say that to those who live here, this is a place of infinite variety—but to an outsider like me, everything just looks the same. Not too big, but not too small. Nothing down-market, but nothing too flashy, either. It is the Bakerloo Line of London suburbs. While in my exhaustion I have decided to hate the whole world, I reserve an extra-special piece of hate for Northwick Park.

As we lurch our way to the end of the street we come to a main road and a large sign saying :

Harrow Town Centre

I have to say that this worries me. I mean, why doesn't it say, for example, "Kenton Town Centre," or even "This Way for Kenton Station"? Brian said it was a five-minute walk to where we want to go, and we've been running for at least three or four minutes—we should be there by now. As we come to a halt, Brian stands on the curb of the road looking around him.

"Is it far?" I gasp, as we are waiting by the edge of the road. Despite the fact that it's after nine o'clock, there is a constant flow of traffic in both directions.

"Not far. We'll be there soon."

He grabs my arm and hauls me across the flow of traffic. Once safely on the other side he has a quick look round before leading me down another side street called Gayton Road. This is pretty much the same as the last street we ran down—more big houses with more big cars parked outside. I follow him past ugly pollarded trees and orange streetlamps until, after a hundred yards or so, he comes to a halt on a street corner.

"Why are we stopping?" I ask as I catch him up. "What's wrong?"

"Nothing. I'm just getting my bearings."

"Getting your *what?"* All the fears I had earlier about putting myself in Brian's hands come rushing back to the surface. "Please, Brian—please tell me you know where you're going."

Brian doesn't answer me directly. Instead he takes another quick glance around him and says, "It's down here."

He starts off down a side street called Gerard Road, and I drag myself after him as fast as I can.

I'm beginning to think it's impossible for Brian to know where he's going. Everything looks the same down here. It's like we've entered some sort of suburban hell, a maze of semis with matching front gardens and indistinguishable frontages stretching on for eternity. In his hurry to get on, Brian is running far ahead of me, and I find myself beginning to panic: What if I were to lose him? What if he were to turn a few corners and leave me stranded in this place? I'd be stuck here forever. As he hurries on ahead, the thought occurs to me that perhaps this is what he's trying to do—tire me out and abandon me, exhausted, in this residential purgatory.

"Brian," I call out. "Brian, wait up!"

He keeps running, seemingly oblivious to my calls. I'm staggering past a front garden that has an ornamental wishing well in it and two tastefully displayed iron wagon wheels. Unlike most of the other semis, this one doesn't have a hedge in front of it—its occupants are proud of their garden decorations—instead it has a low wall made of red bricks. I suddenly realize I can't go on without stopping for a rest.

"Brian!" I shout once more, as I sit down gingerly on the garden wall. And then again, louder, *"Brian!"*

Eventually he stops and turns to see where I've got to, and then after a moment's hesitation, comes trotting back towards me.

"What's the matter?" I say with irritation as he arrives by my side. "Trying to lose me or something, eh?"

"Of course not—we've got to get a move on."

"Well, do you mind telling me where the fuck we're getting a move on *to?* You said it was only five minutes walk, and that was almost ten minutes ago. I'm knackered."

"It can't be much further. Just around the corner perhaps."

I look up at him, aghast. *"Perhaps?* What do you mean, *perhaps?"*

"I mean . . ." He looks about him again, unsurely. "I mean, probably."

I take a deep breath and put my bag down on the pavement. "You don't know where we are," I say, "do you?"

"Yes, I do. Kind of."

"Kind of?"

"Well, I know where we are," he says sheepishly. "I'm just not too sure where Kenton Station is."

If I had the energy right now, I think I'd probably deck him.

"I could have sworn it was just down here," he continues. "It's just that nothing looks the same as it did twenty years ago . . ."

"I don't believe this! I don't bloody fucking bastard believe this!" I put my head in my hands and clutch my hair between my fingers. "It's been one delay after another today. This bastard journey has been going on forever, and now *you're* leading me on a fucking *wild-goose chase!"*

"Sorry," Brian mumbles. "I thought it was just down here . . ."

"Well, it's not, is it? There's nothing down here but Ford fucking Mondeos."

Brian just stands there, looking pathetic, and his feebleness makes me feel even more angry.

"I'm going back," I say decisively. "I'm going back to Northwick Park to see if I can salvage this mess."

"But you can't do that," Brian whines; "it'll be such a waste of time."

"Waste of time . . . !" I am almost beside myself. "What the hell do you call this?"

I stand up with the intention of storming off back the way we came, but as I do so my tired legs buckle under me, and I find myself collapsing back onto the garden wall. In frustration I kick the wall as hard as I can with the back of my foot, and then put my head back in my hands. It seems like everything is conspiring against me today. The timing of this final blow could not have been worse: I'm tired, I'm hungry, I'm fed up, and I'm miles from anywhere. Brian has left me scuppered in the worst possible way. It's almost as if he's chosen his moment. It's almost as if he's waited until I was incapable of resistance. Even Rolf couldn't have planned it better.

I sense Brian sit down next to me on the wall. I glance sideways at him and catch him putting his head in his hands, a mirror of my own posture. "I'm sorry," he says.

"Good," I say.

"I've ruined everything, haven't I? We were doing really well, and now I've gone and cocked it all up."

"Yes," I say. "Yes, you have."

I half expect him to protest at this, but he doesn't. He stays curiously silent. This seems odd to me, so I glance sideways at him, just in time to catch the glimmer of a smile on his bowed face. It's only there for a split second—I'm *sure* it's there—a fleeting upturn of his lips before his expression returns to one of remorse.

I turn back to face the road. What the hell am I going to do? I can't face the idea of giving up, not now, after all I've been through. But what's the alternative? Do I go back to Northwick Park—in which case I'm bound to fail—or do I go on and see if I can find Kenton Station by myself? Or do I trust Brian to lead me there?

I look at him again and realize that I still don't actually know that much about the man. I mean, every now and then he tells me snippets about himself, but I have no way of telling that he has told me the truth. Maybe he's not a tramp at all—maybe this is all an elaborate disguise. Or maybe he's some sort of nutter who's been waiting all day to isolate me, get me alone in some dark street miles from anywhere. Stranger things have happened. There are thousands of possibilities. Here I am, stranded on a garden wall in the back of beyond, and the man sitting next to me could be an ax murderer, a rapist, a religious freak, a mugger, a fraud. I think of that flicker of a smile I saw on his face a few moments ago. A victorious smile perhaps? A treacherous, triumphant, trainspotter's smile. But no, I can't bear to think that. Surely not even Rolf could be *that* evil.

Brian is unaware of my suspicions and just continues talking—keeping up the pretense of remorse for leading me astray. "I was sure I'd be able to remember where the station is," he says. "It's just been such a long time. The place doesn't look the same anymore."

"Of *course* it doesn't," I say. My voice sounds sarcastic.

"It's just so frustrating," he continues. "I mean, I recognize so many of the houses round here. Like that one there on the corner. I used to drive past that house every day in the seventies, on my way to work."

He points at a big white house on the corner of a side street further up the road, and as he does so his face lights up. "Hang on a minute!" he says suddenly, and stands up, excitedly.

I look at him with contempt. "Oh, and now I suppose you're going to tell me you've suddenly remembered the way? Give me a break."

"No, it's not that. Listen!"

He is standing completely still before me, leaning ridiculously to one side with his head cocked in a caricature of a listening pose. He looks like a second-rate actor, hamming it up—he even has a hand cupped to one ear. "Listen out," he seems to be saying. "Listen to the silence, the sound of nothing, because that's exactly what you're about to become—nothing. A failure." And I do listen, because there is nothing left for me to do. I cock my head in sad imitation of Brian, and that's when I hear it. Up ahead of us, somewhere, is the sound of a train.

Chapter 50

8:43 PM—Somewhere in Kenton

It only takes a moment before I am on my feet again, chasing Brian down the street towards the distant clattering of wheels on track. It's almost an involuntary action—I've been running for tubes so much today my feet are programmed to move at the slightest sound of a train. We peg it to the end of the road, and then down a hill to what looks like a dead end, but which reveals a pedestrian footpath when we get to it. Through a barrier, round a corner, and there it is in front of us: a footbridge over the train tracks.

We run up its steep steps, past enormous graffitied lettering, right to the top, and what do we find on the other side? A main road? A tube station with Bakerloo Line trains jamming its platforms? Unfortunately not. All there is on the other side of a the bridge is a large recreation ground, a few trees, some more graffiti, and an empty red telephone box. From the top of the footbridge we can see the train tracks spreading forever in both directions. The train we were chasing has long since gone, and there isn't a station in sight.

"Which way now?" I ask Brian between deep breaths.

"I don't know," says Brian.

"We could follow the train tracks. But in which direction?"

"I don't know. I've lost all sense of where we are."

We stand together on the bridge looking hopelessly down the empty tracks while we catch our breath. We really should be getting a move on, but we both know the consequences of walking in the wrong direction. Kenton Station must be nearby—but if we go the wrong way and end up walking towards Harrow & Wealdstone, it could take us ages.

"I suppose we'll just have to wait for another train to see what the destination is on the front of it," says Brian. "Then we'll know which way the trains are going."

We stand on the bridge looking down on the track. It is the only thing we can see with any clarity, because everything else is dark. On the other side of the bridge the enormous recreation ground is all blackness, with the exception of the dim glow from the inside of the telephone box. For a moment it seems this is all that exists: darkness, a train track, a telephone box.

The wind has picked up now and is blowing in short bursts, throwing handfuls of cold spray against my face. It brings me suddenly to my senses. I turn for an instant to look at Brian, and as I do so I realize with horror just what an idiot I've been. The man beside me is an old, rugged alcoholic—just the sort of man Rolf would despise. There's no *way* he's in league with him. It's like waking up from some horribly paranoid dream.

Brian catches me looking at him and turns towards me, a questioning look on his face. I decide I'd better say something.

"You know, for a while back there I thought . . ." I stop midsentence, and lapse back into silence.

"You thought what?"

"I just thought that, what with us getting lost and everything, you might be . . . you know."

But Brian is ignoring me. Something else has caught his attention. "Here's one now!" he calls out excitedly. "Up ahead—a train!"

I turn to follow his eyes. About a mile away a train is approaching—we can see the light of the driver's compartment looming towards us. After a couple of seconds the iron rails of the track below begin to sing with the sound of the wheels. I have to say, this train seems to be going very fast—it is hurtling towards us at the sort of speed normal tube trains only dream about, and it's only moments before we are able to see right into the driver's compartment. It doesn't exactly look like a tube train, either. It has a nose-shaped front, and there is no sign anywhere on it stating its destination. As it hurtles beneath us Brian leans over the edge of the bridge and manages to catch a single word on the side of the carriages.

Brian looks at me nervously. "Virgin! It says Virgin! This isn't a tube line; this is an overground line!"

"It might be a tube line as well," I say, "you know, like at Upminster this morning."

"But what happens if it's not?"

The possibility hangs between us in the air. Neither of us know where the hell we are. We both assumed that this must be part of the Bakerloo Line, that all we have to do is follow the tracks, one way or the other, to find our way back onto the tube map. Neither of us considered the possibility that this would be anything other than a tube line. If it isn't a tube line, then we're screwed.

"What are we going to do?" Brian asks.

"There's only one thing we can do." Putting down my bag, I hold out my hand, palm upwards. "Have you got 20p?"

Chapter 51

8:47 PM—Kenton Recreation Ground

As Brian and I squeeze our way into the phone box on the corner of the park, I steel myself. I've no idea what I'm going to say. I haven't spoken to Rachel since our argument last night. In fact, the last piece of communication we had was her writing TWAT on my forehead with her lipstick. Hardly a good starting point.

I know she's not going to like me ringing up like this. I should really be calling to patch things up, to tell her that I'm sorry, that I'm coming home. Phoning her to ask for favors is definitely *not* a good move.

I dial the number, *my* number, and stand there next to Brian, nervous as a schoolboy. The phone rings four times, five times. I'm beginning to think that perhaps she isn't in, when suddenly the ringing tone stops and I hear her voice. "Hello?"

"Hello, Rachel."

There is a silence for a few seconds, as if neither of us wants to say anything, for fear of what that something may be.

But then I hear Rachel's voice again. "I was wondering if you'd call," she says. "I've been waiting all day."

"Well," I say, "now you don't have to wait any more."

"Great," she says. She is being sarcastic. "Lucky me."

"Well, I did *try* to call—a couple of times. The first time you were engaged both at home *and* on your mobile—God know's how you managed that—and the second time . . ."

"Oh, Andy, it doesn't matter. The important thing is that you're ringing now. I've been worried sick! I thought something had happened to you. I thought maybe you'd . . . you know. Run off, or something."

"Run off? Why would I run off?"

"I don't know."

There is a pause for a few moments. Neither of us know what to say. I'm confused by what she has just said: she knows what I'm doing today—why would I want to run off? I thought *she* was the one who was going to be doing the running.

Again, it is Rachel who breaks the silence. "Where are you now?"

I try to gather myself. "Well, I was rather hoping you could tell me that. You see I'm lost. Brian's been leading me to Kenton Station, only the stupid bloody idiot doesn't seem to know the way."

"It's not my fault," Brian interrupts from beside me. "It's all changed round here since 1979."

I can hear Rachel's voice change from concern to suspicion. "Who the hell's Brian?"

"Oh, he's just an . . ." I look at the disheveled old man beside me. . . . "He's just a fellow passenger."

"Andy, you're not still doing this trip round the tube, are you?"

"Of course I am. You said last night . . ."

"Forget what I said last night. I just want you to come home, so we can catch our train. I'm sorry I said those things. I'm . . . I miss you." She stops, falls suddenly quiet again, and I am worried she might be crying. Rachel always cries quietly.

"I miss you too," I say, in a hurry to fill the silence.

"And I'm sorry about what I did."

"What you did . . . ?"

"With the lipstick."

"Oh, that . . ." I reach up and touch my forehead. "Don't worry about that. You were right. I was a twat."

"So you don't hate me, then?"

"No, I don't hate you."

"And you'll come home?"

This is exactly the question I've been dreading. "No . . ." I say. "Not just now."

"Why not?"

"Rachel, I'm almost done. I can't stop yet."

"But why not?" There is despair in her voice.

"I just can't. It's something I have to do."

There is a clunking sound on the other end of the phone as if Rachel has just hit something. "God, what *is* it with you and Rolf? You're like a couple of overgrown schoolchildren with all your bets and your silly one-upmanship. Why can't you just call it off and come *home?"*

"Believe me, Rachel, there's nothing I'd rather do—it's just . . . it's rather complicated at the moment."

She is quiet for a few moments, before saying angrily, "So when am I going to see you then?"

"If you can tell me how to get to Kenton, then I'll see you in a few hours. I can meet you on the platform at the Eurostar—if you can just get me out of here . . ."

"You mean you're not even coming home first? You haven't even packed yet."

"Well, I was kind of hoping you'd do it for me."

"Oh, *were* you now . . ."

"Please, Rachel! I promise I'll explain all this when I see you, but right now I have to finish up the last few stations. I'll meet you at Waterloo, okay?"

She groans. "Do I have a choice?"

"It'll be fine, Rachel—you'll see. If you can just direct me to a station . . ."

There is a short silence again, but then I hear her sigh, as if she is giving up. "I'll get the *A to Z,"* she says.

I tell Rachel the name of the street we're on, and listen as she turns the pages of the map. When she finds the right page, she gives me an outline of where we are. From her description it seems we're not that far off Kenton Station after all, and Brian was taking us kind of in the right direction, albeit in a roundabout way. After a couple of minutes I have a clear mental picture of the map and am confident I can find my way.

"Thanks, Rachel," I say. "I've got to rush now, but I'll meet you at the Eurostar."

"Okay," she says. "But, Andy . . . ?"

"Yes?"

"Andy, if you're not there . . ."

I hear her sigh again, and I can tell she is crying this time. I'm getting edgy because I want to go and get on the next train. But she is keeping me here with her tears. And I know what they mean—if I am not there at the Eurostar, she's leaving without me.

Brian doesn't seem to know what all these long silences are about—impatiently, he shakes my shoulder. "For God's sake, man," he says, "we have to go!"

Somehow the jolt of Brian's hand against my arm seems to spur me into action. "I'm sorry, Rachel," I say. "I love you. Really. But I've got to go."

I put the phone down quickly, and then stand there, staring at it as if it's some sort of container with Rachel inside it. I can see her face if I unfocus my eyes—I can see her, standing by the telephone at home, crying.

Brian speaks beside me, and his voice gives me a jolt. "If you're quite finished, can we go now? We've got a train to catch."

I pull myself together. "Yeah," I say. "Sorry."

We pile out of the phone box and hurry off in the direction Rachel told me a few minutes ago. There is a long street heading away from the park, and this is where we go—first at a trot, then at a brisk walk. We follow Rachel's instructions to the letter—up Carlton Avenue, turn right, first left, and before we know it, we are there. Kenton Station is right in front of us, shining out onto the main road like some sort of public transport oasis.

We really have been lucky, because as we race through the barriers and down the stairs, there is a train just sitting waiting for us at the platform. Brian cries out for joy as he leaps into the tube car, but I simply take my photograph of the station sign and step on quietly. I don't share Brian's sense of victory. Sure, we've made it onto the train with only moments to spare, and the next one isn't for another ten minutes. But somehow I just can't manage to be that enthusiastic about it.

Chapter 52

8:55 PM—Kenton–Harrow & Wealdstone–Oxford Circus—Bakerloo Line

What can I say? Here I am again, back on the tube. I suppose, in a way, it feels good. Anxious, but good. We've been up to Harrow & Wealdstone, and now we're on our way back again—back into Central London.

It was easy to find our fourth envelope. It was hidden on the top of one of the train indicator displays—quite safe from prying eyes. God knows how Rolf got it up there, but I had to get Brian to let me stand on his shoulders to reach it. Inside it was my passport—vital for my train journey tonight—and a note with just two words on it: *"Bob—Richmond."* And that was that.

So now, here I am, back on the train to town. The time is a quarter past nine. We now have four out of our six envelopes. We've been on the move for over sixteen hours, and we have just over three hours left to finish the system and win our bet. But do you know what?—despite our numerous delays, despite derailed trains and signal failures and getting lost in the streets around Northwick

Park, I'm actually feeling quite confident. At long last I'm beginning to feel that there's a chance I'm going to make it.

As our tube stops and starts through Harlesden, Kensal Green, and Kilburn Park, I think of Rachel at home, readying herself for our journey to Paris. All day long I've been wondering what I'll say to her when I see her next. This morning, as I rubbed her lipstick off my forehead, I thought of countless clever put-downs and ways to make her feel sorry for all the things she'd said; later on I imagined a more reasoned conversation which would end in her realizing how wrong she was to question both my commitment to her and my ability to get round the tube in time. But I don't want to do any of that now. All I want to do is get on the Eurostar with her, tell her I'm sorry. And perhaps tell her that I love her—face-to-face this time, and without any coaxing from Brian.

And as we race through Maida Vale, Edgware Road, and Marylebone, I also think about Rolf. Perhaps I've done him wrong too. Perhaps he hasn't been following me all day, after all. Or maybe he has. I don't know anything anymore. My head has been so all over the place for the past few hours I no longer know what I've seen and what's just been daydreaming. The whole of today has been such a trip that for all I know, I could have imagined it—the bet, the race, everything. The thought is quite humbling.

All I *do* know is that I have to make it to the end by half past midnight if I'm to have a hope of getting to the Eurostar on time. And while I'm on my way to doing that, I have to acknowledge the fact that I have not made it yet. I still have West London to do, and God only knows what will happen there. Any drop in concentration, any distraction or minor delay, could ruin everything.

So, as our train pulls into Oxford Circus, I have to prepare myself, mentally and physically. There can be no letup now. The final stage is about to begin.

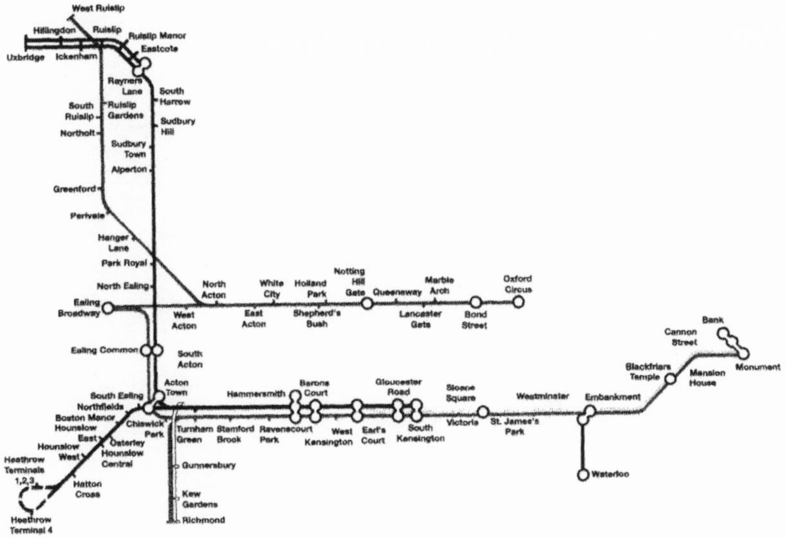

part 5

west london

Chapter 53

9:30 PM—Packing in Belsize Park—All lines

Once she had finished crying, Rachel started packing—*his* things. And as she packed she thought of all the different ways in which she'd like to destroy the London Underground. For the next few minutes this was what she channeled her hurt into—thinking of ways to wreck the tube. She surprised herself with her inventiveness. She decided that if she was ever made Prime Minister, that's what she would do—take the tube, with all its history, its crowds, its announcements, its delays, and erase its existence from the face of London—line by line, station by station.

She would start with the Northern Line, because that was Andy's favorite. She would kill that one slowly. She'd do it simply by turning off all the pumps in the tunnels, and watch it slowly submerge in the water of all the underground rivers that cross the line. Perhaps she'd make Andy watch too—observe as his beloved tube line slowly and irrecoverably drowned. It might take weeks, but it would be worth it. It would *have* to take weeks to make up for all the misery she'd put up with today.

The next line she'd destroy would be the Jubilee Line, because that's where Rolf lived. She'd start with his own station, Willesden Green, wiring it up with explosives which would then detonate the whole of the rest of the line in a massive chain reaction. And to make sure she *truly* got her own back for all of Rolf's intrusive phone calls, she'd put him inside Willesden Green Station just before it blew up—handcuff him to some railings just far enough away so that he would be able to see his precious station explode before he himself was blown to smithereens.

The two blue ones, the Victoria and the Piccadilly, she would fill in with concrete. Tons upon tons of impenetrable, reinforced, top-grade concrete. She'd commission a whole fleet of lorries to bring the stuff in and have them pour their loads one by one into the lift shafts and escalators all along the two lines, until eventually there was nothing of either of them left.

As for the District Line, the Circle Line, the Metropolitan Line, and the Hammersmith & City—hadn't Andy told her that they were all built underneath roads? Well, if that was true, then they'd be easy to get rid of—she'd simply collapse the roads on top of them so that the cars drove where the trains used to go. The stations would become pavements, the rails would be tarmacked over, and the oldest tube lines in the world would instantly become history. Those parts of the train lines that were already out in the open she would leave that way. She'd simply rip up the tracks, use the metal for scrap, and let the bushes grow over the rest.

Rachel stuffed Andy's swimming trunks violently into his bag. Wiping her eyes, she rolled Andy's suit up tight, not caring whether it crumpled or not, and shoved it resentfully into the holdall with the rest of his stuff—his T-shirts, his underpants, his razors and shaving foam. She vented her frustration on his clothing, using her fist like a ramrod to pack it all in, and as she did so she continued her fantasy about destroying the Underground. Just the thought of it made her feel much better.

So, the Bakerloo Line—how would she destroy that? Perhaps she would burn it. Perhaps she would fill it with wood, and charcoal and rubber, all soaked in thousands of gallons of petrol, and then stand at the terminus at Elephant & Castle with a box of matches, making Andy plead with her before she lit one and tossed it in. The tracks would all melt. The tunnel lining would buckle and crack, and the whole thing would cave in on itself, burying the line for good.

The Waterloo & City Line she would dig up, creating a vast scar in the ground. It would lie like an open wound across the City of London and the South Bank—a wound she would never allow to be filled in or covered up. It would become a monument to the ugliness of tube travel and corporate finance alike.

Then she'd take a wrecker's ball to all the stations on the East London Line, smash the tunnel with bulldozers and giant JCBs.

She would simply tip up the Docklands Light Railway, knock it off its perch above the streets of East London, cut its legs out from under it. That would bugger *that* one up.

And when she'd finished all this, when she'd burnt, flooded, blown up, smashed, and collapsed every other line on the system, she'd take the trains from all of them and drive them one by one into the Central Line at top speed, crashing them into one another again and again and again, until the wreckage of it all—the sheer bulk of all the smashed, mangled metal—filled the tunnel completely and impassably forever.

As Rachel shoved the last of Andy's things into the bag and zipped it up, she felt exhausted but much better, like she had purged something from her system. In her imagination she had single-handedly demolished an entire public transport network, and it made her feel good, powerful. And now there was only Andy himself left. Should she destroy him too? Should she tie him to the tracks of her fantasy like some male version of Penelope Pitstop and run him over with a train? Or should she leave him gawping at the destruction she had wreaked, while she waltzed off by herself back home to France?

For some reason she didn't feel like it. It was too close to home, especially on the eve of their wedding, and no matter how annoyed she was, she didn't really want to hurt Andy, not even in her daydream. Make him understand, maybe. Make him see what he'd put her through today. But to do anything to hurt him, even writing any more obscene words on his forehead with lipstick, was beyond her.

With a sigh she hoisted Andy's bag off the bed and carried it through to the sitting room. For the last time she ran through her checklist in her head. Everything was now packed—both her stuff and Andy's. Her wedding dress was finished and was on its way to Paris with Sophie right now. The hotel was booked, the reception organized, the church ready and waiting. She had her passport, her Eurostar tickets, and her credit card in her bag—the rest of the stuff was with Andy. All their friends, and Andy's family, were either already in Paris or on their way.

There was just one thing left to do. Dropping down into the armchair, she picked up the telephone and dialed a cab firm—when she got through, she ordered herself a taxi for midnight. And once this was done, once she'd replaced the handset on the hook, she was finished. She had nothing left to do but wait.

Chapter 54

9:31 PM—Oxford Circus–Ealing Broadway–West Ruislip—Central Line

10:24 PM—West Ruislip–Ickenham—On foot

10:29 PM—Ickenham–Uxbridge–Heathrow–Acton Town—Piccadilly Line

11:29 PM—Acton Town–Turnham Green—District Line

Okay, so here's the deal. I have to finish off four different lines: the Central, the Metropolitan, the Piccadilly, and the District—in that order. I have two envelopes left to collect, the first of which is with someone called Bob at Richmond. I have to travel through a total of eighty-two stops and take pictures of sixty-seven more station signs. And it all has to be done by twelve-thirty. I do some quick calculations in my head. Theoretically, I decide, it is possible. Just so long as everything goes to plan.

So, first things first: the Central Line.

It takes exactly two minutes to run to the Central Line platforms at Oxford Circus. Most people only know what Oxford Circus is like at rush hour, when it is one of the busiest stations on the network, but at this time of night it's almost empty—you can run through its subways as fast as you like. Brian and I are like rats in a pipe—we scurry down walkways and stairs and onto the platform, and within moments we are on a train, speeding westwards.

I like the Central Line. I like it because it's quick, its trains aren't crap, and it runs in a perfectly straight line right through the City and the West End: there's not much chance of a derailing on this service. And at this time of night, when there aren't hundreds of trains clogging up the tracks, it moves through the tunnels like a bullet down the barrel of a gun. Queensway, Holland Park, Shepherd's Bush: we shoot onwards, averaging as little as two minutes per stop. It's exactly the sort of thing that should set me at ease—but somehow it doesn't. I find myself shuffling up and down the car between stops, clutching my fun camera and my A4 blowup of the tube map in my hand, ready to take pictures and cross off stations as soon as we get to them. I can't sit down, and I can't stand still. It's torture.

I think my restlessness is beginning to get on Brian's nerves. "For God's sake, Andy, won't you sit down? Pacing is not going to make the train go any faster."

"Sorry," I say, and sit down beside him, but within moments I find myself tapping the fun camera nervously against the armrest, and I'm worried I might do it some damage, so I stand up again and resume my pacing.

"Look," says Brian, "we're making good time. Why don't you just stop worrying?"

"I can't."

Brian sighs deeply. "You know something, you really must learn to relax. Out of everything, I'd say it was your worst problem in life."

"Oh, would you now?"

"Yeah. You're always running about, worrying about this, worrying about that. It'll drive you to an early grave if you're not careful. I think you should take up relaxation classes . . ."

"Brian," I stop him, "how long have you known me?"

"Not long, but . . ."

"Seventeen hours, that's how long. Sixteen hours and forty-two minutes, to be precise. Well, I've got news for you, Brian: today isn't a typical day, all right?"

He shrugs. "I've spent more time with you today than you probably spend with most people in a month. I figure that's enough time to work out what you're like."

"And just exactly what's that supposed to mean?"

"Nothing."

"No, come on. Tell me."

"Just you're a stresser, that's all."

"A stresser?"

"Yeah. You know, someone who stresses all the time. Sure, today it's this bet, but tomorrow you'll be stressed about how you're going to pay the rent, or the fact that you're late for work, or stuck in traffic, or anything else. Anything to take your mind off your *real* problems."

"Which are?"

"You tell me. Like you said, I've only known you for sixteen hours and forty-two minutes."

"Jesus, you're *impossible.*" I shake my head in disbelief. Who does he think he is—*Cracker* or someone? One day on the train with me and suddenly he thinks he's an expert on the workings of my mind. "And anyway," I say, looking at my watch, "it's now sixteen hours and forty-*three* minutes."

Brian stares at me for a few moments, and then shrugs and turns away—his way, I presume, of leaving me to it. I resume my pacing.

When the train gets to Ealing Broadway, we double back on ourselves and take the other branch of the Central Line up to West

Ruislip. I haven't been up this section of line for over ten years. Normally I'd be fascinated by this trip, but tonight I'm not fascinated in the slightest. I'm worried. *Rightfully* worried, whatever Brian might think. Because I'm afraid that this good run of things can't last. I'm scared that at some point *something* is bound to go wrong.

But it doesn't. We arrive in West Ruislip just before ten-thirty, where we have to leave the tube and run through the streets to Ickenham. But unlike at Northwick Park, absolutely nothing goes awry. We travel along the Metropolitan Line to Uxbridge, where, while we're waiting for the train to turn around and go back, Brian gets out to have a pee. But although I'm terrified he won't finish in time and that the train will start moving off again before he gets back, my fears are totally unfounded, and he returns well before the doors shut. On we go, through Hillingdon and Eastcote to Rayners Lane without a hitch. Then we change onto the Piccadilly Line and travel on to Sudbury, Alperton, and Park Royal. There are no points failures, no signal problems, no broken rails. Our carriage doesn't suddenly develop any defects, and nobody pulls the emergency handle. Nobody throws themselves in front of the train. It's like a dream.

There is *one* slight incident, when we get to Heathrow Airport. We have been sharing a carriage with an exceptionally drunk man, who has been singing tunelessly to himself for the past three or four stops. He seems perfectly harmless. I mean, he's no young yob ready to cause trouble with the first person who looks at him—the man is in his fifties, is wearing a linen suit and a Panama hat, and seems to have a liking for old Dean Martin songs. The few passengers there are in the carriage, sitting alongside enormous suitcases and hand luggage and duty-free shopping bags, seem to view him more as an amusement than a threat. He looks how you'd imagine the man from Del Monte would look if you spiked his orange juice with vodka.

But while the train is sitting at Heathrow, a policeman gets on and starts telling him to empty his pockets. The poor man has to rummage around in his jacket and trousers, and place all his worldly possessions on the seat beside him before the policeman will believe that he's not a danger to anyone. There then follows a lengthy question-and-answer session, made lengthier by the drunk man's insistence that he and the policeman should swap hats, before—finally—the policeman gives up and leaves the train. All the time this is happening our train is stationary. Of course, I don't know that it wouldn't have been stationary anyway, given that we *are* at Heathrow—but it would have been nice not to have the doubt.

From then on everything goes fine. Our train zips through Hounslow, and Boston Manor, and Acton Town without a hitch. By the time we arrive at Turnham Green, everything's looking good. We only have the little spur down to Richmond left to do—Richmond, where we will meet Bob and collect our penultimate envelope. And once we have done that, all we will have to do is catch the last train east, which will take us all the way to Monument, and success.

Chapter 55

11:33 PM —Turnham Green—Piccadilly/District Line

It's 11:33 PM when we arrive in Turnham Green. In other words, we have ten minutes to get to Richmond and catch our last train of the day. Ten short minutes to go three stops to the end of the line: basically doable, but cutting it a bit fine.

Fortunately for us, as we pull into the station, our train to Richmond is waiting for us on the other platform. There is a brief panic as we bundle out of our carriage and sprint through the underpass, but we make it quite easily. I feel a tremendous sense of satisfaction as we tumble onto our new train: our penultimate train of the day. All we have to do now is wait for it to start moving. We're practically there.

Only the train doesn't start moving. In fact, it doesn't look as if it is ever going to move: it just sits there. Brian and I don't notice at first, being glad simply to have made it onto the train before it left—but after a while we begin to get restless. I get up and take a look through the doors.

Further down the platform some sort of commotion is going on:

two men are arguing, and a station attendant in a fluorescent orange vest is trying to calm them down. One of the men is pointing at the other one and shouting something about a set of keys. The other is shouting back, something about a wedding. I decide to ignore them. We don't have time for dramas, and it's not as if the train is being delayed on their account. Trains don't wait for people to finish arguments before they depart a station. If they did, London would grind to a standstill.

"How long have we got?" asks Brian from his seat.

I look at my watch. "Nine minutes. The last train leaves Richmond at 11:43—around the same time as they'll be putting this one to bed in the depot for the night. Hopefully."

I sit down again, glancing anxiously around me. There is no one else in our carriage. Normally trains are pretty busy after closing time—but, after all, it is a weeknight, and this isn't Leicester Square. It's Turnham Green.

After a minute or so I return to the doorway. "For Christ's sake," I mutter, "what's holding us up?"

I look back down the platform, but although the two arguing men are still there, the station attendant seems to have disappeared. I wait, impatiently, for a few seconds before turning to Brian. "I'm going to find out what's going on," I say.

Brian seems alarmed. "But what happens if the train decides to go?"

"It's all right—I'll have time to jump on."

He doesn't seem to like this. "I'm coming with you," he announces, and gets up to follow me out of the doors.

We walk down the platform towards the arguing men, but before we reach them, I spot the station attendant inside one of the other carriages. "There he is." We step back onto the train and approach him.

"Excuse me," I call out, "when's this train going to start moving?"

He turns to me and looks me up and down in that sarcastic sort of way only employees of London Underground can master. "Actually," he says, "it's due to go any moment now, but I'm afraid I'm going to have to stop it."

"Stop it?" I say, incredulous. "Why?"

The station attendant doesn't say anything—just points. In front of him, collapsed on one of the seats, is a man.

"Well, I never!" says Brian.

He is staring at the man openmouthed, and I can't say I blame him. You see, the man on the seat in front of us is completely and utterly naked. Not a thread on him. Added to that, he is handcuffed to one of the handrails.

"Stag night prank," explains the station attendant. "Happens every six months—I don't know why people can't think of anything original."

"Can't we leave him?" I say.

"Bollocks-to-that," mumbles the drunken man. "I've already been to Upminster and back. I want to get off."

I look at the station attendant. "Please? I've got to get to Richmond."

"Sorry," says the attendant. "I can't leave this man like this. I'm going to have to ask you to change here—there'll be another Richmond train along in about ten minutes."

"Ten minutes! But that's no good—I've got to be in *Richmond* in ten minutes."

"I'm sorry, sir, there's nothing I can do. I'm going to have to take this train out of service."

I am dumbfounded. I'd kind of half expected something to happen—but this? This is just ridiculous. To think that I managed to make it through my *own* stag night on Tuesday without a hitch, only to find my wedding is now under threat from some stupid stag night trick meant for someone else—it's enough to drive you spare.

I'm just about to start pleading with the station attendant, when we all hear a shout from outside. The two arguing men have turned the volume up and are now truly bellowing at each other: something about having holes in their pockets by the sounds of things.

"What's going on there?" I ask absentmindedly.

"They're my friends," says the naked man. "They're the ones who did this to me."

"They *are!* Excellent! So they can unlock you, then . . ."

"No," says the naked man. "That's what they're arguing about. They've lost the bloody key."

There is a sudden loud smashing sound from outside. The two arguing men have stopped arguing and started fighting. The smashing sound was the sound of one of them being slammed against the chocolate machine.

Quick as a flash, the station attendant is back out on the platform. "Oi! You two! That's enough!"

But evidently it's not enough. Both men are flailing their arms at each other like a couple of windmills. From what it looks like, neither of them manages to actually hit the other—their wild flapping arms seem more like violent gesturing than blows designed to do harm—but as the station attendant moves in to break it up, he walks straight into one of these wild punches. From our carriage we see the whole thing as if in slow motion: the man's fist connects with the station attendant's jaw, almost lifting him off the ground, and he collapses onto the platform floor in a heap. He is out cold.

The two men stop their fighting instantly and stare at the man they have just decked. Then one of them looks up at the other as if to say, "Look what you've gone and done *now,"* and in a moment their fight begins all over again.

"We should go and help him," says Brian.

"Yeah," I say, "I suppose so."

"Well? Come on, then."

He makes a move towards the door, but on an impulse I hold him back.

"Hang on a second," I say. "Did he say he'd *already* stopped this train, or that he was *about* to?"

Brian turns to me impatiently. "Does it matter? The man needs help!"

Suddenly there is a noise below our feet of the train engines warming up to go. "I don't think he's done it yet," I say gleefully. "I think this train's going to Richmond as planned."

"Well, it's going without me, then," says Brian, making a start for the exit. But he's too late—before he makes it, the doors slide shut, and the train begins to move. Brian starts beating on the glass angrily with his fists, and I have to go over to him and calm him down.

"It's all right, Brian! It's all right!" I point through the window in front of him. "Look!"

At the top of the steps at the other end of the platform two more London Underground officials appear—they are running towards where their colleague is lying.

"It's okay," I repeat to Brian. "Let them sort it out. We're on our way." I look at the tube car around me with satisfaction. "We're on our way."

Chapter 56

11:38 PM—Turnham Green–Gunnersbury—District Line

But not if the naked man can help it.

"Bloody-fucking-hell," he slurs. "I thought I was getting off!"

Staggering to his feet, he reaches up beside him to grab hold of the emergency stop handle, and I have to launch myself across the carriage to catch his hand.

"Stop!" I yell.

"That's exactly what I'm trying to do," slurs the man in reply, looking with confusion at my hand gripping his. "I'm trying to make us stop."

"But you can't do that!" I say.

"Yes, I can." He reaches up with his other hand to pull the lever, but finds to his surprise that his other hand is still handcuffed to the rail. "Oh," he says. "Perhaps I can't."

Suddenly remembering that this man is naked, and I'm now standing very close to him indeed, I push him back down into his seat. "Look," I explain, "this train only has three stops to go—as soon as we get to the end of the line, it will go out of service, and someone will come and set you free. But until then you mustn't do a thing. I've got to get to Richmond, and I only have five minutes to do it."

"Oooooooh!" says the man sarcastically, "aren't we in a hurry!"

"Actually, yes. You're not the only one getting married, you know—I am too. Only I'm not if I don't make it to Richmond and back in the next five minutes."

I give him a quick rundown of my situation. At the end of it he sits there, silent, scratching his naked thigh. "Wow!" he says after a few moments. "That's what I love about the tube. You meet all sorts."

I sit down next to Brian, opposite the naked man. He has no shame about his nakedness. He is sitting there, sprawled out in his seat with his legs spread open as if being naked on the tube is the most natural thing in the world. It's not the sort of thing I want to have to look at this late in the day. And yes, I am looking. A naked man with his legs splayed is the sort of thing that draws the eye, no matter how much you want to look away. After a few moments I take off my jacket and throw it over to him. "Here," I say, "put this on."

Unfortunately it's only a short jacket, so when he hangs it over his shoulders and slides his one free arm into the sleeve, it does absolutely nothing to cover the parts that need covering. I turn to Brian to ask for his coat, but Brian is still angry with me.

"I'm not talking to you," he says, pouting.

"What? Why?"

"You know why." He refuses to look at me, stares deliberately away from me down the empty tube car.

"Okay," I say, "you don't have to talk to me, but give me your coat, will you? I want to cover this bloke up."

"My name's James," the naked man interrupts.

I turn to the naked man to acknowledge him. "Right," I say, "James . . ."

"But most people call me Jim. Or Jimmy. You know, depending how long they've known me."

I ignore him. "Come on, Brian, we're nearly there. All we have to do is make this last connection and we've done it. The last thing we want is for someone to stop the train because there's a naked man on it."

Brian turns to me angrily. "That's all you care about, isn't it? That man back there needed help, and all you're concerned about is your bloody tube journey."

"But he got help. There were two others . . ."

"That's not the point and you know it." He folds his arms petulantly for a few moments, and then, as an afterthought, rapidly takes off his coat and throws it over to the naked bloke, Jim, or Jimmy, or whatever the hell his name is. He does it all without so much as a glance in my direction, as if he's taken a firm decision that I no longer exist.

I stare at him for a while, but it doesn't get his attention, so eventually I give up. And besides, we're pulling into a station. I look at my watch, anxiously. It's now 11:40 and we're not even at Gunnersbury yet. I swallow cold saliva. We've got exactly three minutes to get to Richmond before the last train goes.

Chapter 57

11:40 PM—Gunnersbury–Richmond—District Line

I have a recurring dream where I'm running somewhere urgently, only something seems to be stopping me. The goal is up a very steep hill, and for some reason my limbs are too heavy for me to move properly. Looking down, I find that not only am I running uphill, I am also waist deep in molasses. I'm not running, after all, but *wading,* and slowly my arms and legs are beginning to stick . . .

That's what this bloody train feels like at the moment. I'm sure it's not really that bad, but compared to the hurry I'm in, it feels as though we're going at a snail's pace. Outside I see vague shapes passing—they seem to cling lazily to the scratched train windows, as if unwilling to let us pass them by. I can't help having the feeling that somehow Rolf's got a remote control pointed at our train, and he's just switched us into slow motion.

I remember the last time I was on this line, glorying in the rhythmical sound of the wheels on the tracks—*de-dum, de-dum, de-dum,* the sound went—and the very speed of the rhythm made me feel excited inside. Tonight, though, there is nothing exciting about the sound. *De . . . dum . . . de . . . dum . . . de . . . . dum.* It's like watching an excruciatingly hammy film—one of those old fifties westerns where the cowboy takes forever to die. That's what I imagine his heartbeat to sound like: *de . . . dum . . . de . . . . dum.*

It is 11:41—two minutes before the last train leaves Richmond for the City. I try to ignore the slowness of the train we're on, because I know there's nothing I can do about it—but it's no use. I can feel the seconds ticking away inside me. With every lazy clunk of the train wheels I want to scream—I have an urge to run up the carriages, through the connecting doors, and onwards along the train until I get to the driver's compartment, where I can bang violently on the door and beg the driver to speed up. But I don't. I just sit there, gripping the armrests of my seat until my knuckles go white. And all the while the train seems to be going slower and slower, as if the pace of running around since five o'clock this morning is getting to it—until, finally, in the middle of bloody nowhere, the train comes to a halt.

"What's happening!"

Jim looks up at me from between the lapels of my own jacket. "I think we've stopped."

"I know *that*—but why?"

He is annoyed by the curtness of my question. "How the hell should I know?"

I stand up and walk briskly to the doors, where I press my face against the glass to see if I can see up ahead to what's holding us up. The glass is cold against my cheek. I can't see anything—outside it is just dark.

"Oh, God," I say, "this can't be happening. Please tell me this isn't happening. We're nearly there."

"What's the time?" says Brian, apparently willing to talk to me again.

"Shit! It's eleven-forty-three. Shit!"

"Maybe the last train's got held up," he says. "They do that sometimes, you know, to give latecomers a last chance."

I know he's just trying to reassure me. The thought that tired LU staff, desperate to get home for the night, are going to give a stuff about people missing the last train seems absurdly optimistic to me. If anything, the opposite is more likely, and they'd do what anyone else who has to work late would do—let the train go ahead of schedule so they could clock off a few minutes early.

And besides, we are about to see something that will knock any such optimism on the head. With my face still close to the window I see it before the others. A train. A District Line train, coming in the opposite direction. I look at my watch again: 11:44.

It seems tonight the last train from Richmond is bang on time.

I don't know what to say. None of us know what to say. As the other train speeds past us, we all sit in silence, hardly daring to look at each other. It's virtually soul destroying to think that after all this time and effort, Brian and I seem to have fallen at the last hurdle.

The train passes, and still our own train does not move. We are stuck, welded to the rails. I look up at the others and utter a single, halfhearted word. "Fuck."

Brian tries to soothe me. "Andy, we don't know for sure that that *was* the last train."

"Yes," I agree quietly, "we don't know for sure." Although deep in our hearts we both know it probably was.

"We'll ask when the train gets to Richmond."

"Okay. We'll ask."

"And even if we have missed the last train, you'll still get your envelope. Once we find this bloke Bob, that is."

When our own train starts up again a few moments later, I find it impossible to work up any kind of enthusiasm. What's the point in being excited? I have only two items left to collect—but the fact that I can't finish the system off means I'm going to have to forfeit one of them. Not only that, but I'm still going to have to get into Central London somehow—something that's going to be pretty difficult now the last train has gone. Because whatever happens, I still have to try to catch Rachel before she gets on the Eurostar. Waterloo is a bloody long way from Richmond.

Eventually the train pulls into the terminus. We pick up our bags and make ready to leave. Jim seems unwilling to give us our coats back, but we manage to convince him to hand them over.

"Please leave me one," he whines. "I'm cold!"

"No way, mate," says Brian. "That's the only coat I own."

"Couldn't you at least lend it to me? I'll send it back to you, I promise."

I look at him shivering. "What the hell," I say, flinging my jacket back onto his shoulders. "Have it. I've lost everything else today—what's a jacket?"

The car doors open, and Brian and I step out onto the platform. There are no station attendants to be seen, so we wander up towards the exit to see if we can find someone who can tell us who the mysterious Bob is. We wander to the end of the platform, through the barriers, and up the steps to the ticket office. It's a proper station here, big and airy and spacious, with a lovely high ceiling—I'd stop and admire it if I were here any other day. But today I just can't find it in me to care.

By the ticket office there is a man in a London Underground uniform looking restless. It's the end of the night. He wants to get home. He eyes us impatiently as we approach, ready to check our tickets, and seems surprised when we talk to him.

"Hello," I say, "do you have anyone at this station called Bob?"

He looks at me suspiciously. "Who's asking?"

"My name's Andy. A friend of mine left an envelope for me with someone called Bob, so I'm looking for him."

He smiles suddenly. "Oh! So you're Rolf's friend! Why didn't you say so straightaway?" Reaching into his jacket pocket, he pulls out a green envelope and hands it to me.

I take it from him. Inside the envelope I find my honeymoon reservations. Two weeks in a hotel in Antigua—two glorious weeks that I now won't be able to take, because of a District Line train that was too bloody slow to meet its connection. It's enough to make you cry.

Alongside my honeymoon reservations is a note from Rolf, which reads:

Meet me on Eastbound platform Monument, 12ish, for last envelope.

Bob leans forward to read the note over my shoulder. "Rolf told me what you're doing," he says. "I think it's amazing. It's something I've always wanted to do myself, only I never seem to get round to it. You know how it is."

"Yeah, well," I say, "it's not all it's cracked up to be."

"Still, you're nearly finished, eh? Must be a relief to get it all over with."

"I suppose so. If I hadn't missed the last bloody train."

The ticket inspector looks at me curiously. "Missed the last train?" he says. "I don't follow you."

"The eleven-forty-three back to town. I just saw it leave."

"No, that was the eleven-forty to Earl's Court. The eleven-forty-three is still at the platform. Running a bit late—as usual."

"But . . . but . . ." All of a sudden I'm stammering. "But I've just come from downstairs—there aren't any trains at the platform."

"Yes, there are," says the ticket inspector, pointing. "There."

I look round. "But that's the train I just got off . . ."

He smiles at us sarcastically. "Well, you'd better get back on it, then, hadn't you?"

Brian and I look at each other for a split second, the realization hitting us simultaneously—our train doesn't terminate here, after all; it turns round and goes back again. We were on the right train all along.

In a moment we are tearing our way back to the staircase, terrified the train will leave without us. It's understandable, our fear—this train was due to leave several minutes ago. Without a thought for caution, we hurl ourselves towards the platform, scrambling down the stairs three at a time and falling over ourselves as we tumble into the train.

But as it turns out, we don't really have to run, because the train doors don't end up closing for a good thirty seconds after we're inside the car. But it still feels like a narrow escape. And besides, it takes that long for it to sink in—we've made it. This is our last train of the day. And now, providing there isn't an earthquake or something, we should get to Monument in perfect time.

In fact, there is only one problem left. Jimmy.

Chapter 58

11:47 PM—Richmond–Kew Gardens—District Line

I knew he'd want to pull the emergency handle as soon as the train started moving again. I mean, making the journey from Upminster to Richmond in the nude *once* is bad enough—no one in his right mind would want to go back and do it all again. Even as Brian and I run down the carriages and through connecting doors, I know we'll be too late. The train seems to be moving fine—in fact, it's going quite fast—but I know that if Jim has pulled the lever while the train is in full motion, then the driver won't stop until we're at the next station. That means that Brian and I have to get to him before the train reaches Kew Gardens.

We race down the train, bundling our stuff between one carriage and the next. It's a dangerous thing to do, this. As we step through the connecting doors, we can see the ground racing away beneath us—one slip and we're dog meat. But it's kind of exciting too. I've never done this before—leapt between carriages on a fast-moving train, the wind tugging at my hair and clothes. It's the sort of thing only drunk football hooligans do, or schoolkids messing around while the rest of the carriage watches and tuts their tongues.

We make it to Jim's carriage just as the train is slowing down to pull into Kew Gardens. He is standing up, still wearing my jacket slung over his shoulders, still naked from the waist down, still cuffed to the handrail.

When he sees us, he is furious. "You!" he shouts. "You told me the train was going to stop! You told me someone would come and sort me out! And now I'm going back the way I came! I'm getting married tomorrow, for Christ's sake . . ."

I have to stop him, because the train is entering the station now. "I'm sorry," I interrupt. "I'm sorry, I really didn't know. Now you've got to sit down and cover yourself up . . ."

"I will *not* sit down! I've been sitting down for hours. I want to stand up. I want to go home!"

"And you will—but first I've got to get to Monument Station. Everything depends on it."

"But what about me? You're not the only one who's getting married tomorrow . . ."

"I know . . ." I say, trying to calm him down.

"My wedding's just as important as yours! I have to go home!"

"And you will, I promise. I'll make sure you get out of this, just as soon as we get to Monument. Trust me."

"Why on earth should I trust you?"

"I gave you my coat, didn't I?"

He looks down at the jacket, barely covering his chest. "Oh, yes," he says quietly. "I suppose you did."

"Well, there you go, then! How about I do you a deal? You can keep my jacket if you just let me stay on the train until Monument. Once we get there I'll even pull the emergency handle for you."

"I just want to get these handcuffs off and go home," he says indignantly. But as he does so he looks down, avoiding my eyes, and I can tell there's still a chance he might give in.

"What do you say? Will you trust me?"

No answer.

I put my hand on his shoulder. "Please . . . ?"

By the time a London Underground official comes to investigate the emergency alarm, Jim is wearing Brian's jacket once more over his legs. With the help of Brian's Swiss Army knife I have torn the sleeve of my jacket lengthways so that we could drape it over Jim's handcuffed arm and make it look as though he is wearing the damn thing properly. We have tied Brian's grubby handkerchief round Jim's wrist and the handrail to hide the handcuffs. The only thing we haven't been able to do is cover up Jim's feet, which are still as bare as the day he was born. We just have to hope that the official doesn't notice.

As the LU man enters, I am sitting beside Jim, holding the edges of the coat down round his legs—and Brian has gone to sit further down the carriage in an attempt to look as though he is not with us.

"Okay," says the official, "which one of you pulled the handle?"

"It wasn't us," I say, "honest."

"Not you?" He sneers. "So who was it, then?"

"I don't know. Some kid. He ran down the train after he did it." I point towards the end of the carriage. "That way."

The official looks from me to Jim and back again before he notices Brian further down the car. "Did you see this kid?" he calls over to him.

"Yes. He couldn't have been more than fourteen. Shouldn't be out this late."

The official turns back to me and Jim. His eyes travel down the length of Jim's body—the torn jacket, the handkerchief round his wrist, the coat over his knees . . . and his bare feet.

"Do you often walk around without any shoes on?" he says.

"Er . . ." says Jim, glancing at me briefly, "er . . . yeah."

"Why?"

"Good for the circulation," I say quickly, "isn't it, Jim? Gets the blood flowing." I look down at my own shoes. "I'd do it myself," I say, "only I've got verrucas."

"Verrucas?"

"Yes. Very contagious. I wouldn't want to give them to anyone else who might be walking around barefoot—you know, children. Or dogs."

Involuntary I find myself wincing. *Dogs.* What the hell had made me say that?

The official's eyes narrow at me, suspiciously. "You realize there's a fine for pulling the emergency lever without good reason, don't you, sir?"

"That's what we told the kid," says Brian.

"Yeah," I say, "I suppose that's why he ran away."

"Yes," adds Jim, unhelpfully, "that's right."

The official sighs heavily. "Well, seeing as there doesn't seem to be anything wrong, and seeing how it's after midnight, and this train is running late anyway, I suppose we'd better leave it there."

He turns to leave the carriage, but before he does, he says, "And if you see any more kids . . . or dogs . . . make sure they bloody well behave themselves."

As the doors shut behind him, we all sit for a moment in silence, unsure whether we have got away with it or not. And for a while that's all we do—just sit there. None of us says anything, not even Jim—we just look around at each other, uncertain what to do next. I feel as though I should be leaping out of my seat, planning for the next section of my journey—only there is no next section of my journey. Now that the official has gone, now that the train is moving once again, we are home free. For the first time today, there is actually nothing for us to do. I look over at Brian, then at Jim, and back to Brian again. After all we've been through today, it seems inconceivable that we have succeeded in our quest. But somehow, it looks as though we have.

I watch a smile grow on Brian's face. It spreads slowly, like an inkblot spreading on a piece of tissue paper. "Well," he says eventually, "I suppose this calls for a celebration." He digs into his bag and pulls out three cans of lager: he throws one to me and one to Jim, who fails to catch it with his one free hand, letting it bounce off his knees and onto the train floor. Brian opens the third himself.

Jim grins at us both broadly as he retrieves his can from the floor. "A celebration!" he says. "Great!" And then, less sure, "Just what exactly are we celebrating?"

"Our last train," I explain.

"What . . . you mean you've done it? Been to every single station?"

"By the time we reach Monument we will have."

"Far out! That's amazing!"

"Yes. Yes, it is amazing." I open my can of beer with a brief hiss and raise it to Brian, who nods back to me in acknowledgment.

Jim places his can between his knees. As he pulls the ring, a spray of beer shoots across the car onto the opposite window, and froth starts to flow like molten lava down the slopes of Brian's coat. "Whoa!" cries Jim, "who needs champagne!"

Brian and I give a cheer when this happens, and, encouraged by our applause, Jim places his thumb over the top of the can and shakes the beer up and down, sending a fountain of the stuff high into the air. Beer flies everywhere, onto the ceiling, onto the handrails, the chairs, the floor—tiny droplets form white specks on Brian's clothes and mine like pieces of confetti.

I feel a surge of happiness rising like bubbles within me, and suddenly something within me seems to burst. Before I know it I am on my feet, shaking my own can up and down, spraying liquid all around the carriage and dancing in the beery rain. The smell of hops is everywhere—the very air is sticky with it—and Jim and I are drenching ourselves in a spray of foamy happiness. Brian is on his feet now too, and we're embracing, and before we know it Jim's up with us as well, half his coverings sliding off him as he joins in with our embrace and our cheers: "We've won!" The carriage echoes with our joy, and if it weren't for the fact that Jim is chained to the handrail, I'm sure we'd be dancing—but as we can't, we jump up and down instead, calling out, "We've won! We've won!" And as we celebrate I can barely believe it myself, because we *have* won. *We* have won. We have *won.*

Chapter 59

11:53 PM—Kew Gardens–Westminster—District Line

"So," says Jim a while later, once we have sat down again and Brian has produced another couple of cans from his bottomless bag, unshaken-up this time, for us to drink, "what exactly have we won?"

I smile contentedly. "The world's largest collection of pre-1990s tube tickets."

"Wow! A collection of tickets. You two must be *nuts* about the tube!"

"Don't look at me!" laughs Brian. "He's the bloody trainspotter!"

I laugh too, but at the same time I feel I ought to explain. "The point is not that we won. It's that we didn't lose. If you knew Rolf, and if you knew what I had riding on this, you'd understand just how important that is."

We sit for a while without saying anything, and then Jim says, "I don't know—sometimes losing ends up being the best thing for you. You can never tell till after it's happened. Take me, for example—if I hadn't lost a game tonight, I wouldn't be here now. I wouldn't have met you two, and I'd have missed out on a story I'll be telling my grandchildren. So there you go. Sometimes losing's not so bad."

"Yeah," says Brian, "I've been meaning to ask you about that. How exactly *did* you end up, you know . . ."

Jim holds up his wrist, still handcuffed to the bar. "Like this? I told you, by losing a game."

"But what game?"

"Truth or dare."

Brian shares a look with me, and grins in disbelief. "You mean someone dared you to take off all your clothes and chain yourself to a train?"

"No! Somebody dared me to down ten shots in the pub, one after another." He looks at us both defensively. "Well it *is* my stag night. I was actually quite grateful that that was all I had to do. I mean, drinking ten shots wasn't that bad—they could have come up with something much more embarrassing."

I have to suppress a giggle, which, unfortunately, Jim notices. "Don't laugh! My girlfriend's going to think she's marrying a right nana when she finds out about this." He pauses. "I mean, my fiancée," he corrects himself. "My wife . . ."

"I don't understand," says Brian. "How does drinking ten shots mean you end up naked on a tube train?"

"Well, they were doubles, weren't they. Ten doubles—that's almost a pint. Not only that, but they were all different—you know, one double vodka, one double gin, one scotch . . . they even made me down some crème de menthe. The next thing I knew I was at some station, yodeling over the edge of the platform."

"Yodeling?" I say. "You mean . . ."

"Yeah, yawning in Technicolor. Parking a tiger. Of course, I was sick on my shirt. One of my mates suggested I take it off, and it seemed like a good idea at the time—then they got me to take the rest of my clothes off, which I did without even really thinking about it. Imagine that—they got me so drunk that not only did I *not* put up a fight, I actually did this to myself. Except the handcuffing, that is—*they* did that, as soon as this train came along."

"And then they lost the keys?"

"Yeah. Bastards. Still, like I said, it's not so bad in the end. If anything, being out in the fresh air has sobered me up. Which is a pretty good thing, seeing as how I've got to be at the registry office at ten o'clock." He falls silent for a moment, staring at the floor, before grinning suddenly to himself. "Here," he says, "Mel's having her hen night tonight as well. What do you suppose her mates have done to her?"

"Is that her name?" asks Brian. "Mel?"

"Yeah. Short for Melanie. Best thing that ever happened to me, she is."

"No last-minute jitters, then?"

"Not at all," he says—but it's a reflex action, saying that, and for a moment he stares at the window uncertainly, concentrating, as if he's trying to think of a good reason to have doubts. But then he smiles again, having happily drawn a blank.

"So," he says to Brian, "are you married, then?"

"Divorced."

"Oh."

"Don't worry," says Brian. "I'm not going to give you the speech about how you shouldn't bother getting married. Just don't make the same mistakes I did, and you'll be fine."

"God, I hope so."

"You see," Brian continues, "I spent my whole time working—you know, so that we could afford to have nice things. But, of course, because I spent so much time at work I didn't have much time left for my wife. What I didn't realize was that she didn't really care about having nice things. All she really wanted was having someone around to talk to. And as I wasn't around, well, she went elsewhere."

"Oh," says Jim, "I'm sorry . . ."

"It's all right, it was years ago now. I've had plenty of time to get over it. Or at least, plenty of time to think about it, anyway." He glances at me, briefly, and takes a large swig at his beer can. "You see, marriage is like a garden: it needs lots of attention. If you give your marriage the attention it needs, then it stays beautiful and lovely, and it's a pleasure to be in. But once you get busy doing other things, and you start to let things go . . . well, then it just seems like hard work. I spent so much time worrying about work, and bills, and stuff like that, that my wife started to feel neglected. Eventually she started being pissed off. When your wife's permanently pissed off with you, you know you're in trouble."

It's my turn to take a swig of beer. Brian is directing all this at Jim, but I'm sure he knows that everything he says can equally be applied to me. I can't help thinking that he's talking like this on purpose.

"So," says Jim, "have you got any tips for a novice like me on how to have a good marriage?"

"Yes, as a matter of fact I do." Brian leans forward, as if about to impart some priceless information. "The secret with women," he says, "is remembering stuff. That's where I fell down. You see, women aren't like blokes—they get all het up about days in the calendar: their birthday, their mother's birthday, their sister's dog's birthday, Valentine's Day . . . anniversaries. The list's endless. If you always remember stuff like that, they take it for granted that you must care about them, and so they don't go all funny and insecure on you."

"Oh, dear," says Jim. "I've got a *terrible* memory!"

"Well, do you tell your fiancée you love her?"

"'Course I do," says Jim. "All the time."

"But do you *show* her you love her. Do you buy her flowers? Do you rub her feet when she's tired?"

"Sometimes." Jim looks unsure. "Sometimes I make tea for her when she's too tired to get up."

Brian smiles. "Well, you're all right, then. If you're still doing stuff like that in thirty years' time, then you're on the right track."

I get an image in my head of Jim and his wife-to-be in thirty years' time, sitting naked in a pair of rocking chairs going through their wedding photos together. It's a cliché, I know, a ready-formed image I probably picked up from some advert on television (apart from the naked part, of course—somehow I can't imagine what Jim would look like with clothes on)—but I can't help feeling a little moved at the thought. Because that's what *I* want. Jesus, isn't that what we all want?—a wife, a home, a fat cat asleep in front of your log fire. And to die of a heart attack at the age of ninety while having wild passionate sex with the woman you love. If the alternative is an eternity of learning tube timetables, I know which one I'd choose.

I find myself wishing Jim and his new wife all the luck in the world. I also find myself suddenly talking, which is strange, because I had no real urge to say anything. It's almost as if I'm talking to myself, uttering my thoughts out loud. "I told Rachel I loved her tonight," I say. "In a phone box."

"Oh, yeah?" says Jim enthusiastically. "And what did she say?"

"Nothing. She just wanted me to come home."

"Weh-heh! You know what that means, don't you!"

"No," I say indignantly. "And anyway, I couldn't go home."

"You *couldn't?* Jesus, how can you miss an opportunity like that?"

I sigh heavily. "Well, I had to, didn't I? I had to win this bloody bet."

"Why?" Jim looks at me, confused. "I mean, I still don't understand what's so important about this bet. So you've won a bunch of train tickets—what would have happened if you'd lost?"

"I would have lost Rachel, that's what. If I don't finish the system, Rolf won't give me my Eurostar tickets—and without a ticket, I can't get on the train. Effectively, I've bet my wedding on this."

Jim looks thoughtfully at his can of lager. "Wow!" he says. "How did you explain *that* one to your girlfriend?"

"I didn't. She would have killed me."

"So what did you say to her?"

"I just told her I was doing it for the sake of it. You know, for the challenge. Of course, she wasn't exactly happy about that either, but at least I think she'll forgive me. And that's the problem."

I look up at my two companions. Jim seems confused, but Brian has sunk back into his seat and is smiling gently at me, as if he knows exactly what I'm going to say.

"The problem is that I don't *deserve* forgiveness. How can I stand up tomorrow and make all those vows to Rachel knowing that I've spent the whole of today lying to her? She thinks I'm out playing some stupid childish game with Rolf. If she knew what's really going on—if she knew I've gambled our entire future together—well, she'd never forgive me for that. I don't know what's worse, lying to her or making the bet in the first place."

Jim puts his beer down. "Don't be too hard on yourself, mate. At least you've won your bet, so there's no real harm done."

"Yes," I say, "but there could have been. And now I've got to think of some way I can make it up to her."

Jim seems temporarily to have run out of things to say, but Brian leans forward and puts a hand on my shoulder. "All in good time, son," he says. "All in good time."

For a while this is how we sit, me with my head in my hands, Brian gently patting my shoulder—and Jim watching us as he alternately plays with the chain of his handcuff and sips his can of beer. He seems uncomfortable with the atmosphere, as if my guilt is making him nervous. I can feel him fidgeting beside me, jittering his knee up and down in time with the wheels of the train. Eventually he can't contain his discomfort any longer.

"Dear, oh, dear," he says, overcheerfully, "this is getting far too serious. We're supposed to be celebrating, remember? Come on, let's play a game."

Brian sits up, and takes his hand off my shoulder. "That's a good idea," he says. "What sort of game d'you have in mind?"

"How about *truth or dare* again?"

Brian snorts loudly. "Yeah right! What could we possibly dare *you* that would be worse than sitting naked on the tube?"

"Okay, how about another game, then? What's that game they play on Radio 4—you know, that nonsense game, the one that's named after that tube station?"

"You mean Mornington Crescent?" asks Brian.

"Yeah. What are the rules again?"

I feel a sudden tightening in my chest. It's a painful sensation, like the feeling you get when unexpectedly confronted with some long forgotten fear, and it makes me want to run away. It makes me want to cry out—but instead, all I can manage is a murmur: "Mornington Crescent!"

"That's right," says Jim, turning to me. "Do *you* remember the rules?"

"I thought the whole point was that there weren't any," says Brian.

I grab my bag, frantically. "Mornington Crescent!"

"Are you all right?" asks Brian, catching the urgency in my voice.

I pull out my crumpled A4 blowup of the tube map and hold it up to the light. There it is, in North London, stuck between Camden Town and Euston. Mornington fucking Crescent. I don't believe it. How can I have been so stupid?

Chapter 60

12:25 AM—Westminster–Monument—District Line

All day long I have been crossing off stations on my enlarged tube map. I've been meticulous about it—each time we arrive at another stop, I get out my red marker and put a neat red cross through the station name. That way, I tell myself, I can make sure I don't miss any. With all the running around today, the last thing I need to do is to make a basic mistake like forgetting one of the stations.

The only problem is this: one of the stations was already crossed off before I even started this morning. On the 1997 map I'm using, Mornington Crescent comes with two neat red lines through its name, because the station was closed for rebuilding at the time the map was published. As a consequence, when I glance at the sheet of paper, it's easy to think that I've already been there. When Brian mentioned the station's name a few seconds ago, something inside me froze. As I hold my crumpled map up to the light now, my fear is confirmed: the red cross through the tube stop has not been made by a marker, it is printed. In other words, I haven't been there. Through my own sheer stupidity, I have missed Mornington Crescent.

"Maybe he won't notice," says Jim. "I mean, how's he going to know whether you've been there or not?"

"Oh, he'll know," I say. "Don't ask me how—he just will."

"But surely he'll give you your tickets, anyway. You missed one station—so what? You've still done pretty well."

"Yes, but I'm afraid that in Rolf's book 'pretty well' just isn't good enough."

"But this is your wedding we're talking about here. Surely he'll . . . surely . . ."

He doesn't finish his sentence. I think he must have cottoned on to what Rolf's like—a man who just won't do things by half measures. There are no *almosts* involved with him—either you are a tube enthusiast or you're not, either you go to a station, or you don't. And if you gamble something, you can't pull out at the last minute just because it looks as though you're going to lose. A bet's a bet—especially amongst trainspotters.

While our train rumbles through Embankment and on towards Temple, we all sit staring glumly at the puddles of beer that have accumulated on the floor of the carriage. There doesn't seem much reason to celebrate now. What seemed like an amazing triumph ten minutes ago has turned into a costly and very disappointing failure. And at the center of it all is Rolf. I can almost imagine him now, standing at Monument Station, waiting for us, laughing.

"If he's going to be at the station, I reckon we should just *take* the tickets off him," says Brian after a while. "And if he doesn't want to give them to us, we should use force."

"Great," I say, "is that what you do with your friends, then? Duff them up?"

"Well, he's not exactly been much of a friend to you today, has he? And anyway, who said anything about duffing him up?"

I am about to ask Brian what *else* he means by "using force," when I'm interrupted by Jim, asking me a question.

"I don't want to sound ignorant," he says, "but don't you still have time to get to Mornington Crescent if you want to? I mean, the last Northern Line train doesn't go for a while, does it?"

"You're right," I say, "but what would be the point?"

"To win back your Eurostar tickets. To finish the system."

"To hell with the system. The Eurostar goes at one o'clock—if I were to go all the way back up to Mornington Crescent, there's no way I'd have time to catch it."

"Well, in that case"—he pauses, wracking his brains for me—"can't you buy yourself a new ticket?"

"No chance—this nighttime Eurostar is a one-off. It's been booked up for months."

Jim shrugs his shoulders. "In that case, I agree with Brian—there's only one thing left to do. You should find your mate and duff him up."

Our train carries on, oblivious to the misery of the three of us sitting inside it. We are almost at Monument now. I look down at my bag full of used Kodak Fun cameras, and smile wryly—what use is an *almost*-complete set of pictures of Underground stations? I wonder if I'll ever be able to find a use for them after Rachel has thrown me out. Perhaps I could make a scrapbook for myself, a shrine to my own stupidity.

As we approach Monument Station, Jim turns to me one final time.

"It's coming up for your stop," he says.

"Yes, I know."

"I'm going to pull the emergency handle again once you get off. You know, get myself sorted out. For tomorrow. There's just one thing I wanted to ask: Can I still take your jacket? I'll bring it back to you, if you give me your address."

I tear off a piece of my tube map and scribble my address on the back of it. "Good luck," I say, "with the wedding and everything."

"Yeah, thanks, and you." He places my address in the top pocket of the jacket. "Oh, and, Andy . . ."

"Yes?"

"You will let me know how it all turns out, won't you? When I bring the jacket back? I hate not knowing the end of a good story."

"Yes," I say. "I'll let you know."

But as the train pulls up at Monument, right on schedule, just before half past midnight, I already know how this story is going to end. There's going to be a lot of groveling to do. I'm going to have to grovel to Rolf, for a start, and beg him to let me have the tickets, even though I know it will be useless because there's no one I know with a harder heart than Rolf. And facing Rachel is another matter. If I ever manage to catch up with her, I'm going to have to grovel to her as well. I'm going to have to let her know exactly what has been going on today. And I'm going to have to tell her that she was right, that I *am* nothing but a sad and inadequate trainspotter, after all—and a second-rate one at that, a failure.

As I get off the train I form a crude plan in my mind. Basically, I'm going to have to get those tickets off Rolf somehow. I'll start by asking him nicely, and if that doesn't work, maybe I'll try bartering with him. I'm sure I must have something Rolf wants, some piece of tube memorabilia he'll be willing to swap for my tickets—even a tattered copy of an old tube map should be more valuable to Rolf than a couple of Eurostar tickets he won't even use. I still have Rolf's safe-deposit key, which I could refuse to give back to him. And if all else fails, I might have to resort to Brian's duffing-up plan, after all. Whatever happens I have to get the tickets out of him quickly because it's already twelve-thirty, and half an hour to get from here to Waterloo Station at this time of night is cutting it just a little bit fine.

As Brian and I step onto the platform at Monument, this is what I intend to do—get the tickets from Rolf by whatever means necessary, whether it be persuasion, trade, or even violence. There is only one problem with the plan. A quick look up and down the platform shows it's completely empty. Rolf is nowhere to be seen.

"Maybe he's on the westbound platform?" Brian suggests.

I pull out the note he left for us at Richmond. "Nope," I say, "he quite clearly says he'll be on the eastbound."

"Well, he's not bloody here, is he?"

Together we stride towards the exit stairs. I can see a station attendant coming down them now and talking briskly into his radio—Jim must have gone ahead and pulled the emergency lever. But we don't have time to stay and watch.

We pass the station attendant and hurry on to the stairs. It is there that we find an explanation for Rolf's absence. Stuck on the wall, taped up with electrician's tape, is a note written in Rolf's unmistakable handwriting. It reads:

Fed up with waiting. Gone home. R

"Fed up with waiting!" I say, incredulous."Fed up with *waiting!* The bastard!"

"He can't have been waiting that long. He was only supposed to meet us half an hour ago."

"The bastard!" I repeat. "He's not fed up with waiting at all. He just wanted to piss off with my tickets! The total, utter bastard!"

"So what are we going to do?"

"He must have known I'd missed out Mornington Crescent, and so he couldn't be bothered to wait. I'm going to bloody kill him when I see him . . . !"

"Andy," Brian interrupts, putting his hand on my shoulder, "listen to me. What are we going to do?"

I stare back at him blankly, because for the first time today neither of us has an answer. I'm going to miss the train to Paris, that's for certain—without a ticket they won't even let me on the platform. And Rachel will go without me; I have no illusions about that. I honestly can't see any way out of it.

For a brief moment a perverse thought enters my head: in the face of all this failure, there is still one thing I could win, and that is my bet with Rolf. I have already lost everything else—Rachel, our wedding, our future—everything that could possibly matter to me. But, if I wanted to, I could still make it to Mornington Crescent. I could still, if I wanted to, prove to my sad, trainspotter friends that I am El Tube Supremo—a man who can't get married, but who can conquer the Underground any day of the week.

I stare into Brian's tired, tramp's eyes, and his question remains. What are we going to do? Now, that is all that matters. What *are* we going to do?

Chapter 61

12:56 AM—Eurostar platforms, Waterloo International Terminal

Outside, in the darkness, it begins to rain. It starts out in the west of the city, in Uxbridge and Hillingdon, but quickly begins to move its way eastwards. It pours relentlessly on the roof of the station house at Perivale, streaming down its crescent-shaped facade and through a broken pane in the 1920s glass frontage. It sweeps on towards Acton, Shepherd's Bush, and Latimer Road, where it gushes down the viaduct in a miniature torrent before draining away to the road below. Soon it reaches the West End and the City, where it drums on the roofs of the cut-and-cover stations, splashes heavily on exposed tracks, and leaves streaks of water on the windows of the last trains as they hurry in and out of the short tunnels on their way to their depots for the night. Even the deep-level stations begin to feel it, as the underground rivers start to swell, and the now empty stations begin to hum faintly with the sound of the pumps draining the extra thousands of gallons harmlessly away.

Out in Richmond it falls on the hapless head of Bob the ticket inspector as he hurries from the station wrapped up in his overcoat.

In Kingsbury it soaks through the Gucci shoes of the beautiful Italian woman where she's left them on the back porch of her new lover's home. At Cockfosters the obese station supervisor, who forgot to bring his coat to work, curses as he locks the station gates behind him and runs to his car. It pours all over carriages 690 and 891 where they sit in Northfields depot, and it drips steadily on the chocolate machine at Upminster Station through a tiny but expanding crack in the roof over the platform. And at Morden, right at the southernmost tip of the tube map, it forms little streams, which trickle under the canopy, forcing the young homeless boy who sits there to huddle further back against the station wall.

Rachel can see the rain through the domed glass roof of the Eurostar platforms at Waterloo, but she can't hear it. The noise of the train engines, warming up for the nighttime journey to Paris, cut out most other sound; and besides, the impressive domed glass roof with its blue metal supports probably has some built-in soundproofing to prevent the sound of the elements outside from coming through.

In fact, the only reason Rachel notices the rain at all is because her eyes are well and truly peeled. She has been looking all around her for the past fifteen minutes, hoping with increasing anxiety that Andy will appear somewhere on the platform. As a consequence, her powers of observation are sharpened. With each passing moment she sees more and more, details she has no interest in, but which she takes in anyway while she scans the station for her fiancé.

She is surrounded by luggage—not only hers, but his. Every now and then she sits down on the edge of a suitcase, but feeling restless, stands up again. Anyone looking on would be able to see that she's nervous. Anyone would be able to tell she's waiting for her lover—perhaps a married man she's about to embark on an illicit affair with, or even a casual acquaintance with whom she has had a brief but sweet encounter which she hopes will develop into something further. Whoever it might be, it is obvious that the man she's waiting for is important to her. And from the desperation on her face it is also obvious, to anyone looking on, that she has been stood up.

She glances at her watch: just over three minutes to go. The Eurostar train stands before her, its doors beckoning. She should really have got on by now, found their cabin, stowed the suitcases—but for some reason she wants to see Andy coming down the platform before she does so. She tells herself that she's waiting here out of principle: why should she carry all the bags on by herself?—she has done everything else today; it's Andy's turn to do something. But really all she wants to do is reassure herself that he is coming, and deep down she knows this.

She looks at her watch again. She's getting worried now. She sets about moving the bags over to the edge of the platform by the doors of the train, so that she can haul them in at the last minute if need be—but then she finds she is in the way of some people who want to embark. She spends the next few moments shuffling her bags to one side so that the newcomers can get on. Once she has finished, she looks up at them. They are a couple. A young couple, holding hands.

Everywhere Rachel looks there are people hurrying for the train. Not *serious* hurrying of the sort you find at rush hour, where businessmen and little old ladies alike sprint down platforms in panic, puffing and red-faced from the unaccustomed exercise. No, this is another sort of hurrying. This is people rushing because they are excited, because they are about to go on a journey and they can't wait for it to begin. This is groups of holidaymakers, on vacation already, drunk on the expectation of the days to come. Or couples, on romantic weekend breaks, impatient for the privacy of their couchettes.

Oh, *where* is Andy? Why is he doing this to her? She hasn't seen him all day—he could at least bother to turn up for their train. It is supposed to be romantic, going to Paris like this together on a night train—it is supposed to be symbolic of what they are about to do, embarking on a new life together. But all the romance has been knocked out of her. She is angry. She has been waiting for Andy all day, and she refuses to wait for him any longer. She meant what she said on the phone earlier. If he doesn't turn up, she's going without him.

She glances at her watch again, her anxiety, her frustration and anger, growing. The time is 12:58½. Damn Andy and his big ideas! She always knew that leaving for Paris the night before their wedding would be cutting it too fine. She wanted to catch a train this afternoon, to give them time to prepare once they'd got there, but then Andy suggested this limited overnight journey, and it seemed so romantic she got carried away. She should have listened to her doubts. There's nothing romantic about waiting on a platform by yourself. There's nothing romantic about missing your wedding because your partner has left everything too late.

She decides she'll give him thirty more seconds, and if he doesn't appear on the platform, she'll start loading all the luggage onto the train herself. She is beginning to feel betrayed again, like she has lost out to Andy's mistress—that whore, the tube. Perhaps she should avenge herself. Perhaps she should just get on the train now, wander along the carriages and sleep with the first single man she comes across. There's bound to be some young businessman going to Paris for a meeting in the morning, or perhaps an older man, with rough hands and Gauloises on his breath, some French cologne she won't be able to mask when she stands at the altar in the morning. Perhaps she'll do this, so that she can hold her head up as she speaks her vows, because she won't have been walked on, after all, despite Andy's best efforts.

Twelve-fifty-nine arrives. She looks down at her two large bags and her suitcase: she'll easily be able to haul them onto the train at the last moment. She'll leave it another few seconds before she writes Andy off.

God, she'd hate to think what her friends would say if they ever found out Andy has stood her up at the station. Patrice *told* her it was bad luck to spend the night with Andy on the eve of their wedding day. Esther the dressmaker said the same thing—don't spend the night before your wedding with the groom. It seems that when it comes to weddings, the whole world becomes suddenly superstitious. Well, she has news for them all. It doesn't look like she's going to have the luxury of bad luck, after all. Thirty seconds to go, and her husband-to-be is nowhere in sight.

Is this last-minute jitters, then? Is jilting her at the station platform merely a rehearsal for a more dramatic betrayal tomorrow morning? Or is this Andy's way of stamping his authority on their marriage right from the very beginning: keep the bitch waiting, make sure she gets used to it. Whatever it is, she isn't having any of it. It is time to make up her mind now. Either she's going or she's staying.

She hears the engines start up with a roar which sends tiny shudders along the length of the train. A guard is walking along the platform towards her, checking the train one final time before it departs. She is the only passenger still on the platform. All the doors are shut but her own. The guard has the whistle in his mouth. This is it—the train is leaving.

With one final look down the empty platform, she gives a sad, resigned sigh and reaches down for the bags. Slinging the holdalls over her shoulder, she clutches the handle of the suitcase in her hand and steps towards the door of the train.

Outside the rain increases. At the side of the station where the taxis gather to pick up arriving passengers, it runs in torrents, but none of it runs in towards the platforms, choosing instead to follow the path of least resistance round the curve of the building and down towards the river. In the road it forms fields of tiny splashes like flowers, each one dying almost instantly, only to be replaced by a hundred more. It hammers on the roof of the Eurostar platforms, but the glass is hard and new, and not even the slightest drop can penetrate. And gradually, as the train finally pulls out from beneath its glass and metal dome, the rain begins to die away.

Chapter 62

12:57 AM—Waterloo–Northern Line and Mainline Station

By the time my tube pulls in at Waterloo underground, I'm starting to panic. My heart is pounding, and I'm beginning to pant like I've just done a sprint. I think I'm getting high on all the excess oxygen, because I'm getting slightly dizzy, which is just having the effect of making me panic even more. As the train decelerates, I start hitting the door release button even before we stop, blind to the fact that it makes no difference, that the doors will open automatically anyway. I can't help it because I'm itching to get out. It is 12:57. I have three minutes before the Eurostar departs.

As soon as the doors begin to slide open, I am through them, tearing along the platform, running up the stairs, through the corridor to the escalators. I go faster than I ever have done today—it is as though I have been newly charged, filled up with a fresh and unstoppable energy. And as I run, as I hurry from steps to corridor to escalators, I feel strangely free. Brian is not with me. I have no maps, no instructions from Rolf, no fun cameras—I have left them all behind. I don't even have my jacket, because I've given that to naked Jim, and I have abandoned my bet, because it is no longer important. All that is important is getting to the Eurostar train before it leaves.

For some reason the escalators are not working, so I have to scramble up them, checking my stride at the initial steps which vary in height from the others. It's a long staircase—about the same length as those at Charing Cross and Leicester Square—and it is only my excess of adrenaline that takes me all the way to the top. Once there I throw myself forward to the gates. I don't have time to fumble for my tube ticket, so I clamber clumsily onto the top of the barrier and then jump down on the other side, ignoring the shouts of the single ticket inspector standing guard.

There is a clock above the ticket machines, and a glance at it as I rush past sends my heart through the roof of my mouth. Although my own watch says I still have a minute or two to go, this clock claims it is one AM exactly. But I don't have time to worry about this, because there is no telling what is right and what is wrong until I make it to the train itself. Racing through the ticket hall to the exit marked "Eurostar departures," I bundle my way up a last set of escalators and out into the vast open space of the mainline station on the south bank of the river.

When I get there I find that the station is almost completely empty. I've never been to the Eurostar platforms before, and so for the first time since Brian took me on that wild-goose chase at Northwick Park, I feel unsure of where to go. There are over twenty-five platforms at Waterloo—I haven't the faintest idea which one is the right one.

In desperation I look all round me, searching for a sign to point me in the right direction. But for some inexplicable reason, there isn't one. No signs, no symbols, no official to ask. How the hell am I supposed to find this place?

Spying a cleaner sweeping the floor in front of Burger King about fifty yards away, I call over to him.

"Oi, mate! Eurostar! Which way?"

The man points behind me to an unmarked escalator, this one going down, and at once I realize my mistake. The entrance to the Eurostar terminus is actually right beside me—in my panic I have been blind to it. Typical, isn't it? It's only when you're really in a hurry that you can't work out where the hell you're going.

Without waiting to thank the cleaner, I tear off down the escalator and find myself in a small additional station concourse, set out a bit like an airline departure lounge. In front of me is a row of ticket barriers with a sign above them saying "Waterloo International." I suddenly remember that I have no means of getting through, that my tickets are somewhere in North London, sitting in a green envelope in Rolf's pocket. And any hopes I had of leaping the barriers or somehow bundling through unnoticed are quickly dashed. There are no less than five inspectors guarding the entrance. As far as I can see, I am the only passenger they have to keep an eye on.

Swallowing quickly, I stride over to the first of the inspectors.

"Has the Eurostar left yet?"

"You'd better hurry," he says briskly, "it's going any second."

"Christ! I've got to get on that train!"

I make a lunge towards the gates, but the inspector bars my way with his hand. "Er, can I see your ticket, sir?" he asks.

"Not enough time," I say, trying my best to hurry past him.

"I'm afraid I can't let you through until I've seen your ticket. And your passport, for that matter."

"But I don't have my ticket . . ." I begin.

"Then I'm afraid you can't come through."

"No, you don't understand. I'm getting married in the morning in Paris. I *have* to be on that train."

"I'm sorry, sir, you can't come through without a ticket."

"But my wife-to-be is on that train!"

"I'm sorry, sir . . ."

It's like listening to a scratched record. I'm getting desperate.

"Look, I'm an EU citizen," I say, waving my passport in his face. "I have to be on that train. I don't have a ticket because"—mentally I fumble around, trying to find a suitable excuse—"because my wife has them! That's right, my wife has them. And she is through there, on the train, waiting!"

He looks decidedly uncomfortable for a few moments before agreeing to let me through, on the condition that he accompanies me onto the platforms. But as he lets me through the gates, I don't hang around for him. Let him chase me if he wants. I've got a train to catch, and that's all that matters.

I don't notice much else as I run through the departure lounge, past waiting rooms and coffee stands that have long since closed their shutters. I certainly don't pay any attention to the ticket inspector, who keeps calling out as he struggles to keep up with me. I am focused on finding the stairs to the platforms, and when I do I take them three at a time. I can hardly believe that I'm here, stumbling up the escalator to catch my last train of the day—this special, for-a-limited-period-only, night train to Paris that I have been longing to catch ever since today began. And at last I am out in the open, bursting out of the ground beneath the great glass dome of the Eurostar terminal, and rushing out onto the enormous modern platforms. My heart is exploding with the adrenaline that is rushing round my system, and I am breathing so fast I can barely control it.

But no matter how fast I run, no matter how fast I breathe, it doesn't make any difference. I am too late. Despite all my best efforts—my running up escalators, leaping over barriers, lying to ticket inspectors—as I hit the Eurostar platforms I can tell straightaway that I am too late. Because as I run towards the right platform, I can see the train pulling out of the station. It is leaving the safety of the great glass dome even as I run forward, and accelerating away southwards in the direction of Paris. It has gone. The Eurostar has left without me.

Chapter 63

1:02 AM—Eurostar platforms, Waterloo International Terminal

Waterloo Station. Tube stop for the Bakerloo, Northern, and Jubilee Lines. Home of the old "Necropolis" railway and the "Drain" line. Central focus for trains on the South Bank. Eurostar departure point. Station interchange. Terminus.

It seems an appropriate place in which to fail. All about me is glass and blue-painted high-tensile metal: the new age of rail transport. Not citywide transport, like I have been traveling on all day; not even *country*wide transport, like the great trains of the nineteenth century, spreading out like a net from London through the industrial heartlands and out into the furthest corners of our island. No, this at last is a truly international railway—a railway which links Britain with the rest of Europe—the future. It's a future with all kinds of risks, all kinds of possibilities, but it's a future which seems to be moving on without me.

It is three minutes past one on the morning of the day that I'm getting married to Rachel. I *walk* along the platform at Waterloo. I *walk* past the one or two trains which have been left at the station, locked up for the night under the shelter of the great glass dome. I walk, alone, towards the place from which I would have embarked upon the Eurostar, with Rachel, bound for our new life together.

About halfway down the platform, sitting on the edge of a suitcase, is a solitary figure. She looks small, vulnerable, in these grand surroundings, and somehow out of place, like a mermaid washed up in a big city she doesn't understand. Or perhaps she understands it all too well. It is a place so vast and so busy that it is easy to lose yourself here by mistake. It is a place where people daily sacrifice the things that are important without even knowing that they are doing it. It is a place where everyone, almost without exception, is just a little bit insane. And here she is, sitting on a platform, alone, having just given up the chance for escape.

I walk slowly over, and sit down beside her on the suitcase.

"We missed the train," I say.

"Yeah," she says, "story of my life."

"Story of *our* lives."

We sit for a while, both of us staring down at the other two bags by our feet. One of them is open, as if she has just delved inside it to find something and hasn't bothered to zip it back up again. It lies like a burst sausage, displaying its insides unashamedly: socks, knickers, bras, moisturizer, tampons, cotton-wool buds, shampoo—a melange of personal items jumbled together without order or reason. The sight makes me feel slightly uncomfortable, like I'm intruding on something private.

"You said you'd go without me if I didn't turn up," I said, after a few moments.

"I know."

"Why didn't you?"

"I was going to. But then I remembered something my father

used to say to me when I was a girl: *Courage, tout n'est pas perdu.* It means, 'Don't give up on a lost cause.'"

She plays with the strap of her bag as she speaks, turning it over and over in her hand. Further down the platform the Eurostar official is standing, arms folded, keeping an eye on us.

"Actually, that's not quite true," she says. "I don't think you're a lost cause—not yet, anyway. And I don't give a toss what my father used to say. I was so pissed off with you when you didn't turn up that I was going to get on the train whatever happened. I just wanted to get out of here. And I wanted to teach you a lesson. But when it came down to it, I just couldn't."

"Why not? You had every right to."

"Well, what would be the point? We're getting married tomorrow." She looks at me for the first time since I sat down. "We *are* still getting married?"

"Yes," I say. "If you'll still have me."

"Don't be ridiculous—of course I'll still have you." She sounds irritated. "What a stupid thing to say."

I realize that the time has come to be repentant. After all, as far as Rachel is concerned, I have been a bit of a fool—running round the Underground all day without any proper explanation of what the hell I'm doing. If we had the time, if we were staying home in London, now would be the moment to start groveling. Now would be the time to explain the truth about my bet, to tell her how important our wedding is to me, how much I love her. But we are not staying in London. We are going to Paris, so these things will have to wait.

Standing up, I hold out my hand in front of Rachel. "Come on," I say, "let's go."

She stares at my hand blankly for a couple of seconds. "Where are we going?" she asks.

"To Paris," I say. "Where else?"

"But we've missed the last train."

"Then we'll go to the airport and see if we can catch a late flight."

"Can we do that?"

"I'm sure we can. Gatwick is open all night—there's bound to be a plane we can catch, standby. And if there isn't we'll think of something else."

Taking my hand, she pulls herself up beside me. We pick up the suitcase and the bags and wander down the platform towards the exit, still holding hands. It would be much easier to walk with our hands free, but neither of us wants to. There is something sincere about holding hands like this, like we're children again, best friends on a school outing together. And there is a softness in Rachel's fingers that I haven't felt in a long time.

"Is the Underground still open?" she asks, stepping closer beside me so that our arms brush each other while we walk.

"I don't know," I say, although somewhere deep down I probably do.

"We'll need to get to Victoria somehow and get a train to Gatwick. Maybe we should run—see if we can catch the last tube."

She says it innocently, and I am reminded that she has no idea how much running for trains I have done today. You've got to smile, really.

"I've got a better idea," I say.

I want to drop her hand and put my arm around her shoulders as we walk. I want to stop right here in the station concourse and kiss her. But I don't, because it's too soon. Instead I lead her outside, to the front of the station, where the rain is just about audible as it patters on the glass roof. And there, once I have put down the case I'm clutching, I hold out my hand to hail a black cab.

Chapter 64

With Rachel

I don't know how we are going to get to Paris, but I know we will. If there isn't a plane from Gatwick, perhaps there will be one from Heathrow, or one of the other London airports. Perhaps we can hire a car and catch a ferry across the Channel—not nearly as romantic as a night train, but practical, and there won't be any traffic at this time of night. Or perhaps we'll just take this taxi all the way there. Whatever we do, it hardly seems like a problem. The options are all there.

After today, after the struggle of racing between one line and another, the prospect of sitting in a cab for a while seems quite luxurious. I will enjoy leaning back into the spacious leather seats. I will enjoy the fact that someone else is doing the traveling for me, making the decisions, worrying over our route. Despite my failure today, I feel as though I have earned it.

And once we take off into the night, I will be free for the first time to do whatever I want. Perhaps I will tell Rachel all about my travels. Perhaps I will tell her about Brian and how he supported me, about our train derailment and our delays, about how we met naked Jim and my paranoia about Rolf. And perhaps, at last, I will even tell her about the bet, about all the things I staked and how I won them back, one by one. After all, I will have to tell her about it at some point.

But deep down I know I shan't tell her any of this, because now is not the time for talking. The past twenty-four hours has been stressful for both of us, and tomorrow will be a day not only of joy but of anxiety. I have a feeling that to talk about my journey on our way to the airport would be inappropriate. Now is not the time for explanations, apologies, justifications. Now is the time for gentleness.

Once the luggage is all loaded into the trunk, I tell the driver to take us to Gatwick Airport and, taking Rachel's hand once more, climb into the back of the cab. I feel like a teenager, still amazed by how soft and warm her fingers feel against mine, and it's like waking up from a dream—a troubled dream, filled with stress and missed opportunities. I feel fully conscious—more so than I have felt all day. At last my eyes are firmly and calmly fixed on what is really important to me, and for the first time in my life, I can truly say that I would be happy if I never saw another tube train again. I'm not just saying that. Tube fanatic or not, there are some moments when you have to take stock and realize exactly where your priorities lie.

As our cab pulls away from Waterloo Station, I kiss Rachel again, and settle back to enjoy our journey. Outside the rain continues as we roll through Kennington, Brixton, Streatham—it forms streaks across the windows of the car. Every now and then a streetlight drifts past the window, lighting up Rachel's face with an orange glow. She looks tired—tired but beautiful.

Gradually the clutter of shops and houses begins to fall away. Once past Croydon and Purley the road widens, and before long we are passing over the M25 and out of the confines of Greater

London. Concrete gives way to fields, buildings give way to wide open spaces. There are no more buildings, only trees and hedgerows. There are no more people. Rachel and I hold hands in the back of the cab, occasionally smile sleepily at one another, and watch as the Surrey countryside opens up before us, vast, and empty, and dark.

Epilogue

Willesden Green—1:30 AM

As Brian's cab pulled up on Willesden High Road, he was ready to drop. That final station had just about done it for him—he'd almost missed the last train to Mornington Crescent, and he'd had to run all the way just to make sure he got there in time. It was a good job that it was he who'd done it, and not Andy, because he'd only just made it—at the speed Andy ran he wouldn't have had a hope.

Of course, Brian hadn't really seen much point in going to Mornington Crescent tube station, anyway, not after it was too late to pick up their last envelope. But Andy had insisted. And he didn't see much point in being here in Willesden Green either, but again, Andy had insisted—and since this whole thing had been Andy's project in the first place, Brian didn't really see how he could refuse. So here he was, for Andy. He had Andy's bag of fun cameras. He had Andy's map and red pen. And in his hand he had a small key that Andy had thrust at him before he ran off to catch his train to Waterloo—the key to a safe-deposit box.

As the taxi came to a stop, Brian looked up at the block of flats before him—Rolf's block of flats. It looked just like where *he* used to live back in the days when he was still together with his wife. That was in the days before they'd moved to Kenton, when he used to think that there was nothing that would ever come between them. The thought made him smile sadly. He'd been about Andy's age then, and just as self-obsessed.

Pulling out the tenner Andy had given him for the fare, Brian handed it to the driver and told him to keep the change. Then, once he was out of the taxi, he picked up the bags and made his way over to Rolf's front door. He was glad he'd come now—perhaps he'd be able to do Andy a favor while he was here. After all, he had been hearing all about this Rolf bloke all day. And there were one or two things he wanted to say to him.

The door buzzed open only a few moments after he rang the bell, almost as if he was expected. Brian stood for a moment, wondering if a voice was going to come over the intercom asking who he was, but it didn't, so he pushed the door open and started making his way upstairs. Rolf's flat was on the second floor. When he came to the top of the stairs, Rolf himself was nowhere to be seen—but the door was slightly ajar, so Brian let himself in.

The flat he entered was unlike any apartment Brian had ever been in. Its shape seemed standard enough—a long hallway, with rooms coming off on either side—but it was the decor that was unusual. The walls of the hallway were covered with hundreds of postcards—their images were of tube stations—and old 1930s tube posters. Brian noticed immediately that each of them was framed in exactly the same way, and they were all so evenly spaced on the wall that from a distance they almost looked like they were part of the wallpaper design.

To his right was a room filled to the ceiling with junk: roundel signs, station nameplates, train seats, straphangers—it was like a transport scrapyard in there. He was about to walk in and have a look around when he heard a sound from down the hall—the sound of a television. He hesitated for a moment, looking back at all the junk. But then he shook himself. He wasn't here to mess about in Rolf's front room—he was here to collect Andy's Eurostar tickets and give Rolf a piece of his mind. It would be best if he just got on with it.

Briskly he made his way down the hall towards the room where the television was playing. He couldn't help picturing what he was about to find. From the way Andy had described Rolf, he half expected to find some cape-wearing villain in a black cap sitting in a leather armchair, poring over some sort of arcane timetable information by the light of a solitary candle. But when Brian put his head round the door, the sight that greeted him was not what he expected at all. Rolf was sitting on his bed with a plate held under his chin, nibbling on a slice of slightly burnt toast. He was dressed in blue-striped pajamas and a grubby, white terry-cloth bathrobe, and on his feet were a pair of comical chipmunk slippers, the soles wearing through. It wasn't exactly sinister. No candles, no cape, no cap. Even the program he was watching wasn't strange or mysterious or obsessive in the slightest—it was a rerun of some seventies American cop show on Channel 5. Not one of the classics like *Kojak* or *Starsky and Hutch,* but one that never really made it over here. One that got pulled after the first series.

Brian pushed the door open and stepped inside. "Rolf?" he said.

His monosyllable was greeted with a startled shriek, as Rolf dropped his plate, sending buttery toast crumbs all over the bedspread. "Oh, my God! Who are you?"

"Relax," said Brian, "I'm a friend of Andy's. I've come to collect his tickets."

Rolf sat perfectly still, like some startled animal caught in the headlights of an oncoming truck. "Andy sent you?"

"Kind of, yes."

"So I take it he finished the system, then?"

"No, he didn't. But *I* did." Brian walked over to the side of the bed and emptied the bag of fun cameras on it. They formed a pile on top of his duvet—a pile of bright yellow boxes, which in Rolf's bedroom somehow looked too bright, and too cheerful. "I've been with Andy all day, and I have to say that it has not exactly been fun."

"Yeah," said Rolf, unsurely, "I heard there were a few delays."

"A few! There were delays everywhere. It was the worst day on the tube I've ever seen. You know, you should be ashamed of yourself, making Andy do this on the day before his wedding—it's criminal."

Rolf picked up one of the fun cameras and looked at it. "I didn't make him do anything. It was him who suggested it."

"But you're supposed to be his friend."

"I am his friend." He turned the fun camera over in his hands. "But there are some things that are more important than friendship."

There was something faintly pathetic about the way he sat on the bed, half-buried in fun cameras, and Brian had to resist the urge to treat him like a sullen child who needed a good clip round the ear. "Listen," he said, "there's something I want to talk to you about . . ."

"Fine, but before you do, you couldn't just tell me about these delays, could you? I suppose they were signal failures as usual?"

Brian was thrown for a moment. "Well . . . yes. Amongst other things."

"Like what other things? Points problems?"

"Like a derailed train . . ."

"A derailment! Where?"

"South Kensington, if you must know."

"Which line—Piccadilly or District?"

Brian didn't answer. Despite what Rolf might think, this wasn't what he was here for. He might have to give him that clip round the ear, after all. Right now, for example, Rolf was reaching into the drawer in his bedside table and taking out a pad of paper and a pen. Brian stared at him. "Rolf," he said, "what are you doing?"

Rolf glanced up at him momentarily. "I like to keep abreast of these things. So, tell me, what sort of time was this?"

"About five-ish, I think."

"And it was on the Piccadilly Line—northbound or southbound?"

"Southbound."

"I don't suppose you got the train number, did you?"

Brian snorted loudly to himself. This was unbelievable—the man was taking *notes.* He hadn't met him more than two minutes ago, and already Rolf was asking him about derailments and signal failures and train numbers, and noting everything he said in a journal. The ironic thing was that Brian actually did know which train it had been—it was the same train that Rolf had left his third envelope on, between carriages 690 and 891. Not that he was going to tell Rolf that, of course, because that would only be encouraging him. And besides, Brian had had enough.

Ignoring his last query, he looked Rolf straight in the eye. "Let's stop playing games," he said.

Rolf stopped what he was doing and put his pad of paper down. "I don't follow you."

"I'm *on* to you, Rolf. I know your secret. I know what all this is about."

"Are we still talking about the derailment . . . ?"

"You know exactly what I'm talking about. This bet. This whole thing with Andy—it's not about the tube at all. It's about Rachel."

Rolf swallowed hard. "Rachel . . . ?" he said.

"Yes, Rachel. Why else would you go to so much trouble to hijack Andy's wedding? And why else would you be willing to bet this priceless collection of tube tickets you're so proud of? You wouldn't risk that unless you were after something. Or rather, someone. Andy might not be able to see it, but it's bloody obvious to anyone else—and I tell you, it's not on."

"So Andy told you about my ticket collection, then?" Rolf said hurriedly.

Brian reached forward and grabbed hold of Rolf's jaw. "Don't change the subject," he said, squeezing the man's chin in his hand. "I know your sort, Rolf. I've had intimate experience of people like you, and I'm not going to let you do anything to spoil Andy's wedding. From now on I want you to think of me as Andy's guardian angel. And if I ever hear that you have done anything to jeopardize their marriage, I swear I'll come after you, so help me God. So before you do anything hasty, I want you to remember two things. The first is that I know where you live. The second is that I've got absolutely nothing to lose. Got that?"

Rolf nodded.

"Right, now I've got that out of the way, let's finish up so I can get out of here. Andy asked me to give you this." Brian let go of his chin, and rummaged in his pocket to find the safe-deposit key Andy had given him at Waterloo. Holding it up for Rolf to see, he then tossed it over beside all the fun cameras on the bed. "So, if you'll just give me the tickets, I'll let you alone."

Rolf's face went suddenly pale. "The tickets?" he said nervously.

"Yes, the tickets. That *is* why I'm here."

The trainspotter hesitated. "Can't we wait till tomorrow? I mean, I should really check the photos first, make sure they're all there."

"No, I can't wait until then."

"But I have to check the pictures."

"No," said Brian commandingly. "You don't have to check anything. I've been quite patient with you until now, so just stop arsing about, and give me the tickets."

"But I can't. They're in a safe-deposit box. That's what this key's for." He pointed to the key on the bed, and Brian noticed that his hand was shaking. "I can't open it until the bank's open . . ."

Brian was confused. There was something about this that didn't make sense. "You mean, you put Andy's Eurostar tickets in a safe-deposit box?"

"Eurostar tickets? What are you talking about?"

"Andy's Eurostar tickets. In one of your green envelopes—Andy said I could have them."

"Christ!" said Rolf, visibly relieved. "I thought you were talking about my collection of tube tickets!" He reached over to the chair where his coat was hanging and pulled out the last green envelope from the inside pocket. "You can have this, no problem. I suppose you'll be going to Paris for the wedding? Andy did invite me, but I didn't feel up to it . . ."

"Rolf," said Brian abruptly, "shut up." He snatched the envelope from Rolf's hand, and stopping only to give a short but menacing look in Rolf's direction, walked out of the room, along the hall, down the stairs and out onto the street.

Twenty minutes later, Brian was in Kilburn. He had just found himself a space to lie down in a shop doorway. As he opened his bag and unrolled the blanket he'd been carrying around with him all day, he smiled. It had been a long time since he'd tried to be threatening, but he was relatively happy with the result. He especially liked the way he'd referred to himself as Andy's guardian angel. Not that he thought Andy needed looking after, mind you. It looked as though he'd pretty much learned his lesson.

Brian wrapped his blanket around himself and sat down on the hard pavement. His legs ached from all the running today, and there was a dull pain between his toes where the athlete's foot had taken hold. And he had to shift around for a couple of minutes before he could get comfortable—the combination of hemorrhoids and lumbago made it difficult to find a position which wasn't painful in some way. But he didn't much care about any of that. As he'd said to Andy earlier, it was all a matter of degree—and today was better than most days, so why should he complain?

Reaching for his bag, he put the green envelope and its contents safely at the bottom. Who knows, perhaps he'd use those Eurostar tickets sometime next week—he'd always wanted to go to Paris.

And since he was rummaging in his bag anyway, he decided to have one last beer before he went to sleep. After all, he hadn't really drunk much today, and there was nobody here to tell him off. It would be nice—one last drink before bedtime.

He was just pulling the ring of a can when he noticed Andy's tube map poking out of the top of his coat pocket. It was strange to think that this was the only souvenir he had of today's journey: a piece of A4 paper covered in little red crosses. It was crazy really, he should have had something more—a picture or something. They'd had all those fun cameras all day, and they hadn't taken a single picture of each other, just pictures of tube signs. They hadn't even said goodbye properly—just a brief hug before Andy had had to run off. Never mind. He'd think of Andy if he ever got round to using those Eurostar tickets. In the meantime, he raised his can in a silent salute to his friend. Congratulations, Andy—best luck for tomorrow and for the rest of your life.

He took a large sip, and then put the can down, and as he did so the tube map caught his eye once again. He took it out of his pocket and looked at it. It was really very crumpled now and slightly worn through use—a bit like some people he could mention. It was time to put it, and himself, to bed.

He had to scrabble about a bit in his bag to find Andy's red pen, but when he did so, he held the map down fast against the paving stones. Mornington Crescent already had a cross through it, but it was a printed cross, not one of Andy's. It wouldn't be right to leave it like that. Pressing the pen firmly against the paper, he put two strong lines through the station name. Two hundred and sixty five stations—over twenty hours of solid traveling—and at last it was finished. Brian smiled to himself. It *was* an achievement, but he was glad it was over. Folding the map up, he put it back in his pocket. And, with a final sip of beer, he laid his head down on the cold paving stone to try to get some sleep.

KEITH LOWE is thirty-one and an editor in the United Kingdom. *Tunnel Vision* is his first novel.